WHEN STORMS COLLIDE

WHEN STORMS COLLIDE

A REALM OF ISTMERE NOVEL
BOOK THREE

MICHELLE FROHMAN

1st edition 2025 published by Acorn Hill Press LLC

ISBN: 979-8-9883045-6-2 (e-book)

ISBN: 979-8-9883045-7-9 (paperback)

ISBN: 979-8-9883045-8-6 (hardback)

Cover design by MerryBookRound

Editing by EJL Editing

Map by Cartographybird Maps

Formatting by Michelle Frohman

Art by Marialuna Grassi

www.michellefrohmanauthor.com

Author Note

This story explores themes that may be troubling to some readers. For a full list of content warnings please visit www.michellefrohmanauthor.com

For Mom—
My biggest supporter.
I never could have completed this trilogy without your undying support and without you shouting my accomplishments from the rooftop.

For Dad—
We are alike in so many ways.
Without the drive to better myself that you have instilled in me, I never could have made this dream come true.

THE MYRENE SEA
MYRENE
THE REALM OF
ISTMERE
MAPPED
IN THE PRESENT AGE
DRAKELLIA
SIRALETH
SIRALETH PORTAL
SIRALETH DOCKS

THE STONE
PALACE
AKRA
PRINS
DRAGON'S
HOLLOW
THE
SHADOW
PRINS
PORTAL
PRINS
DOCKYARDS
DRAGON'S
WAY
THE SIRAWAY SEA

Pronunciation Guide

Alastir: A-luh-STIR
Araneoch: ARE-uh-nay-awk
Amiyah: Uh-my-uh
Kotova: Kuh-TOE-vuh
Kolya: KOHL-ya
Noctani: KNOCK-tahn-ee
Saanvi: SAHN-vee

Akra: A-KR-uh
Istmere: IST-mear
Prins: Prin-Z
Siraleth: SEAR-uh-leth

PROLOGUE

Akra, Istmere

6 Months Ago

It had been years since Annelise had stepped foot in The Stone City. A sense of both familiarity and dread settled deep within her gut at the thought of seeing it once more. The moment she had received the raven, she had known who it was from. Zion was the only one who knew of her location, after all. Annelise packed her things on the Island of Myrene and took off in her narrow boat, braving the Myrene Sea by herself. By the time she pulled the worn, ramshackle vessel up onto the rocks on the outskirts of Prins, she was exhausted.

Sailing directly into the dockyards wasn't an option.

To everyone else but Donika... she was already dead. Only her daughter knew the truth. That she had been spared in the battle of Siraleth, and that Donika hadn't been able to kill her.

Whether it was a moment of weakness or a swell of emotion towards her mother that stopped her blade, Annelise may never know.

She had spent time in those years since in the mortal realm, but her heart always called her home to the realm of Istmere. To her own people. No matter what, Istmere was always where she returned to. The only souls she had kept in contact with from her past life were Zion and Isaac. Isaac didn't know of her current hideout, and Zion wouldn't send for her unless it was urgent.

She had unfurled the stained parchment with shaking hands as she read the sparsely worded letter.

Diana has been discovered and captured—she awaits sentencing in the Stormvault.

Those twelve words had set Annelise's heart thumping so fast she thought it might beat right out of her chest. She knew this day would come, but she had hoped they had more time. Alastir, the seer, had prophesied at least a decade would pass before the prophecy came true. The prophecy that the last Stormshade of the Kotova bloodline would end the strife and peril that had waged war in Istmere. That over a decade would pass before Donika found her sister.

Over a decade of endlessly hunting for her, scouring every inch of this realm and the next.

It had been too long since she had last visited Diana in the mortal realm. The spell that bound her magic was sure to be wearing off by now—if it hadn't already. She knew that the next time she went to maintain the spell—to reinforce it—she would likely need to wipe her memories as well. But that was dark magic—not something Annelise relished in performing.

But she would do what needed to be done to protect Diana from all of this. From her own blood, seeking to kill her. From a realm that had once been a safe and loving place, but had morphed into something hateful and volatile. From a mother who didn't know how to care for her but was trying to do what she thought was best.

She knew that they had moved from New York to Silver Oaks, and that meant Diana's magic had awakened. Annelise had told Laurel that if her magic showed signs of awakening, to bring her to Silver Oaks. The portal to Istmere stationed there served as a magical beacon to all Shades. There would be Shades in that town who could help Diana.

Annelise had cursed herself for letting it get this far, for not having gone to Diana to explain things sooner. She had thought she could keep her safe in the mortal realm forever, changing the prophecy and what Alastir had seen. Changing what the Mother had planned for them all.

Her own demons kept her from revealing herself to Diana. They both needed protection from Donika. The guilt of all her decisions threatened to swallow her whole.

She gathered her skirts and set off at a clipped pace, up the steep bank and towards the open plains that would lead to Prins.

She needed to hurry.

There was no telling how long Donika might keep her alive, toying with her. Donika wasn't one to make quick work of someone, especially not her own sister. She had waited years for this moment, and if Annelise knew anything about Donika, it was that she would want to savor this moment. She would hold her in the dungeon for some time, torturing her and playing with her until her spirit was broken.

Zion had warned her that this was going to happen, but she hadn't wanted to listen. She had thought her interference would only make matters worse. When Zion had sent word that Donika had sent the young Nightshade soldier to the mortal realm after her, she had immediately gathered herself and left. It had only been a matter of weeks before the second letter had come, informing her of Diana's capture.

So much had happened in that short time.

Annelise's skirts kept tangling around her legs. She grasped the long skirt in her fist and hoisted it to her knees as she sprinted across the plains, backpack jostling against her spine. She wouldn't allow it to slow her down. The only weapon she had on her was a dagger stuffed into her boot—but her plan didn't involve daggers.

Not necessarily.

When she arrived at the city proper, she slid the cloak out of her pack and fastened it around her neck. She pulled the hood up to obscure her golden strawberry hair. She wasn't sure anyone would recognize her any longer—it had been too long since anyone in this realm had known her—but she wasn't willing to take any chances.

She slowed her steps as to not draw attention to herself, sticking to the far sides of the road and creeping between the shadows under the merchant shops that she passed. She exhaled a sigh of relief as she turned left onto the queen's road—the road that would lead her to Akra.

To Zion and Diana.

She had no intention of bursting through the front doors of the castle, that much she was certain of. She would need to use her secret access to the castle to find Zion... but she would need to be careful. She had sent the raven back, but there was no telling if Zion would be expecting her immediately. If he would be there waiting for her. She could only pray to the Mother that he would sense the surge of her energy running through their binding as she stepped foot into the castle and drew closer to him. Their nearness a physical thing deep in their cores. They may not have seen one another in a long time, but the binding still simmered inside of them.

Even after all this time, he was still her other half.

Annelise neared the castle and instead of taking the twisting roads that switch backed across the mountain's face, she crossed the river towards the back of the castle. Taking the mountain pass. It had been many years since she had seen these paths; tears welled in her eyes at the memories that flitted behind her eyes. The memories she had created here.

The last time she had set eyes on The Stone Palace, she had been carrying Diana away from this place, trying to find a better life for her.

A safer one.

Her plan had worked for some time, but in this, she ultimately failed.

She pulled her hood tight as she approached the back of the castle, the dark void at the base of the mountain coming into view. She kept her head down and her steps quick as she approached the portcullis.

Donika's rooms weren't on this side of the castle, but that didn't mean anyone who might see her through their window wouldn't report back. Luckily, her brown cloak blended in with the dead of winter, the colorless grass and the stark trees. It served as a form of camouflage, and she could only hope that as she approached, no one had seen her.

She advanced towards the entrance only known to a few and could see that the portcullis was already open in a giant yawn, the darkened corridor visible beyond.

Zion was expecting her, then.

She hastily stepped inside, a swell of emotion threatening to choke her as she bent to the lantern that had been left at the entrance. She struck a match against the stone and lit the lone flame inside.

The packed dirt floor of the tunnel came into view as she moved forwards, the lantern light flickering warmly against the ancient stone walls. She pulled the chain to close the portcullis behind her, allowing no one else who might know of this secret passage to enter. She didn't want to chance being followed into the secret passages from behind.

She inhaled deeply to steel herself before moving onward.

After entering The Stone Palace without an invitation… there would be no going back.

Donika would never spare her a second time, and if her plan didn't work out as she hoped it would, it would be the last plan she ever made. She prayed to the Mother that she never encountered Donika during her short stay in The Stone

Palace. Her daughter would surely smell the magic on her, despite her own spell binding. Her disdain for Stormshades had only grown over the years, and Annelise's own spellbinding had begun to wear off weeks ago.

When she had received Zion's letter, she hadn't had time to reinforce it. Besides, she might need her storm magic to make it out of this mess alive.

Despite her past mistakes, she would do anything to protect Diana. To save her from her sister. The same couldn't be said about Donika, and the guilt only a mother could experience made nausea roll fresh in her stomach.

How could you love a monster?

Annelise wasn't sure she did anymore, and that fact brought a fresh wave of guilt all its own.

Annelise had one hand on the lantern—lighting the path before her—the other hand trailing against the stone wall to her right. The knowledge of these passages might have died with those that had lived in her tenure in the castle, and it was distinctly possible they were in disrepair. She risked these fragile stones caving in on her, trapping her.

But Zion had to have traveled these passages to open the portcullis for her.

The thought reassured her as she ascended one staircase after the other, quickly out of breath. She wasn't used to traversing these passages any longer. The wind was nearly taken out of her lungs at the sheer number of steps she had to ascend simply to make it to the ground floor.

She pushed her hood back to wipe the sweat from her brow. Despite the cold winter air, the flame from the lantern and the exertion of scaling the tunnels left her panting and her skin warm.

She stopped at the door to the round antechamber, pressing her ear to the wood and listening. Once she had determined the chamber was safe to enter, she twisted the iron knob and the door squeaked open.

The chamber and passageway beyond weren't dark as she had expected—the torches on the walls were lit and they filled the cavity with warm flickering light. The chamber also wasn't empty, and she gasped as she saw a figure step into view from the shadows, her hand clasping her chest tightly.

For only a moment, she imagined it was Donika step-ping from the shadows, waiting for her. That Zion had told her she was coming... that he had successfully lured her to the castle after all these years. So she could kill her for certain this time, finishing the job.

"Easy, bird. It's just me." Zion's deep timbre filled the antechamber and her muscles relaxed.

Bird.

It had been so long since she had heard him call her that. Too long.

'Always taking flight' he had once said. The nickname suited her more than he ever could have guessed. He had called her bird long before she had left to be with Osiris, and still long after.

Zion was a good man. A forgiving man. He understood they were better off as friends.

"Zion," she breathed, collapsing into his arms.

The warmth of his golden skin was a soothing balm to her. She had missed his touch after all these years. She could sense the binding magic pulsing deep in her core, as if it had missed its other half, too. No matter how many miles or realms she traversed, she and Zion would always be bound.

Until death.

It was their secret. The only thing they had kept only to themselves.

Would that knowledge have stopped Donika from killing Annelise? Knowing her father would die, too? She shook her head to clear her thoughts. There was no use thinking on it now. The past was in the past, and Annelise was determined to keep it buried.

"You made good time," Zion remarked, a smile in his eyes as he pulled away from her only enough to meet her gaze.

"How is she?" Annelise asked, breathless.

A smile turned up the corner of Zion's mouth before he answered. "Strong. Like her mother."

Annelise shook her head, worry still fresh in her gut. "What does Donika want with her?"

"You know what she wants." He sighed, running a hand across his shorn black hair.

Annelise favored this look on him—it suited him. When they had married, he had grown his hair out into boundless curls that he wore tied at the nape of his neck.

The shorn haircut made him appear younger.

"The Kotova grimoire will *never* choose her. Never. It would rather go undiscovered for centuries before it chose someone with a black heart."

"I tried to warn her," he replied. "You know her biggest weakness—family. She feels slighted by you still. She is a Kotova by blood, but she thinks the bloodline never claimed her. *You* never claimed her."

Donika would never forgive her for leaving their family to come to The Stone Palace for Osiris. It hadn't mattered that it wasn't her choice—that she was summoned. That she hadn't *wanted* to leave.

The result of those events was Diana, and Donika hated her from the very moment she saw her. Donika was driven by the jealousy that consumed her, and she saw it as a betrayal. That Annelise left because she and Zion weren't good enough. That wasn't the case at all. She had written to Donika. Thought of her each and every day. But The Stone Palace was no place for a child, and she tried to restrict her visits to when she had training for the academy.

She didn't want her spending more time here than necessary. She had wanted to protect her. By the time she had fallen pregnant with Osiris's child, they had hastily sealed their marriage to make things official before anyone else knew. She and Zion hadn't been romantically involved for years at that point, but that didn't matter to Donika.

Before Osiris found out her true nature—that she was a Stormshade and had hidden it from him—she stood to be crowned queen of Istmere.

"Has she found it yet?" Annelise asked, biting her lip.

Zion shook his head. "No, she hasn't. She sent her soldiers to the mortal realm in search of it, but she found nothing. It hides from her still. I believe it is fiercely loyal to Diana."

This brought a smile to Annelise's lips. She had known the grimoire would choose Diana when she had sent it to search for a new ward. The grimoire was quite picky due to its sentient nature, and she knew that Diana would care for it well, as she had all these years.

"How long has it been?" she asked, meeting Zion's gaze once more.

"Almost a month. We have time yet, before she tires of her playthings," he replied.

"Play*things*?" Annelise asked.

She was under the impression it was only Diana who had been captured.

"She has taken her friend captive as well. A Shade. Fowler... Tess Fowler," Zion replied.

Annelise nodded to herself. "I know the family. Only a month... that's more than I had hoped for. But then again, after all this time, Donika would want to savor it. I wouldn't be surprised if she kept Diana imprisoned for *years*. If my instincts are correct, we have time to infiltrate the castle staff and formulate a plan. Who do we have on our side to aid us?" she asked.

"Surprisingly, the boy who was sent to retrieve her from the mortal realm and his friend. He has done a poor job of hiding his true feelings, and I'm sure Donika suspects where his loyalties truly lie. The boy has been playing the part to try to remain out of her crosshairs, though I'm not sure how much longer that will work."

"Hardly much of a boy," Annelise mused with a short laugh, remembering that Nikolai had to be at least twenty-two by this point.

She hated the idea that he had feelings for Diana. He had double crossed the resistance, and Isaac was *furious* with him. He was the reason Diana was in this mess in the first place.

No.

Annelise shook her head. Not Nikolai's fault... no.

That blame fell on her.

She might not have brought her daughter here and served her up to Donika on a silver platter, but she was the reason Diana was even in Istmere in the first place. Placed right beneath Donika's nose.

Donika couldn't chase her to the mortal realm. Diana was safe there. If she had never come to Istmere to search for answers, she would still be back in Silver Oaks. She would still be *safe*.

The error and blame here fell squarely on Annelise's shoulders.

"So, Nikolai and his friend. Who else?" she asked.

"We still have Theo and Ezra. They will help with the plan. I have to be careful with Avery—she might not swing towards our side any longer. And, of course, the spies from the resistance: Luca, August, and Elijah. We have to be careful with Corian." His eyes narrowed as the name left his lips.

"That snake?" she asked.

"He still *slithers* by her side. He is in her ear at all times, and has climbed the ranks significantly since you have last seen him," he replied. "I suspect him of sharing her bed, though I have no proof of that."

Annelise nodded. "I'll be sure to not underestimate him."

"He walks dreams, as Diana does," Zion told her.

Annelise raised her brow. "A dangerous man, indeed. Did you bring the glamours?"

"Of course," he replied, turning to rifle through the pack at his back. "I'll need to get more, but this should suffice for now. Donika doesn't travel throughout the castle much except the wing with her quarters and the throne room. Be vigilant to avoid those areas."

"And you've secured my position?" she asked, taking one of the vials of glamour liquid and popping the cork stopper, throwing the drink back in one shot.

"Yes. You'll be on staff in the kitchens. You'll have access to the soldier's food and have ample opportunity to drug them. But we need to be careful which potions we choose. We need them to make it to their posts and out of Donika's sight before they collapse. We need to be sure suspicion does not fall on us."

"It will take some trial and error," Annelise mused, thoughtful.

In her mind, she raced through the pages of the Kotova grimoire, a number of spells already coming to mind that would suit this job *perfectly*.

"I will keep a close eye on Donika, but we should have some time to perfect the plan. Keep your glamours fresh and let me know the moment you need more. Never cross her path, bird."

"I understand," Annelise replied.

She reached out and gave Zion's rough hand a gentle squeeze.

"I've missed you, Zion."

"I've missed you, too. I've wanted to see you—I only wish it were under different circumstances," he replied, squeezing her hand back.

"Me too. Be careful, Zion. I know you remain at her side for now, but the moment she senses the tides are turning, she will turn her back on you, too. History means nothing to Donika when she thinks she has been betrayed." Annelise's mouth tightened as she raised her chin.

"Same to you," he replied, his voice raspy.

Annelise could see out of the corner of her eye that her hair was a duller shade of golden brown, the red and pink undertones almost completely leached from it. Her features felt sharper, her nose longer. Zion handed her a kitchen apron, and she pulled it over her head, tying it in the back to secure it.

She spun with her arms out. "How do I look?"

"Perfect. As always." His voice was almost... sad.

Zion would love her with any face she wore.

She grabbed her pack and moved towards the tunnel that would lead into the heart of the castle, confident that her glamour would hide her from prying eyes. She needed to get Diana out of the Stormvault as quickly as she could, which meant she needed to get to work perfecting her potions.

She turned back towards Zion with a soft smile on her lips, beckoning him to follow her.

"It's time to go save the realm."

Akra, Istmere
Present Day

I was swallowed by the darkness, but not even that seemingly endless oblivion could handle my uncontrollable magic. As I reached what I thought was the end of all-encompassing shadows I had never known before—a peace I desperately reached for—I was spit back out, coughing and sputtering in the dirt.

The last thing I remembered was gazing into Nik's black, lifeless eyes. The only sound that filled my ears now was the persistent, hollow ringing after my newly unbound magic had detonated on the plains of Siraleth. I wiped the smoke and filth that obstructed my vision from my eyelids, my sleeve coming away bloody and stained with ichor. My gaze found Tess first, and I exhaled an initial sigh of relief before the devastation before me became apparent.

Not only apparent… no. That didn't adequately describe what I witnessed before me.

It threatened to *consume* me.

Whatever was left of this part of Siraleth had been leveled.

By *me*. By my magic.

Bodies were strewn about the rubble, pools of rain and blood scattered across the battle ground. Donika's men weren't the only bodies my eyes snagged on as I took in the scene before me.

Resistance members.

Friends.

This wasn't the first time my magic had lashed out and slaughtered innocents.

Tess moved to my side and my lip quivered as I pushed to my knees, hot tears streaming down my cheeks to leave trails of clean skin in their wake. I turned towards her—but despite her lips moving—I heard nothing.

The ringing in my ears only intensified.

The storm had passed when the shadows claimed me, but I wasn't sure how long had transpired between then and now. Donika and her men were nowhere in sight.

Nik was nowhere in sight.

My heart was suddenly heavy, as if I were being crushed by the weight of what had happened. Donika had stolen Isaac's storm magic and left him a hollow, lifeless version of himself.

My mentor, my friend.

He was gone. He was Noctani. A lifeless monster bound to Donika by black magic.

Donika's Noctani had then set their sights on Nik. The image of his black, depthless eyes would haunt my dreams. Haunt my every waking thought. A vision of him that would flash behind my eyelids every time I closed them.

We had been happy.

We had been *bound.*

But Donika had ripped that away from me, too. As if taking everything else from me hadn't been enough.

The numb sensation in my chest was suddenly replaced by anger. I curled my nails against the cobblestone street until they turned red with fresh blood, a growl escaping my throat. I couldn't sense my storm magic. The only thing I experienced simmering in my core was molten rage.

But that was better than feeling nothing at all, right?

If there had been one ounce of magic left in my body, it would have torn through me in this moment. But I had extinguished any and all of it when I had shattered. It would be days before my magic came back to me, as it had during the battle outside the safe house in Prins.

And I was thankful for it.

I needed the silence.

With the bond being broken, there was no way I could control my magic. My unfettered fury threatened all of those around me.

Broken.

But I was alive. Annelise had said that if Nik died, I would die. That was how the bond worked. But Nik wasn't truly *dead...* was he? If he was, I would be too. And fate had decided I wouldn't greet the Mother today.

If it was only broken, it could be repaired. If Nik was truly dead, I wouldn't be kneeling here in the dirt, grinding my teeth against the tears that flowed freely down my soiled cheeks. My gaze searched the wreckage and I could see Zion and Annelise stir from where they lay among the debris.

My magic may have sent Donika and her men running for now, but we needed to get the hell out of here. They could easily come back to finish us off, and I wasn't about to hang around to find out. Warrick had betrayed us. Instead of trusting us, he made a deal with Donika to free his family that had been captured in the battle at Prins.

How naïve.

As if Donika would ever set his family free, no matter what he offered her. He led her and her monsters straight to us at the cottage in Siraleth and ambushed us. We thought we were going to save Isaac, but in reality, we were far too late to do that. Where was Warrick now? I didn't remember seeing his traitorous face in the melee that preceded my eruption.

Tess offered me her hand, and I took it gratefully, allowing her to pull me to my feet. My knees buckled, but firm hands grabbed me from behind and held me upright. A quick glance over my shoulder confirmed it was Puck who had caught me, his eyes a silent apology as he slung my arm over his shoulders, supporting my weight.

I was too weak to walk on my own.

I had expended all of my energy and magic and was lucky my last ember hadn't been consumed as well when I had detonated. I said a silent prayer to the Mother that I hadn't killed my best friend. My mother. My stepfather.

Only those that had rushed in to save us. To join in the battle against the Araneoch and Noctani, knowing there was no way we could win. The lifeless eyes of the resistance members who met their end by my own magic stared up at me as we crossed the remains, picking our way across the rocks. A part of me wanted to return to the cottage underground. To the safety of the expansive library and the Gothic bedroom I had begun to call home. But I knew that wasn't possible.

My magic had broken any and all spells that kept Donika away from her childhood home, and that would be the first place she searched for us, anyway. No one spoke, and Zion and Annelise joined us as we limped towards the spires that reached into the sky that would lead us into Prins.

Where could we go that was safe? Isaac was one of Donika's puppets now, and none of the established safe houses could provide us protection. He would surely divulge the location of all of them. One particular body stood out to me among the rubble and I nodded towards it. Puck obliged, turning to allow us to venture towards it.

Warrick's lifeless eyes stared up at the sky in surprise, his mouth slightly ajar. What had he thought would happen? That he would free his family and live happily ever after? There was no happily ever after... this wasn't a fairytale.

This was a nightmare.

I bent down to pry the sword from his cold, dead grip. Even in death, his grip was steel. When his fingers finally gave way, I fell backwards into Puck, the sword firmly grasped in my bloody hand. I unbuckled the scabbard from his waist with my other hand and Puck helped me to pull it free.

Warrick had betrayed us. Betrayed me. If it weren't for his selfishness, Nik would still be here. Warrick himself might still be alive. He hadn't trusted us enough to confide in us. Instead... he had turned to Donika. He trusted the deal he made with her, and it cost him his life.

I buckled the scabbard across my waist. When I faltered from weakness, Puck slid the sword into the scabbard himself, grasping my arm once more.

We walked on in silence.

It wasn't until we had passed through the towering marble arch into Prins that one of us finally spoke, breaking the fragile silence that had settled over us.

"Do we have a destination in mind?" It was Tess whose voice rang out among our group.

Zion ran a hand down his face, his brow furrowed.

"Any ideas?" he asked, his gaze immediately landing on Annelise.

Her eyes were downcast, a million thoughts swirling behind her ocean blue eyes.

"I have a friend in Prins. A friend I haven't seen in... a long time. It's as good a place to hide as any. With all the safe house locations compromised and Donika sure to be scouring Prins for us, I think we need to disappear for a while."

"And Saanvi and Kenna?" Puck asked, adjusting my arm across his neck. I could tell he was tired, and I hoped wherever this friend of Annelise's was, it wasn't too much further.

"We will have to send word once we are safe," Zion replied, nodding towards Annelise. "It is on this side of The Shadow?"

She nodded, her lip disappearing between her teeth as she concentrated.

"It has been a long time since I have been there, but it is on the coast. Between the Siraleth mountains and those that encase The Shadow. Towards the Myrene Sea. We can't leave the Kotova grimoire behind." She shook her head. "I can go back to the cottage and retrieve it, then let Kenna and Saanvi know of our plan. Head towards the coast and I will catch up with you or send Kenna ahead."

Despite feeling as if I had descended into a catatonic state, I nodded at Annelise. I was thankful she was willing to go back to retrieve the grimoire. After my magic had been entirely expelled, I simply didn't have the energy to go myself. And she was right... we couldn't leave it unprotected. It would only show itself to another Kotova, which left only the two of us to go back for it.

"Good. This friend lives in the middle of nowhere, then." Zion's gaze never left Annelise.

She nodded solemnly.

"To the middle of nowhere, then," Tess agreed with a humorless laugh.

Annelise turned back in the opposite direction, towards the cottage. I watched as her lone figure disappeared into the mist. With how exhausted I was, it wouldn't be difficult for her to catch up with us.

Zion led the way as we got a head start and traveled the main path in Prins towards The Shadow. Halfway through the center of the city, we turned left, away from the Prins Dockyards. We passed through the area where homes and shops were built right into the mountainside, and it wasn't long before the buildings became sparser. The tall grass of the Prins plains and forest beyond greeted us. The mountains enclosed us on the left and right as we made our way into the thicket of evergreens, a long, flat plane visible before us.

I felt comfort in the safety of the blanket of trees the forest provided us, and dreaded the inevitable exposure we would experience once we had to cross the planes. If I remembered correctly from my studies of Istmere in the grand library, there were two large rivers we would need to cross to make it to the western coastline of Istmere. Towards the Island of Myrene.

If we were traveling that far, that is. Despite my fatigue and the gripping thought that I couldn't possibly go on, I hoped that we were. I wanted to put as much distance between Donika and myself as humanly possible, and I dreaded the thought of Nik hunting us down and finding us.

I wasn't sure I would be able to fight him if it came down to that. Back in Siraleth my numbness had quickly turned to rage, but the longer we walked, the emptier and more hollow I felt. The war against Donika was not in our favor, and every time we made a step forward, it was always two steps back. If not more.

Donika had storm magic now.

She wouldn't be as powerful as I was—having been born to the magic, and hers having been stolen—but she would be a force to be reckoned with all the same. She had set out to steal my magic with her serpent staff, but I guess stealing Nik's and drawing him to her side was the next best thing for her.

She would never stop trying to break me, and she wasn't entirely unsuccessful this time. Deep down, I did feel broken. I couldn't see a way to save Nik. To defeat Donika and save Istmere.

I was so very tired. *Bone deep* tired.

Defeat weighed heavily on me as we walked, and our eyes were on the sky as we passed through the open plains towards the dense forest beyond. Donika's spies could be anywhere.

A black crow appeared overhead, squawking and beating its wings furiously as it sailed ahead of us. Puck gave my shoulder a reassuring squeeze.

"Kenna," he breathed. "She will fly ahead and scope things out for us. That means Saanvi and Annelise can't be too far behind."

His words brought me little reassurance as we entered the thicket once more, the sounds of the river beyond drawing us forward. We stopped to rest and hydrate momentarily, and I wished desperately that we had a canteen to fill. We would need to cross the water to continue on anyway, so I waded into the fresh stream until I was knee deep. I cupped the water to drink deeply at first, but as I noticed the blood and dirt staining my hands, my stomach roiled. I scrubbed and scrubbed my fingers until my nails were raw and my skin was cracked. I moved onto my face next and fully submerged my skin until I could scrub the flesh there as well.

I wanted to wash away the events of today, to forget that everything had happened and return to the bed in Siraleth with Nikolai. To remember our limbs twined together, his skin against mine.

But the only thing I felt was empty.

Tess watched soundlessly from the bank as I scrubbed my skin clean. When I was finished, we met on the other side. Everyone else was only soaked to their knees, but I had soaked through my tunic in my attempt to clean my skin of all reminders of today. A shiver ran down my spine as a coldness settled in my bones, one I feared would never leave. Tess wrapped her arm around me and held me close, rubbing vigorous circles into my arms to warm me. My teeth chattered as my eyes met hers.

"I think you're going into shock." Her voice was barely above a whisper.

"I don't think anything can shock me at this point," I muttered, casting my eyes downward.

"We need to get her moving," Annelise's voice cut in as she moved to my side. I hadn't realized she had even returned to our group, the grimoire tucked safely under her arm against her side. She shook her head back and forth with worry. "Her magic will likely return in the morning, and I hope to reach our destination before nightfall."

Tess nodded as she looped her arm through mine. Puck moved to my other side, but I raised my hand to ward him off.

"I can walk on my own for a while," I told him through chattering teeth.

"Are you sure?" he asked, raising an eyebrow skeptically.

"I'm sure," I told him resolutely.

Tess walked by my side, but her arm threaded through mine did little to warm me. We took the shortest possible route from one woodland to the next, trying to minimize the amount of time we were out in the open. The resounding caw from above would intermittently keep us on track—wherever it was we were going.

It wasn't until we reached the second river that my weakness won out, and my knees buckled, giving way beneath me entirely. I caught myself on the heel of my palms, skidding into the dirt of the forest floor. Puck wasted no time scooping me up and pressing my cold body to his chest.

"She's burning up," he said, his worried gaze meeting Tess's.

Words were silently exchanged between them with only a glance, and we picked up our pace as we approached the coastline and traveled towards the mountains of Prins. The peaks were still visible from here, covered in snow and reaching into the clouds far beyond.

My skin was hot to the touch—as if I were being burned from the inside out—and the snowy caps beyond brought a chuckle to my lips. How could I be hot, my skin burning hot, when there was snow covering the mountain range still within sight? The air was still cool against my skin.

My eyes suddenly heavy, the last thing I remembered was Tess grasping my hand and squeezing it tightly. My hair blowing in the soft breeze from the Myrene Sea. Then I was swallowed by the darkness once more.

2

When I woke, the smell of salt and brine filled my nostrils, a soft breeze passing over my skin. The sound of waves crashing against rocks roused me softly and for a moment I could pretend that everything was ok. That I could stay here—by the sea—forever. Forget about the war I had waged against my sister. Forget about the suffering of the people of Istmere.

Forget about Nik.

But despite the numb sensation that pervaded my body, I knew none of it was true. That reality would come back to swallow me whole. It would drown me if I let it. That maybe Donika had finally broken me, and I had nothing left.

When I peeled my eyes open, I was met with the ceiling above me, made of driftwood that had to have been pulled from the shores. An insect net surrounded my bed and when I sat up, I could see the Myrene Sea off in the distance. It crashed softly against the small cliff that separated us from the salty waves. My eyes searched the shore to the right, where I could make out two figures sitting, huddled together against the sand.

There was a home to the left with a thatched roof and worn wooden siding. It appeared spacious for a home built by the sea with nothing else around it. One that had seen many years and was well loved. To be this close to the sea, we had to be in the furthest reaches of Prins, the unscalable mountains between us and Akra.

This was the safest place from Donika for the time being.

We would need to regroup and forge a new plan, but the only thing I wanted to do was sleep. I wasn't sure how much time had passed since the darkness claimed me, but I was still tired despite hours of rest. The fever I had spiked on the way here had broken, but my legs were still sore and exhausted.

And most importantly, I still couldn't sense my magic.

That would mean that only a day or so had passed. I groaned as I swung my legs over the side of the bed and moved to stand.

"She wakes," a feminine voice sounded from my left and I startled, my hand moving to my chest in surprise.

"I didn't see you there," I told her, swallowing back the stale taste in my mouth.

"I didn't mean to frighten you," Annelise replied, a smile playing on her lips.

As if there was anything to be happy about right now.

"The others?" I asked, my gaze drifting out towards the two figures resting in the sand.

Annelise nodded towards them. "Kenna and Saanvi have joined us. Puck and Zion are hunting. There isn't exactly a market in these reaches of Prins, and there are more mouths to feed now."

"And Tess?" I asked, turning towards her with a raised eyebrow.

"I had to practically bribe her to give me a moment alone with you, she has been steadfastly by your bedside since we arrived. She is in the house"—She nodded behind us towards the driftwood cabin—"to give us some privacy."

"And whose house is this?" I asked, leaning against the cot I had been resting on.

"An old friend," Annelise replied, that same smile playing on her lips once more.

I squinted my eyes at her in confusion. "A lover?"

"God, no," she all but barked, rousing to stand from her chair. "An old friend. You will meet her soon enough."

I bristled.

Everything was smoke and mirrors with Annelise, and I was sick of her secrets.

"Care to join me for a short walk to stretch your legs?" she asked, brushing her pants off and walking towards the shore, expecting me to follow.

We never did get a chance to talk after everything had happened. I wasn't sure I had even had a moment to process the fact that my mother was *alive* let alone the events that had unfolded after that. I was drowning in my own emotions. Anger, sadness, bitterness, all tangled up into one tornado that threatened to sweep me away.

But I had lost my vengeance. My fight.

I was hollow without Nik here. Empty at the thought that he was a blood-sucking Noctani and there was *nothing* I could do about it.

I pushed off the cot to follow Annelise, her strawberry blonde hair whipping behind her in the salty breeze. Siraleth was by the sea as well, but it wasn't nearly as drenched in the seaside air as it was here. Everything was touched in a layer of salt, even the wind itself. I could taste it with every breath I took.

I wasn't ready to speak with Annelise, but I didn't have much of a choice. It was only the small group of us here, and there was no avoiding one another. We walked towards the shore, Saanvi and Kenna raising their heads as we approached, their gazes trailing after us as we ambled down the coastline.

It wasn't long before sand was filling my boots and the feeling of it against my toes—inside my sock—was beginning to drive me crazy. I paused to ditch the boots, rolling up my socks to stuff them inside, tying the laces together so I could hang them across my shoulders.

Annelise laughed softly and my gaze met hers. "Just like your father."

"My father?" I asked, one hand raised to shield my eyes from the sun so I could read her expression.

She nodded. "Osiris loved the beach but hated the feel of the sand. How it permeated everything, and always came with you wherever you went next."

I guess we did have that in common.

I motioned with my hand for her to continue on and I followed at her side, the sand now slipping freely between my bare toes. It was warm against my skin from the baking afternoon sun.

"What did you want to talk about?" I asked, breaking the delicate peace that had settled between us.

I couldn't imagine things would ever be *easy* between us, but right now, they were especially strained. She had lied to me since the moment we first met, and everything had gone to shit. When I had first thought she was dead I had craved her in a way I never thought I would. I wanted to hear all about her life. To *know* her. Now that she was alive and right before me, I didn't feel the same. She was simply another person who had lied to me and betrayed me.

"I wanted to... explain," she began, casting me a sidelong glance.

I kept my eyes on the sand.

"I'm not sure there is anything to explain. You lied to me, pretended you were someone else... and here we are. You left me in the mortal realm and never came back for me, despite telling my mother you would."

She flinched at the word *mother* as if it physically hurt her. As if she had any right to the word herself.

My mother was the woman who had *raised* me. We might not have seen eye to eye, but she did the best she could for me under the circumstances. She was raising a Shade, not a normal teenager after all. Where was she supposed to turn when Annelise had simply... disappeared?

"I wanted to come back for you," she replied, her voice tight.

"But you didn't," I countered, my voice cutting.

Annelise threw her head back, blinking away the tears that threatened to stream down her cheeks. Her skin was as pale as a seashell against the coastal sun, her cheeks pink. "I did come back, once."

Once.

Now I was the one biting back my tears as they stung the back of my eyes. I wasn't ready for this conversation—wasn't sure I ever would be. I stopped abruptly, my feet planted in the sand, my head shaking back and forth.

Annelise stopped as well, her gaze meeting mine. "You were happy. I didn't want to destroy what you had built for yourself there. What your *mother* had built for you there. You were so beautiful. Radiant. I knew the moment I laid eyes on you that I couldn't take you back to *this.*" She spread her arms wide, her head shaking back and forth. "This was no life for a young girl with her entire life ahead of her."

"Bullshit." I ground my teeth together, my eyes falling back to the sand as I dug my toes in.

"Diana, I am telling you the truth. You had to have been six, maybe seven. You were with your new family, devouring a cone of mint chip at the creamery in New York. You know the one... the one you always went to with your father."

I did know. I bit my lip against the swell of emotions that surged forth.

"I couldn't take you away from that. *I couldn't.* There was no life for you here, all that waited for you here was *death.*" Her words were barely above a whisper.

"You had to have known the spell would wear off. The one that kept my magic spellbound. That my powers would eventually resurface. What was your plan, then? What did you plan to do?"

"I planned to spell you again. I had been keeping an eye on you, and when your mother took your family to Silver Oaks, I knew she was following my instructions. That the spell was wearing off, and you needed to be around other witches your own age."

"But you didn't spell me again," I pointed out.

She shook her head. "I couldn't. I ran out of time, which was my mistake. I couldn't get close to you—Fletcher Price and Antonia Finch were preventing that. Then Nikolai showed up and I knew I was too late, that there was no going back now. That everything had been set into motion already."

"Everything?" I asked, my brow raised at her.

She nodded. "The prophecy. The events that Alastir had seen unfold."

"And when I was imprisoned in the Stormvault?" I asked, my eyes narrowing.

"I risked *everything* to get you out. To get you to safety. Donika told me that if she ever laid eyes on me again, it would be for the last time. She spared me in Siraleth, she would not spare me a second time."

"*Spared.* As if she were doing you a kindness," I scoffed, my brows pinching together. "Donika doesn't have a kind bone in her body."

"Whatever her reason was, she *did* spare me that day. I was banished from Istmere. I posed as a servant in the kitchens to regain entrance to the castle, and it was a risk. Zion helped, but he knew if Donika laid eyes on me at any point, glamour or not, I was as good as dead."

"You posed as a servant to be able to set me free... but why did you then lie to me about who you truly were?" I asked, the hurt bubbling to the surface and bleeding into my every word. "Why not simply tell me you were my mother?"

Her eyes were pleading as she met my gaze. "I wasn't sure you would want to know it was me. So much time had passed... I was scared."

"*You* were scared? How about the eighteen-year-old you left with mortals, not knowing she had powers let alone magic that could turn on her and *kill* her? How about the eighteen-year-old who was prophesized to end a decades old war in a realm she had *never been to*, never even heard about?"

"It was a mistake. I see that now."

I swallowed hard—the taste of bile strong in my mouth as I bit my tongue. "Oh, well I'm glad you've been illuminated to that fact."

Annelise wouldn't meet my searing gaze.

"And the grimoire?" I asked. "How did it choose me when you were still alive? You were its previous guardian, were you not?"

"I was," she replied with a nod. "I knew you were coming of age. I knew you had discovered your magic once you had moved to Silver Oaks, so I sent the grimoire to you. Or rather, I sent it to find a new ward, knowing it had only a few left of the Kotova bloodline to choose from. It chose well... as I knew it would."

"But didn't you need it? You are a Stormshade, too," I asked, confused. "And why can nobody else see it or look upon it? When Donika sent her soldiers to find it back in the mortal realm it wasn't hidden, it was simply sitting in my dresser drawer. And yet they still couldn't locate it."

Annelise nodded, her gaze still captivated by her own hands gripped before her. "I had the book for a long, long time. The book of shadows served me well, and I had taken everything from it that it was able to give to me. It was time for it to move on." Her lips quirked into a ghost of a smile. "The book of shadows is... unusually discerning. It commonly only lets its ward gaze upon its pages and learn its spells. With its sentient nature it would have sensed those searching for it. Hidden itself to ensure it couldn't be found until it *wanted* to be."

That made sense as to why Donika had sent soldier after soldier but come up empty each and every time. The grimoire didn't want to be found until I had returned to the mortal realm to retrieve it myself.

"You didn't need the book anymore... so your magic is bound, then?" I asked, a pinch of jealousy in my voice.

I should have known.

Of course Annelise's magic was bound, there was no way she didn't have control of her own storm magic. She was far too controlled. Too calm and collected.

She nodded in response, her gaze tentatively meeting mine.

"Zion?" I asked.

I had guessed correctly, apparently. A rose flush appeared against Annelise's cheeks.

I wasn't the only one she had taken advantage of, then. Zion had been in love with her—bound to her—and she had *still* left him to be with Osiris. A new wave of rage filled me as I shook my head back and forth.

"At least one of us is bound, then," I scoffed. "But if Nik died, I was supposed to die. But here I stand."

Annelise nodded.

"That means Nik isn't dead... that has to mean he can be saved. The binding isn't gone. It's not missing. It's *broken*. Something that is broken can be repaired..."

"We can't know for certain," Annelise replied, her voice tight.

"The spell was awfully certain. If he died, I die." I set my chin as I narrowed my eyes at her.

"If there is a way, I will help you find it," she replied.

"I don't want your help," I bit back, the words slipping free on instinct.

Annelise flinched, and a long moment of silence passed between us.

"Diana... what I wanted to say to you was that *I am sorry.* I have messed this up irreparably and I know that I don't deserve your forgiveness nor do you have to give it to me, but I am sorry nonetheless."

"As long as you're sorry," I sneered, crossing my arms over my chest.

I knew I sounded childish. Petulant, and immature. But I was so enraged, all I wanted to do was lash out. If my magic had come back by now, the sky would be dark, rumbling with thunder and fury. But my well of magic was still depleted, and I found myself thankful for that.

"There is nothing I can do to fix the mistakes I have made in the past. All that we can do is move forward." She sighed, running a hand through her mess of golden pink waves.

"You're right about that." I stepped back, my arms still crossed over my chest, putting a barrier between us.

I could sense myself building a wall to safely tuck my emotions behind as I wiggled my toes in the sand, attempting to ground myself. If I didn't separate these emotions from myself, they would consume me.

I turned to head back towards the driftwood cabin, but one last thought kept me rooted where I stood. I turned towards Annelise once more, her hair whipping in front of her from the ocean breeze, obscuring half her face.

"You knew I wasn't an ordinary witch. You knew I was a Stormshade. You knew my magic could turn on me and kill me. Steal my power. You had the means to bind my magic, and you kept that to yourself, too." I turned to go but her reply had me turning back once more.

"I told Isaac. I told him what to do, what to teach you. I tried my best to help you and remain hidden." Her hand outstretched, grasping my arm as if to stop me. I jerked out of her grip as if she had burned me.

"Your *secrets* are more important to you than anything or anyone else. You knew I could bind my storm magic, but you let it go on unbound for *months* only because you wanted to stay hidden. Revealing that there was a bloodline would have revealed your true identity. You are no better to me than Donika herself."

As soon as the words had left my mouth, I regretted them, but it was too late to pull them back now. I stormed off towards the house, tears falling in big, wet droplets against my freckled skin, leaving my mother staring after me on the ocean shore.

3

I hardly wanted to storm into the driftwood cabin without knowing whose house it truly was. I lingered outside the door, hoping Tess had been watching us through the stained glass window.

Sure enough, the door squeaked open and Tess descended the steps, grasping my shoulders and pulling me close.

"You're awake," she sighed against me, squeezing me tight.

"Not for long if you don't let me breathe." I laughed against her, all the rage that had been simmering below the surface immediately forgotten with her presence.

Everything else may have gone to shit, but I still had Tess.

We walked over towards the pavilion that I had awoken in. It was set up as makeshift sleeping quarters, with a few beds sparsely decorated with plain, simple pillows and blankets. Each bed was covered in a mosquito net, and I imagined there were a great many other flying insects that loved the sea as much as we did. Tess leaned against one of the beds, inhaling deeply and filling her lungs with the salty air.

"If we weren't in the middle of a war, I could definitely stay here forever," she sighed wistfully.

"I could, too," I agreed.

There was something peaceful about this piece of land, and the ramshackle house nestled among the rock cliffs.

"How was that?" Tess asked, nodding towards where my mother stood off on the shore, her back turned towards us, facing the incoming tide.

"Just peachy," I replied, jumping up onto one of the beds and crossing my legs. "How long have we been here?"

"About a day," Tess replied, jumping up onto the bed opposite me.

"My magic should be back any time now, I expect." I ran a hand through my mess of auburn curls, finding that it wasn't nearly as matted as I had expected it to be after the battle in Siraleth. Though that isn't to say it wasn't still in rough shape.

"I suspect that is true," Tess agreed. "What did mommy dearest have to say?"

I pinned her with a deadpan glare which had her curling over with laughter.

"How she planned to come back for me, but never did because I looked 'so happy' with my mortal family. How she's sorry, but apparently keeping her identity a secret from me was more important than helping me with my storm magic. Oh yeah, and she is bound. At least one of us has control over our storm magic."

"She is?" Tess asked, her hand flying to her throat. "How could she let you go through that, let that storm hurt you… and she had the solution in her back pocket the entire time."

I shrugged. "Your guess is as good as mine."

I let out a deep sigh as I leaned back on the palms of my hands. I was utterly and completely drained from everything that was happening, and all I wanted to do was curl up into a ball and forget all of my problems. My body was drained of energy and magic, and I felt as if the fire had been sucked straight out of me. My head was *throbbing*.

"I know it isn't any consolation at this point, but she's the one who missed out. You are the most amazing person I know, and she would have been lucky to have seen you grow up."

"Thank you, Tess." I pushed off the bed and crossed the space between us, grasping her shoulders and pulling her into the circle of my arms.

If I could only stay like this, my head on Tess's shoulder and her arms around me, everything would be alright. There would be no war in Istmere. No malevolent sister trying to torture innocents and steal my crown. No mother who abandoned me with a million empty excuses. No unbound, uncontrollable magic to contend with. And Nik would still be here—human—not some magic siphoning vampire.

I thought I had cried my last tears with Annelise and what was left behind was a hollow void. I pulled away only enough to see Tess's face.

"I think I need some rest," I told her, my words lacking any emotion. Despite having woken up from sleeping a full day, I felt as if I could barely keep my eyes open.

"I think that's a good idea," she replied, pushing off the bed and moving towards the house.

My brow furrowed in confusion. "Aren't we sleeping out here?" I asked, gesturing to the beds beneath the pavilion.

"We are, but there's a real bed in there that I'm sure you can take advantage of." She motioned towards the driftwood cabin. "Come on."

"But whose house is this?" I asked, skeptical.

Annelise was certainly *close* with whoever it was. I wasn't sure what to expect when we crossed the threshold. Tess led me up the steps as she spoke.

"Annelise didn't tell you? It belongs to Amiyah. She's been begging to meet you. She'll be happy to know you are finally awake."

"And who—exactly—is Amiyah?" I asked as Tess reached for the wooden doorknob.

She turned her head back towards me, her eyes soft.

"Tyr's mother," she replied, as she turned back towards the door. "She's Annelise's sister. Your Aunt."

I expected a surge of emotion, knowing this house belonged to *family*. To another member of the Kotova bloodline. But I still felt empty.

This was simply another secret Annelise had kept, and I didn't have the energy to be bitter anymore. I only wanted to close my eyes.

Tess pushed the door inward, and we walked into the main living space, which was decorated with every single seashell that could fit inside the small cabin. They adorned every surface and hung from every wall, all shapes and sizes. There were bowls piled high with sea glass, and a coffee table made of worn oak that had a sea glass mural embedded in its surface. The couch was linen and worn, the windows open, the shutters rustling in the soft ocean breeze.

I wasn't sure what I had expected, but this wasn't it. Annelise didn't strike me as a collector of things, so it surprised me that her sister was. I wondered if Tyr grew up in this house, or if this was something special, for only Amiyah and her beloved trinkets. The living space opened into a small galley kitchen with three doors off to the right, two bedrooms and a small washroom. It might not be much, but it was loved, and lived in. I could imagine Annelise coming to visit, walking the beach until she found the perfect shell to bring inside and add to Amiyah's collection.

The first door on the right opened and Amiyah appeared, her brows raising as she took me in, her long grey-blonde hair cascading down her back.

"My, my, aren't you the spitting image of your mother? It's wonderful to finally meet you, Diana."

Amiyah moved forwards but didn't embrace me, she simply grasped my hands between both of hers and gave them a tight squeeze, her eyes soft when they met my gaze.

She was older than Annelise, but not by much. Her once sandy hair had begun to grey, her green eyes creased with the start of wrinkles. Her skin was tanned from the sun, each freckle merging into another to create a canvas of color across her skin. I held her gaze, and whatever last vestige of emotion left within me leaked out as a hot tear rolled down my cheek.

"I'm sorry."

It's all I could think to say. All that could be said. Tyr was her son, and he was dead. He was dead because he had saved *my* life, sacrificing his own for mine.

"There is nothing to be sorry for, my dear." Her grip was comforting.

I was surprised to find Amiyah wasn't nearly as cold as Annelise. Not nearly as calculating. She was all warm sun and carefree comfort. I immediately felt safe in her presence. She felt like *home.*

I wiped my cheeks with one hand while the other was still grasped within hers and took a staggering, shuddering breath.

"We will talk later. For now, you need rest." Amiyah motioned towards the second bedroom on the right and I could feel the loss of her grasp deep within my chest as she turned to open the door for me. Her touch brought forth a healing all its own. I wondered if healing ran in the family. After all, Annelise was a skilled healer too. Something about Amiyah brought forth an emotional healing, and I instantly felt as if I had known her for years.

"Rest as long as you need, Diana. We can talk when you wake. You are safe here."

I nodded, wiping my nose with the neck of my dirt and blood-stained shirt. I was too tired to be embarrassed, and the wrought iron bed with the lumpy mattress never appeared more comfortable than in this moment. Tess gave me a reassuring smile that never reached her eyes as I closed the door between us, leaning against it.

There was an outfit of fresh clothes laid out on the bed before me, but I didn't have the energy to change. I made my way over to the bed and curled up atop the comforter, my knees pressed to my chest, my arms woven tightly around them.

In the silence of the seaside bedroom, I finally let myself cry, every drop staining the pillow beneath me with salty tears and dirt that remained from the battle. I cried until I was numb. I rocked myself to sleep beneath the thatched roof of the beach house, too tired to crawl beneath the comforter.

I had Tess and I had the resistance, but it didn't matter.

I had never felt so utterly and entirely alone.

I was in an out of sleep for what felt like days. At some point I had sensed my magic return, slowly stirring me from the fitful sleep I had fallen into. The spark of energy lit within me, but I didn't have the energy to grasp it. All emotions of anger and vengeance had been sapped from my body with the last of my tears. I was cold and hollow, as if the energy within me had depleted entirely and that the cup had never been refilled.

Tess had been checking on me frequently, and she had called for Puck to drag me to the small washroom between the two bedrooms. She had stripped the dirty clothes from my limp body, joining me in the tub and scrubbing my skin clean as my eyes fell closed. She had washed and braided my hair in a simple plait down my back before dressing me in fresh clothes and laying me atop the bed once more.

She hadn't spoken, and I had found comfort in that. That she knew I had to mourn in my own way, and that I wasn't ready to speak about it all yet. That the reality of the situation had finally taken its toll on me, and it had left me weak and fractured.

I hadn't expected Donika to ever break me... but in this moment, I thought that maybe she had.

The thought of Nik's black, depthless eyes sent me back into a deep slumber. Unconsciousness was the only relief I could find from the constant grief of his loss.

I had never loved anyone before Nik, and the love I had for him was *all-consuming*. It was fire and I was the kindling, no hope of withstanding the flames. I would never see his glacial blue eyes again. Feel his rough, calloused hands as they slid against my skin. The flush of heat that rose to my cheeks when his hips pressed against mine.

I stifled a sob into the pillow as I rolled over, determined to banish every thought of Nik from my mind. Tess had heard my cries and silently entered the bedroom, curling up on the bed with me.

She held me until sleep took me once more.

4

When I woke next, Tess was sitting in a worn oak rocking chair at my bedside, a book in her hands. The thought of Tess voluntarily reading something that wasn't a fashion magazine stirred me from my haze and I sat up, wincing at how sore my muscles were.

"Sleeping beauty finally wakes," Tess said with a smile that only turned up the corner of her mouth.

"How long have I been asleep?" I asked, my voice rough as sandpaper, sounding more akin to a croak from disuse.

Tess mused for a moment before answering. "Three days. No... four. Four days. On and off."

Her gaze lifted from the book to hold mine.

Silence fell between us as I realized I had let almost an entire week slip by. The only bathing I had done was the bath Tess had forced me to take, and my auburn curls were matted into a braid that hung messily over my shoulder. I rubbed the sleep from my eyes before stretching, the true passing of time tangible within each muscle that protested.

"What are you reading?" I asked, raising an eyebrow at her.

Her gaze met mine once more over the book.

"You know, there isn't that much to do to pass the time here on the outskirts of Prins. Nothing but the sea, really. It's peaceful. I understand why Amiyah loves it... but I have been bored out of my mind."

The ghost of a smile crossed my lips as I imagined Tess helping around the small cabin. Fishing with Puck in the Myrene Sea. Taking long walks with Zion as he hunted for our next meal. All the while... I slept.

"I know you needed this time to yourself," she began, straightening in the rocking chair and placing a receipt in the spine of the book, resting it on the driftwood nightstand, "but it's time to wake the hell up."

"I am awake," I protested, running a hand through my mess of hair. No amount of detangler was going to help me fix this mess.

"No, you aren't," she insisted, her expression turning stern.

"Tess—" I wasn't sure how to explain. How to put into words the loss I was experiencing. The cavity that had opened in my chest.

She shook her head, defiance in her eyes. "You are a survivor, Diana. You have had your time to grieve, but now it is time to *wake up*. This isn't you. Seeing you like this..." tears filled her amber eyes as she held my gaze, her head giving a soft shake.

"I'm sorry."

The words were empty. Hollow. What else could I say?

"I know you didn't mean to scare us. I know you didn't mean for any of this to happen, but you are a *fighter*. To see you slip into a coma… it has had us all on edge. This didn't even happen when we spent three months in the Storm-vault being interrogated and tortured. Have you given up? Do you want to go home?"

The word 'home' made me flinch. I paused before an-swering, the reality of the situation settling in my gut as if it were a weight. I gave my head a gentle shake.

"This is my home now."

Tess's lips formed my favorite smirk as her eyes sparked with mischief. "That's what I like to hear."

Tess needed me.

Istmere needed me.

I had lost Nik to this war but that didn't mean I was ready to give up yet. I couldn't go back to the mortal realm—my tail between my legs—and leave Istmere to Donika. Mother only knows what she has been up to since our last run in. She would never stop torturing and perse-cuting the innocent people of Istmere.

As long as she was alive, she was never going to stop.

I was going to stop her.

It was time this war came to an end, and Donika would meet hers at the end of my blade. A sharp pang reverber-ated in my chest that Nik's gift to me, Stormslayer, would be the blade to end this all—that he wouldn't be here to see it.

I sensed my storm magic surge within me unbidden, and I knew it was time. I had grieved long enough, and my magic propelled me out of the sheets and towards my feet as if it had a will all its own. It was storm magic after all. In a way, it did. No other magic in the realm had such sentient tendencies.

"First things first... you need a shower." Tess exaggeratedly plugged her nose as she slung her arm over my shoulder. "I'll set out some fresh clothes for you. Meet us outside when you are ready?"

I nodded, thankful that I would have a few more moments to gather myself before I had to face everyone. I barely recognized the bathroom. The last time I had been in here I had been in a haze. I stripped down and entered the shower, letting the hot water run down my skin until it was flushed from the heat. I turned the water even hotter, letting the sensation invigorate me. Once I had surely burned off my first layer of skin I toweled off, dragging the brush through my hair until it fell in wet, heavy strands down my back.

I found the white T-shirt and black shorts Tess had left out for me. I shrugged into them, pleasantly surprised that the clothes were baggy enough that I could still scent the salty ocean wind against my skin.

I opened the door to find that everyone had congregated a way down the beach. There was a long teak table set out on the sand, wooden backed chairs arranged around it. The sun beat pleasantly against my skin as it warmed me even further, and I finally felt as if I was coming back to life.

I wasn't sure if I would be able to get through this war without facing Nik as Noctani, but I was praying to the Mother that I could. If I could end Donika and thus end her Noctani as well… all the better. I wasn't sure I wouldn't falter beneath his cold, dead eyes. I didn't think I was strong enough to face him when he was in this form.

Zion sat at the head of the table, his leg propped up on his knee as his head fell back, soaking in the sunshine. Annelise sat to his right, her gaze never leaving mine as she watched me approach. Tess and Puck were on his left, and Puck followed Annelise's gaze to where I stood, a smile crossing his lips.

"It's good to see you up and about, Diana." He pulled the chair out next to him and offered for me to sit.

Across the table sat Saanvi and Kenna, Amiyah at the other head of the table. I sat, my bare feet burying themselves in the warm sand as I rest my hands across the tabletop. The rays of sun beating down on me had already begun to dry my hair—frizzy wisps curling against my cheeks.

"What are you all discussing?" I asked, my gaze meeting each of those seated at the table. When my gaze fell on Amiyah, it lingered only a moment before falling to my hands folded before me.

I couldn't help but drown in guilt when I met her honeyed gaze. Her only son was dead, and if it weren't for me and this war, he would still be here. With her.

"We were discussing what to do next, but only as your advisors," Zion spoke, his gaze boring into mine.

A pang resonated in my chest as I realized the one advisor I truly needed was *also* Noctani, trapped in Donika's clutches.

Isaac.

I pressed my eyes closed, my hand moving to my chest as if it could quelch the physical pain I was experiencing there. But it was no use. The sun stung the back of my eyelids and all I could see was red as the light bled through.

"And what, exactly, do you advise?" I asked, my jaw tight as I opened my eyes once more to meet his gaze.

In Isaac's absence, Zion stepped up to take on the lead advisor role in the resistance, though our forces were scattered across Prins at this point. I was thankful that it was only a small group of us that had been ambushed in Siraleth, and the majority of the resistance was still safe in the city.

"Our initial plans will need to be... revised... but the fact still stands that we need to march against Donika, not wait for her to come to us," he responded. He leaned towards me, inclining his head. "We are down two of our strongest Shades, but we still have *hundreds* willing to march. Maybe even thousands."

"Aren't you forgetting one key detail?" I asked, shielding my eyes from the sun as my gaze squinted beneath the rays.

"And what might that be?" he asked, raising a brow.

He would listen to whatever it was I had to say, and I was thankful to have his support in a time like this. He couldn't replace Isaac, but someone needed to step up to take the charge alongside me. I couldn't do this alone, and I was thankful that I didn't need to.

"I'm unbound," I bit out.

Without the binding, I had no control of my storm magic, and thus, no hope of controlling my magic against Donika. A storm could easily turn on me and kill me. Or steal my magic for itself if it chose to do so. Without the binding I was *useless,* and it wasn't as if I could simply bind to another. A magical binding was a one time thing.

Puck shot to his feet as realization crossed his features. He leaned over the table, his gaze hardened on Annelise. "But she isn't dead..."

"So?" I asked, my gaze shifting to meet his. "I can't do any magic without the binding. How do you expect me to stand against Donika?"

"That's not what I meant," he answered, shaking his head as his gaze returned to Annelise's. "You said during the binding ceremony that if he died, *so would she.* She doesn't appear dead to me."

Annelise and I had already discussed this on the shore a few days ago. My gaze fell, eyes traveling back and forth over my hands as I reasoned out what Puck was saying.

"The binding isn't severed, it isn't gone. It is *broken.* Something that is broken can be fixed." Puck spoke the same words I had spoken to Annelise on this very beach. She had said she would try to help me any way she could...

My thoughts were wild with possibilities as Zion stood to join Puck.

"Now, we don't know exactly what that means," he said, his hand reaching out as if to calm us all down. He didn't want us getting too excited.

"We *do* know, Zion." I stood to join them, Kenna and Saanvi nodding out of the corner of my eye. "If he were *dead,* I would be too. But I stand before you. If he isn't dead, *he can be saved.*"

"Diana, we don't know that—" Zion started, but Amiyah cut him off.

"She is right, brother." I almost flinched that Amiyah still saw Zion as her brother, after everything Annelise had put him through. "You know this, Anna. You have seen it."

"What are you talking about?" I asked, my blood pumping fast enough through my veins that I could hear my own heartbeat drumming in my ears.

"Let's all sit down," Zion replied, motioning for us to return to our seats. "We need to calm down."

"Annelise..." Amiyah's voice was a plea as we all sat. Annelise avoided her sister's gaze.

"We don't know for certain, Amiyah," Annelise replied, her voice curt. Her gaze remained fixed on the table before her.

"Simply because the spell has been lost to time, doesn't mean it never existed, Anna. *Enough* with your secrets." Amiyah's voice was cutting, and I sat back in surprise.

This was at odds with the soft, quiet woman that had greeted me when I had first arrived here. She was filled with Kotova fire, same as me. Same as all of us, apparently.

"What are you talking about?" I asked, my gaze on Annelise. "What secrets do you keep from us now, *Mother*?" My words dripped acid as she flinched back from me.

"There is a spell..." she began, her eyes tentatively meeting my gaze. She shrank back at what she found there. I raised a brow at her, daring her to continue. "A spell that once belonged to the Kotova grimoire."

"And what spell might that be?" I asked, crossing my arms over my chest. My eyes narrowed on her, unsurprised that more of her secrets were coming to light.

"An... antidote of sorts," she finished, not bothering to elaborate.

"An antidote for *what,* exactly? Being Noctani? Because there is no mention of that *anywhere* in the Kotova grimoire. I have combed it front to back numerous times, and there is no mention of the monsters Donika has created."

"No... not for Noctani." It was Amiyah who spoke, her disappointed gaze resting on her sister. "For siphoning."

"An antidote—for siphoning? I don't understand." My brow furrowed as I turned to meet Amiyah's gaze.

"What can be done can also be undone. All magic must find a balance. The grimoire... it may have been in my sister's possession these last years, but the book of shadows is no stranger to me. I have seen and studied the spells hidden within its leather binding. Those that might have resided in it, but reside there no longer..."

"You ripped another spell out of the grimoire?" I accused, my voice seething as I stood. My gaze seared into her. "Not just the key? You ripped *more* spells from that sacred book?" My nails dug into the table hard enough that they turned white. My magic surged forwards and pressed against my skin from the inside, begging to be released. I closed my eyes, calming myself. I couldn't allow my unbound magic to release itself.

I took a steadying breath. "How could you?"

"I was trying to help a friend," Annelise replied, her gaze flitting to Zion for support. Zion's fist curled against the table, and he did not return her gaze.

"Out with it. That's the same excuse you used last time, when you had knowledge of a spell we *desperately* needed. I won't ask again. Where is the spell to reverse siphoning?" Venom dripped from my words as I sensed the fire within me surge back to life.

There might still be hope to save Nik, if only my mother didn't hide this, too.

"I'm not sure where it is now, but I know who would," she replied, swallowing hard. "Alastir."

"Alastir, the seer?" Amiyah asked, her brow wrinkling.

"Yes, the very one." Annelise still refused to meet her sister's gaze.

"Whatever is done can be undone. If magic has been siphoned, even if it wasn't the same spell from our grimoire, it can be returned to the source." Amiyah nodded as she spoke, as if trying to convince herself, too.

Maybe we could save Isaac too.

Save all the innocents Donika turned into Noctani.

"And what will happen when the magic is returned to the source?" I asked, my nails still digging into the table.

Amiyah shook her head. "There's no way to be certain all will go back to normal."

"But there is a chance," I said, the words coming out as a statement more than a question.

"Yes, there is a chance," she replied.

Saanvi spoke up for the first time from across the table, hope sparking her autumn gaze as her lips curled into a smirk. "Looks like we're going back to Prins."

I had enjoyed what little time we had spent at the seaside cabin and was sad to be leaving it behind so soon. We hadn't brought anything with us, and the pack that Amiyah offered me was light. There was only enough room for some food and water, along with a change of clothes. I strapped Stormslayer back onto my thigh and swung the pack over my shoulder, heading into the living room to meet with the others.

I wasn't ready to face the tension with Annelise yet. She was staying behind with her sister. We would see her upon our return with the antidote spell, in hand.

Hopefully.

Zion agreed to stay with her as well. That left Tess, Puck, Saanvi, Kenna and me to make the trek back to Prins. I was counting all my lucky stars and praying to the Mother above that Alastir would know of the spell we sought—or at the least—where we could find it.

Kenna had turned into the black raven, soaring ahead of us to guide our path and search for any obstructions or trouble we might encounter on the way. Her black wings unfurled as she took flight, but that wasn't the last we had seen of her. She continued to circle back over and over, as if to say we were moving too slowly.

I was thankful for the watcher and felt safer on the journey with her gliding through the cloudless sky ahead of us. The last thing we needed was another ambush from Donika, or to run into any of her other monsters. The thought sent a shiver down my spine with the acknowledgment that Nikolai was now one of them.

I swallowed back the grief that threatened to grip me and pushed it down once more. I couldn't retreat back into myself again and forget about recent events. My friends were counting on me.

Istmere was counting on me.

I couldn't let them down.

I hadn't remembered the journey to the seaside cabin taking us this long when we initially came, but then I recounted how I had slipped into unconsciousness for more than half of it. By the time the sun had sunken behind the horizon we had only made it past the first river crossing. We set up camp for the night and Kenna returned to us. We took shifts keeping watch through the darkness. By the time the sun crested the horizon in the morning I was thoroughly sore from a long night of sleeping on the cold, damp forest floor.

It had to be mid-morning by the time we made it to the second river crossing and traversed the empty plains towards the main city of Prins. I was both nervous and excited to be closer to the prospect of an antidote, and prayed we weren't being sent on a pointless mission. Tess walked ahead with Puck; their heads bent together as they spoke. We stepped onto the city streets and headed towards The Shadow. As she had the first time we crossed, Saanvi seamlessly turned into a lithe black cat—an emerald hanging from her collar—to guide us through.

She slipped down the staircase and into The Shadow, glancing at us over her shoulder to ensure we followed closely behind. We had crossed The Shadow so many times at this point I no longer needed a guide, but we kept our heads down and our mouths shut all the same.

Donika could have spies in the city and we needed to remain off her radar. I made a mental note to pick up some glamours when we visited Alastir, though I didn't have any coin on me and doubted the others did, either.

Saanvi led us through the darkened tunnel and the spelled door beyond it that led us up and out before turning back into her regal human form and slipping into step beside me.

"Sometimes I wonder what it would be like to be a Nightshade, and what my animal form might be," I told her.

"Something fierce," Saanvi replied, nodding to herself as she thought. "Maybe a lion... or a jaguar?"

"Or a honey badger," I mused with a laugh.

Saanvi smiled, turning towards me as we continued to walk. "Sure, you can be a honey badger, My Queen."

Her use of my title surprised me, my foot catching in the space between two cobbles, momentarily tripping me before I regained my balance.

"Please, call me Diana."

I had been jealous when I had first met Saanvi, thinking there was something more going on between her and Nik. Those thoughts were quickly quelched when I saw the camaraderie between them. Saanvi was smart and loyal—I was thankful to call her a friend and to have her at my side.

"Ok, Diana," she replied, a blush rising to her cheeks and painting her tawny skin in the most beautiful shade of rose. "Thank you, for trusting me to come on this mission with you."

"Of course. You are one of my best advisors, and nobody knows the streets of Prins the way you do."

"Being a cat certainly helps. I can slip in and out easily without being seen. It's a common enough animal that hardly anyone pays attention to me."

"A trait I wish we all possessed. I would give anything to be invisible," I replied, biting my lip. "I fear even if we are successful in this mission, we have no chance at winning the greater war."

"I don't have those same fears," Saanvi said, lifting her chin. She met my gaze as she tugged on her long, midnight braid. "I have every faith in you—bound or not."

My brows pinched together as I glanced back at her. "Without the binding, I have no magic," I protested. "I would be essentially... useless."

Saanvi shook her head fiercely. "Never useless. You might not be able to call on your storm magic, but the prophecy never said anything about using *magic* to defeat Donika. Only that it would be an unusually powerful Stormshade of the Kotova bloodline that would do it."

My gaze fell to my boots as we walked, realization dawning on me.

Saanvi was right.

"But without my storm magic, I'm practically mortal," I argued.

"I'm not sure it will matter. You are wicked with your blade." She nodded towards Stormslayer strapped against my thigh. "And you're forgetting one vital piece of information," she replied.

My gaze pulled from the cobblestones to meet her amber eyes once more. "And what might that be?"

"Donika is not without weaknesses. Blood. Family. *This* is her weakness, and we will do everything in our power to use it and exploit it. Even if we can't save Nik—"

I cut her off with a glare that had her chuckling.

She cleared her throat before speaking again. "Even if things don't go as planned and you remain unbound, Donika is weakened by her blood ties. By her family. She couldn't bring herself to kill her mother, despite having every opportunity to do just that. She knows Zion betrayed her—turned on her—but she never sent a contingent after him when the soldiers she did send couldn't find him in the woods. And you. She has had the opportunity to kill you many, *many* times. But she hasn't."

"While that may be true, I think she might have been waiting until she finalized the siphoning spell. She wants my magic."

"But does she want your magic more than she wants you dead?" Saanvi asked, her brow raised. "She already has storm magic. She has Isaac's. She claims to want you dead, then why is she dragging her feet? Why toy with you when she ambushed us in Siraleth instead of cutting your throat?"

My gaze fell to the cobblestones once more as I gave what Saanvi has said some thought. If it was true and family was Donika's weakness, she might hesitate. All it would take is one moment of hesitation for me to run Stormslayer across her throat and end this. Zion and Annelise would be marching with us, and they would serve as further distraction. She had the opportunity to kill them in Siraleth, too.

But she hadn't.

Maybe Saanvi was right, and we had finally identified Donika's only vulnerability.

"I think you might be a genius, Saanvi." A smile spread across my lips as I felt—for the first time since Nikolai turned—that there was hope to put an end to this war.

"I wouldn't go that far." Saanvi laughed. "But I appreciate the sentiment, nonetheless."

"I would much prefer to march against Donika while bound, but if worst comes to worst, we might only need to distract her long enough to finish the job. She does love theatrics, after all."

"She sure does," Saanvi agreed as we crested the narrow hill that brough us into Dragon's Hollow and towards Alastir's shop. Saanvi gave me a reassuring nudge as I tucked a stray curl behind my ear. "But I don't think we will need to worry about that too much. I think we will find the cure to this Noctani bullshit and we'll be marching against Donika with Nikolai and Isaac in tow."

"I sincerely hope you're right," I breathed.

The flapping of wings and the stirring of air interrupted us as Kenna landed before us, seamlessly turning into her human form without as much as a missed step.

"Did I miss out on the girl talk?" she asked, tossing her sleek onyx hair over her shoulder. It was such a contrast to her pale, milky skin.

"Not exactly," Saanvi replied as she cast me a knowing glance.

"Have either of you been to Alastir's before?" I asked as we began the trek back down the hill, Alastir's shop coming into view in the distance.

"Sure have. We've been trying to get the stubborn old bastard to join the resistance for years until he finally told us not to come asking again or he would curse us," Kenna replied.

My eyebrows rose in alarm.

"He is an incredibly powerful seer with a vast amount of spells in his repertoire, he could most certainly curse us if he wanted to," Saanvi replied with a shrug.

Nik had also asked Alastir to join the resistance, but he had claimed he was too old for war. Maybe there was still hope yet to sway him to our side. He had been the closest friend and advisor to my father Osiris. He hadn't been surprised when

I had shown up on his doorstep in Prins searching for stolen spells.

Tess glanced behind her, checking to be sure we still followed closely behind, before approaching the door to the charm shop and swinging it open. The last time we had come here it had been the middle of the night and the shop hadn't been open for business. Today the shop was open. A few Shades milled about selecting potions off the shelf or ringing out with their purchases at the front counter.

Alastir was nowhere in sight. The gentleman operating the till was much younger than the seer we came searching for. My eyes fell on the doorway in the back of the shop that led up to the apartment above, and I fell into the memories of that night. How Donika had found me with Corian by her side. How they had pulled me into a dream. How that same night Nik and I had given into our feelings and touched each other on the gym mats of the training room for the first time in weeks.

The voice of the cashier pulled me back from my reverie as I blinked several times to refocus.

"What can I help you with?" he asked, his eyes roving over each of us as he realized we hadn't brought any items up to the till to cash out.

"We are looking for Alastir, is he in?" Puck asked, placing a hand on the counter and leaning against it in a way I could only describe as arrogant.

It almost made me laugh. *Almost.*

"One moment," the cashier replied, moving towards the room that sat in the back of the shop. It appeared to be an office of some kind.

When the cashier returned—alone—I swallowed back the lump in my throat.

"He isn't available at the moment," he replied, his lips pressed together in a thin line. He didn't offer us anything else.

"Can he make himself available?" Puck asked, a threatening note in his voice. "I'm afraid it's incredibly important, ole chap."

Tess rolled her eyes as she crossed her arms over her chest. I had to stifle a groan at Puck's attempts at intimidation. He couldn't play the part that Nik did, he was too... British.

"Afraid not." The cashier replied, offering nothing further than a searing gaze.

"Please, Sir. You don't understand—" I spoke, moving to the front of the counter and pushing an indignant Puck out of the way. "This is of the utmost importance and it is *crucial* that we speak with Alastir right away."

We couldn't stay in Prins; Donika's soldiers would find us. If we didn't find Alastir—and soon—we would have to return to the seaside cabin empty handed. And that simply wasn't an option. Time wasn't on our side, and I could sense the minutes ticking down.

As far as I was concerned, all plans of going to war were put on hold until we found the antidote to the siphoning spell. Or some other kind of cure. I had made up my mind about that the minute Amiyah had mentioned the spell. All magic had a balance, we simply needed to find it.

Surely Alastir had seen this. Seen that I wouldn't go to war without Nikolai by my side, and that we would be coming to him to seek out the spell we needed.

"What is it you wish to speak with him about?" The cashier asked with a smile.

He hadn't been nearly this nice to Puck, and I narrowed my eyes at him.

Pursing my lips I said, "you don't have the clearance. I will speak with Alastir, and Alastir alone. If he isn't here, I implore you to tell me where we might find him."

I plastered a fake smile across my lips and my teeth ground together as I tried my hardest to push down the magic that surged to the surface every time I lost my temper. A wave of relief washed over me as I sensed it return to my core, to the ember of energy that lived there.

The cashier frowned. "I'm sorry then, afraid I can't help you," he replied, that false smile returning to his lips that never reached his eyes.

I slammed my fists against the glass counter in frustration and the beakers and potions that sat atop it rattled together.

"When he returns... will you let him know that Diana is looking for him?" I asked through clenched teeth, meeting the cashier's stern gaze with one of my own.

Recognition lit his eyes before he leaned over the counter towards me. Puck's arm shot out to stop him, but I gave him a reassuring nod, his arm falling back to his side.

"Are you… you're not… Diana Kotova, are you?" he asked in a voice merely above a whisper.

"Oh, mother above…" Tess exhaled as her arms dropped to her side in a huff. "So much for staying hidden…" she muttered as she moved towards the front door of the shop and glanced up and down the street.

"Who is asking?" My eyebrow arched in question as I turned back towards the counter.

"I'm under strict instruction that if *Diana Kotova* came here—" the cashier began, before he was cut off by Saanvi.

"Good lord, man, *stop* saying her name." Her hand grasped the blade fastened at her waist as she narrowed her eyes at him.

He had the decency to blush with embarrassment, his mouth falling closed.

"Go on," I urged, motioning with my hand for him to spit it out.

His voice fell to a deep whisper. "I am under strict instruction that if… *you*… were to come here, that I give you this piece of paper."

He rifled through the drawer on his left until he removed his hand, a folded piece of parchment within his grasp. I snatched it out of his grip, unfurling it and flattening it to the glass countertop.

1178 Wilder Way.

I gazed up in confusion.

"What is this?" I asked, uncertainty creasing my brow.

The cashier reached out, sliding the paper his direction so he could read it. "An address." He wordlessly slid the paper back.

"But *where*," Puck seethed, appearing as if he might punch the cashier in the face at any moment.

"The Shadow," he replied, his gaze flitting between each of us once more, as if realizing who we were in truth.

"*Where*, in The Shadow, mate?" Puck asked through his teeth, losing whatever modicum of patience he had left. "It's not as if we frequent the place or have google maps."

The cashier took a step back, away from Puck, as his gaze moved back to me.

"It's by the mountains," he replied with a deep swallow.

"Mate, I am trying my *hardest* here not to rearrange your face. You do realize that The Shadow is completely closed in on *both* sides by mountains, correct? Please, please, for the love of whatever mortal God or the Mother above it is that you pray to, do not make me ask you another question." Puck had lost his last vestige of composure and his hand curled into a fist at his side.

We were wasting too much time, and the longer we spent lingering around in Prins the greater the chances were of us being spotted and captured. The cashier held his hands out as if to calm us, but a muscle ticked in Puck's jaw as he took a deep breath, moving forward.

"It's on the left. The left coming from here. You go down the stairs, past the brothel district, past the Old Cat pub and keep going, towards the Siraway Sea. It's near the edge of The Shadow on that side. That's all I know," he spit out, speaking fast enough the words were practically running together, his palms lifted towards us defensively.

"Thank you. You have been *most* helpful," Puck replied, his words dripping with sarcasm, as he retreated towards where Tess stood at the threshold of the shop.

Back the way we came, then.

Alastir had seen us coming. He had known I was going to come to Dragon's Hollow searching for him, and he had left an address for us. What else had he seen? Was it Alastir at this address, or the answer to our questions?

Either way, we had better get going. And quickly.

I turned away from the counter to join the others on the cobbled street outside the charms shop, the crinkled parchment with the lone address tight within my grip.

6

We retraced our steps out of Dragon's Hollow and back towards The Shadow, the morale of the group slowly dwindling. It wasn't until we had crested the hill and had come back down on the other side that I realized I had forgotten to get any glamours.

If we couldn't find Alastir, we would need to return to the seaside cabin. We couldn't risk staying in Prins and being seen. It was far too risky, and the Noctani and the rest of Donika's soldiers were likely on high alert, searching the realm high and low for us.

Saanvi stayed in her human form as she led us down the steep stone staircase back into the depths of The Shadow once more. We passed through the heavy, spelled door and traversed the long alleyway beyond it.

The hair on the back of my neck raised as if my magic could sense something in the air, and I shot Tess a sidelong glance.

Her eyes flashed with worry, telling me she sensed the same thing. The sooner we found Alastir and got out of The Shadow, the better.

Puck led the way towards the Siraway Sea, into the brothel district where the buildings were shuttered closed. The only light escaping those townhomes was the open door as patrons passed in and out. We kept our heads down and walked onward, trying our best not to draw any attention to ourselves. The cobblestone road turned and brought us into an area of The Shadow I had never explored before. When we passed the Old Cat pub, I knew we were heading in the right direction. The street curved around the ramshackle buildings and the mountains could be seen immediately beyond, through rips and tears in the awnings strung overhead.

"Any idea where we are going now?" I asked at Puck's back, a nervous trickle crawling up my spine.

"Your guess is as good as mine. Our friend at the charm shop wasn't the most helpful, to say the least," Puck replied as he cast a glance over his shoulder.

"I think I have an idea where," Kenna replied, her nose crinkling.

She was using her heightened sense of hearing and smell to investigate the surrounding area. I wondered if she could hear some of the conversations from inside the buildings we passed. Oh, to be a fly on the wall in The Shadow. I could only imagine.

"By all means, dear raven, lead the way," Puck winked at her, motioning for her to walk ahead of him.

She rolled her eyes at him, giving him a playful shove before turning left towards the higher walls that enclosed The Shadow in its entirety. We were close to the edges of The Shadow now, and to exit, we would need to backtrack significantly. A sensation of unease settled deep within my gut at the thought. We weren't near any of the staircases that led up or down to either side of Prins.

"And where are we going, exactly?" Saanvi asked, her brow raised at Kenna's back.

"You'll have to wait and see," she replied, a coy smile playing across her lips.

Tess shot me a glance, and I shrugged. There was an awfully flirty tone to the words exchanged between Saanvi and Kenna lately, but I had always thought they were merely friends. The vibes had changed recently, and I was starting to think that was no longer the case. It made my jealousy of her when we had first met all the more laughable.

"You and your secrets," Saanvi murmured in response, a smile lifting the corner of her mouth as her eyes glanced at her boots against the cobblestones.

I sensed another tickle on the back of my neck, as if we were being watched. I cast a glance behind us to see if we were being followed, but the narrow street behind was empty.

I turned forwards once more, shaking the thought from my head. I was anxious to find Alastir and ask our questions, then get the hell out of The Shadow. I prayed the shop worker hadn't sent us on a wild goose chase. The only solace I had was that Puck had scared him shitless despite his initial failed attempts, and I doubted he would lie to us after that.

"Do you feel that?" Puck asked, stopping before a shop window and turning his head, eyes downcast.

"Feel what?" Tess asked, moving to his side.

"I feel like… like someone is watching us."

My eyes darted up and down the street. "Yes."

I *hadn't* imagined it.

"I've felt weird since the moment we descended into The Shadow," Tess agreed.

I nodded. The sensation was growing in intensity, as if it were a crescendo. It started off small and slow, but the strength and intensity was building within me, and my magic surged to my fingertips. I bit my lip and tried my hardest to push it back down, but a crack of thunder sounded overhead and I squeezed my eyes shut.

Shit.

"Maybe nobody heard it?" Kenna offered with a half-hearted shrug.

"Yeah, right. The Goddamn sun is out. Not a threat of clouds in the sky. Seven devils," Puck swore, running a hand through his mess of curls.

"I'm sorry. I can't control it…" I trailed off, shaking my head. I tried my hardest to concentrate, pushing my magic back to my core.

"I don't like this," Puck replied, his eyes on me. "We need to get out of here. Now. Someone knows we're here."

That same sensation had grown and was pronounced in my core, as if an *incredibly* powerful magic wielder was nearby. As if my own magic could sense it.

"Couldn't agree more," Tess replied, turning back towards the way we had come.

As we spun to follow on her heels, the sensation tickling the back of my neck hit a climax. Seven men moved into the mouth of the street, one by one stalking into view. The man at the front of the pack was one that I recognized, and a breath escaped my chest as I took a step back away from them.

Kane Price.

Not only was he a member of Donika's army, but he was Fletcher's brother. Fletcher... who I had killed in the battle at the Prins safe house with my unbound magic. After he had slain Tyr.

I swallowed hard, taking another step backwards. We were outnumbered. Rage flickered in Kane's gaze as he slinked forward, his steps slow and methodical. A club was held in one hand, a broadsword in the other. His men were equally well-armed, and all I had were my throwing knives and Stormslayer strapped against my thigh.

"Is this the part where we run?" Saanvi asked, her hand on her whip as she uncurled it against her side. She already had her sword gripped in her other hand.

"I would say so," Puck replied, motioning with his head for us to take off in the opposite direction. "Let's go."

I pulled Stormslayer free, the dagger instilling a sense of surety in me as I held it tight in my grip. We took off in the opposing direction, our boots slamming against the cobblestones as we ran. Kenna led the way, but none of us were sure of the best way to escape from this vantage point. We didn't know where we were. We weren't lost, exactly, but we were in a part of The Shadow none of us were familiar with, and Kane and his men were close on our trail.

I could sense the magic rolling off Kane as if it were a physical, tangible thing. He was more powerful than Fletcher, and the thought had a lump forming in the back of my throat. Would we be able to beat them if it came down to hand-to-hand combat?

"Kotova!" Kane roared behind us, the sound of his boots against the cobbles growing closer and closer.

They were faster than us, that much was clear at this point. They were gaining on us faster than we could out-run them. I wouldn't be surprised if Kane was familiar with these streets. We followed Kenna as she banked right, towards the center of The Shadow, away from the Siraway mountains we had been heading towards. The street narrowed, and we had to pass through single file before it opened again on the other side and we took off at top speed.

We were racing through the streets of The Shadow, causing quite a raucous, eyes drifting towards us and heads peeking out of shops to see what the commotion was about as we stormed by.

We darted around another hard left and Puck almost lost his footing, sliding against the stone road and scratching his forearm, leaving behind a streak of hot, red blood. He was on his feet again in a matter of seconds, catching up to us. He was faster than we were, and I feared he was holding himself back as to not leave us behind. I pumped my arms at my side harder and harder, pushing myself to the limit.

I was never the fastest runner, but I *had* been training. At least I wasn't being left behind by the entire group. Tess held herself back for me too, and I knew that nothing I could say or do would change that fact. She was all legs, and she could outrun any of us on her worst day.

"Where are we going?" Saanvi called out from behind me as we turned left again.

"You think I've got a clue?" Kenna turned her head as she called back to us. "I'm just trying to lose them!"

One more turn led us to a dead end, and we all skittered to a stop barely in time to prevent us from toppling over, one after the other as if we were a row of dominos.

"*Shit.*" My breaths came in short, fast pants as I tried to fill my lungs with gulping heaps of air again.

"Turn back!" Kenna called from the front.

"Too late." Tess replied, swallowing hard as we turned towards the way we had just come.

Kane had cornered us, twirling the club in his hand, a sinister smile across his lips.

"Kane, it doesn't have to be like this…" Puck tried, his hands out as if he could put some distance between us and Kane's men.

"I've never much liked you, *Petyr*," Kane spit out, Puck's full name dripping with disdain as it left his mouth. As if it were not a name at all, but a curse.

"The feeling is mutual, trust me. But we don't want any trouble," Puck replied, his right hand moving to his Katana strapped across his back.

His hand rest against the hilt, but he didn't pull it free. Not yet.

"My quarrel isn't with you, though I've been given instructions to bring the whole lot of you in. Dead or alive." Kane raised the broadsword in his hand and pointed it at me, his murky brown eyes narrowing. "You. Now *you*, I will bring in dead."

I swallowed hard. "I understand your pain, but I had no choice. It was me or him, and I wasn't about to lie down and let Fletcher kill me," I replied, voice gruff.

"I don't give a shit. A life for a life. You killed my brother, so now I will kill you. I'll give you the mercy of making it quick." His voice was full of rage as he moved forwards again.

Puck stepped in front of me, sliding his Katana free of its sheath and holding it in the space between us. His expression was a warning. "You won't take her."

"We'll have to see about that, won't we?" Kane asked, his smile menacing as his eyes fell on me. "Nikolai wants to see you again. Begged Donika to let him be the one to capture you. Best I can do is bring him your limp, lifeless body."

The mention of Nikolai had my blood singing in my veins and my magic moved forwards forcefully, pressing under my skin so urgently I almost *wanted* to let it loose. It was too unpredictable, and I could hurt one of us as easily as I could hurt Kane or his men. I pressed my eyes closed as I pushed the magic down, my hand gliding to the back of my belt, and the throwing blade tucked beneath my leather jacket.

My fingers found the hilt of the throwing dagger and as I slid the dagger free, my eyes snapped open, my throwing arm surging forward.

The knife struck home barely shy of its target, sinking into the flesh below Kane's left shoulder and lodging into the thick muscle. He tore it free and threw it to the cobblestone, where it skittered away from him into the shadows.

His mouth opened in a snarl that was half human, half wolf, his fangs protruding from his mouth and splitting his lips in a menacing grin. Blood trickled down his chin and the wound in his shoulder, soaking through his shirt as he surged forwards, his blade meeting Puck's as he moved to stand before me. To guard me.

Everything felt as if it happened all at once, my blade meeting that of one of Kane's men as I narrowly ducked under his blow. The force with which his blade hit mine had me faltering, almost slipping to my knees. I pushed back with all my strength, the man taking a few steps back, an expression of surprise crossing his features.

I darted forward swiftly, using speed to my advantage. But Kane's soldier fell away before my blade could hit home, barely catching the material at his shoulder. The training gear split open, revealing the thin slice I had made against his skin with my blade beneath.

I turned with the blade in my hand as he raised his own between us, but this time I was ready for the jarring force with which our blades met. My other hand slid to the back of my shirt to grab the other throwing knife stashed there. As my hand closed around the hilt of the small knife-edge, I eased the force with which I was pushing Stormslayer, allowing the soldier to fall forwards towards me.

I easily slid the throwing knife into his chest and he fell to his knees, slumping over. I bent to retrieve the sword he carried and pulled it from his limp grasp. As I stood to full height, I sensed someone behind me. I ducked barely in time to see a blade go sailing over my head.

Once second later and that blade would have separated my head from my shoulders.

I turned quickly on my heel, the sword I had taken from the fallen soldier cutting across the man's knees. He fell back with a cry as I stood, sliding my other hand with Stormslayer tight in my grip across his throat. I pushed him to the cobbles with my boot and wiped the blade against my jacket.

That was two men down.

I turned to see Puck still fighting Kane, their skills evenly matched. Kenna and Saanvi had each taken down one soldier as they battled another together, and Tess fought at Puck's back, protecting him. I watched as Kenna sunk her blade deep into the belly of the soldier she and Saanvi fought, pressing against his shoulder with a bloody hand to dislodge him from her blade.

I turned towards Tess to help her dispatch the last soldier, leaving only Kane still standing.

He fell to his knees before Puck, bowing his head in defeat.

"Please, please allow me to live." His voice was hoarse as his eyes were cast down to the puddle of blood that pooled around his knees. His shoulder wound from my throwing knife was bleeding in earnest now.

"Afraid I can't let you run back to Donika and reveal you saw us here, mate. You understand." Puck's voice was sharp, despite the sarcasm in his words.

"I meant what I said," Kane said, his eyes meeting mine. "Nikolai wants to see you. He's been asking about you."

"How dare you speak his name," I seethed, stepping forward and pressing Stormslayer to his throat hard enough for blood to trickle down and darken the collar of his shirt.

"He leads the Noctani now. He is more powerful than he has ever been before, and he is searching for you," Kane replied, his gaze raised to mine. He shrunk back at whatever he found there.

My lips were bared over my teeth and I felt more animal than human as his words found my ears. Nik had been taken from me, and Kane wanted to use him as a bargaining chip to save his own life. Was there truth to the words that he spoke? Was Nikolai leading the Noctani and searching for me? Whatever we did from here, we *couldn't* let him find me.

Nikolai wasn't mine anymore. He was *Noctani*. He could steal my magic with his fangs and leave me completely mortal.

The sound of Nik's name in my ears ripped something open within me that I had thought I had sealed shut. Rage simmered, barely contained right beneath the surface.

How dare he speak Nik's name as if he knew him?

Without another thought, I sliced the blade across Kane's throat in one fluid motion as my emotions threatened to flood me. The wall I had carefully built between me and my emotions was failing. Tears of anger welled in the back of my eyes, but I blinked them back.

I would not cry again.

What I hadn't seen in the blindness of my rage, what I had failed to notice, was that Kane had lifted his hand in his last moments. Had that been a blade that had caught the light?

I turned from his limp body against the blood-soaked cobbles, my boots soaking through with his blood as it pooled around me.

Saanvi was behind me, on her knees against the cold, wet street. Her hand was splayed against her stomach as her mouth opened in a gasp.

One of my throwing knives was buried in her chest.

7

Time slowed down as I turned to face Saanvi, her face stricken with pain as she grabbed the hilt of the throwing knife and pulled it free. Blood bloomed across her tunic immediately and Puck kneeled at her side, pressing his hand to the wound. Kenna ran towards her, falling to her knees and grasping her around the shoulders.

"We need to get her to a medic or a healer, and *quickly.*" Puck's voice was strained as the blood pooled around his fingers.

"I didn't—" The words were swallowed before they could even come out.

I hadn't even seen Kane pick up my throwing knife where it had been discarded. I should have been paying closer attention. My ears were ringing as I frantically searched up and down the cobblestone street, thinking of anywhere we might be able to go for help. We were still deep within The Shadow, far from any of our contacts in the resistance.

"What do we do?" I asked, raking a hand through my hair, my gaze falling back on Saanvi as she slumped against Kenna.

Tears streamed down Kenna's dirt-stained cheeks as she squeezed Saanvi tight. This couldn't be happening. I couldn't lose another person I loved.

"I'll run for help," Tess offered, standing from her squatting position and moving towards the mouth of the alleyway.

She stepped over the dead bodies strewn about the cobblestone, her boots splashing in the darkened puddles of their blood.

"There isn't time," Puck replied through clenched teeth.

I shook my head back and forth. This couldn't be happening. This was *my fault*.

As Tess neared the mouth of the alley, her eyes fell on something, or someone, and she stepped backwards slowly. Her gaze cast back towards us before she unsheathed her dagger, grasping it tightly in her fist.

"Gotten yourselves into quite the pickle, haven't you?" The familiar voice sounded as he rounded the corner, taking in the scene before him.

He crossed his arms over his chest, a knowing smile across his lips. His dagger hung from the strap on his thigh, his jacket clinging against his muscles as he gave his salt and pepper hair a shake.

"*Phineas Wolfe.*" The name left my mouth sounding as if it were a curse.

I couldn't think of a worse time for him to show up. We needed to get Saanvi medical attention, and quickly. We didn't have time to deal with him or his men. He had warned us not to come back to The Shadow, and I feared what would happen to us now that we had.

"The one and only, darling," he replied, a glint of mirth in his eyes.

"Please, just let us go," I ground out, my voice pleading.

I wasn't beneath begging in order to save Saanvi's life. We couldn't let her die here, in the depths of The Shadow, surrounded by blood and grime.

Phineas raised a brow in my direction. "Appears you are in dire need of assistance. Might I offer you some?"

"What's the catch?" I asked, deadpan.

I didn't trust Phineas for one second, and whatever he offered would come at a price. He was in the business of stealing spells and information; I doubted he would willingly do something out of the kindness of his own heart.

"No catch, love, you simply need to come with me," he replied.

"We aren't going anywhere with you," Tess responded, her lips thinning.

"Not sure you have much choice in the matter." He nodded towards Saanvi as her body slumped against Kenna even further, Puck still putting pressure on the wound at her chest.

One of Phineas's men appeared right over his shoulder, his hand moving towards the sword in its scabbard across his back. Phineas gave an infinitesimal shake of his head and the man relaxed his hand back to his side.

"What will it cost us?" I asked, my jaw clenched.

"Ah, you are correct that it won't be free. But it is a fair price, if I do say so myself." He laughed, but the humor didn't reach his eyes.

What was he playing at?

"And the price?" I asked through gritted teeth.

"You tell me everything you find out when you track down Alastir."

I couldn't keep the surprise off my face as my mouth parted. "How do you know we are searching for Alastir?"

"Let's just say I have eyes and ears in this realm. I make it my business to know *everything*."

I swallowed hard, my feet moving to gaze at the puddle of blood I stood in. I wasn't sure what he would need with the information we were searching to get from Alastir, but it seemed harmless enough. We were hunting for a cure or an antidote for Noctani, to return the witches to their natural states. What nefarious things could he do with that information? If he or his men had already spotted us on this side of the realm, as had Kane, we were running out of time.

"Done. Now help us get her out of here," I replied, my voice tight.

"Diana—" Tess spoke, but my glare cut off her words.

We needed to do this for Saanvi, and if that meant Phineas would need to sit in on our meeting with Alastir, then that's what we would do.

Phineas's gaze moved from Tess to me, and he shrugged. "Very well then."

He motioned for his man to join us, and he moved forward, helping Saanvi to stand and slinging her arm over his shoulder. Puck held her other arm around his neck, his hand still pressed to the wound.

"Can you walk?" he asked, his voice barely above a whisper in Saanvi's ear.

She squeezed her eyes shut for a moment, pushing her feet beneath her. As soon as she did, her knees gave out.

"We have to carry her," Puck said, grasping Saanvi behind the knees and lifting her into his arms. Phineas's man moved forward to wrap a strip of fabric across her back and chest to put pressure against the bleeding wound.

"Where are we going?" I asked, a weight of uncertainty filling my gut.

"You'll see," was all Phineas replied, a lilt of a smile lifting the corner of his lips once more.

He turned out of the mouth of the alleyway and walked down the street at a clipped pace, not bothering to glance behind him to ensure we were following. My palms were sweating as I slid Stormslayer back into the sheath at my thigh, rubbing the sweat off onto my soiled pants.

Tess cast me a wary glance, but I only shook my head in response. We couldn't trust Phineas, but it was our only choice. He could easily be leading us into a trap. If we tried to take Saanvi up and out of The Shadow to get her help, she might not make it. Her face was chalky, her eyes squeezed shut. The natural golden pallor was draining from her face as Kenna walked beside Puck, grasping her thin hand within her own.

Saanvi would be alright. She had to be.

I cursed myself for leaving a throwing knife. It was a mistake I would surely never make again. I had been so incensed by the sound of Nik's name coming out of Kane's mouth that I had been distracted. I had allowed him to harm one of us in his final act.

We had left their bloody bodies in a heap across the alleyway's dead end and it was sure to stir up some questions. So much for keeping a low profile in The Shadow. We needed to help Saanvi, find Alastir, and get the *hell* out of here before Donika's men found us. We were practically leaving a physical blood trail behind us.

I pinched the bridge of my nose hard enough for black spots to mar my vision. This had all gone to shit, and we didn't have much time left. We needed to get out of Prins sooner rather than later and return to the seaside cabin to regroup. We needed a new plan. We were leaving ourselves vulnerable wandering around the realm for this long, unprotected.

We twisted and turned along the streets of The Shadow, going back the way we had come when we were fleeing from Kane and his men. We made our way towards the Siraway mountains and the sea beyond, the area where the shop worker had told us we might find Alastir. Maybe we would get lucky and we could kill two birds with one stone, help Saanvi and speak with Alastir all at once.

Kenna whispered an incantation under her breath as we took another twisted turn, her eyes closed in concentration. She didn't have healing powers as Annelise and Amiyah did, but I prayed to the Mother whatever healing magic she *did* have would help.

The uneasy sensation of being watched settled deep within my core once more, and I picked up my pace, joining Phineas as he stalked ahead of us.

"Are your men following us?" I asked, my brow lifted at him as I pulled up at his side.

He shook his head. "It's only Baron with me today." He nodded back towards the man who walked at Saanvi's side with Puck and Kenna.

"Something doesn't feel right," I told him, my hand against my stomach to quell the growing nausea. "It felt like it did when Kane and his men were watching us, stalking us. Someone is here."

Phineas glanced at me, holding my gaze for one long moment before putting two fingers in his mouth and letting out a sharp whistle. His speed increased, his long legs moving faster, and I increased mine as well to match pace with him. I practically had to run to stay at his side. A bald man with a long goatee exited the door ahead of us, and I skidded to a stop. Phineas said nothing as the man joined us, walking among our group.

After the next corner we turned, a man with a fedora pulled low over his brow joined the group, meandering out of the pub as if he were only a drunk patron on his way home. He kept his head low, his eyes darting left and right. Something soared in my vision to the left and I turned my head sharply to see a boy no older than fifteen scaling the rooftops. He was matching pace with our group as he jumped from one rooftop to the next, watching us from above the tattered and ripped awnings that shielded the street below.

Phineas's men.

He would not let us be outnumbered. Whoever was following us had better turn back now, as more and more of Phineas's gang came out of the woodwork to form a pack around us. Whatever we were going to find out from Alastir, Phineas wanted that information. *Badly.*

Phineas came to a stop at a closed shop, his hand on the door knob. He stopped suddenly and I almost skidded into him. He whispered a spell quietly enough that I couldn't make out any of the words, and the door popped open beneath his touch. He ushered each of us in as he pushed everything on the large wooden table that spread across the open space onto the floor.

It was a modest shop with three large wooden tables, two of which were covered in beakers and bottles of liquids. There was a young man restocking the shelves against the left wall and he dropped a beaker and balked when he saw us come in. The bright green liquid spilled across the concrete floor.

"So sorry, sir. I will go get him."

The young man scrambled up the staircase to the right of the cashier counter and disappeared onto the second floor.

Get *who*, exactly? A healer?

My heart was beating out of my chest as they laid Saanvi across the table. She had lost consciousness at some point during the journey here, and her head fell limply against the worn wood beneath. Her hand was still clasped within Kenna's, unwilling to let go.

Phineas moved towards the shelves on the left and scanned them quickly, muttering under his breath.

"Aha! Here it is," he exclaimed, reaching out and snatching a test tube full of pink liquid off the shelf.

He moved to Saanvi's side, helping Puck to sit her up.

"Time to wake up, love," he said, shaking her shoulders not-so-gently before giving her a few slaps across the cheek to try to rouse her.

Saanvi stirred, grumbling complaints escaping her lips as she peeled her eyes open.

"Drink this." Phineas's voice brooked no argument as he tipped the test tube of pink liquid to her lips.

Saanvi coughed and sputtered, choking on the pink liquid as she made a face of disdain. She ran a hand across her lips, catching the droplets that had run down her chin. "That is *awful.*"

"Nothing that is going to save your life is going to taste good, I fear." Phineas took a step back, his hands on his hips as he watched Saanvi.

"What was that?" I asked, moving to his side.

"A healing potion. Won't be enough to close the wound itself, but it works by healing the wound from the inside out," he replied. His eyes narrowed on Saanvi to watch for any changes in her condition.

I nodded in response.

I was relieved he was helping us, but make no mistake, Phineas Wolfe was a dangerous man. We couldn't trust him. He had betrayed my mother and stolen the key spell from the Kotova grimoire, and he had insinuated it wasn't the only spell he had stolen from my book of shadows.

"I'm coming, I'm coming," a gruff voice sounded from the stairwell.

My eyes floated up to watch as the older man descended the stairs, one hand on the railing and one hand clasped to his chest. The young man that had been stocking the shelves was right on his heels. How had Phineas known where to find him?

"I never thought I would see you here again," he spoke to Phineas as he made his way to the wooden table. His wrinkled hand moved the tunic of Saanvi's shirt aside to inspect the wound in her chest.

Phineas simply laughed. "It's good to see you again, Alastir."

8

Exactly the man we were searching for. How had Phineas led us right to him?

Alastir had descended the staircase and moved straight to Saanvi's side, pushing us gently out of the way. He gradually laid her back down, procuring a translucent green stone from his pocket and placing it on Saanvi's chest right above her wound. He got to work quickly, grabbing the mortar and pestle off the counter and filling it with all sorts of herbs and powders with a dash of liquid to form a salve.

He pulled the tunic away from Saanvi's chest and it stuck to her skin, causing her to wince in pain. He liberally spread the salve across the wound as he muttered an incantation, the words unfamiliar to me.

"Didn't you see us coming?" I asked, leaning my hip against the front counter as we watched him work.

"Don't sass me, girl," he replied, his gaze deadpan as his eyes quickly flickered up to me before returning to Saanvi. "You know very well I only see what the Mother deigns to show me, and she did not show me this."

When he was finished applying the salve to Saanvi's wound, he grabbed the quartzite stone and place it in her grasp, his hands encompassing hers. More spells flowed from his lips as we waited on bated breath to see if we had gotten here in time to save her. The knife had to have nicked something vital in her chest with the amount of blood that she had lost.

Saanvi's head fell back as her muscles released, no longer able to hold her own head straight. The creases of pain that had marked her expression were gone. I moved forward in shock—my hand out—but Alastir stopped me.

"Needn't fret—the girl lives. This is part of the spell. She will heal faster in slumber."

I glanced at him, eyes wide, before nodding in response.

If there was anyone that could save Saanvi at this point, it would be Alastir. He was not only a powerful seer but a powerful Shade with abilities far beyond what we could comprehend. I moved back to the counter, resting against it and releasing the air I had been holding in my chest.

Saanvi would be ok.

Puck had begun rifling through the beakers and test tubes on the shelf and one crashed to the floor before him, spilling neon green liquid across the floor.

"Sorry, mate," he cringed as he turned to Alastir, who was watching him with narrowed eyes.

"Petyr, step away from the shelf." Alastir pushed away from the table to move towards him.

"If people don't stop calling me that…" Puck mumbled as he stepped away from the shelf as Alastir had asked, crossing his arms over his chest.

"Thomas, you'll grab the mop to clean this up?" Alastir asked, unclasping his cloak at the neck and draping it across one of the chairs that had been pushed away from the table. The young man nodded, disappearing into a back room to gather the supplies.

Alastir turned to Phineas with an unreadable expression in his gaze, and my eyes flitted between the two of them. How had Phineas known *exactly* where Alastir was? And how did they know each other?

"Time for those answers?" Phineas asked, the ghost of a smile across his lips. "I did hold up my end of the bargain, after all."

"You did," I replied through my teeth, crossing my own arms over my chest in a protective manner.

Phineas nodded towards the door with his head, his salt and pepper curls falling across his brow. His men quickly filed out of the small shop, out of ear shot. He pulled a chair out from the table and sat, his legs spread wide, a smirk across his lips.

"Go on then, don't let me stop you."

I wanted to wipe that smirk right off his smug little face.

"What is this place?" I asked instead, Phineas's gaze narrowing on me.

Alastir's forehead creased as he met my gaze. A moment passed before he answered.

"This used to be my home," he replied, a sad lilt to his words. "I grew up here. Raised my children here."

Children? I hadn't known him to have any. And I hadn't known that Alastir grew up in The Shadow. Many Shades who weren't as well off did, but I hadn't imagined that he was one of them. He ran a successful charm shop in Prins out of a generously sized town house.

"I didn't know." My voice was soft.

I could see the emotion flood Alastir's gaze as it flitted to Phineas once more. What was the connection here?

I turned towards Phineas—my gaze shrewd. "How did you know where Alastir was?"

"I knew he would be home," was all he said.

Home.

Not *his* home, but home. As if they had shared it together.

My gaze darted between the two of them once more, the puzzle pieces slowly falling into place.

Alastir sighed. "I was raised here by my parents. When I had my first child, I raised him here, too. Only a certain sort of clientele frequents a shop in The Shadow, therefore I moved the main store to Prins and had my youngest, Thomas, take over operations here." He nodded towards the young man mopping up the spilled liquid across the room. I hadn't even noticed him reappear from the storage room.

Thomas was his son.

"And your oldest?" I asked, my brow quirked.

Deep down, I already knew the answer. A long moment of silence passed between us as we waited for his reply. Finally, he sighed, running a hand through his beard.

"Phineas," he replied, his eyes crinkling at the corners.

Whether it was with affection or disappointment, I couldn't quite tell.

"So you knew to come here, because this was your home, too?" I asked, glancing back towards Phineas.

He nodded in response, eyes downcast. I had never seen him without his smug expression, and the vulnerability that crossed his gaze surprised me.

Alastir was Phineas's father.

It took me a moment to wrap my mind around it—how it could all make sense. Alastir was kind and gentle, but also *incredibly* powerful. Phineas was nothing but trouble.

"If Alastir is your father, why would you need to get the information from us? Couldn't you simply ask him yourself?" I asked as I watched him prop one leg up on his knee and sit back in his chair.

"I could," he replied, "but he wouldn't tell me. My father stopped telling me what he sees many, many years ago."

"Because all it brings is *trouble*," Alastir hissed. He turned his attention back towards me. "You made a bargain with him? To save the girl?"

I nodded in response. My gaze met Tess's from across the room and she appeared equally surprised by this turn of events as I was.

"But you are the one who sent us after Phineas a few months ago. You told us he held the answers we searched for when we couldn't find the missing spell from the Kotova grimoire," I replied, reasoning it out in my head.

"Yes, my son deals in stolen spells. I happened to know that one was in his possession. Whether he knew it or not," Alastir replied with the ghost of a smile, pulling a chair out from the table and sitting across from his son. "I know what my son is. I'm not proud of it."

Phineas appeared as if he was going to say more but stopped himself, biting his lip and turning his gaze away. Saanvi stirred on the table, her legs moving, her lips murmuring, before becoming still once more. Her chest rose and fell in a steady rhythm.

"So what did you bargain with my son to save the girl's life?" Alastir asked.

He looked very, very tired.

I swallowed, steeling myself for what I was about to ask. I hadn't managed to discuss Nikolai without ripping the wound wide open, and I had lost my temper at the mere mention of his name slipping from Kane's lips. That is what had gotten us into this mess in the first place.

"You might not know, but—" My words were cut off by Alastir's interruption.

"Nikolai is Noctani."

I closed my eyes, pressing them together tightly. "Yes, Nikolai has turned Noctani. The mother showed you that?"

Alastir nodded once.

"We were told by Annelise that there was a spell that lived in the Kotova grimoire once, a spell to reverse siphoning magic. That whatever magic is done can also be undone. Amiyah said the spell has long since been ripped out and has been lost to time. But if anyone were to remember it or know where it was located, it would be you. You are our only hope for creating a cure for Noctani... an antidote for it."

Alastir's shoulders slumped under the weight of the request before his narrowed gaze met Phineas's.

"What could it hurt for him to know?" I asked. "He wanted any information we got from you. I don't see the harm in him having the cure for Noctani. This is a *good* thing."

Alastir shook his head as if I didn't understand. "It isn't that simple. Spells can be twisted and turned based on the will of the Shade. A spell can easily be reverse manufactured."

A sigh escaped my lips as I turned to Phineas. "You wouldn't."

"Alastir, I wouldn't." There was a pleading note to Phineas's voice, one I had never in my life expected to hear from him.

This side of him was... unexpected. He was the cocky, arrogant spell thief, but we had a front-row seat to his family drama. Phineas delt in knowledge, maybe he simply wanted the bragging rights of being one of the few Shades in the realm to have this information.

"My trust for you was burned out long ago," Alastir replied, his gaze falling to his boots.

Phineas appeared stung by his words. "It was the deal they made," he replied, his voice tight.

"It was," I confirmed.

Would I live to regret this? Would Phineas twist the spell and turn it into something dark, something evil? Would he reverse it to create even more Noctani? But to what end?

It was a risk we were going to have to take. I needed to bind my magic once more, and I needed Nikolai. We needed to end this war with Donika. Phineas couldn't be a priority of mine.

"Does this mean you have a cure? You have an antidote?" I asked Alastir.

Hope was clear in my voice as my gaze flickered to meet Tess's across the room once more. If he was this worried about Phineas having the spell, that had to mean that he had it, right? Or he knew where it was located at the least.

I hadn't let myself hope before. I hadn't wanted to set my heart on this only for it to be shattered when this turned out to be a dead end. More than anything, I wanted Nikolai back. I wanted to save him. More than I even wanted to end this war—as bad as that was. I was *broken* with the piece of the binding shattered within me, and I wasn't sure I could make my move against Donika when I didn't feel whole.

"The spell you seek is the reversal of siphoning. It would reverse the very essence that made the Noctani what they are. I cannot guarantee that it would restore the Shade to their original state, or that the Shade would even survive it." Alastir's gaze was sharp, his voice gruff. "Do you understand what I am saying, girl?"

If he called me girl one more time...

I bristled. "*Diana.*" I replied through my teeth. "You'll have enough respect for your rightful queen to call me by my name, at the least."

Alastir cleared his throat. "My apologies. I meant no offense. It's only that this is a... tricky spell... to put it simply. I cannot make any guarantees about its success and I don't want your expectations to be misaligned."

"Have you ever done it before?" Tess asked, moving towards me from across the room and stopping at my side.

Thomas had left at some point to dispose of the mop and bucket.

"I have not." Alastir shook his head. "The siphoning spell originates from the Kotova grimoire, but it no longer resides there."

"We already know that," I replied, my jaw tight. "My mother ripped it out."

I could curse her for ripping out the spells I needed most in my time of need.

"Do you have it?" Tess asked.

Alastir shook his head. "It is not in my possession."

"But you know where it is?" Her eyes hardened.

Alastir's gaze fell on Phineas and it took every bit of strength within me not to leap across the room and fasten my bare hands around his neck.

"I don't have it, Alastir," Phineas replied.

There was no hint of untruth in his voice, but this wasn't a man we could trust.

"You don't... but you did," Alastir replied.

Phineas averted his gaze in confirmation.

"Where is it now?" I asked, my patience wearing thin. "Who did you sell it to?"

Phineas squirmed under my gaze and my hand darted to Stormslayer's hilt at my thigh, ready to unsheathe her at a moment's notice. Alastir raised his hand as if to stop me, but I could see Puck closing in on Phineas out of the corner of my eye. Kenna hadn't left Saanvi's side, but her eyes darted about the room as she watched everything unfurl.

Right before Puck could grab Phineas across the shoulders from behind, he pushed back out of his chair as if he could sense him. It skidded across the concrete and into Puck. He whirled on Puck, a dagger held between them.

"There's no need for blades," he said, despite holding one firmly in his own grasp.

"Sure," Puck shrugged, his Katana glinting off the sun that peered through the shop window. "No need for blades, simply tell us who you sold the spell to and we will be on our way."

Simply knowing that we wanted it—needed it—Phineas would want the spell for himself. We were walking a fine line here. My blood was pumping through my veins thickly enough that my head was pounding to the rhythm of my heart. I would not let Phineas stand in the way of possibly curing Nikolai. I would do whatever it took to get my hands on that spell.

"Afraid the spell isn't... accessible right now." Phineas appeared sheepish as he took a step back... away from Puck.

Towards me.

I moved fast enough that I wasn't sure if anyone saw, and I had Phineas's back pressed against my chest, Stormslayer held across his throat. Everyone always thought Puck was the greater threat and underestimated me.

Big mistake.

I pressed the blade against his Adam's apple and a trickle of blood spilled down, soaking through the collar of his white tunic.

"This all feels so familiar, doesn't it? My blade to your throat? You'll tell us who you sold the spell to, and you'll tell us now." My voice brooked no argument.

Phineas nodded, but that only made the blood trickle faster, my blade sinking deeper into his skin. He raised his hands in defense, letting his dagger clatter to the floor.

"It's with Corian." His voice was breathless as he slumped against me. "The spell is with Corian, Donika's dream walker."

9

Great. The spell was in the *one* place we couldn't go retrieve it.

It was in The Stone Palace.

I let Phineas go, and he dropped to the floor, his knees giving out. He crawled to stand, rubbing against the place where the blade had cut into his skin.

"Lot of good that does us," Puck said, shaking his head and throwing his arms up in exasperation.

It made sense that Corian would want to purchase that particular spell from Phineas. They didn't have the siphoning spell itself, that was still safely tucked away in the Kotova grimoire where it belonged. That was the spell Donika had been desperate to get her hands on. Corian had probably gone searching for a siphoning reversal spell from Phineas knowing he could twist it and use it as a jumping off point to create his own twisted Noctani spell.

As Alastir had implied.

He might have created the Noctani out of that exact spell.

I released a frustrated exhale as I gripped the back of one of the dining chairs tightly enough that my knuckles turned white.

"We can't get that spell." I muttered, my gaze on the floor.

"Alastir?" It was Kenna's small voice that drew our attention back towards the table.

I lifted my head, glancing at Alastir only to see that his eyes were white, completely glazed over. No iris or cornea was visible at all, only the milky shade that now stared back at us blankly. Was he having a vision?

Phineas moved to his side, gripping his shoulder as he gently shook him.

"Alastir, Alastir! What do you see?"

"He's having a vision?" I asked, moving to his side.

Phineas nodded in confirmation, his mouth taut in a thin line.

Alastir was somewhere far, far away as the vision took him. His hand twitched and his head nodded absently. It only lasted a matter of seconds before the milky white mask of his eyes cleared and his hazel gaze coming back into view.

"I remember," he spoke, his voice brittle has he re-adjusted to his surroundings, his gaze sweeping the room. He cleared his throat, his hand on his chest before he spoke again. "I might not have the spell in my possession, but I remember. The Mother... she showed me."

He stood from his chair and it pushed back with a screech against the concrete floor. He hurried to the counter where he grabbed a pen and parchment, scribbling down all that he remembered from the vision. His hand moved quickly across the paper, and a silence fell across the room. As if we all held our breath collectively.

Why would the Mother choose to show him the spell? Was it because he had already seen it, he simply needed his memory refreshed? The Mother *didn't* choose sides, and a vision such as this was a rarity, indeed.

When Alastir finished scribbling down the spell on the paper, he said nothing. He went to the shelves and searched for ingredients, pulling them off the shelves and placing them on the countertop.

Saanvi stirred, her eyes opening.

"What's going on?" Her voice was weak. She pulled the bandage away from her chest wound to find it most-ly healed, only the last of the scab still visible beneath. "What the—" but her words were cut off by Alastir.

"You'll need to rest. You can't travel with the spell that I used. It might be outwardly healed, but the body is fast at work draining your own energy and magic to do the healing. You'll need to stay here for a few days until your magic can replenish and the wound can finish repairing itself."

Saanvi met Kenna's gaze. Tears pricked her eyes as she pulled her to her chest, holding her tight against her. A soft smile graced my lips at the sight. I couldn't be more thankful to Alastir for saving her.

"And the antidote?" Saanvi asked, her eyes searching the room for me.

"We don't have the spell," I explained, "but Alastir might still be able to replicate it."

"I make no promises," his voice was stern, his concentration on the shelves before him as he stroked his beard. "I need bloodroot... there isn't any here."

His gaze flitted to Phineas. "Fetch me some."

"Me?" he asked, surprised. "Why me?"

"You, son, are the most familiar with The Shadow. Not only do they not know how to find the exit to this disastrous place, but I cannot send one of them out to fetch something that they don't even know what it is. Now *go*." Alastir's voice was commanding as he continued to study the shelves.

Phineas silently grabbed his jacket and shrugged it on. As Alastir's son, he had to be well versed in charms and potions himself, knowing exactly what ingredient it was Alastir needed. He silently left the shop, slamming the door behind him and rattling the windows. His men followed him as he set off down the cobblestone street, out of sight.

The moment the door closed between us Alastir moved to the counter where I was perched, his eyes bright with excitement. "Listen to me carefully, it won't take him long to find the bloodroot. We only have a matter of minutes."

My brow furrowed in confusion. "What is going on? What aren't you telling us?"

Alastir shook his head, as if he didn't want to speak the words he was about to say. "Siphoning is *dark* magic. Blood magic. To reverse it, we need the same. Magic is all about balance. Give and take. Is this a price you are willing to pay?"

I gulped, the consequence of the decision weighing heavily on me despite already knowing the answer. "Yes." The word was barely a whisper.

"I do not know the price, but there *will* be a price. Of all the spells Phineas could get his hands on, this one is especially dangerous. I know you made a deal with him, but you might need to keep some of this a secret. This spell can easily be twisted for one's own gain, and blood magic is unpredictable when altered."

I nodded in response. "I understand. But what if he finds out? What will be the price of betraying him?"

Alastir raised his brow. "You don't want to know."

I nodded. I couldn't think of the repercussions of that right now, we needed to perform this ritual and create this antidote. We didn't have any other choice.

"What do you need from me?" I asked, studying the parchment where Alastir had scribbled the spell.

"Your blood."

"*My* blood?" I asked, confused.

"Kotova blood is some of the most potent and powerful blood there is. Donika used her own blood to create this spell, we need your blood to undo it."

I nodded in understanding.

Alastir grabbed a glass and placed it on the counter, reaching into his belt to procure a small knife. Without preamble he grasped my hand, cutting the palm. I winced, holding it over the glass as the blood poured forth over my skin. His eyes darted towards the shop door before returning to me, squeezing my hand to encourage the flow of blood.

Once enough blood had filled the glass, he pressed his own palm to mine, blood smearing between our hands.

"*Sana quod laesi. Sana quod laesi. Sana quod laesi.*" The incantation flowed from his lips rapidly. When he removed his hand from mine, the only indication that there had ever been a cut was the smear of blood left behind.

"Quickly, go upstairs and wash that off." Alastir nodded towards the staircase that led to the second level. He wiped his own hand on a dish rag, stuffing the bloody rag into a drawer behind the counter. "Thomas, bring this upstairs and place it in the vault."

Thomas, who I hadn't noticed appear again, nodded in understanding. He grasped the glass in his shaking hands and followed me up the staircase. Right off the landing to the second floor was a small washroom, and I ran my hand under the sink until it was clean. I wiped my hands off on the washcloth, leaving it hanging over the lip of the sink. I quickly descended the staircase, Thomas on my heels.

"We cannot perform the spell with him here. I will have to figure out a way to get rid of him. The blood magic gives off a distinct essence that he will sense immediately."

"I understand." My throat was thick.

"There is another ingredient I seem to be missing that I will have to send out for as well. Dragon's breath. I could have sworn it was right here," Alastir spoke as he moved towards the shelf, his hand lingering on an empty spot where the container must have been.

It was only another moment before Phineas approached, his men remaining outside as he opened the door to the shop.

His hand was filled with a green and red root with a white flower. He placed it on the counter before Alastir.

"Will it only be enough for one cure?" Puck asked.

Isaac. He was thinking of Isaac.

"Do you need more than one?" Alastir asked, his gaze meeting Puck's.

"Yes," I answered for him. "We need two."

"Who else—" but his words were cut off as his eyes glazed over, turning milky. It only lasted the span of a exhale before they cleared. "Isaac."

His expression turned grim as he grabbed a larger beaker from the shelf and placed it on the counter. "Isaac was a good friend of mine. Tried to convince me to join the resistance more times than I can count."

"And each time you declined?" I asked.

"As I've told you before, I am too old for war," he replied thinly.

He didn't appear to be *that* old. But at some point, Shades slowed in their aging. If he was the advisor and best friend of my father Osiris, he had to be at least in his sixties at this point, if not much older. I was too afraid to ask.

Alastir ground together a mixture of ingredients in the mortar with the pestle, pressing them together until all that was left behind was a brown, indistinguishable powder. He poured the powder into the beaker, filling it with a mixture of different colored liquids.

"I still need Dragon's breath," he said, glancing at Phineas.

Phineas crossed his arms over his chest, raising a skeptical brow. "I think not. One of them can go out and get it. I won't leave again. I am owed this antidote just as much as they are. We made a deal."

"I'll go," Puck offered, not wanting to argue further.

We didn't want to raise suspicion by continually sending him off for ingredients, it was best if we went ourselves this time.

"I'll go with you," Tess offered, "can't be out here alone in a time like this."

"We all should go," Saanvi offered, swinging her legs over the side of the table. "We could easily be ambushed—we need strength in numbers."

"*You* won't be going anywhere," Alastir spoke without glancing up from his concoction. "You won't be leaving this shop for two days, at least."

Kenna bit her lip, clearly hesitant to leave Saanvi here alone.

"I'll go with you," I spoke, moving towards the door. "Three is better than one."

Puck nodded in confirmation, his hand on the knob.

"And what, exactly, are we searching for?" Puck asked.

"A plant with dark red leaves and bright red flowers. You can't miss it... its unmistakable. Though it only grows in Dragon's Hollow."

"Seriously?" Tess murmured under her breath, exasperated.

By the end of this day, we would have gone back and forth enough times that we could have made it from one end of Istmere to the other.

"Back to Dragon's Hollow, then..." I said reluctantly as Puck opened the door.

We stepped out of the shop and out into The Shadow once more.

10

We weren't exactly sure of the way back to the staircase that led out of The Shadow from Alastir's family home. What we did know was the general direction we needed to move in. Tess and I followed Puck, allowing him to take the lead. We had pulled our cloaks over our heads and kept our gazes turned down, hoping not to draw any attention. It would have been helpful if one of us were a Nightshade and could use our heightened sense of smell to guide us.

Luckily, we didn't pass the spot where we had slain Kane and his men again. We made it out of The Shadow and back into Prins as the weather took a turn. The sky overhead was turning an ominous grey color, the clouds roiling together angrily. A single raindrop fell against my cheek and I lifted my hand to wipe it away, raising my gaze towards the sky.

I couldn't be certain that this storm was a natural one and not of magical origin, and the thought had a shiver running down my spine. But we were already halfway there, and there was no turning back now. Alastir needed the Dragon's breath from Dragon's Hollow to complete the Noctani antidote, and there was nothing that would stop us from retrieving it.

I felt a hope begin to wedge itself deep in my chest, and I tried to shake it away. Alastir had said he wasn't sure if this spell would return the Noctani to their original state. Or if they would even survive it. The thought that I could lose Nikolai forever made my gut twist and my head throb. The fact that I wasn't dead *had* to mean something. I feared if the antidote killed the Noctani, then I would die too. I didn't think there was any other way to get around the binding, despite it being broken in its current state.

I sent a silent prayer up to the Mother that the antidote didn't kill them. That would be a worst-case scenario, and one we couldn't afford.

We swung right on the cobbled streets as the sky opened up, sending a light rainfall down upon us. My feet splashed in the shallow rain puddles as we walked, cleansing Kane's blood from my boots. By the time we had crested the hill into Dragon's Hollow I was tiring, and I could see the same in Tess and Puck. It had been an incredibly long day, and nightfall was threatening to descend. We had been back and forth what felt like a million times, and we hadn't thought it would take us this long. We hadn't planned to stay the night in this part of the realm.

We had to make it back to Alastir before the sun set at the least, we had no place else to stay overnight except for his home. We couldn't risk an inn, despite my craving for a plush bed at the moment.

"Where should we begin searching?" Tess asked, pulling her cloak tighter around herself to help warm her skin and ward off the chill that had settled in the air.

"The fields where we used to train?" Puck asked, brow raised. "There are all sorts of flora towards the forest, I can't quite remember ever seeing Dragon's breath though."

"We might not have noticed it if we weren't searching for it," I reminded him. "And it could have been the wrong season."

"That's true," he conceded.

Thunder cracked loudly overhead, followed by a slow and steady rumble that vibrated through my feet and up my spine. Lightning streaked through the sky and hit one of the buildings behind us, sending sparks flying and a loud crash through the air.

"We'd better hurry if for no other reason than to get out of this weather," Tess grumbled, forging onward, down the other side of the hill.

It was only about a twenty-minute walk through the rain-slicked streets before we glimpsed the old training fields in the distance. Puck had been right, there was flora of all shapes and colors sprouting and blooming on the outskirts of the forest.

I wave uneasiness rolled over me as I recalled that this exact forest was where we had seen Donika's Araneoch monsters for the first time. Tess cast me a glance that told me she was thinking the same thing. We trudged towards the forest edge and scanned the plants for dark red leaves with bright red flowers.

"Is it this?" Tess asked, holding up a bright red bloom with petals.

I shook my head. "No petals… it's more… elongated and spiky."

She nodded as she returned to the flower patch and kept searching.

The flowers were growing densely together and it was difficult to see them all individually. I found I had to kneel in order to push some out of the way to see what was growing beneath. The edges of the forest were decorated with shocks of blue, purples, reds, and yellows. Summer in Prins was beautiful, but the same chill Tess had sensed earlier from the oncoming storm was settling deep in my bones.

"This?" Puck asked, a long red flower in his grip.

"Yes!" I exclaimed, standing despite my knees protesting from all the kneeling. "How much did you find?"

"There isn't much," Puck confessed as we approached, kneeling down to where he had plucked the flower. "Did he say how much of the flower and its leaves he needed?"

I shook my head. "We should take all we can find and make it quick."

My gaze met the horizon as the sun was beginning to set, disappearing behind the tall pine trees and casting the sky in an eerie yellow glow against the storm clouds.

Puck nodded at me in agreement. We didn't want to be caught sneaking around in The Shadow after dark, but it appeared that's *exactly* what we were going to have to do. We were lucky to have left at first dawn this morning, but it still hadn't been enough time with having to backtrack across the realm multiple times.

Lightning struck a nearby tree, and it cracked and moaned, falling to the forest floor a mere thirty feet from us. Tess and I hurriedly helped Puck pick all the red stems and leaves we could find before stuffing them into Puck's pack.

"This will have to be enough," Puck declared, "nightfall is almost upon us. We've run out of time."

"Let's get the hell out of here," Tess agreed, starting towards the streets of Dragon's Hollow.

"What the—" Puck spoke, but the three of us stopped in our tracks as we saw what awaited as at the entrance to the training field.

No.

No, no, no.

This couldn't be happening.

We didn't have the antidote yet.

Where the cobbled streets met the tall grass of the training field was a pack of Noctani. Their hair was dripping with rainwater as if they had been prowling the streets for some time in the storm. At their lead was a shock of blond hair, and my tongue was thick and leaden in my throat. I swallowed back the horror that threatened to choke me as I took a step backwards.

I didn't want to see him like this.

I wasn't ready to face him yet, not that I was sure I ever would be. He had the ability to steal my magic—and by the looks of it—we were outnumbered. My vision wasn't clear beneath the heavy rain that spit from the sky, but it appeared as if there were at least six or seven of them.

I hadn't wanted to face Nik until we had the antidote in hand.

It was too soon.

We needed to escape him, because killing him wasn't an option. Isaac wasn't with them, and that fact brought with it only a small amount of relief. Over Nik's shoulder I could see Antonia Finch, our old art teacher. She was the only one left from the Shades that had stalked us in the mortal realm and tried to bring us back to Istmere for Donika.

Fletcher, his brother, and his men were all dead.

Ms. Finch's eyes were an endless depth of black, and tears stung the back of my eyes at the sight. She hadn't wanted to fight for Donika, but she had ended up Noctani in the end; despite her best efforts. She was too weak to stand up for herself, her only options were to obey Donika—or lay down and die.

I swallowed hard, taking another step back. My gaze darted between Puck and Tess, and they glanced back with equally bewildered expressions.

I couldn't fight Nikolai.

I couldn't.

"What do we do?" I asked, panicked.

I grabbed Puck by the arm, desperate. He could read it in my eyes. Even if we tried to fight them, we would lose. Any one of them could steal my magic and bring it back to Donika. It wasn't a risk we could take.

I wouldn't lose my magic, and I wouldn't lose Nik. Neither was an option.

Puck turned back towards me, rainwater spilling down his face as the intensity of the storm surged. "We run."

Without hesitation I took off at a sprint toward the south corner of the field, grabbing Stormslayer from its sheath at my thigh and pulling it free. My throwing knives were still secured in my boot and at the back of my belt, but I desperately wished I was more heavily armed. I had no qualms about using force against the other Noctani if it meant making it out of this alive.

Nik was the only one I didn't want to raise my sword against. I wasn't sure I even could, if it came down to it.

The Noctani took off too, their speed far eclipsing ours as they cut off our passage into Dragon's Hollow. We skidded to a stop, sludge flying where our boots had dug into the mud.

"*Shit.*"

"Shit, indeed." Tess murmured, her sword held tightly in her grip.

Corian hadn't been embellishing when he had said they had increased speed and strength. With how quickly they had cut off our path I would guess they were twice as fast, at least. Maybe more.

Shadows slithered out from Nik's hands and I had to choke back a cry as they slid across the field, wrapping around my legs. For once his shadows didn't bring me comfort, and the only thing I could think of was how Donika had used her shadows to torture me.

Hurt me.

It would be foolish for me to expect anything different from Noctani.

"We only want to talk," he called out, his voice sounding as smooth as honey, a sinister smile lifting his lips.

My gaze traveled from those lips up to his black, endless eyes, and my magic surged forth of its own volition. I was too volatile. It was all too fresh. The last time I had seen Nik as Noctani my magic had detonated, and we couldn't risk that happening again. I didn't have control of my power, and if I unleashed it here, I had no clue what would happen. I didn't want to risk Puck or Tess. I didn't want to risk hurting Nik.

The group of Noctani had found us fairly easily. Who knew how many others were out prowling the streets of Prins searching for us? How many soldiers Donika had sent to find us?

"Whatever happens here, you need to get that Dragon's breath back to Alastir," I murmured to Puck, my voice low.

"Don't talk like that," he snapped. I could sense his searing gaze against my back. "We aren't leaving you here."

"You might have to, if it comes down to a fight we can't win. Our only hope is to finish the antidote. *We need to finish the antidote*, do you understand me?" I replied through clenched teeth.

"No. What good does the antidote do if we don't have *you* anymore? I won't leave you here." Puck's voice was grim.

"Do not make me command you, Puck."

"You wouldn't dare." This time, his voice was *venom*. "I will stay to protect my queen at all costs. I will not sacrifice you and your magic to save Nikolai. It's not what he would have wanted."

"And if your queen commands you to run, to leave with the Dragon's breath and finish the antidote?" I asked, my voice strangled.

"Then she will be shit out of luck, because that isn't an option. Who gives a shit about the antidote if you are dead?"

"*Me.* I give a shit," I snapped back.

"Stop it!" Tess cried, "both of you!"

The Noctani were fast approaching from across the field, closing the distance between us. They were close enough now to be within ear shot, listening to our every word.

"I can distract them enough for you two to get away," I said, lowering my chin and focusing my gaze on Nikolai.

He would be the biggest threat of the group and fighting him without killing him would be *incredibly* difficult.

"That's a terrible plan," Tess spat, adjusting her footing as the Noctani continued to approach.

There was nowhere to run. Nowhere to hide. It would come down to a fight, and I didn't think they would kill me. They would take my magic and bring me back to Donika. It would buy us some time, at least.

"Listen to me. Both of you. We cannot fight them. We can't kill them all and take Nik alive."

Nik released a laugh so deep his head tilted back against his shoulders, his face pale against the stormy sky.

"Maybe not, but we will try." Puck flicked his Katana through the air, threatening the Noctani not to come any closer. "I won't run without you. I promised him, Diana. I promised him I would take care of you. Keep you safe."

"From *him*?" I seethed—my teeth bared. "The circumstances have changed. They won't kill me, Donika wants that too much. She would never let her Noctani take that from her. The two of you on the other hand... "

I let my words trail off, hanging in the thick, tempestuous air.

"Enough." Nik's voice was cutting and deep as he raised a hand.

The Noctani stopped in their tracks behind him. Their dead, black eyes tracked our every breath. Our every movement. Nik's sword was strapped to his back. His wet hair fell over his brow. His lush mouth twisted into a smile. Everything about him was the same *except those eyes*. Every glance towards him that met his blackened gaze threatened to undo me. How could this have happened? How could I have let Donika turn him into one of her twisted little monsters?

Nik inclined his head as his gaze remained focused on me.

"What's the matter, Firecracker? Didn't you miss me?"

11

This couldn't be happening. I desperately prayed this was only a nightmare, but when I squeezed my eyes shut tightly and opened them once more, the group of Noctani still stood before me. Nik's head was cocked to the side, that familiar lazy smile across his lips.

His hand moved to his chest, right above his heart. Did it still beat?

"You wound me, Firecracker."

He took a step closer, and I took a step back. He lifted his brow at me.

"Are you afraid of me?" he asked, his voice that same velvety tone he used when he would flirt. I could taste bile rising up the back of my throat and I tried my best to swallow it back down.

I shook my head. "No, not afraid. I don't want to hurt you."

He laughed, his head falling back as his mouth opened, showcasing those sharpened white teeth.

Fangs.

"Hurt *me*? You could never hurt me, Firecracker. Not when I'm like this."

I took another step backwards towards Puck and Tess, and he tracked the movement. He inclined his head ever so slightly, but he stayed put.

It was Puck whose voice broke the heavy silence that had fallen across the clearing. "Just leave. We don't want to fight you, Nikolai. Take this opportunity and turn back." His voice sounded as if it were a desperate plea.

"I don't want to fight you either, *brother,*" Nik replied.

Puck flinched.

"My quarrel isn't with you." Nik shook his head. "We simply need to take Diana with us." Nik reached for the hilt of the broadsword strapped to his back, sliding it free. The sound echoed across the clearing, rising above the pelting rain.

"You can't take her." Puck's voice was stern as he adjusted his grip on the Katana, stepping in front of me even more to obscure me from Nikolai's gaze.

My own gaze flitted to Tess, and she could see the tears gathering in my eyes.

"I'm afraid this isn't multiple choice. There is no other option."

Before Nik even finished speaking, he had made his move. He surged forward with the broadsword swinging down towards Puck. He moved fast enough that it was difficult to track his movements, but Puck had met his sword with his own, pushing him back with all his strength.

But Nik was faster.

He was *so much faster*.

We stood no chance against the increased speed and power of the Noctani. They moved forward all at once, Ms. Finch's arms reaching out towards me. I slashed Stormslayer towards her and she stepped back, a surprised expression flitting across her face. She stepped back, and in her place another Noctani surged forward, one I didn't recognize. Stormslayer met the blade of the other Noctani as I pushed her back, her blonde hair plastered to her forehead from the rain.

The thunder boomed overhead once more as the sounds of fighting filled the clearing. I could see Tess engaging with another Noctani out of the corner of my eye before focusing back on the one before me. This was truly a nightmare. I hadn't wanted to fight them, but I could see there was no other option.

A Noctani was sneaking up behind me and I turned quickly, plunging the dagger into her neck. They were coming from every angle. We were outnumbered. I cut a glance towards Puck, who had been disarmed, and he and Nik grappled with Nik's broadsword.

What a fucking mess.

I turned from the Noctani, sliding my blade out of her neck to face the next one. This man was much taller than me, his muscled arm grasping a club in his fist. My vision snapped away quickly—to an image of that club buried deep within my skull—but it was gone just as quickly as it had appeared.

Had it been a vision? Or had it only been my own fear, materialized?

I dodged the club as it came towards me, right before it could crush me beneath its weight. I kicked the Noctani in the back of the legs, but he didn't budge. I brought Stormslayer into an uppercut towards his chin, but he batted my arm away as if I were merely a toy. The hand not holding the club swung towards me—too quickly for me to dodge—and it slammed into the side of my face. I could taste blood as it filled my mouth, my head turning under the force of his fist.

Before he could get another hit in, I flattened to the mud, rolling to escape his grasp. His club swept towards me again, and I narrowly avoided it, stepping back into the clutches of two other waiting Noctani. One grasped my arm and twisted it behind my back hard enough that I heard a crack in my shoulder, my arm going limp and Stormslayer sliding from my grasp. My legs were kicked out from under me before the Noctani pinned my other arm behind me. I hung my head, the tendrils of my auburn hair darkened from the rain dripping onto my cheeks.

"No!" Tess cried, lunging towards me.

In that single moment of distraction, Nik was able to get the upper hand. He slid the broadsword free from Puck's grasp and hitting him in the temple with the hilt of it. Puck's body slumped into the mud before he lay there, motionless.

I pressed my eyes closed, unable to watch as he approached Tess from behind. She was too focused on me. He smacked the hilt of the sword into the back of her head as her gaze remained locked onto me. She slipped to her knees before sprawling in the mud.

He hadn't killed them.

He hadn't killed them.

He hadn't killed them.

I kept repeating it to myself over and over again as he moved towards me, wiping the mud on the broadsword off on his wet tunic. If he had wanted to, he could have. They were merely unconscious. The rain hadn't let up, and the storm raged above us in earnest now. My magic pulsed right beneath the surface, begging to be set free.

I wanted to release it *badly*, but I had no idea what would happen if I did. It had been disastrous every time my unbound magic had lashed out before, and I doubted it would be any different this time. But what other choice did I have?

Before I could reach for it as a last resort, take the risk of using my unbound magic to get out of this mess, Nik placed a hand on my shoulder.

I recoiled away from his touch.

Was this the part where he sunk his fangs into me, draining me of any and all storm magic?

A tear slipped free and ran down my cheek, but with my hands bound behind my back I couldn't reach up to wipe it away. I didn't want them to see me cry. I was completely and utterly defeated.

Nik's hand found my jaw, and he grasped it, turning my face up towards his. He ran his thumb along my cheek, capturing the single tear with his finger. He stared at it for a long, interminable moment before slipping the finger into his mouth to taste it.

"Please," I begged, "please just let me go."

He narrowed his eyes down at me. "Afraid I can't do that, Firecracker."

Nik tilted his head to the side as he gazed down into my face, before slamming the butt of his sword against my temple. Everything went black.

12

The familiar sensation of dream walking settled over me, but I hadn't remembered falling asleep.

I had been knocked out.

But now I was in The Stone Palace, and Corian and Donika stood before me. Corian's gaze locked onto mine, and I could see in his expression—in the lines of his face—that he could see me standing before him. He turned back towards Donika, not revealing my presence.

To what end? What was he doing?

Donika ascended the dais and sat atop her gilded throne, parting the skirts of her intricately beaded dress as she sat. She tossed her blue-white hair over her shoulder, reaching out to pet one of the grey wolves who sat at her side.

"Any word from him?" she asked, not bothering to lift her gaze to Corian, who stood before the dais.

"Not yet, but I suspect his presence alone will have ensured her swift capture. The sight of him would rattle the bitch, surely. Willing or not... she will go with him," he replied.

Donika smiled. "Yes, I suppose that would be quite a shock."

"Indeed," Corian mused, his mouth pulling into an equally sinister grin. "You'll have her back in your possession by week's end, I'm sure of it. And you'll have her magic, too."

"Everything always works out exactly how it's supposed to," she told Corian, her gaze still on the wolf she lovingly stroked.

"Always, My Queen. There was never any doubt you would be the true victor," he responded.

"Once Diana is back in my possession, I will need to deal with my mother and father," she spat the words as if they disgusted her. As if the thought of her own family made her stomach turn.

"May I have the pleasure, My Queen?" Corian asked, bowing his head towards her. "It would be an honor."

Donika's gaze flickered up as she shook her head. "No. Their deaths belong to me, and me alone."

Corian lifted his own head to meet her piercing gaze. "I understand. Have you changed your mind about sending the Araneoch out to escort them back?"

Donika shook her head once more. "I have faith that Nikolai will fulfill his orders. He is much more useful to me like this. His life force is bound to my own blood. I couldn't have planned it any better."

"I couldn't agree more. Do you wish to see them now?" he asked.

"Yes. Bring them in." Donika set her chin towards the doorway to the throne room.

I turned my head and watched in horror as the Noctani filed into the room to line up next to one another. There were so many of them. Hadn't she only had ten the last time I had seen them in a dream? How had she succeeded in making so many in only a few weeks?

My heart skipped a beat as I saw Isaac file in among them, his expression devoid of all emotion.

"Isaac!" I called out.

I knew he couldn't hear me—that there was nothing I could do—but the name escaped my lips, regardless. I slapped my hand over my mouth—forgetting myself—as Corian turned towards me with a sneer on his face.

Donika didn't notice.

"This is all of them?" she asked, a brow raised as she descended from the dais.

She inspected the Noctani one by one, turning their chins and lifting their arms to examine each and every part of them. Once she was satisfied, she stood back to take them all in.

"Yes, My Queen. All but those that are a part of Nikolai's delegation," Corian replied with a self-satisfied smirk twisting his mouth.

Donika nodded. "I must say, Corian... I am impressed. We have quadrupled our numbers in such a short amount of time. She stands no hope against me now."

When Corian didn't respond, Donika turned towards him, a curious expression on her face.

"What is it?" she asked, her hands on the hips of her expensive gown.

Corian snickered before his gaze fell on me once more.

I backed up until I hit the row of windows that lined the throne room, my breathing shallow as his eyes watched me. Followed my movements. Tracked me across the room.

I had to get out of here. I couldn't let him leave a token on me. It would lead him right to my location, wherever the hell that was. I shook my head back and forth, desperately trying to wake myself up. Corian wasn't holding me here against my will; I had found this dream all on my own.

"We have a visitor," he replied smugly.

Donika's brow raised in surprise. "Oh, we do!" She clapped her hands together. "How delightful. It has been too long since I have seen my dear sister. Are you able to connect me?"

Corian shook his head. "Unfortunately, my magic was depleted by the last batch of Noctani soldiers. It will need to recharge before I can do that level of magic. But I sense her here. I see the fuzzy outline of her. She can hear you, My Queen."

Interesting that his dream walking abilities were muted when his magic was depleted. He could still see me here, but it wasn't in focus. As if the magic didn't have a strong foothold.

Donika turned towards where Corian's gaze had been searching, her eyes narrowing, although I knew she couldn't see me.

"My dear sister, are you impressed with the army I have assembled here? Surely you know there is no hope for you now. Wherever you are, your time is limited. Nikolai will fetch you and bring you back to me, and he will not fail in this task. He will drain you of every ounce of your magic until it belongs to me, and then I will kill you."

I ran for the throne room door, but no matter how hard I pulled on the iron handles I couldn't make them budge. Wake up, wake up, WAKE UP! *I bit my lip hard, hard enough to draw blood if I weren't asleep, and the pain brought me back into sharp focus.*

The dream began to fade around the edges.

"I simply want you to know that I look forward to our reunion. A little Stormshade who can't even control her own magic never stood a chance against me. And that prophecy?" Donika threw her head back and laughed, the whites of her teeth startling me.

She had fangs.

Was she... was she Noctani too?

Had she turned herself into a siphoning monster on top of all the other misdeeds she was guilty of?

"That prophecy can go fuck itself. In no realm could you ever best me. Istmere is mine, and you will never take it from me."

The dream was fading faster now, and I could see on Corian's face he knew he would lose me at any moment. He turned towards Donika, whispering something I couldn't quite make out.

"Nikolai will never—"

But her words were cut off sharply as I was plunged into the light. I was slumped against the wall of a small room. No... not a room.

A cell.

I had promised myself I would never be a prisoner again and my anger and vengeance swelled within me. There was nowhere for it to go, and I had the distinct impression I would implode from the pressure. This wasn't the Stormvault, but it must have been made from ash and iron all the same. It suppressed my magic.

I approached the bars of the cell, peering down the corridor. It wasn't nearly as large or vast as the Stormvault was, and with no windows, I could only assume we were some-where underground. There was a Noctani guard standing at the end of the hall, but I didn't recognize them. Nikolai had knocked me out and taken me prisoner... but he hadn't taken me back to Donika.

Not yet, at least.

I pulled on the bars with all my strength, but I wasn't able to budge them. My shoulder stung with a sharp pain and I remembered that it had been pulled out of its socket. Someone had to have pushed it back in while I slept, as it was merely sore now. I wasn't sure what time of day it was—or when I had been knocked out—but I prayed that I was the only one they had taken. That Tess and Puck had made it away safely. Nikolai had said that he only meant to capture me... would he have knocked them out but still let them go? Or would he have killed them?

If it was the former, I hoped they had the sense to go straight back to Alastir and Phineas to finish the antidote. That was the most important thing right now. Especially if Nikolai planned to steal my magic and turn me into a mortal. They had the Dragon's breath—it was the final piece to create the antidote for Nik and Isaac.

Isaac.

Seeing him in the dream... mindless and empty... brought a physical pain to my chest. We needed to save him. He had taught me so much about my magic, there was no way I could ever repay him. He was more than merely a mentor to me. He was family.

But something nagged at the back of my mind about the difference between Nikolai and Isaac. During my dream walking, Isaac appeared to be completely under Donika's control, with no thoughts of his own. Nikolai appeared... sentient in a way. He remembered me, remembered that he used to call me *Firecracker*. Did the bond between us have something to do with the difference between them? I hadn't met enough Noctani to be sure, but something about Nikolai on that field in Prins was... different from what I imagined. He wasn't himself—that much was clear—but he also wasn't as... bloodthirsty, as I had been expecting.

I ran a dirt caked hand down my face and before I placed it back onto the bars before me, I noticed it had come away bloody. I brought my fingers to my bottom lip, and sure enough, it was split open. A slow drip of blood was running down my chin. I had bit my lip in the dream to try to wake myself, but it appeared I had bitten my lip in reality too.

As my surroundings became apparent to me, so did the soreness in my body. Not only was my shoulder sore, but I must have a black eye as well with how painfully it throbbed. I wouldn't be surprised if I was covered head to toe in bruises from having the shit kicked out of me on the training field. They had tried to subdue me without truly killing me, and they had succeeded.

But Nikolai... he had slammed the sword into my head.

He had *hurt* me.

My breath caught in the back of my throat as I sank to the floor, curling my knees into my chest. The movement must have made enough sound to draw the attention of the guard at the end of the hall, because a voice rang out.

"She wakes! Master, she wakes!"

Master? Was that what Nikolai was now, master of the Noctani?

I was instantly sick, my stomach roiling at the thought. Nausea rose in my gut, turning my mouth dry. I wrapped my arms around my knees and buried my face between them. What a fucking nightmare this had all devolved into.

I could hear a door opening and closing, the sound of heavy boots against the concrete floor.

The approaching figure held a lantern in his hand, the light searing through the back of my closed eyelids. I made the mistake of glancing up and instantly regretted it. I scurried to the back of the cell to put as much distance between us as possible.

Those endless, tourmaline eyes were the source of my every nightmare recently. They had once been a glimmering, glacial blue. No matter how many times I saw what Nikolai looked like now, I would never get used to it.

He inclined his head towards me, confusion creasing his brow. "Firecracker, you have no reason to fear me."

"No reason to fear you?" A humorless laugh escaped me. "You're Noctani now. You *hurt* me." I spoke through a clenched jaw, my hand subconsciously traveling to my temple where a headache throbbed.

His gaze fell to the floor before flitting back towards me once more, as if he were choosing his words carefully. "But that was necessary."

He appeared so... confused. I narrowed my eyes at him. "How so?"

"You wouldn't come with me," he explained simply. As if it were the most obvious answer in the world.

I nodded slowly. "Why would I willingly go with my captor?"

"I am not your captor, Diana." His brows drew together once more.

"What would you call it?" I asked, incredulous. I couldn't believe we were having this conversation right now. As if I would willingly *want* to go with him while he was in this state.

"I—" he started, but the words never came. It was as if he was trying to speak, but the words wouldn't come forth. "I—" he tried again.

After a moment of struggling, he closed his eyes, recentering himself. "I don't know." Those black eyes opened once more and locked on me. "Come closer... I've missed you."

"Stay away from me," I replied, disgust clear in my voice.

Confusion twisted his features once more. "Why are you mad at me?"

"Mad at you?" Now I stood, my hands at my side, nails digging into the palm of my hands hard enough that the biting pain would help to clear my thoughts. "I'm not mad at you, Nikolai. You are a *monster*. You have been sent to steal my magic and bring me back to Donika so that she can *kill* me."

"That's not—" but the words were cut off again, his mouth opened as if he was trying to push them out. "Dammit!" He grabbed the chair across from my cell, smashing it against the concrete wall until it shattered into a million broken pieces. My arms covered my face to protect it from the flying debris.

"It's as if I can't say the right words. I think them... but they won't come out of my mouth." He ran a frustrated hand through his blond waves, pulling the hair tightly in frustration. "I would never hurt you."

Was he fighting his link to Donika? Was his tether to me still intact, allowing him to resist her compulsion? I could only pray that his magical bond with me still lingered somewhere deep within, even if I couldn't sense it anymore. That the fact that we were both still here meant the bond hadn't been broken, and that it was stronger than whatever hold Donika had over him.

"But... you have." My voice was barely above a whisper as the moment he slammed the sword into my temple flashed before my eyes. "You gave me a black eye. Maybe even a concussion."

He shook his head. "You have it all wrong. You'll see."

"You need to let me go." My voice had turned into a plea.

"Don't you see?" he asked, his black eyes wide. "*I can't.*"

But I was here—wherever that was—and not in the Stormvault. Was he fighting it? Was there a piece of the Nikolai I knew hidden within the monster that stood before me now?

I pressed back against the stone wall, the cold leeching through my body as I rest my hands against it. "Please, Nikolai. *Please* let me go."

He shook his head as shadows slithered from his fingertips, through the bars of the cell. They glided towards me until I couldn't see anything at all except darkness. I recoiled from those shadows, not knowing what to expect from him.

"You'll see. This is how it has to be... but you'll understand, eventually. Until then... "

His voice trailed off as his darkness wrapped around my face. I tried to claw the shadows away, but they simply re-formed where my hand had trailed through them.

I couldn't see.

Couldn't breathe.

And not until my limp body hit the cold, damp floor and my consciousness slipped away from me once more did I truly feel that my heart had been irreparably shattered.

13

When I woke a second time, I was in the same cramped cell, but this time it wasn't empty. I was lying on a cot with a brown knit blanket thrown over my legs. There was a bowl of what appeared to be soup and stale bread propped on a stool in the corner. A stack of books sat beside it, a lone lit lantern as well. The warm light filled the cell, and the aroma of the food reached my nose right as my stomach grumbled.

He hadn't stolen my magic yet, and for that I was thankful. I could still sense it simmering in my core despite it having nowhere to go due to the ash enchantments. If I had any hope of escaping him and the rest of the Noctani, I needed to keep up my strength. And I *needed* my magic. Even if it was unbound. I rose to approach the bowl of food, my body protesting and a groan escaping my lips at how sore I was.

A headache still throbbed at my temple, and surely Nik's suffocating shadows hadn't helped the situation. What had he meant when he said he was trying to say the right thing? Why couldn't he speak the words he wanted to? Was it due to his link to Donika that he appeared to be fighting?

He had claimed he would never hurt me... but he had.

Twice now.

The thought had tears stinging the back of my eyes, but I pushed them down as I settled on the floor in front of the stool. I ripped off pieces of the bread, soaking them in the soup to soften them and hopefully prevent any of my teeth from chipping.

As I ate the meal in silence, I perused the books that had been left in my cell. I was surprised to find they were some of the volumes that graced my own shelves back in the mortal realm.

Had Nik brought these for me?

No... it couldn't have been him. He had *captured* me. *Hurt* me... knocking me out twice now and keeping me prisoner. He had no reason to be kind to me. It was only a matter of time now before he stole my magic, leaving me entirely mortal before dragging me back before Donika. Whoever had brought this meal for me had to have brought the books, taking pity on me for being stuck in this cell all alone. But if not Nik... then who?

Corian had seen me in that dream, but he hadn't initially revealed my presence to Donika. Had he wanted me to see how their army had grown? How hopeless the resistance was now? It was something I had already feared, but the dream had solidified it. In this moment, I truly did feel hopeless.

My bond was broken, and I didn't have control of my magic. The resistance numbers were scattered across Prins after our last battle. Isaac and Nikolai were Noctani. And I was a prisoner... again. It surely didn't appear as if we were on the winning side of things.

I finished the soup as I contemplated my next move. The items in my cell could be used as weapons now. Surely the fire from the burning lantern that flickered at my knee could be of use. I pushed the empty tray of food towards the cell door and settled back onto the cot with one of the books.

The door at the end of the hallway creaked open, and I wasn't surprised when Nikolai appeared. His shock of blond hair was concealed by his hood, which was pulled up over it, concealing part of his face.

"Are your accommodations to your liking?" he asked as he stopped before the cell door, his brow raised.

I met his gaze. "My... accommodations?"

"I brought these things to you in hopes it would add some... comfort... to an uncomfortable situation. You had fallen asleep on the cold concrete floor and... " his words trailed off as his gaze flickered towards the door at the end of the corridor.

"*You* brought me these things?" I asked, my brow furrowed.

"Of course," he smiled, but the smile never reached his eyes. I couldn't see the dimple in his right cheek. It was hollow, and my stomach sank at the thought.

"But... why?" I asked, confused.

Why would he want to make me comfortable? I was his *prisoner*. It didn't make any sense.

He inclined his head as he examined me. "I care for you, Diana."

Care for me.

Not love. No... it would never be love again. Not unless we succeeded with the antidote, which I wasn't sure was even an option at this point.

"I thought Noctani didn't care for anything." My words were soft as my gaze fell.

I didn't have the energy to be angry in this moment, and I didn't think my heart could break any more than it already had. Tears pricked the back of my eyes and I pinched the bridge of my nose as I fought them back.

Nik didn't appear to be as mindless as the other Noctani. He wasn't as... catatonic. I didn't think he was under Donika's complete control the way the Noctani in the dream had been. He appeared as a darker version of himself... fighting off his Noctani instincts and compulsion. This second interaction with him solidified my idea that the bond we shared had to be playing a hand in the version of him that stood before me now.

If I ever got out of here, I would have to ask Zion and Annelise. The bond was strong blood magic—it was entirely possible that it altered whatever Noctani spell Donika had conjured up since the bond came first.

I released a heavy sigh as my hand fell back to my lap.

"Nothing has changed," he said slowly.

"Nothing has changed?" My voice came out raw. "*Everything* has changed, Nik."

He shook his head. "It doesn't have to be like that."

A humorless laugh escaped my lips as I tipped my head back against the wall of the cell. "Doesn't it? Were you not sent to capture me so that Donika could *kill me*?"

"I would never let her—" his words broke off as if he were choking, his hand moving to his throat. "I would never. Let. Her. Kill. You." He spoke each word separately, as if the strain of speaking them was a physical thing.

My eyes narrowed on him.

"I'm not sure you have a choice in the matter." My gaze met his once more.

"There is always a choice." He clenched his teeth together, and a muscle feathered in his jaw as he spoke, the sharp points of his fangs visible amid the glow of the lantern.

"You are Noctani," I reminded him, placing the book on the cot beside me. "You are devoted to Donika."

A long moment passed before he answered. "Yes."

"Then I'm not sure why we are even having this conversation. Donika wants my magic, and she wants me *dead*. And if she can get you to do it, all the better for her. She takes a sick pleasure out of turning my loved ones against me."

Nik's gaze dropped to his boots as he gripped the iron bars before him, hanging his head.

"Everything is so... confusing." He bit his lip, and I could see his blackened eyes moving back and forth in thought.

He was at war with himself. The Nikolai that stood before me absolutely didn't reconcile with the Noctani I had encountered previously, and what I knew of the Noctani from dream walking and seeing Corian's creations.

"What do you mean?" I asked, my gaze intent on him as the wheels spun in my mind.

If our bond was allowing him to fight Donika's compulsion, I could certainly use that to my advantage.

He lifted his head only enough to peer at me beneath his hood. "My heart tells me one thing, my brain another."

He pushed back from the iron bars with startling speed and stepped back to the end of the hall. If I had blinked, I would have missed it.

"Where are we?" I asked, moving to stand. "Tell me where we are!"

"Enjoy the books," he replied as he reached for the iron handle of the door.

"Nikolai, where are we!?" I cried, rushing to the front of the cell and gripping the bars as he had moments ago.

But he didn't answer, the only sound in response was the heavy wooden door shutting between us.

I wasn't sure how much time had passed since Nik had last visited the cell, but it had to have been days. Meals were brought to me on a steady rotation, almost always the same thing. I wasn't able to discern where we were or get any information out of the Noctani who came to monitor me. They were able to hold conversations as Nik was, but their answers were vague and controlled.

But something else wasn't right. At least a week had to have passed since I was captured, but we hadn't moved yet. Weren't his orders to steal my magic and bring me straight to Donika? What was he waiting for? Why were we still here? Did he have something else in mind for me?

I passed the time with the books he had brought me, and when I finished those, more were brought with my meals. He hadn't returned, and the Noctani that were sent down to the prison cells were strangers, I recognized none of them. I hadn't seen Antonia Finch since that fateful brawl on the training field. I was hoping she might come down so that I could see if I could appeal to her, having known her in the mortal realm.

I had no idea how long I had been knocked out for when I had been taken here. I had no idea if we were still in Prins or if we were in Akra. Wherever we were... it had an underground dungeon. With no windows or light to break the monotony, I was going stir crazy. At least the last time I had been held prisoner I had Tess with me.

I hoped she was safe, somewhere far from here. I knew she wasn't stupid enough to try to track me down and break me out with only Puck at her side. I prayed she stayed on task and completed the antidote, returning to the seaside cabin to regroup from there.

A chill had crept into my bones deep enough that I wasn't sure I would ever be warm again. My fingers were turning a ghostly shade of white. No matter how hard I tried to warm myself by the lantern with the single blanket I had been given, a shiver racked my bones.

I was almost done counting the marks on the ceiling when the door at the end of the hall opened. My head turned, surprised to find Nikolai there.

"Where have you been?" I asked, teeth chattering.

"Missed me?" he replied, that devilish smirk lifting one corner of his mouth showing off one fang.

A shiver ran down my spine for an entirely different reason. It was a combination of fear and longing. He was *right there*, but at the same time he was *gone*. It was all too confusing.

His eyes roamed over my body, taking me in. "Are you cold?" A note of concern entered his tone.

I simply nodded—my hands still tucked beneath the blanket.

"I'll have someone bring down more blankets," he replied, his tone serious now. All traces of teasing gone. He was like the old Nik one second, then he was entirely *Noctani* the next.

"You could let me out of here... "

The ghost of a smile graced his mouth, but there was no humor in it. "Not sure that's a good idea, Firecracker."

That wasn't a no.

I pushed to a sitting position, wrapping the brown blanket over my shoulders as I approached the bars of the cell. He took an involuntary step backwards away from me, and I arched my brow at him.

"What, are you scared of me Nikolai?" A smile lifted my lips as I narrowed my eyes at him.

If this was my one opportunity to get out of this cell, I was going to take it. If I could prey on his weaknesses, appeal to his softer side that had shown itself these last few days, then I might have a chance.

"Never." His voice was a challenge.

"Then why not let me out? Surely there is somewhere warmer up there we can go and talk," I replied, nodding towards the ceiling of the prison.

I was desperate to get above ground.

Nik bit his lip with a fang, stuffing his hands into his pockets. It was such a *human* gesture, but he wasn't human at all anymore. Or was he?

"If I don't get rid of this chill in my bones I'll die. Not only will you have robbed Donika of the pleasure but my magic will return to the earth. I don't think Donika would ever forgive that."

His gaze snapped up to mine, his eyes roaming my face as he warred with himself.

There was a piece of him that was still fighting. Maybe there was a chance to escape this after all.

"You aren't safe from the others," his voice was ragged as he ran a hand through his blond hair.

"Then don't bring me near the others," I suggested, a wicked smile on my lips. I tried my best to ignore the cold that threatened to rattle my teeth.

I put on my best flirty voice as I gazed at him beneath my eyelashes. "I would kill for a warm bath and some clean clothes. Please, Nikolai. You know you want to."

"I do." He swallowed hard, his voice almost... strangled. "Will you try to run? I know you, Firecracker."

I shook my head. "I won't run."

Not yet, anyway. I needed to find out where we were. Needed to find some kind of weapon to use against him, then escape without any of the other Noctani noticing. He was faster and stronger than me, and I wouldn't make it out alive unless I was armed. There had to be weapons above ground wherever we were, and I needed to find one. Discreetly.

To do that, I needed *out* of this cell.

"If you do, I'll have to punish you." His voice was all velvet now.

He might be Noctani, but he was still a man. I could surely use his inner primal instincts to my own advantage.

"We wouldn't want that," I teased, shuffling the blanket away from my shoulder to reveal my collarbone.

It was so damn cold down in the dungeon, I wouldn't be surprised if the expanse of skin he saw there had turned blue. He slowly moved towards the iron door and fished in his pocket for the ring of keys. My heart almost stopped beating in my chest as he finally pulled them out, finding a long brass key and inserting it into the lock.

My chest tightened as the lock clicked and the door sprang open between us.

I was treading in dangerous territory here. A lick of fear ran up my spine as I walked across the threshold, Nik's hungry eyes locked on mine. He was glancing at me as if I would be his next meal, and the thought made me swallow hard.

There were two ways that could go.

This plan of mine could easily go wrong, and I needed to be careful. Nikolai was Noctani, and he was dangerous. I only needed to find a way to escape, and once I had I wouldn't look back. Nik led the way to the door at the end of the corridor. My heart was beating so fast I thought it might jump right up my throat and out of my mouth.

This was it.

Once I was upstairs, I would have to be careful. I might only get one chance to escape him, and when that opportunity presented itself, I needed to be ready.

Nik held the door open between us as I glanced down the hall on the other side of the door apprehensively.

"After you, Firecracker."

14

What I found beyond the heavy wooden door to the prisons was not what I had expected. We were, in fact, underground. Beyond the prisons was a completely normal appearing home. It must have belonged to one of Donika's spies because a cell in the basement seemed... odd otherwise. I made my way down the corridor which was plastered and covered in an old cottage style wallpaper. It led to a lounge room of sorts, Noctani milling about.

One that I didn't recognize turned towards me, a hiss escaping her throat as she bared her fangs at me. Nik moved fast enough that I didn't even see him—within a blink he was in front of me—his arms out as if to protect me.

"You will not touch her, Giselle," he hissed through clenched teeth.

"And if I do?" she asked around her own bared fangs. "You tread a fine line, Nikolai. Donika will not be happy to hear about this."

Nik moved again, and I found it difficult to track his rapid movements in the contained space. One moment his hands were exactly that, but in the next they were claws and he scraped the long talons across Giselle's face, raking across her skin.

She fell back with another hiss, cowering into the corner as she cradled her cheek. Blood poured forth from the wound and I found that I couldn't draw my eyes away from it. They might drink blood, but it still ran through their veins.

Interesting.

Another Noctani moved forwards in defense of Giselle and lurched for me. Right before he was able to close his hand around my throat Nik pushed him back with a roar that had gooseflesh raising across my skin. The Noctani man wasn't deterred, he lunged again and this time Nik thrust his clawed hand forward, sinking it into the other Noctani's chest.

When he ripped his hand away the Noctani's heart was clasped between his bloody fingers. I stepped back as my mouth opened with an inaudible cry. Nik's gaze locked on each and every Noctani as they backed away from him, eyes downcast. He dropped the heart with a sickly thump and leaned down to wipe his hand off on the clothing of the dead Noctani, keeping his own pristine.

"Donika will only know what I choose to tell her," Nik seethed as he returned to my side.

His hands had returned to normal—the claws retracting—and he placed one against the small of my back. I flinched, but he didn't seem to notice. Adrenaline running high, he pushed me towards the staircase that would lead to the upper level. As I ascended the steps, he turned back to address them once more.

"None of you will touch her, she is under my protection. I am in charge here, in case you have forgotten. I will not think twice before I gut you, leaving your entrails for the Araneoch to feast on. Do not cross me. If any of you as much as harm a hair on her pretty little head, I will ensure you suffer for it."

A heavy silence fell as my chest tightened. I had never heard him speak like that before, a cruelty in his words I didn't associate with him. I shook my head, trying to clear my thoughts. No matter how much he might seem as if he were *my* Nikolai at times, he wasn't. He was Noctani, and I'd be better off not to forget that.

We reached the top of the stairs where it opened into a large kitchen area. The blinds were drawn shut against the outside. I internally cursed that I wouldn't be able to discern where—exactly—we were. If it was even day or night. The blinds were the blackout kind, not allowing a peep of sunlight to come through even if it was daytime.

Nik guided me past the kitchen area where another Noctani was sitting silently, towards a second staircase that led to the second level. I had counted nine of them so far. That was more than what had shown up on the training field that day they captured me. There were too many of them in this house. I swallowed back the bile that rose in my throat at the thought.

The last time I had seen Donika's Noctani forces she had only about ten in total. With ten in this house alone, and at least forty in her court that I had seen when I was dream walking last week, her numbers were flourishing.

My gaze was fixed on my feet as I ascended the stairs. I didn't have time to be upset about the state of things, I merely needed to focus on getting the hell out of here. I hadn't seen any weapons lying about thus far, but my eyes were always searching for something that might help me to escape Nikolai. If we were engaged one-on-one, my chances were much higher. But with the house filled to the brim with Noctani... my chances at escape overall weren't looking great.

Nik led the way to the end of the hallway and opened the door, allowing me to pass inside first. This must be where he was staying. The bed was rumpled, black satin sheets clearly slept on. There was one large window, but the blind was drawn shut as they had been on the first floor. There was a fireplace filled with crackling flames that almost brought a laugh to my lips.

Did Noctani get cold?

To the right was a large washroom, the massive basin set down into the ground similar to a wading pool. Wherever we were, this house had to have belonged to someone quite wealthy. Had they killed the owner to take it for themselves as a hideout? Or turned them Noctani?

A million questions raced through my mind as my gaze scanned the room. There were no visible weapons here, either.

Nik broke the silence as he cleared his throat. "I'll get a new set of sheets, you can make use of the washroom if you'd like... " he held his hand out, gesturing me to go ahead.

I nodded, a soft smile on my lips despite the pit in the bottom of my stomach. "Thank you."

The last thing I wanted to do was thank him. I wanted to rake my hand across his cheek and jump from the second-story window... but I couldn't make my move yet. I needed to bide my time and wait for the right moment. He had already shown weakness towards me which meant he would again. I needed to wait. I would only get one shot at this.

My skin crawled at the thought of sharing the bed with him, but I was desperate for a good night's sleep out of the cold of the dungeons. Nik began stripping the bed, and I moved to the washroom, locking the door behind me.

Not that it would do much good.

The marble floor was cold against my dirty feet and I quickly moved to the faucet on the tub to fill the wading pool with steaming water. I found a number of salts and soaps on the shelf near the vanity and emptied them into the pool, filling the bathing chamber with a crisp citrus scent. I stripped my dirty clothes off as I waited for the pool to fill with water, glancing at myself in the gilded mirror atop the vanity.

My eye was still black and blue, likely from when Nikolai had knocked me on the temple with the butt of his sword. My cheek was also bruised, my lip swollen. It had been at least a week since I had been thrown into the dungeon and I still looked like shit. I gripped the sides of the vanity as I hung my head.

I would get out of this... I was too determined not to. I wasn't about to go down without a fight. I was Diana Kotova for God's sake. I was a survivor. I wasn't going to die like this.

No... I would fight until the end.

But until then... I would outsmart these Noctani and escape.

When the pool was filled with steaming water, I turned the nozzle off and waded down the marble steps. The hot water seared against my skin, causing my flesh to redden instantly. The sensation invigorated me.

I scrubbed my body clean, washing my hair and pinning it to the back of my head with a clip I had found on the vanity. I leaned back, enjoying the soft bubbles against my skin.

The door creaked open and my eyes narrowed. I was sure I had locked it. Nik entered, a stack of clean clothes resting on the palm of his hand. I lifted an eyebrow at him.

"You think I don't have a key to every lock in this house?" he asked, setting the clothes down on the stool by the vanity. He moved towards the bench in front of the window and sat, his hands clasped between his knees.

I shook my head. "It wouldn't be like you to be unprepared," I replied.

"No." He agreed, his gaze trained on me.

He watched as I poured water over my shoulders, basking in the warmth of the pool. He didn't miss a single movement. I inclined my head, a thought occurring to me. I had been able to draw out pieces of him before. His humanity. It was as if the real Nikolai was still trapped inside, only a wall existed between that man and the Noctani that stood before me.

Could he remember specific moments from his life before he was turned?

I leaned back, my feet kicking up in the water and my breasts cresting the surface, my nipples hard. His eyes traced down my body with hunger, his gaze darkening further. I hadn't thought that was possible with how black and endless they already were. Did he remember that night in Siraleth? The night he took me in the bathtub, water sloshing over the sides as we came together?

"Diana—" There was a note of warning in his voice.

It didn't escape me that this was the first time he had called me Diana since capturing me. It was always *Firecracker*.

"Yes?" I asked innocently, running a slow hand down my body. He groaned when it disappeared between my legs.

I needed to weaken him. I needed him to trust me enough for me to find an opening for escape. If seduction was the way to gain that trust, then so be it. I would need to use every weapon in my arsenal to my advantage.

His lips spread into a devilish grin, his fangs showing and sending a shiver down my spine. I still held a healthy dose of fear for those fangs, which could steal my magic from me at any moment. As if in response to that thought my magic surged to the surface, simmering below my skin.

"Don't tease me." His eyes narrowed as he spoke, the grin never leaving his mouth.

Those lips. Oh, how I had missed those lips. I wanted to feel them skim across my skin, take my breast into his mouth...

It hadn't taken long for my fear and repulsion of him to turn into desire, and I cursed myself for it. Why was I feeling this way when I should be disgusted by him? I was doing this for myself as much as I was doing it to manipulate him.

"I would never," I answered, running that same hand back up my stomach to cup my breast.

I gave the nipple a twist and my head fell back, my lips parting.

Nik moved quickly, one moment he was sitting on the bench beneath the window, the next he was in the pool of water beside me. His hand was on my back, encouraging my body to float. His clothes were soaked through, clinging to him in a way that made my own hunger stir.

Oh, how I had missed him. Missed his touch.

I bit my lip.

This wasn't Nik.

I had to keep reminding myself of that. I couldn't reconcile the Nik who was Noctani, bashing me over the head until I was unconscious, and the Nik who had showed me softness and kindness, bringing me books and meals in my cell. It was all so different from the one before me now, a hunger in his dark eyes that I was all too familiar with.

I waited on bated breath for him to touch me, his shadowed eyes scanning my body with reverence. His lips parted as his gaze passed over my stomach and my breasts which were now aching beneath his gaze, before coming to a stop on my face.

I had been in the bathtub before him, as I was now. Back in the underground cottage in Siraleth. Back when we were bound.

Did he remember?

"I will not touch you unless you ask, Diana."

My own lips parted on a gasp. *He did remember.* Those were the same words he had spoken to me on the training mat in the safe house. When I had still been so angry at him but had already resigned to the fact that I forgave him.

That I loved him.

I spoke the same words back to him that I had that day. "Touch me, Nikolai."

Whatever restraint that had been holding him back broke in that moment. I could see a flash of the old Nikolai—the Nikolai that I loved—before he lowered his mouth to my skin.

15

A chill ran up my spine when his lips touched me. Tasted my skin. It was a shiver laced with both fear and *want*. I was walking a thin line, but I found in this moment that I didn't care. That I wanted him.

No... needed him.

His lips felt much the same as they had before, but entirely different at the same time. His tongue darted out of his mouth to taste the skin on my stomach, sucking and teasing. I let out a groan of my own as he moved upwards, his one hand supporting my back and the other finding my breast. He cupped it gently, sucking it into his mouth. I could feel his fangs trace over my nipple and another shiver ran down my spine, my core throbbing.

My hand found his hair where I gripped it tightly. His gaze found mine, my nipple still in his mouth.

"Fuck." The word slipped past my lips at the sight of him.

"You like that?" he asked, already knowing the answer.

I nodded fervently. Despite being in the now cooling water, warmth pooled between my legs. His right hand continued to help me float as his other dragged up my calf, then my thigh. The air strangled in my throat as he moved towards where that heat was growing, his fingers teasing but never touching.

"Nikolai." The word was both an admonishment and a prayer as it escaped my lips, and he laughed darkly.

He lifted me and I hadn't been expecting it—I clung to him as he stood. I wrapped my legs around him as he ascended the stairs of the pool, exiting the washroom altogether. He deposited me onto the bed where I crawled back towards the pillows. He stood over me, his hungry gaze tracing up and down my wet body. His clothes clung to him in an entirely inappropriate way, his cock hardened and pressing against his wet pants.

His eyes burned as he watched me take him in.

"I didn't think... " I spoke, my words trailing off.

"That I could still get hard for you?" He reached for the hem of his wet shirt, pulling it over his head and letting it fall to the floor. "Look at you." He ran his tongue across his lips, licking them. "As if there was any doubt." He shook his head, water droplets spraying. As if the thought, the very idea was silly.

I made an impatient noise in the back of my throat as his hands went to his belt buckle, undoing it with agonizing slowness. I was bare before him and he took his time stripping down, watching me *want* him. *Need* him.

He unbuttoned the pants and slid them down his legs, stepping out of them. The sight of his hard length popping free had my core tightening. He was so Goddamn beautiful. Even like this.

He bent his knee on the bed before me, grabbing the back of my thigh and pulling me towards him. His gaze heated as he took in my breasts, my hardened nipples, then down even further as his gaze found the want between my legs. He kneeled before me, his mouth grazing the skin of my thigh before settling between my legs.

A gasp escaped my throat as his mouth met my center with no preamble, and I gripped the wet satin sheets in my fist.

Holy. Shit.

He had never had me like this before.

His fang grazed my bundle of nerves and I almost screamed, a noise of pleasure buried deep in the back of my throat as I pressed my lips together. He lifted an eyebrow, that wicked smile across his lips as he continued. One of my hands moved from fisting in the sheet to fisting in his hair, and that only made him work his tongue even harder against me.

Inside of me.

I was gasping against the sheets, one of his hands finding my stomach to press me down into the bed as I writhed beneath him. He worked me with his mouth, soft in some places and harder in others, driving me towards that cliff that I wanted desperately to fall over.

I could feel my pleasure building, but before it could crest he met my gaze, running his tongue across his lips to savor the taste of me. I thought I might come undone right then and there. He lifted off his knees to press his body over me. The hard length of his cock nestled between my thighs. My hand moved from his hair to grasp it, working my hand over the length of him as he groaned.

His mouth found my neck, and a gasp escaped me, but for an entirely different reason than pleasure.

My neck.

That was where the Noctani bit their victims to steal their blood and their magic. My limbs locked up, my hands finding his chest and trying to push him away, but all he did was laugh against me. He kissed my neck softly, gently, sucking at the skin there. My body reacted despite my mind's warning, leaning into him.

No... I couldn't let him bite me.

The thought was present in my mind as he opened his mouth, his fangs grazing against the delicate skin where my neck met my shoulder.

"Nikolai—" my voice came out as a warning, but desire was thick in my veins and I couldn't bring myself to push him off me.

He sucked the skin there one last time before sinking his fangs into me.

"Wait—" the words barely left my lips but were stopped when an all-encompassing *pleasure* enveloped me.

This couldn't be what it was to to have your magic stolen. This was pure, raw ecstasy. After the initial sharp bite of pain as his fangs pierced the skin, I experienced nothing but bliss as he lapped his tongue against me. Drinking the blood my body offered him.

He held me against his mouth with one hand while the other traveled down my body, between my legs, before inserting a finger inside of me. I moved against him, my thoughts foggy with want as he worked his finger in and out of me before inserting another, stretching me.

My blood dripped down my neck and onto the wet, satin sheets as he pulled back, licking it as it dripped down his lips. I could still sense my magic deep in my core, pressing against me with that familiar warmth.

It had been insistent at first, but now it didn't seem to mind. And neither did I.

He hadn't stolen my magic, only my blood. *But he had bitten me.*

I was utterly confused, unsure of how the magic of the Noctani worked as he continued to work his fingers in and out of me. My hips moved against him, all thoughts of stealing my magic gone as I wrapped my arm against him, holding him close to me. His bite had left me in a hyper aroused state, as if I were floating on a cloud of pleasure and it was all I could think of. All that filled my thoughts. I wanted him buried inside of me.

"More," I pleaded, my hand finding his hard length once more and pumping.

He growled against my neck as he lapped up the last bits of blood that pooled there. He removed his fingers from my wet center, replacing them with the head of his cock. He wasted no time thrusting all the way into me, a cry escaping my lips.

He had never been this rough with me, but I didn't mind at all. I pulsed around him and he groaned, pulling all the way out of me before thrusting in again. His name escaped my lips as he held me down, pinning my hips against the bed as he moved over me and inside me roughly.

My head fell back with each thrust, and I bit my lip to stop myself from crying out. The sensation of him filling me... his hands on my body... the way his fingers teased right above my center as he thrust in and out of me...

"Wicked little witch," he crooned, watching as my eyes fluttered shut. "Don't hold back, Diana. Let them hear how much I please you. Let them hear how much you love my cock buried deep inside of you. Let them know you're *mine*."

I was going to come.

I opened my mouth to say as much but he continued at that merciless pace, my breasts bouncing hard as he thrust into me with such power. His fingers continued to tease that bundle of nerves and I fell over the cliff, digging my nails into his back hard enough to draw blood. His mouth found my breast, taking it into his mouth and biting.

My head fell back with a cry as the pleasure became too much, too all-consuming. He drank from my breast as I came again, riding against him as if there was nothing more I wanted in the entire world. He hummed against me as his tongue lapped my blood, the vibration sending another wave of pleasure through me.

I came again. And again.

"That's it," he encouraged, lifting his head.

Blood trickled down his chin as he grinned up at me, his fangs exposed.

"Fuck—" The word escaped me on a whimper as he thrust into me harder, chasing his own pleasure.

He pumped and pumped, slamming inside of me relentlessly until he came, spilling into me and capturing my mouth with his. It was the first time he had kissed me since turning, and the taste of my own blood mixed with his pleasure sent me over the edge once more.

I let out a cry against him as he held my mouth with his, my own blood smeared across my lips before he fell against me. He remained inside of me, entirely spent. I wrapped my arms around him, holding him against me as a small smile crossed my lips. The feel of him against me, inside of me… it felt so natural. So right.

Reality slowly crept in as I remembered the wet, bloody sheets against my back. Sticking to my thighs. My wet hair plastered against the pillow. The taste of my own blood on my lips. Blood caked on my breast and neck.

Nik had bitten me, but my magic still simmered in my core.

What had I done?

16

L ater that afternoon—if it even was afternoon—we were lying in bed. Our bodies were wrapped together blissfully. The only thing missing was the sun streaming in to cast a warm glow against our skin.

And Nikolai's humanity. That was missing, too.

I was splayed across his chest, the bedsheets tangled around my torso. His skin pressed against mine. I wasn't sure whether it was day or night, or how long I had been locked up here. I wasn't sure I even cared in this moment. With his eyes closed peacefully, I could almost pretend that everything was back to normal.

Almost.

"Why are you looking at me like that?" he asked, quirking his brow as he peered down at me with one eye open, one eye remaining closed.

I shrugged against him. "It's nothing."

I couldn't help but wonder about his life since turning into Noctani. I knew he had gone to the castle to see Donika, to receive his orders, but I wasn't sure how much I could ask. I feared that whatever I *did* ask might set him off.

He sat up against the headboard, pulling me with him. He gazed at me with those black tourmaline eyes and a shiver ran down my spine. I wasn't sure if it was fear or lust. Maybe it was a combination of both.

"Ask me," he said.

His voice sounded almost... gentle for the first time since I had been captured by him.

"What has it been like?" I asked.

I figured it was best to try to keep it vague rather than asking specific questions that might set him off. His personality since turning Noctani was... volatile. He had suffocated me with his shadows one moment and then brought me books in the next. He had ripped a Noctani's heart out with his bare hand simply for trying to take me. His gaze fell on the window beyond the bed and his brows pinched together in thought.

"It hasn't been as bad as I would have thought. I dare say I have enjoyed most of it."

I cleared my throat. "How so?" I kept my gaze trained on him as I pulled the bedsheets against me.

I pressed back against the headboard next to him, and his hand fell from my back to the mattress between us. A muscle feathered in his jaw as he wove his hands together in his lap.

"I'm stronger and faster than I ever was as a human. My magic is... unparalleled." He allowed a sliver of shadow to escape his fingertips and it slithered towards me, caressing my exposed thigh before retreating. "I didn't want to see Donika again, but it wasn't as bad as I thought it would be. The hardest part about going back to The Stone Palace was seeing Zachariah."

"Your father?" I asked, studying him.

He didn't meet my gaze, but he nodded.

"Yes, my father. I hadn't seen him in... years before I was turned. I remember being so *angry* with him when he showed up in Siraleth. I had thought turning Noctani would simply erase all of that. That all of that anger festering inside of me would simply disappear. But it didn't. When we got back to Akra, all I wanted to do was prove myself to him all over again. Win back his trust. Show him that I was stronger and more powerful than ever before, exactly as he wanted."

He shook his head, a curl of his blond hair falling over his forehead. He tilted his head back to rest on the headboard, his gaze on the ceiling.

"He and Donika are working together. That... *angered* me even more. That the only reason I joined Donika's army in the first place was to please him, but it was still never enough. He forgot about me entirely, simply taking my place by Donika's side when I couldn't do it myself. I only wanted him to be proud of me, finally."

I wasn't sure what to say. I didn't think Nik would ever be able to make his father proud knowing what I did of Zachariah. He wasn't a good man. He killed his own wife because she stood in the way of how he wanted to raise his son. Stood in the way of his quest for power.

Nik glanced at me and a smile tugged at the corner of his mouth. He almost appeared as if he were *my* Nikolai when he did that, but it never reached his eyes.

"He was very surprised to see me like this," he said, waving his hand to indicate his Noctani state. "I guess that wasn't the initial plan when their army came to Siraleth. Merely a consequence of Donika trying to... torture you. Best you."

"I'll bet he was surprised," I sighed.

"I wish I could have had a better relationship with him, and now that I am Donika's most powerful weapon and it still isn't enough... " he paused, thinking. "It's as if I'm mourning my human self and my relationship with my father all at the same time. I knew he was out there in Istmere somewhere, but I never expected to be working with him again. Especially not in this capacity."

"Working with him, how?" I asked, my voice soft.

"He and Corian are Donika's number one and two. Now I have been thrown into the mix and it throws that balance off kilter. She didn't trust either of them to find you... only me. Zachariah felt... slighted, I think. To not be her first choice for once. And now we all work together for Donika, doing her bidding."

"Her bidding?" I repeated, phrasing it as a question in itself.

I was treading a fine line here.

Nik nodded enthusiastically. "What she tells me to do, I do it. Except sometimes... sometimes... " He opened his mouth to speak but the words wouldn't come.

It was as if he physically couldn't say what he was trying to, that the words were cut off in his throat.

"This." He heaved a frustrated sigh, running a hand through his hair. "I don't belong entirely to myself anymore. I belong to Donika. And sometimes I can't say... what... I... am... thinking." I could see him physically struggling to get the words out, as if under a spell.

From my time spent with him, I gathered that it was a side effect of being bound to Donika. That her blood made him what he was, and her magic that runs through his veins won't allow him to betray her. But that didn't stop him from fighting against it. I had never seen the other Noctani fight against it, and the only discernible difference between him and the rest was that he had been bound when he was turned.

I placed a hand against his shoulder. I was surprised that each time I reached out and touched him, I found his skin warm and soft. It was utterly at odds with what he had been turned into—I expected his pale and chalky skin to be cold and clammy.

"But you haven't brought me back to her yet, even though that is what she told you to do."

His gaze sparked with anger. "No, I haven't. When it comes to you, she won't tell me what to do. She can't. *You're mine.*" He all but growled those last words. "The idea of her putting a hand on you... "

Confusion and exhaustion threatened to pull me under. My eyelids were becoming heavy as I slumped against the headboard.

"You'll keep me safe?" I asked.

The hope in my own voice threatened to choke me.

He nodded fiercely, his hand coming up to palm my cheek. "I will never let her kill you."

Those two things weren't necessarily the same thing, and the difference wasn't lost on me. There was only so much Nik could do to defy Donika. There were certain things he couldn't even say—certain things he couldn't do. It was only a matter of time before his loyalty to Donika overrode his need to keep me all to himself. At some point, Donika would make him bring me to her. And he would obey.

I needed to escape before that happened.

Nik shuffled back down onto the bed, pulling me with him. His chest warmed my chilled fingertips and I curled against him, my head resting in the crook of his neck.

"I am glad I got to see my father, though. Despite everything. He always wanted status for me, and what better status could I get than the strongest Noctani in Donika's army? To prove ourselves, she put us through a series of tests. I passed with flying colors." He laughed to himself, the vibration of his chest running through me.

I didn't answer. I didn't need to.

Even without humanity Nik was trying to please his dad, as he had while growing up. There was no pleasing Zachariah. Not when Nik was in love with me. He might not have those types of emotions right now, but he did feel some form of *possession* towards me. I was counting on that to save me, in the end.

When I finally fell asleep, the sheets still stained with our blood from earlier, all I could think about was how much the lines had blurred.

And how here and now... I didn't think I minded it at all.

17

Time was moving in slow motion during my stay in the Noctani safe house. Each day was different. Some days, Nikolai would allow me downstairs with him to explore the first floor. Some days, he would make me stay locked in his room.

One thing was certain, he never let me interact with any of the other Noctani.

Ever.

Nik was the only one I had been in contact with and I was beginning to think I was losing my mind a little bit. Nik was still somewhat himself, but he also... wasn't. He remembered things from our past and he craved both my blood and my body, but without the bond in place, I couldn't discern what his true feelings were. And any time I tried to ask, he would shut the conversation down.

The blackout shades were pulled down on all the windows and locked closed at all times, and I could never tell if it was daytime or nighttime. That in and of itself was making me go stir crazy. Nik had told me that while Noctani weren't affected by the sun as vampires might be, they did largely prefer the night. This observation allowed me to discern that they appeared to keep a nocturnal schedule. I could guess when it was day or night based on their sleeping schedule, but I could never know for sure. It had me out of sorts.

Nik had left early today and was already gone when I woke. I made quick use of the washroom in all its decadence before dressing and approaching the door. I had tried to use my magic to unlock it time and time again. Despite it appearing to be a regular wooden door, it must have been laced with iron or ash. My magic was useless against it. I tried the same with the windows, but never had any luck.

Nik had been wearing a jacket with big silver buttons yesterday, and while we romped around in bed together I had torn the jacket from him, ripping one of the buttons off and shoving it under the pillow for later. He had tossed the jacket to the floor, long forgotten about, and hadn't picked it up today, either. When I moved to the bed and fished under the pillow for the button, a sigh of relief escaped me that the back of it was a long pin.

I hadn't thought I would get this lucky.

I quickly moved to the door and dropped to my knees before it, fishing inside the lock with the sharpened back of the button. It was a little short, but it was all I had. I scoured this bedroom searching for something I might use to pick this lock, but there was nothing. Nik likely hadn't realized the button could be used as a lock pick, either.

I pressed my ear to the door to listen for a click. I had never picked a lock before, and it hadn't been part of my training with the resistance. I was fishing around blindly for anything that might give, holding my breath as I sent up a silent prayer to the Mother.

"Please, please unlock," I muttered to myself, a line of sweat creasing my brow as I worked.

Right as I was about to give up, as I was about to search the room for another tool I might use, I heard the click. My eyes flew wide as I turned the knob, the door creaking towards me as it opened.

I was on my feet in a heartbeat, quietly treading down the hallway. I didn't have any weapons, and I hadn't seen any I could steal during my supervised visits on the first floor. If I was going to escape, my best bet was to do it while Nik was either gone from the house or asleep.

I was fairly familiar with this area of the house, having cased it each and every time I was let out of Nik's bedroom. At the end of the hall was another bedroom and washroom before the steps descended into the main living space. The hallway was covered in a thick, worn carpet and I used it to my advantage, trying to remain as silent as possible despite my clunky boots.

My heart was beating fast enough that I thought it might jump into my throat as I inched towards the staircase carefully. I had never made it this far before, and there was no telling when Nik would be back. I had no idea if there were Noctani milling about on the first floor. I was blindly hoping to get lucky one more time.

My next step had the floorboards creaking beneath the carpet and I pressed my eyes closed, internally cringing. I waited in silence for one long moment, but no one came. The board creaked once more as I shifted my weight off it with my next step, and as I sent another prayer up to the Mother, the door at the end of the hallway flew open.

Shit.

I lifted my eyes, expecting a horde of Noctani to appear before me, but it was only Giselle. The beautiful Noctani who had challenged Nik down by the entrance to the cells. Whose face now bore the scars of his claws.

I took a deep, steadying breath as I took a step backwards away from her, the floorboard creaking beneath me again.

Curse that fucking floorboard.

"What are you doing out of your quarters?" she asked me, quirking her perfectly manicured eyebrow up at me.

I opened my mouth to speak, but before the words even had time to come out, Giselle was before me, her hand wrapped around my throat. She lifted me off the ground and I kicked against her, pulling at her hand. Her nails dug into my skin.

"Let... me... go... " I gasped between ragged breaths.

I couldn't breathe. Couldn't think. Another few moments and I would black out.

She cocked her head to the side as she narrowed her gaze on me. "I have no plans to let you go. I will do what he failed to do. I will bring you back to Donika." She paused for a moment, her nostrils flaring wide. "You smell like him."

I tried to reply, to kick free or claw her hand away from my throat, but all I managed to do was flail through the air.

She released me with a disgusted expression, her lip curling. "To think he would take a *witch* to his bed."

I coughed as air rushed back into my lungs, pressing the palms of my hands against my knees as I tried to fill my lungs with air.

"What is so special about you?" she asked, crossing her arms over her chest.

I rubbed the sore skin around my neck, my gaze finally meeting hers. "Are you not still a witch, only one tainted with dark magic?"

She laughed at this. "I am so much more than that, you cannot even begin to comprehend." She ran her gaze over me, and I could see the jealousy simmering in her onyx eyes. She was tall and lean, with a small waist and long, impossible legs. Her dirty blonde hair was cut to shoulder length, her black eyes lined with kohl.

"And yet, it isn't you he takes to his bed." I said, taking another step back to put distance between us.

Her gaze filled with rage in an instant. "Not yet, anyway."

Her words had my stomach doing somersaults, and I tasted bile rise up the back of my throat. Would Nik take another into his bed now that we weren't bound? Now that he might not even be capable of love? I'm not sure if it is something I could forgive... and the thought of him with another almost had me emptying my stomach right onto the carpet between us.

Giselle could see that her words had rattled me. She took a step towards me. "He will tire of you, and when he does, he will move on to me. I can blow his mind like you never could, *Stormshade*." She spat the word as Donika did. As if it was a curse.

"And yet I have been here for what, two weeks? Three? And he *hasn't*."

I never saw her raise her arm but between one blink and the next, her palm was against the side of my head, smashing my skull into the wall. It gave beneath me, my head crashing through and hitting the stud behind the plaster. I saw stars behind my vision, but I never pulled my gaze from her.

She was *fast*.

"How dare you speak to me like that," she raged, a fistful of my hair in her grip as she wrenched my neck back.

No.

No, no, no.

Not my neck. Not my magic.

I aimed to push away from her, to fall to the ground and scurry back into the bedroom, but her grip on me was relentless, and she was much stronger. I needed Stormslayer, and I needed it *now*.

She bared her fangs, black veins pulsing out from her eyes. Her head snapped back, preparing to break skin, when I was suddenly wrenched away from her.

Or rather... she was wrenched away from me.

I was seconds away from her drinking my blood and stealing my magic as Nik was supposed to do, but she was thrown to the end of the hallway. Her head cracked painfully against the stairway banister. I fell to my hands and knees when her grip on my hair was yanked free, and I inhaled deeply, trying to steady myself.

Nik was standing above me, his black boots and training pants the only thing that would focus in my vision. When my gaze traveled up to meet his, the only thing I could see in his depthless eyes was simmering, unfettered rage.

"How dare you put your hands on her!" His voice was cold as ice as he slowly moved towards Giselle.

She cradled the back of her head, crawling away from him until she hit the other side of the wall. The only place for her to go now was down. Nik's footsteps were slow and measured, and Giselle cowered away from him.

"Was the scar across your pretty little face not enough of a warning?" he seethed.

Pretty? I shook my head, clearing the thought.

I couldn't be jealous, and of a Noctani, no less. I was losing my Goddamn mind. I moved to stand, my head pounding and my ears ringing with every beat of my heart. Spots swam before my vision once more, but I tried my best to blink them away.

"I'm sorry, Nikolai." Giselle exposed her neck to him, as if she were a wolf and he were her Alpha.

Maybe she was a Nightshade. Was it possible that the Noctani were more animal than human now that they had been corrupted with black magic? Had they formed some type of... pack among themselves?

The hierarchy was clear. Nikolai led them, and no one else would stand against him. He was the strongest as a human, and he was the strongest as Noctani.

"Sorry?" he asked, inclining his head towards her. "Weren't you sorry the last time?"

He kneeled before her, reaching his hand out to push a lock of her dirty blonde hair behind her ear. The gesture was almost... intimate. It had jealousy simmering hot in my gut. As his hand skimmed the back of her neck, his nails became elongated claws, and they dug in.

Giselle threw her head back, an animalistic howl wrenching free from her throat as her head fell back. My jaw fell open as I scrambled backwards away from them. Tears stung the back of my eyes as I reached the bedroom door, my hand on the knob. I wanted nothing more than to close it between us and free my vision from the horror before me, but I couldn't bring myself to glance away.

He had paralyzed her.

Severed her spinal cord.

I wasn't sure that was something even a Noctani could recover from. Blood dripped down the back of her neck, staining the carpet with fat, wet droplets. This... this wasn't Nikolai. The Nikolai I knew was never cruel. Never reveled in such savagery and cruelty.

He leaned into Giselle, his lips whispering against her ear. "This is what happens to those who think to touch what is *mine.*"

With his claws still digging into the back of her neck, he closed his fist, snapping her neck in one swift movement.

Her lips parted on one final cry before her eyes glazed over. He released her, and her bloodied body fell to a heap on the carpet before us.

I turned to retreat into the bedroom, but Nik was already there behind me. He was so damn fast. I flinched away from him, but there was nowhere to go. Giselle's dead body lay across the hallway, blocking the route to the staircase.

I had lost my only opportunity to escape.

"Are you scared, Firecracker?" he asked, raising his brow at me as he leaned down towards me.

Yes. I couldn't separate the two... the Nikolai I once knew and the one standing before me. They weren't the same, but there was so much of them that *was.* The dimple on his right cheek popped as he glanced down at me, and I thought I was going to be sick all over again. What was I doing?

My hand remained on the doorknob, but he grasped it, bringing my palm over his chest.

His heart beat beneath my palm, a rapid, furious pace.

"Am I not your Nikolai?" he asked, raising his brow at me. "Does my heart not still beat?"

It did... but that didn't mean he was *mine.*

No.

Dark magic had made him something... other.

But despite knowing that, despite every instinct in my body telling me otherwise, I melted the moment his lips brushed the skin on my cheek. He wrapped his arms around me, fitting my body to his. He was still so... warm. And he was *right here.*

I shook my head, trying to clear the thought. Things were getting too muddled, and I needed to keep my wits about me.

When he took me to the bed that night, there was only one thing that was flitting through my mind over and over again. He had left the door unlocked.

18

From the time of my capture to now, the lines had blurred for me—and I had nobody to blame but myself. I had set out to get out of the dungeon, and I had done exactly that. But now I was more confused than ever, wondering exactly how soulless and evil the Noctani truly were when Nikolai still appeared to maintain a sliver of his humanity. Whether that was due to being bound before being turned, I couldn't know for sure.

Nik could remember vivid moments from our past together. He could be gentle and sweet. But he could also be angry and unpredictable. It was as if there were two sides to the same coin, and it was a toss-up which one I was going to get. He had hurt me, suffocated me with his shadows, hit me in the head with his sword, stolen my blood without my consent. But I hadn't been on the receiving end of the cruelty I had seen him possess against the other Noctani.

Not yet, at least. I wasn't sure how much longer he could manage to fight the compulsion.

He lay with his arm wrapped around me. With his eyes closed, I could almost pretend that this was normal. That *he* was normal. His eyes were closed in sleep, his mouth slightly parted. I could almost pretend he wasn't Noctani at all, and we were enjoying a day in bed together back in Siraleth.

But that wasn't the truth.

The truth was Nikolai *was* Noctani, and there was a part of him that thirsted for not only my blood but my magic. He had drunk from me multiple times, and each time all I had felt in that moment was unbridled pleasure. The initial sting of his fangs wore off quickly, replaced with nothing but pure ecstasy. He hadn't turned me into Noctani, and he hadn't stolen my magic.

He was still in control of his own choices to a certain degree. But something had also been irreparably changed in him... because the Nikolai I knew would never be cruel. Never hurt me. Never blacken my eye and tighten his hand around my throat without a second thought.

I turned, biting back the tears that threatened to fall at the thought. I wouldn't be able to lose him a second time. I needed the antidote, and I needed it *now*. Alastir had said not to put all my eggs in one basket... but I had, and I desperately needed Nik to return to normal.

After the incident with Giselle, he had to address the Noctani once more to ensure they stayed away from me. For the remainder of the day, he had kept me locked in his bedroom at the end of the hallway.

But when he had come to bed that night, he had forgotten to lock the door behind him.

I needed to escape quickly and quietly. After determining yesterday before my encounter with Giselle that the windows were sealed shut permanently, that left the only other option—the front door.

I hoped now that Nik had threatened the others, the common spaces were more likely to be abandoned, the Noctani having returned to their own rooms.

If only I could be as lucky.

I hadn't yet found any weapons that I could use against Nik, but I had decided that when I *did* make my move, I would risk summoning my magic if need be. I wouldn't go down without a fight, and I doubted Nikolai would forgive me for trying to escape with his new volatile personality.

Once I had made the decision to go, I needed to go.

A piece of me didn't want to leave him, though I knew there was no other option. I couldn't stay here like this forever, remaining his prisoner. I needed to cure him, because I couldn't stomach fighting him when the time came.

And we needed to save Isaac.

I needed to escape before Nik decided to take me to Donika, after all. Or one of his Noctani crew decided to go against him and take me themselves. Once we cured Nik... we would be bound once more. That was, if everything went to plan. I was living on borrowed time playing house here, and it was time to go.

Once my magic was bound, I could kill Donika and end this war once and for all. The people of Istmere deserved to live in peace. They had suffered enough over this last decade. I needed to refocus my priorities, which had been entirely lost these last few weeks.

I rolled to the side of the bed, away from Nikolai's arm, and it fell to the bed between us. I waited until I was sure he hadn't woken, then I stood. The bed creaked as my feet met the floor, and once more I waited to ensure he hadn't woken.

He had brought me clothes and had dressed me in a silk slip last night, the material clinging to my curves. I certainly couldn't leave in this, especially if I needed to cross all the way back to the seaside cabin within the next two days. No, I needed a tunic and some type of riding pants or trousers. I silently padded to the dresser and pulled the drawer open slowly. It creaked despite my carefulness.

I waited again, but Nikolai still didn't wake.

I breathed a soft sigh of relief before taking out a white tunic that buttoned up to the neck, pulling it on over the slip, and a pair of black pants. I pulled on the pair of boots I had come here in, my eyes on Nikolai's still form.

He was almost... *too* still in sleep. As if he were dead.

I guessed, in a sense he was.

But his heart still beat, and blood still ran through the veins of the Noctani. The essence that had changed them was magic, which made me all the more hopeful that they could be returned to their natural state.

I couldn't find a cloak among the mess of clothes on the floor, and didn't risk rifling through them and waking him. I wasn't sure what I would find when I left this house, or where I would be. I knew it was time to go.

I prayed to the Mother that it would be warm enough that I could make it back without layers, but the summer nights in Istmere were temperamental and unpredictable. It wasn't like the mortal realm.

I moved to the door, and though I had promised myself I wouldn't, I turned back.

My breath caught in my throat as I took him in one last time.

Tears stung the back of my eyes as I thought that this might be the last time I ever saw him. He looked so peaceful, his head laid across the pillow. His hair softly billowed out around him. He was bare from the waist up and I could see his tattoos clearly beneath the light of the lantern on the bedside table.

I couldn't leave him like this forever... in this state. I silently promised him that I would cure him at all costs as I turned, my hand on the knob. I twisted the knob and eased the door open and waited, to see if the movement had woken him.

It hadn't.

I shakily inhaled as I put one foot in front of the other, creeping towards the staircase as quietly as I could manage. I only needed to avoid that fucking floorboard. I skirted around it, sticking to the walls of the hallway, and made it to the top of the staircase before pausing. I listened for any Noctani that might be in the room below, but heard nothing.

It was now or never.

I gently descended the stairs, cringing each time my boot made one of the steps creak. I cursed that this house was older, full of squeaks and groans. I hoped anyone that might hear chalked it up to the old bones of the house. Once I had made it to the bottom of the staircase, I glanced around.

Thankfully, the room below was blessedly empty.

On silent feet, I walked towards the front door, and my breath caught in my throat once more when it finally came into view.

This was it.

This was my chance.

My footsteps quickened, my hand reaching out for the knob of the front door when a wind stirred my hair.

Within a blink, a form stood before me, towering over me. An angry expression masked his face. He narrowed his eyes at me, those black tourmaline gems studying me. Assessing me.

"Where do you think you're going, Firecracker?"

19

My heart leaped into my throat and I set my jaw.

"Nikolai, you need to let me go." I kept my voice steady. Authoritative.

His eyes blazed. "I'm afraid I can't do that."

He reached out for me and I backed up, narrowly escaping his grasp.

"Diana—" my name in his mouth was a warning, his hand still extended towards me.

"I'm sorry, Nikolai." I turned, rushing away from him and towards the dining area, but he beat me to it, backing me into the narrow kitchen.

There. On the peninsula was a small dagger.

My small dagger.

Stormslayer.

I had told myself I would risk my magic if it came down to it, and it had. Nikolai had found me trying to escape, and I wouldn't get a second chance. It had been a luxury that he had allowed me to stay with him in his bedroom here, but after this... he would simply throw me back in the dungeon.

I reached out to my magic, and it filled my core, extending to my fingertips. As if Nik could sense the rush of energy, he lunged forward. Unlike in the training field that day he had captured me, this time I was faster. I used my magic to propel me and I stepped out of his grasp. I pushed my magic out once more and sent the dagger flying off the counter and into my waiting grasp. I held it between us as I circled, herding Nikolai's back towards the front door.

"You are going to use my own blade against me?" he asked, raising a brow.

"*It isn't your blade,*" I ground out, shaking my head.

"I had it made for you, did I not?" he replied, cocking his head to the side.

"You did, but Stormslayer belongs to me. Let me pass, and I will not hurt you," I said. I had meant to be stern, but I could hear my own voice shaking.

"Diana." He smiled, a patronizing edge to his voice. "You couldn't hurt me even if you tried. But I know you, and you won't hurt me, regardless. You don't *want* to."

"I might not want to... " I answered, steeling myself for what I was about to do next. "But I will do what needs to be done."

I lunged, slicing Stormslayer down towards Nik. As I predicted, he hadn't been expecting it, and he hadn't moved out of the way in time. Stormslayer buried in his right shoulder and I pulled it free, a thick stream of blood cascading down his bare chest. His hand moved to the wound as if he couldn't believe it was truly there before he turned back towards me, teeth bared in a snarl.

I didn't give him any more time for small talk, I lunged again. I had a weapon, and he didn't, so that gave me the upper hand—even if he was a weapon in and of himself.

I sliced Stormslayer through his forearm and he backed up with a hiss. I lunged towards the front door, crossing the space as quickly as I could. I had almost cleared the entryway, my hand reaching for the knob when I was snatched back by my hair.

I cursed.

I had wanted to tie it back but there wasn't a hair tie in sight in this Godforsaken house. He wrenched me back by the hair and I let out a hiss of my own, slamming Stormslayer into his arm. He released me with a grunt, and I lunged for the door again. This time I drew on my magic once more to propel me forward faster.

I had to get out *now*.

The other Noctani were sure to hear the commotion and come, and I didn't stand a chance against all of them. The use of my magic was sure to create a storm any minute now, and as the thought crossed my mind, I could hear a soft rumble of thunder growing in the distance.

I turned back towards Nik—extending my hand as I allowed my magic to surge forth—sending him flying backwards. He hit the dining table with a crash and fell to his knees, but I didn't stay to see how long it had taken him down for. I wrenched the door open and crossed the threshold, blinded by the afternoon sun. It had been days since I had seen its welcoming rays, but the sudden flash of light stung. I wanted to lift my arm to shield my eyes but I didn't, pushing onward, trying to put as much space between me and the house as possible.

I could hear Nik close on my heels, cursing.

I pulled more magic from my core and faced him, throwing him back with an amethyst burst of energy once more. He hit the side of the house, which was incidentally made of brick, cracking his head against it. I cringed internally, but I knew an injury such as this one wouldn't kill him. It would barely wound him in his current state.

I propelled myself forward pulling on more of that magic that simmered in my core, the sky darkening rapidly overhead.

"Diana, you cannot run from me," Nik ground out from behind me.

Good. His voice was further away.

"That is exactly what I intend to do," I muttered, not turning.

The streets here were sparse, only a few homes scattered about at this end of the road. I pushed myself down the street, pumping my arms at my sides and pushing my body to its absolute limits. I wished I had Tess's spidery long legs in this moment.

A hand grasped my arm and tore me back against something hard.

Nik's chest.

He held me against him, his arm around my throat cutting off my airway. He was going to suffocate me. I slammed my boot down on his foot but he didn't flinch. I brought Stormslayer down to stab into his thigh, and that caused him to release me with a howl.

Blood trickled down the wound in his chest, his forearm, now his thigh. His hair was a mess, matted across his forehead as he narrowed his eyes on me, rage simmering in the darkness.

Thunder boomed loudly overhead, and I jumped, startling. A rain drop fell from the darkening sky and kissed my cheek, sliding off.

"Come back to the house with me, Diana. I don't want to hurt you." His words were sweet but his voice was sinister.

He was angry. Beyond angry.

"I can't do that." I swallowed hard.

The raindrops spattered around us. They bounced off my cheeks, soaking into my tunic. Soaking through my unruly mess of hair. Stinging my skin. I reached out to the storm above with my magic—but as I expected it to—it reared back. It sent a strike of lightning down close enough that I had to jump to avoid it. The cobbles where I had stood only moments ago were darkened, smoking.

"Have you not had an enjoyable time here?" he asked, his smile malicious.

I shook my head. "You held me here against my will. Drank from me."

"Ah," he said, taking a measured step towards me. I took a step back. "You let me do those things."

"I didn't have a choice," I spit out, tightening my grip on Stormslayer.

His smile widened. "Didn't you?"

He could see how a part of me had *loved* it. The rough sex, the blood drinking. There was a part of me that did... but I didn't want *this*. I didn't want Nik when he was Noctani. I wanted *my* Nikolai back. My protective, cocky, stubborn Nikolai who would never dream of hurting me. This abomination before me wasn't that man, despite how easy it was to pretend.

A tear slid down my cheek, mingling with the rain that now lashed against us. I was soaked through, the tunic sticking to me in an uncomfortable way. A sob racked my body as I felt myself losing him *again*. The Mother above had a cruel sense of humor.

How many times would I have to lose him? How many times could I endure?

I didn't want to leave him here, but I *had* to. I had to trust that I could get the antidote and cure him. That everything would be ok.

I opened my mouth to speak, and another cry escaped me. He moved forward, to capture me or console me I would never know. I reached out to the storm above and I grasped a thread of its magic, pulling it down towards us with all my strength. Lightning struck, and this time I knew to shy away, shielding my eyes.

When I turned back Nikolai was on his knees, grasping his arm as he grimaced, his fangs exposed as he threw his head back with a cry.

Thank the Mother I hadn't killed him.

Thank you, thank you, thank you.

I took a step back.

"This isn't you. I only want the old Nikolai back. The one who was *mine*," I cried, my vision blurred from the tears and pelting rain.

That first time, when my magic had detonated, and he had escaped, it had felt as if *he* was the one who left me. But it was me leaving him now. I was leaving a piece of myself here—wherever that was.

A piece I would never get back.

I turned, Stormslayer tight in my grasp as I took off down the street.

Soft words spoken behind me met my ears, but I didn't stop, didn't turn, I just kept running, tears streaming down my face.

"I still am yours."

20

I didn't stop until my legs were tired to the point they physically couldn't carry me further. I cursed myself for not keeping up with my running training more, but I never was one for endurance activities. I had no idea where I was, only that I was in a remote portion of Istmere, and I was tired top the point of possible collapse. I wasn't sure where I was headed, either, only that I needed to put as much distance between me and that house as possible.

Nikolai hadn't followed me.

I had left him there, shirtless and bleeding on the cobblestones. The thought left a sickening lump in the pit of my stomach. Had bile rising up the back of my throat, but I swallowed it back down, out of breath. I was in desperate need of rest and water. The roads were small and narrow, with sparse houses scattered about.

It was most rural—I certainly wasn't in the city.

I pushed my exhausted legs to carry me further, across a small river with a narrow, rickety bridge. The roads ended here, but I continued on through the wood, knowing I would either end up in a city or on the coast at some point. I was fine with either. I was terribly lost but for some reason the thought didn't scare me. I was relieved to have escaped that house with the both of us still alive.

I had successfully escaped Nikolai *without* him stealing my magic, and I was thankful for that. I wasn't sure why he hadn't stolen it at the first opportunity, or any of the ones that had come after that. Maybe it was a deeply buried kernel of his former self? I tried not to think too hard on it. The thought of the old Nikolai brought tears to my eyes, and I was too tired to cry. Too spent from the events of the last three weeks.

It wasn't until I had crossed another river, stopping to drink as much as I could fit into my belly, that I stopped to rest for the night. I had nothing but the damp, baggy clothes I had left in. I curled at the base of a tree, hoping that I could make it through the night despite the chill settling deep in my bones.

When the sun rose and its warm rays beat against my face, I thanked the Mother for what little sleep I had managed to get. And for protecting me through the night while I was alone. I gathered myself and carried on, finding another road after a few more hours of weary travel.

By the time I hit a cobbled street and a few small shops came into sight, I recognized where I was. This was the westernmost part of Akra, the small town at the base of the mountain that housed the castle. Luckily, I was on the southern side of the lake, and the castle wasn't within my sightline. If I kept traveling this road, I would eventually end up in Prins.

I didn't have any coin on me, but I was starving and dehydrated. Exhausted down to the bone. I ducked into a small tavern that had a rickety, wooden sign out front proclaiming *the best Dragon's Ale in the realm.* I trudged inside, closing the door behind me.

There were few patrons sitting at the bar and scattered among the tables in the tavern, but no eyes turned towards me when I entered. I sent another silent prayer to the Mother. Nobody was searching for me here. Not yet, at least.

I sat at the bar, dragging out a stool and settling onto it.

"Looks like ye had a long day, eh?" the bartender asked, slinging the dish towel over her shoulder.

She was short and stout, with long braided hair that was a muted gold, her eyes a striking green. I nodded, meeting her gaze.

"I don't have any coin—I only need to rest here for a moment if that's alright." I gave her a soft, encouraging smile.

She nodded. "O' course. Why don't I get ye a meal, on the house."

She called towards the back of the tavern where a burly, curly haired man acknowledged her with a grunt before turning back to the stove.

"I don't want to be any trouble," I told her, guilt settling in my gut. I didn't want to take anything for free.

"Don't be silly," she said, sliding a tall mug of Dragon's Ale before me with a smile. "We take care o' each other in these parts."

I nodded, returning her smile. "Thank you. I can't tell you how much I appreciate it."

"It's no worry, darlin'," she replied, grinning wide and I could see she was missing one of her bottom front teeth. "Ye can repay us by slaughterin' that bitch on the mountain." She winked, placing a plate of bread before me.

"I-I-" I stuttered, but I wasn't sure what I was even about to say before she held up a hand, cutting me off.

"Yer secret is safe with us. It's a pleasure to serve the true queen." She grasped the towel across her shoulder, resuming drying the glasses behind the bar top.

"How—" I cleared my throat. "How did you know?"

I had never met this woman before. Never been to this part of Akra. I was weary that I had been recognized immediately, cautious that Donika was still out searching for me. At this point Nikolai and his Noctani might be, too. I doubted Donika would think I were in Akra though—right under her nose. So close, but still out of reach.

"Blazing red hair"—She gestured towards my mop of curls tangled in a mess at the nape of my neck—"baggy clothes. Fire in yer eyes. You look as if ye escaped something right awful. It's an easy guess. Not to mention yer the spittin' image of yer mother."

She knew Annelise? I wasn't sure I believed her answer, but I let it drop. I munched on the bread she had placed before me, devouring the chicken and rice when she had brought that out, too. I enjoyed my meal in silence, watching the other patrons in the bar chatter among each other. I was so thankful to eat something that wasn't soup or stew for the first time in weeks. I downed the tall glass of Dragon's Ale as if it might be the last I ever had. The way things were going for me recently... it honestly might be.

"Who do I owe my thanks to?" I asked the bartender as I brushed my hands off on my pants, pushing the stool out and standing.

My legs protested at moving once more, but they held.

"Fleur," she answered with a smile.

For only a moment it appeared as if she was taller. Slimmer. Her skin unblemished, her beautiful hair unbound down her back and shining a bright golden sheen. No missing teeth. I blinked, and the illusion was gone.

A glamour.

A smile turned up the corner of my mouth. "Thank you, Fleur. I'll be sure to remember your kindness and hospitality. I can't thank you enough."

"Welcome back any time, ye are." She nodded. "Say 'ello to Annelise and Amiyah fer me."

A knowing glint twinkled in her eyes. I opened my mouth to say more, but she simply disappeared back into the kitchen. I shook my head, smiling as I made for the tavern door. I had better get going if I wanted to make it across The Shadow before nightfall.

My clothes had finally dried but were left starched and crisp from the rain, rubbing against my skin uncomfortably. I was chafing, and it was only a matter of time before I broke out in a rash. I couldn't wait to get out of these Goddamn clothes.

I didn't stand out too badly as I strolled into Prins, my feet throbbing from the blisters that had formed there. I had a full belly and renewed energy, hoping I could make it to the outskirts of Prins by sundown. If I kept this pace, I should be back at the seaside cabin by midday tomorrow.

I hoped Puck and Tess were there.

For a moment, it crossed my mind that maybe I should find Alastir's family home in The Shadow. But I shook my head to myself. I couldn't be sure Tess or Puck were still there, and I didn't want to run into Phineas looking like this. He was too all knowing. A collector of information. He would use anything against anyone, me included. I didn't want rumors of my capture spreading across the realm.

No... I needed to make it back to the safety of my family. If Tess and Puck weren't there, Zion would send a raven to let them know I was back safely.

I strangely didn't mind traveling alone and wasn't as frightened of being recognized. Nobody expected the rightful queen of Istmere to be traveling the streets in baggy, soiled clothing with her hair uncombed and no entourage. It was easier to fly under the radar, though I did wish I had a glamour like Fleur. I wondered if she was someone from the resistance, having known both my mother and aunt.

As I reached The Shadow the sun had begun its descent in the sky. I made quick work of descending the staircase, picking through the now familiar streets to the other side. The sun had slightly fallen over the horizon by the time I ascended the stairs on the other side. I was thankful I hadn't run into anyone untoward and praised myself for remembering the way all on my own.

I didn't want to travel alone under the cover of night, but I hadn't any money for a room at an inn either. I would *kill* for the fluffy down bed at Eight Bells right about now, but I knew it wasn't in the cards. I would need to spend another night under the stars, curled at the base of a tree. I pressed through the southern part of Prins, making my way through the streets beneath the soft glow of the torches and lanterns that hung outside people's homes and outside the merchant shops.

I was utterly exhausted I wanted to sleep for at least two days when I finally got back.

Maybe three.

It had to be almost midnight by the time I collapsed at the base of a tree in the forest leading back towards the seaside cabin. I curled up into myself to keep warm. The summer night was especially brisk against my skin, but I was thankful my clothes were at least dry this night.

I fell asleep to the soft sounds of the birds chirping in the trees, safe and peaceful beneath the blanket of stars for the first time in a long, long time.

21

When I woke the next morning, there was a chill across my skin. My body had curled in on itself against the chill of the morning air. My hair was wet, plastered to the side of my face from the morning dew. I squinted my eyes against the rising sun and startled when a figure came into focus before me.

She stood tall, her arms crossed over her chest, her raven black hair falling down her back. She crooked a brow at me as I pushed my back against the tree I had fallen asleep beneath the night before.

"Seriously?" Kenna asked, reaching down to offer me her hand.

I gratefully took it, standing to brush the pine bristles off my clothing.

My entire body ached. From running from Nikolai, from pulling on my magic, from breaking my own heart. I

215

stretched, the muscles complaining as I raised my arms towards the sky with a groan.

"I couldn't make it any further last night," I explained, stifling a yawn. "I was utterly exhausted. I can't tell you how thankful I am to see a friendly face."

Kenna nodded, a smile lifting the corner of her lips.

"And you thought nobody would find you here?" she asked, glancing around.

All that surrounded us was the forest floor, the clearing visible ahead that would lead to the first river crossing towards the cabin.

I nodded. "Not many other options, I'm afraid."

Kenna's smile fell, her expression turning grim. "I take it things didn't... go well? When you escaped?"

I shook my head, my gaze falling to my worn boots. That was an understatement. I bit my lip, holding back the swell of emotion that threatened to spill forward. I wasn't ready to unleash all of that yet. I needed to get back to the cabin first.

Back to Tess.

"You can tell me all about it on the way back. The others are waiting." She nodded her head towards the clearing before taking off, not glancing back to ensure I followed.

Kenna had always had a brusque nature, but I enjoyed that about her. She was all business, no fluff. I inhaled deeply to steel myself before I trailed after her.

"Were you on patrol?" I asked, raising my hand to shield my eyes from the sun as we entered the clearing. The sun beat down mercilessly overhead, but I welcomed the warmth as it pooled against my skin. Last night on the forest floor had been so cold.

"I was on the night patrol, almost packed it in and headed back before I spotted you," Kenna explained. "We've all been taking turns—we haven't stopped searching for you since the moment you were captured. The resistance has been out in full force, too. Though I'll happily report to Zion, they can return to hiding."

"We all?" I asked, a morsel of hope growing in my chest that Tess and Puck were back at the cabin, too. That it would only be a few more hours before I would see them.

Kenna nodded. "Tess and Puck returned about two and a half weeks ago. They explained that the Noctani had taken you. I have to be honest... we weren't sure we were going to find you, Diana."

A humorless laugh escaped my lips. "I wasn't sure I was going to be able to escape."

"And all in one piece?" she asked, slowing her pace to walk by my side. She raised her brow at me in question.

"Yes, all in one piece. My unruly and unpredictable magic remains intact, thankfully."

Kenna's lip turned up in a half smile. "Good."

"When did you and Saanvi return from The Shadow?" I asked, lowering my hand once we had walked under the cover of trees in the forest beyond the clearing.

"When you didn't return with the Dragon's breath, we went searching for you," she replied, glancing at me out of the corner of her eye.

My gaze remained fixed on my boots, watching the path before me.

"And did you find Tess and Puck?" I asked.

She nodded. "We did. We caught up with them, then returned to the cabin to let Zion and Annelise know what had happened. Then we sent patrols out immediately. Tess wanted to go after you herself, but we didn't know where to begin searching. We thought to use a locator spell, but all your things remain back at the underground in Siraleth. You hadn't left anything behind in the cabin that we could use to track you. The grimoire itself wouldn't work for such a spell, not truly belonging to anyone."

I nodded in understanding.

"I wouldn't have wanted you to come after me without reinforcements, anyway. They took the three of us down as if we were *nothing*. As if we were merely toy soldiers. Knocked Puck out, and Tess too, before taking me."

"Where did they bring you?" she asked.

I thought for a moment. "I'm not exactly sure. It was a remote location in the northwest corner of Akra, in a home taken over by the Noctani. I'm not sure what happened to the previous owners, but it was outfitted with a dungeon in the basement. There were cells." A chill crept over my skin at the thought of the cold, damp concrete I had slept on those first few nights. "It appeared they had been there for some time."

"Would you be able to lead us back there? To the house?" Kenna asked.

I shook my head. "I don't think so. I left in a... hurry. I wasn't thinking those first few miles. I'm not sure I'd be able to find it again even if I tried."

I never wanted to return there, not even to find Nik. After everything that had happened, it felt as if leaving him was a betrayal in and of itself. The guilt of that and everything that we had done while I was captive sat heavy in my gut.

"And... you're ok?" Kenna asked, her eyes on the marks at my neck. My wrist.

I pulled the tunic up around me, covering the bite marks that were surely bruising by now.

"I am," I assured her, my smile tight.

"You have nothing to be ashamed about. Nothing to hide from us. You are a fighter, Diana. A survivor. Whatever you had to do to survive, it doesn't matter now. You're here. You're safe. And you still have your magic."

I nodded tightly in agreement, though I wasn't ready to believe the words quite yet. I hoped I felt that way someday... but guilt and shame stirred heavily in my core.

"Saanvi is ok?" I asked, my gaze meeting hers once more, changing the subject.

"She is. She's a fighter, that one. Just like you," Kenna replied with a wistful smile.

"I'm happy for you two. I didn't know—" but Kenna cut my words off as she raised her hand.

"Nobody knew," she said. "We didn't want to tell anyone. But seeing her there, the throwing knife so close to taking her life, I didn't care in that moment who knew about us. Only that I needed her to be ok."

"I'm happy for you. The both of you." I smiled, relieved I could find something genuine to be happy about among this mess of a situation we had found ourselves in.

"Thank you." She smiled, a dimple popping on her left cheek.

We had reached the river crossing and while I was filthy beyond belief, we didn't stop to bathe. I was anxious to get back to Tess and Puck. I was still weak, and Kenna helped me across the water, the tide pulling against me and threatening to sweep me downstream.

My pants were soaked through, my boots squeaking with each step I took. The second river crossing couldn't come soon enough. The sun was high above us now, the birds chirping as we delved deeper and deeper into the forest. Kenna's eyes watched the sky, and I knew she wanted to take her raven form, craved taking to the skies to glare down from above. But she remained beside me to guide me back.

"Did you... " I started—not sure I wanted the answer to the question I was about to ask. "Did you return to Alastir after you found Puck and Tess? Did you finish the antidote?"

The ghost of a smile crossed Kenna's expression. "We did." Her words were tight.

I cocked my head to the side in confusion as a swell of emotion burst in my chest. "That's great news, so why does it sound as if you aren't too happy about that?"

"You'll see. I'll let Tess explain." She averted her gaze and my stomach dropped.

"What is it?" I asked, grabbing her arm to stop her.

I couldn't wait until we got back to the cabin. I had never been a patient person, and news like this would eat me alive inside. If something was wrong, I needed to know.

Now.

She scooted out of my reach. "I don't know all the details." She motioned for us to continue. "We are almost there—I promise Tess will explain."

I nodded skeptically, eyes narrowing. "They brought the Dragon's breath back to Alastir?"

"They did," Kenna replied. "Puck thought Tess was insane that she stopped to collect even more of it before returning. All he could think about was notifying the others that you had been captured. But Tess *insisted* you would never forgive any of us if you didn't complete the spell and bring enough of the ingredient back to Alastir to complete the spell."

A single laugh escaped my lips. "She was right. This can't all be for nothing. We need to save Nik and Isaac. That is the priority right now. Has there been any sightings of Donika or her men?"

Kenna shook her head. "We had assumed she had sent the Noctani force after you and withdrew the other soldiers once news got to her that you had been successfully captured. But they never brought you to her?"

I shook my head, my brow furrowed. "No. It's... complicated."

Her eyes traveled to the marks on my neck once more. "I can only imagine."

Her gaze wasn't judgmental, it was understanding. As if she would have made similar choices had she been in the same situation. I was thankful that Kenna had been the one to find me.

I had left the seaside cabin with such haste, and on bad terms with my mother. I was anxious to see her again, too. I wanted to ask her about the bar maid I ran into who knew her and Amiyah. I had enjoyed a rare bit of hospitality in Akra, and I wondered at the connection between the two of them.

The soft breeze mussed my hair as the sounds of the ocean crashing against the rocks filled my ears. We were close now.

My muscles were so sore I couldn't wait to take a long, hot bath in the little tub at Amiyah's house. I knew we would be calling a council meeting right away, but I hoped I had at least a few moments of rest to clean up before we did.

As we neared the clearing and the trees grew sparser, we were spotted. Puck shouted to the others something I couldn't quite make out from this distance. A figure was running through the sand, barreling straight towards us. Tess reached me and practically crashed into me, knocking the air from my lungs as her body slammed against mine, holding me tight to her chest.

"Diana. Thank the Mother you're ok," she breathed, squeezing me as tightly as her arms would allow.

"Can't. Breathe." I bit out between staggering breaths.

She laughed, releasing me only enough to gaze into my face.

"Diana, you had us so scared. You have no idea how happy I am to see you." Tears filled Tess's eyes as she pulled me to her once more.

"You have no idea how happy I am to see *you*," I told her, squeezing her back.

The tears that I had held back since leaving Nik spilled forth now, soaking through the material at Tess's shoulder and leaving behind stains of dirt and salt. A sob racked my body as she held me tightly.

Kenna left us, allowing us a moment alone at the forest's edge.

Tess held me there for a long time while we cried. I let everything out until there was nothing left, and I was dry and empty once more.

I wasn't sure how many more times I could do this.

My heart was fragile beyond reason. My emotional cup was pretty empty right about now.

Donika would pay for this. She would pay for almost breaking me. She would pay for the torment she put me through. Her reckoning was coming, and it would come at the end of *my* blade.

I pulled away only enough to see into Tess's eyes once more.

"Please tell me you have it," I croaked. My words were fragile. Brittle.

Tess's expression turned downcast, and my heart threatened to stop beating in my chest.

"Tess? Kenna said you had it... " My words were a plea. A prayer.

Please have it. Please. I can't take any more disappointment.

She nodded solemnly. "We have it."

My brows knitted together in confusion. "Then what's wrong? Why doesn't anyone sound happy about that?"

Tess took a steadying breath, her grip tight on my shoulder as her gaze roamed over my face, taking in my appearance. The dirt on my clothes. The stains on my pants. The ill-fitted clothing I had stolen from Nikolai. The marks on my neck. The purple bruises that had begun to fade on my face.

"We have the antidote, but there's a catch. And you're not going to like it."

22

"A catch?" I asked, my breath caught in my throat.

I knew it was too good to be true. I wanted *one thing* to work out *for once*. It was always one step forward, three steps back, and I wasn't sure how much longer I could endure it.

We needed a win. We needed the tides to turn in our favor.

Tess nodded. "I'll explain everything, but first, let's get you bathed and fed."

She slung her arm around my shoulder, guiding me towards the cabin.

"We need to convene the council," I told her.

"I agree, but first you need to take care of yourself. Give yourself a minute, Diana. You just got back from escaping capture. Mother only knows what you endured while you were there, and while I can't wait to hear all about it, you need to take a beat. You smell, babe."

She laughed, but it didn't reach her eyes.

The pit of dread in my stomach was growing, expanding within me as I rifled through all the reasons getting the antidote might not be such a good thing. Whatever it was, we would deal with it. If there was a way we could save Nik and Isaac, and the other innocents that Donika had experimented on without their permission, we had to take it.

I followed Tess inside and she set a fresh set of clothes out for me in the bedroom I had stayed in when I had first come to the cabin. After Nik had first been turned Noctani and I was utterly broken inside.

I released a heavy exhale as I stripped out of the clothes I had stolen from him, both happy and sad to be rid of the reminder of that time we spent together. I left them piled on the bathroom floor as I scrubbed my skin clean until it was pink and raw. I didn't want a single reminder of it left on my body. Not an ounce of blood or dirt leftover. When I had finished and pulled the curtain aside, the clothes I had come back in were gone.

Those clothes were the only thing I had left of him at this point, but I detested them all the same. I didn't need to see them again. I needed to move forward, not think about what had already transpired in the past. There was nothing I could do to change it now.

I dried off, shrugging on the clothes Tess had left for me. Thankfully, they fit much better. I hadn't seen Annelise or Zion yet, but Amiyah was in the small kitchen when I returned to the main living space. Tess and Puck were perched at the dining table, their eyes turning towards me as I cracked the door open.

"Better?" Tess asked, a knowing smile on her lips.

"Yes, thank you. I'll be even better once I eat something," I replied, my hand resting on my stomach as it gave a knowing growl.

"Glad to hear it," Amiyah called from the stove. "I hope you're hungry."

I fell into one of the seats at the table across from Tess. *"Famished."*

My mouth watered as she set a roasted chicken before us, along with a bowl of bright green vegetables. My nose filled with the aroma, and my stomach grumbled once more. I was thankful for the food, and thankful to be back here with family.

"Eat up you three. We'll be outside when you're ready." Amiyah gave me a soft smile as she brushed her hands off on her apron, pulling it over her head and leaving it on the counter. She exited down the narrow driftwood steps, leaving us alone in the cabin.

I could see through the small window over the couch that Saanvi and Kenna were walking down the beach, hand in hand. The table by the coast where we had the last council meeting was visible from here, and Annelise and Zion sat there talking, their heads bent towards one another.

I helped myself to a generous portion of the meal Amiyah had prepared, knowing that I would need my strength in the coming days.

Tess spoke around a mouthful of food. "I figured we could discuss some of the... less savory topics. Just us. Before re-grouping with the others."

I smiled my appreciation. "You don't want the others to know he bit me?" I asked, my brow raising in challenge.

Puck choked on the bite he had been chewing, not expecting me to come right out with it.

"I don't care, but I figured *you* might." She shrugged, as if we were talking about something completely normal.

Once he regained his composure, Puck's gaze fell to his plate, his eyes dark. "Are you ok?"

I nodded. "I'm ok, Puck."

"But he... he hurt you."

I flinched. "He did."

Puck's head fell back, his gaze turning toward the ceiling as he bit back whatever emotion threatened to overtake him. Nik might have been my love, but he was Puck's closest friend. It wasn't only me who had to carry the burden that Nik was... different now. Corrupted. Irrevocably changed. A monster.

"He hurt you, too," I reminded him.

Puck laughed humorlessly. "He did. Knocked me and Tess out. But... he didn't kill us. And he should have. That's what I would have done if I were in his shoes."

I nodded. "There is a piece of him. I'm not sure how small that piece might be, but there *is* a piece of the old Nikolai left inside of him."

"That gives me hope, at least," Puck replied, picking up his fork.

"Kenna told me that you finished the spell after I was captured," I replied between bites.

Tess nodded, swallowing. "My idea."

"Good girl." I grinned.

Tess could read me like a book. She had always known me so well.

"Then we returned to Alastir's, running into Kenna and Saanvi, who were out searching for us on the way. We faked the potion with Phineas and took the real antidote back with us," Tess explained. "Once we had the antidote, we came back here right away, sending out patrols to search for you as we gathered numbers to find you."

"But it looks like you didn't need us at all," Puck's lip turned up in a half smile.

"How did you escape him?" Tess asked. "Why didn't he bring you to Donika? Why did he let you go?"

I chose my words carefully. "I... betrayed him. Deceived him. *Seduced* him. But I don't know who I fooled in the end, him... or me."

"Oh, Diana. You did what you had to do to survive," Tess told me, her voice full of understanding. "But he... he bit you?"

I nodded. "But my magic remains."

"Why did he bite you but not steal your magic? Isn't that the whole point?"

A blush rose to my cheeks unbidden. "It was... part of the seduction." I was embarrassed to speak the words in front of Puck.

Puck's gaze held mine. "But he had ample opportunity to take your magic. To bring you to Donika, as he was instructed. And he didn't."

"No, he didn't," I agreed. "It's as if there are two sides to him, and they are at war with each other. He can be malicious, but amiable. Cruel, but reverent. But *never* kind."

Puck's gaze fell once more.

"It sounds as if it's more complicated than we initially thought," Tess mused.

"You can say that again," I scoffed, pushing my plate away from me.

"Was Isaac there? Anyone else you recognized?" Puck asked.

I shook my head. "No, only Antonia Finch. I didn't recognize any of the other Noctani."

"I wonder where Isaac is," Tess deliberated, biting her lip.

I told her about how I had seen him in my dream walking at the castle, but I wasn't certain if that was where he remained. Isaac was powerful, too. Nikolai might have been selected to lead the Noctani, but Isaac had to have an important position within the ranks as well. He might be by Donika's side, leading her Noctani forces at the castle.

"Will you finally tell me what the catch is with the antidote?" I asked.

"Once we regroup with the others." Tess nodded towards the door. "Are you ready?"

"As ready as I'll ever be," I grumbled, pushing away from the table and placing my dish in the sink.

I wasn't sure what the council would have to say about what was to come, but I knew what my priority was. I couldn't risk moving against Donika and killing Nikolai or Isaac in the process. We needed to cure them first, then put an end to this war once and for all.

I followed Tess and Puck out of the cabin and down the steps, towards the table resting on the shoreline. Amiyah had joined Annelise and Zion, and when Saanvi and Kenna saw us making our way over, they joined us at the table too.

I reluctantly pulled the chair out at the head of the table next to Zion, a smile in my eyes as I took him and Annelise in. I was happy they were safe and sound back here. I can't imagine how worried they must have been.

"Diana." My mother's voice drew my attention, her voice gentle. She moved around the table and captured me in her arms.

Despite everything that had transpired between us before I had left, I let her. I took comfort in the feeling of her arms around me, her embrace tight. I couldn't bear the thought that I had almost never seen her again, and I had left things unfinished. I had left our relationship strained and full of resentment, and I wanted to fix it so desperately. I squeezed her back, and her eyes were filled with tears when she pulled away. She took her seat beside Zion once more.

Zion grasped my hand in his, eyes soft. "Welcome back, Diana."

"Thank you," I replied, my voice quiet.

"There was never a doubt in my mind that you would escape. You're strong, like your mother. Resourceful."

I cleared my throat. "It was a close call, that's for sure."

Zion nodded. "You don't need to divulge the details to us. All that matters is that you are here, and you are safe. Now, we need to talk next steps."

"Agreed," I replied, nodding. "Where are we with numbers? Kenna told me you pulled on the resistance in hiding to search for me."

Zion released my hand as he turned back towards the group. "The numbers are strong. I sent out letters and ravens, and it's better than we thought after the attack on the safe house at Prins. We have large clusters of Shades spread across the realm, three thousand strong, ready to march for you."

Three thousand. We had thought our numbers were diminished after the battle at Prins, but that attack had turned even *more* towards our side. More Shades wanted to fight for their own freedom.

Wonder sparked in Zion's gaze as he continued. "You are a beacon of hope for the people, Diana. Those that had given up are now turning to take up arms in your name. Those that have suffered under Donika, lost a family member or friend, they are ready to march in honor of the true queen. Many of the Shades in Istmere simply needed a strong leader to follow. They aren't afraid anymore."

My magic swelled in my chest at his words, pressing against me and filling me with a fiery energy. The hairs on my arms stood up, a soft smile on my lips as I held Zion's gaze.

"That's better than I could have ever hoped for," I told him. "There's just one thing we need to do first."

He nodded in understanding. "I'll let Tess and Puck take it from here."

I turned towards them, my hands fidgeting in my lap.

It was Puck who spoke first. "We returned with the Dragon's breath so Alastir could finish the spell. We made three different antidotes. Two true antidotes that we have with us, and one that Phineas took. He doesn't suspect our deceit, and we didn't want to stick around to wait for him to find out."

Puck pulled a glass tube of bright red liquid out of his jacket and placed it on the table.

"Is this it?" I asked, my gaze focused on the fluid within.

He nodded. "This is it. We have two of them, but we have the spell to make more. We would only need more of your blood. Alastir has sent us with everything else we need."

"And?" I asked, raising my brow. "You said there's a catch?"

Puck's gaze flitted to Tess, and she glared daggers back at him before she spoke.

"I guess *I* have to break the news, then. Remember how Alastir had said that he couldn't guarantee that it would work? That it might not return the Shade to their natural state, or that they may not even survive it?"

I nodded. "Yes, I remember."

Tess cleared her throat before continuing, her eyes on the antidote at the center of the table. "That's because you don't... *drink*... the antidote."

My brows knit together. "You don't drink it? I don't understand. Then how is it administered?"

Tess's voice was raspy as she spoke, her soft brown hair billowing gently in the sea breeze. "It is administered by submerging a blade in the liquid."

Dread pooled deep in my gut.

"And?" I prompted.

"And driving the coated blade through the Noctani's heart."

23

My eyes were darting back and forth, my mind racing. This must have been what Alastir meant when he said he wasn't even sure the Shade would survive it. I had a million questions running through my head, but we couldn't risk going back to find Alastir again.

My gaze met Tess's.

"This is the only way?" My voice was thin.

Tess nodded solemnly. "Alastir confirmed it. The only way to cure this type of spell is with an equally dark and bloody one." She nodded towards the antidote before Puck. "This spell contains your blood. That is enough for the two antidotes we have. There is no other way."

This... changed things.

I had expected another pit to form in my gut, but my heart had simply stopped entirely, suspended within my chest. If we didn't succeed, if we didn't cure Nikolai, he would be dead. There would be no going back.

I pushed back from my chair, my hands on the table as I stood. My gaze traveled to Zion.

"What do we do?" My voice was quivering.

I wished more than anything Isaac was here to guide us. He was my mentor, and he knew more about this type of magic than any of us... except for maybe Annelise. My gaze flitted to hers and she nodded.

"I've had the Kotova grimoire in my possession for decades, and I trust Alastir with my life. If he says this is the only way to reverse the siphoning spell, it is the only way." Her hands were neatly folded in her lap as she spoke, but my gaze snagged on her finger, picking the skin off her thumb with anxiety.

Like mother like daughter.

"Then we need to test it on someone else first," I offered, my gaze drifting around the table.

It was Saanvi who spoke. "The ingredients required for the spell aren't commonplace, one of which being *your blood*. We have two antidotes in our possession, and it might take days if not weeks to create more. Do we even have that much time?"

Zion nodded at her in agreement. "We don't, not the way Donika's numbers are escalating. Our spies confirmed that her numbers have tripled, quadrupled, even since the beginning of this war. If we wait much longer, we risk her creating so many Araneoch and Noctani we have no hope of standing against them. We can't continue to let her grow her forces. We need to act."

"Then we move against her now," Kenna suggested.

My eyes met hers as I settled back into my seat, my hand splayed across my chest. My heart was still beating and I could feel the steady rhythm beneath my palm.

"And when we kill her, we have no idea if her Noctani will continue to live or if they will die with her," Tess countered with a shake of her head. "The dark magic and the blood she used to create them resides within her. If she dies, there is a possibility that they may return to their natural states... or to the earth from which they came. But there is also a possibility that they will die, corrupted by the spell that turned them. We have no way of knowing. If we move now, Nikolai could end up dead, anyway."

I nodded, my eyes darting to each of them. "That's not a risk I'm willing to take."

When Annelise spoke next her voice was cold, brittle. "Is that what Nik would have wanted? Risking the lives of the entire resistance—and the fate of Istmere—just to save him?"

My gaze was cutting when it met hers. Zion's hand gripped my knee, keeping me in my chair as my magic surged forth, pressing against my fingertips so fiercely I singed the wood table, leaving behind ten fingerprint marks. I pulled my hands back hastily, burying them in my lap.

I swallowed hard. "Nik would have wanted to see this through. And are you forgetting, Mother, that if he dies, so do I? Who will take the throne then?" My voice dripped acid. "Will it be you? Was the whole point of this not to reinstate the rightful heir to the throne? Istmere will descend into chaos without a succession in place. If Donika dies and so do her Noctani, *then so do I.* The fact that Nikolai and I still live serves as proof that even if the magic has been twisted and darkened, *we are still bound.*"

"I'm sorry for suggesting it," Annelise put her hand out, pleading. "That isn't what I meant. Only that we are losing focus. The greater threat is the war against Donika, not the Noctani alone."

"And we will resume our plans to march against The Stone City once we have cured Nikolai and Isaac and have them safely by our sides, marching with us." My eyes narrowed on Annelise. "Let's not forget I can't march against Donika with my magic unbound. I do not plan to march against her with strength and numbers alone. We need Nikolai so that my magic can be used in the fight to come."

I could see that she regretting having spoken, risking shattering the gentle peace we had achieved upon my return. I understood her reasoning, but there was nothing left to discuss. We needed my magic bound, and we needed Nikolai.

That was my first priority.

"So we have to risk it, then. Trust Alastir. That the antidote will work and we will restore him. We only have two in our possession, and we need to use them wisely." Puck's voice was gentle, bringing the conversation back to what our next steps would be.

I closed my eyes, letting the sound of the crashing waves waft over me. I inhaled deeply through my nostrils, allowing the smells of salt and brine to center me. I nodded, my gaze finding Puck's when I opened my eyes once more.

"Yes. We will have to take the risk that Alastir is the most seasoned magic wielder in this realm, and if there is any chance of saving Nikolai, it rests with him. I have to be the one to do it." I bit my lip, my gaze falling to the table.

"Diana, no," Zion protested, his chair pushing back in the sand as he gripped the sides of the table, knuckles white. "You cannot be the one to wield the blade. If it doesn't work and we lose him?" He shook his head. "You would essentially have killed yourself."

Annelise nodded in agreement. "I have to agree. If there is any life after this one... you can't carry that burden with you. I don't think it's a wise choice, Diana."

It was Saanvi who cleared her throat and spoke, silencing all of us. "In fact... it has to be Diana. When Alastir finished the spell and gave it to us, he was certain to tell us that it *had* to be the blood of the antidote that wielded the weapon. Diana's blood was used to create it, therefore Diana must wield the blade."

I took a deep breath, exhaling through my nose.

It was settled, then.

I would either cure Nik, or kill him... there was no other choice.

Whatever happened next, it would change everything. I would either have Nikolai back in my arms, my magic bound, or he would be dead, and our chances of defeating Donika diminished.

"Now the question is, how do we find them?" Zion asked, settling back down into his chair.

"I don't think I can find the house he kept me in again," I replied, shaking my head. "I think our best bet at finding them is to lure them out."

"And how will we do that?" Kenna asked.

"I'll be the bait," I replied, my jaw tight.

He would come for me—I knew he would. He couldn't stop himself. Not only did he lose me for himself, but he disobeyed Donika's direct orders. He wouldn't let me get away a second time.

"Then we move in force," Zion said with a nod. "We will call on more resistance members. We need to have numbers to match theirs, at the least. We have no clue how many they will have with them, but we need to be a small enough group to not draw notice as we travel."

I nodded. "And what will we do with the other Noctani? They are innocent, too. Most of them, anyway. Donika made them what they were without their consent."

"I'm afraid they may be a casualty of war," Annelise answered.

Leave it to her to speak the cold truth. My gaze fell to my hand where I picked at the nail on my own thumb.

"I hate to agree, but she's right," Saanvi said. "We can try to spare them, but there will be casualties as we try to administer the antidote to Nikolai and Isaac."

"We have to try to keep Isaac safe and busy until Diana can cure Nikolai, then Isaac next. She is the only one that can cure them both with her being the only one to wield the weapon," Kenna added. "Keeping them busy without killing them will be a task in and of itself. We can't save them all, Diana."

The way I saw it, they were still *my* people. They were still innocent residents of Istmere, fallen victim to Donika's ministrations and experiments. They were no more at fault than we were. It felt wrong to cure Nikolai and Isaac because of our personal relationships with them but sacrifice the others for our greater purpose.

Zion could see the emotions warring on my face and his hand found my shoulder, squeezing it. His hazel eyes were soft as they held my gaze.

"Being queen means making the hard decisions. We cannot win this war without Nikolai the way things stand right now. We will try to fight them off, but our mission is to keep Nikolai and Isaac safe until you can administer the antidote to both of them. You aren't alone, we will be there with you."

I nodded, my breath catching in my throat. I knew he was right, but that didn't make it any easier.

"How many will we take with us?" I asked.

"I will send a raven to Prins. Should five on top of the seven we have here be enough?" Zion asked.

Amiyah had been quiet the entire time, letting us hash out the next steps ourselves and not interjecting. But she spoke now, her voice cutting. "If you think you are marching without me, you are mistaken."

The ghost of a smile crossed Zion's face, and he nodded. "Eight, then. An additional five should be plenty."

When I smiled at Amiyah, her eyes sparked with emotion. The fact that she would march with us, even after what had happened to her son Tyr, had gratefulness swelling deep within my chest. We were stronger together, and I was confident the group of us would be able to hold the Noctani off long enough to see this through. We only had to pray to the Mother that there would be no Araneoch.

"It's settled then," Zion pushed away from the table. "I'll send the message. We march to Akra to lure them out the morning after next."

"Why not tomorrow?" I asked.

"You've only just gotten back. You need your rest, Diana. The trials to come will be a strain for us all." He gave my shoulder one final squeeze before retreating to the cabin.

"How can we be sure Isaac will be with them?" Kenna asked. "He wasn't with the group that captured you and held you hostage."

I nodded. I had been thinking the same thing. "We can only hope that he is. If he isn't with them, we will cross that bridge when we come to it."

Isaac was a father to Kenna, and I was equally anxious to ensure his safety.

"It's settled then," Tess said, a hopeful half smile gracing her lips.

Nothing had gone to plan as of late, and I was anxious to get this over with. I was glad Tess still had hope... but at this point... I wasn't sure.

We would need more than luck to get through this.

We would need one hell of a fucking miracle.

The morning after next came quicker than any of us expected, leaving us little time to prepare. Amiyah and Annelise helped to cover us in skin spells that would ensure fast healing and increased speed and strength. Despite the added protection, we would still be much slower than the Noctani.

I sharpened Stormslayer, dreading the fact that the very blade Nikolai had forged for me might be the blade to kill him. I shook my head, trying to clear those thoughts. I needed to be positive. I needed to be strong and clearheaded going into this.

Everything would go to plan.

It had to.

I strapped the freshly sharpened Stormslayer to my thigh sheath, securing my throwing knives in my boots and strapping a scabbard with a sword across my back, just in case. The others were equally well-armed.

Seeing everyone in fighting gear—strapping themselves with weapons—had me feeling as if we were already marching into the lion's den. I sent a prayer up to the Mother that we wouldn't encounter more of Donika's soldiers and we could successfully lure out the group of Noctani from their hiding spot.

We had lured them out unintentionally once before by simply walking the streets of Dragon's Hollow... how hard could it be? I was nervous to veer close to The Stone City again, but we couldn't exactly meet the Noctani on the streets of Prins, in the middle of civilian territory. We wanted to keep the casualties as low as possible which meant we needed to protect the innocent people of Istmere. There were families and children in the realm who needed protecting, who didn't have a place entrenched in the fighting.

As we passed through Prins, the other resistance members Zion had called upon would meet up with us. The greatest number of Noctani still resided within the castle walls, my dream walking had assured me of that much. We were all skilled fighters and we wouldn't be caught by surprise again.

We would be leaving the seaside cabin empty for the first time in a very, very long time. I tasted salt in the back of my throat as I glanced back at Tyr's childhood home, wishing he was marching with us today.

He deserved to be here, too.

We had transferred the bright red antidote from the glass tube to plastic bottles, easier to carry on our person and minimizing the risk of breaking the glass and losing the potion altogether. I carried one bottle in my jacket pocket, the other was with Zion.

As soon as we had lured them out, I would need to cure the blade with the antidote, suspending it in the liquid. Then I would fight Nikolai. Then Isaac.

Nik might not waste the opportunity to steal my magic a second time. I needed to be extra careful to stay away from his fangs. He was stronger and faster than me. I would need to use all the skills he had taught me to evade him. The only problem was... he was the one who had trained me. He would likely be able to predict my moves.

But the same held true for me—I knew his fighting style. I would be ready.

The group of us were silent as we crossed the first river, traversing the forest and clearings towards the second crossing. A calmness had settled over our group. As if we all accepted the fate that was about to come to fruition, no matter what it was.

The calm before the storm.

My anxiety had my magic pressing against me, begging to be released. I kept my breathing steady and pushed it back gently, over and over again. I needed to keep my focus... I couldn't keep splitting my attention trying to keep my magic at bay. I missed the sensation of being bound, my magic listening to me acutely and responding to my every whim.

We filled our canteens at the second river crossing, unsure of how long we might be away from our makeshift camp. We had a large breakfast to ensure we wouldn't need to stop again until we were almost out of Prins. I hoped we might be able to stop into the tavern in Akra at some point to see Fleur again. She had been kind to me in a time of need, and I wanted to thank her once more.

As soon as we entered Prins, eyes were darting in our direction. The eight of us were dressed in dark training leathers, strapped to the hilt with weapons of all kinds. We were marching to war—and this time—we weren't hiding it.

We weren't lying low.

We *wanted* them to find us.

The resistance members Zion had called on joined our group right before we passed through The Shadow. There was a sense of security with our numbers being this strong. We stopped to camp for the night right outside the border of Prins. We would journey towards the far reaches of Akra first thing in the morning when dawn began to kiss the sky with pink rays.

We traveled in silence, a heavy weight settling on all of us now that we were close to our destination. What happened next would likely determine the outcome of this war and the thought had me swallowing back my anxiety. I kept my eyes on my boots, my mind racing through every possible scenario as we breached the tree line.

We had made it to Akra in merely two days' time.

Zion dropped his pack to the earth, settling himself against a tree as he watched the sky above with careful eyes. His gaze flickered to Kenna momentarily, and they engaged in a silent conversation. Kenna nodded, shifting into her raven form and taking to the skies above us.

She called out once, then disappeared into the cloud cover.

"Now what?" Tess asked, coming to my side and dropping her own pack.

Zion clasped his hands between his bent knees as Annelise joined him.

"Now... we wait."

A hand against my mouth had my eyes snapping open, a scream on the tip of my tongue was snuffed out by the thick, leather glove covering my lips. My eyes flew wide in alarm, my head shaking back and forth.

Nikolai bent before me, his hand clasped tightly over my mouth, his knee against the cold, hard ground as he crouched. He brought a slender finger to his lips.

"Shhhh, Firecracker. We don't want to wake the others."

I tried to snap my head to the side—to see the rest of the camp—but Nikolai held me firm.

Where were the others? Weren't Puck and Saanvi on the first watch? Had he killed them?

We had gone to bed that night knowing the Noctani were close. We could feel a cold chill in the air, creeping into our bones. The forest was devoid of all sound, a sign that there was dark magic among the woods. No birds chirped in the trees—no deer grazed the forest floor. It was utterly deserted.

Nothing living wanted to venture this close to the soulless creatures Donika had created. I had settled into my bedroll, anxious for dawn to come, never expecting Nikolai would find us so quickly. It hadn't even been one full nightfall before he had made his move.

"If you promise not to scream, I'll remove my hand." The pressure on my mouth eased as Nikolai leaned back, his eyes narrowed at me.

"What did you do to them?" I asked, sitting up in my bedroll and closing the distance between us.

Nikolai didn't move back. He studied me with those black, endless eyes. His gaze traveled from my brow, down my nose to my mouth. His gaze stopped, a smile lifting the corner of his own lips.

"I never imagined I'd see you again this soon. Couldn't stay away, could you, Firecracker?" he asked.

He reached his hand out, tucking a piece of stray curls behind my ear. When I flinched, his smile turned down.

"What's wrong?" His brows furrowed in confusion.

What's wrong?

It was my turn for my eyes to narrow, incredulous. My gaze traveled sideways to see there were full bedrolls beside me, soft snores filling the surrounding air.

"What did you do to them?" I asked, my voice barely above a whisper.

I wasn't worried about waking the others. I *needed* to wake the others. I simply needed to give the appearance that I didn't, lulling Nik into a false sense of security while I reached for my blade. Stormslayer was tucked beneath my makeshift pillow, the antidote was in my pack, which Tess was currently using as a head rest. Her breathing was soft, undisturbed. He hadn't hurt those in camp who had been sleeping, at least.

Nik cocked his head to the side.

"Puck and Saanvi," I explained slowly.

His tourmaline eyes sparked with something akin to recognition before he stepped back, his hand moving to his sword and sliding it free of its scabbard. I was on my feet in a heartbeat, Stormslayer sliding easily from beneath the pillow, held tightly in my grip.

Puck and Saanvi had *let* him in.

Alone.

They had baited him into camp, hoping he would come to steal me away, and now he was cornered. Footsteps stirred the brush as Puck and Saanvi jumped into the clearing, wielding their weapons in the space between us.

Tess stirred, and I kneeled at her side, shaking her not-so-gently. I needed the antidote, and I needed it *now*.

A wicked smile spread across Nik's lips, his fangs protruding from his mouth a sharp reminder of who he truly was in this moment. His sword moved to Tess's neck, and I stilled.

Tess peered up at him, unmoving.

"Not another movement from you," he snarled.

"You wouldn't hurt her," I protested.

His gaze flitted towards me. "Says who?"

Everything felt as if it happened all at once.

Once moment Nik was entirely outnumbered, caught in our web with no reinforcements. In the next moment he slid the sword away from Tess's throat, nicking the skin and leaving a thin line of blood trickling down her collarbone. Puck and Saanvi had burst through the brush, but so had the rest of the Noctani.

We were now surrounded by them, the cover of darkness making it difficult to see exactly how many of them there were. I did a quick scan, and there had to be at least seven of them. Maybe eight. We were evenly matched.

"You think I'd come here alone?" he asked, his head tilting to the side, his gaze never leaving mine.

"I came to take you back, Diana. And I won't fail again. You're *mine*." His teeth bared, sending a shiver running down my spine.

My palms were slick with sweat, my grip on Stormslayer sliding beneath my clammy hands. Tess still lay against my pack, but Zion had moved slowly in my periphery. He held the bright red antidote in his grip, shielding it from view inside his coat. He nodded towards me, but I didn't dare shift my gaze from Nikolai.

Annelise was on her feet now, too. Kenna had joined Saanvi, and Amiyah and the shades from the resistance were armed and ready, closing in the perimeter. We were scattered in a circle, holding our collective breath waiting for someone to make the first move.

"You wouldn't kill me," Nikolai protested, his eyes narrowed at me, fire brimming within their black depths.

I swallowed hard, a lump in the back of my throat as I spoke. "No, Nikolai. I wouldn't kill you. I want to *save* you."

"*Save* me?" He laughed, his head falling back and his eyes closing. His golden hair glimmered beneath the light of the moon, casting him in an eerie glow. "Why would you need to save me, Diana? I have *never* been stronger. *Never* been faster. Never been *more clear-minded*."

I shook my head, biting my lip against the urge to turn back. I dug my heels into the dirt at my feet, my legs bent, shoulder width apart.

"You aren't yourself."

"I've never been more myself," he argued, the sword in his grip slicing down between us.

I shook my head, my magic pressing against me painfully.

I hoped that with our numbers, I wouldn't have to release it. I was *so close* to being bound once more. From saving Nikolai from being cursed as a Noctani.

Footsteps drew our attention as we all turned towards the figure entering the clearing.

His head was bent, his hair shorn low against his head—but when he lifted his gaze to meet mine—I couldn't mistake that gaze. Despite it now being swallowed by darkness.

Isaac.

He moved into the center of the clearing, his gaze landing on each of us as he moved forward.

We all remained still. Waiting.

He examined me with a predatory affect, his head bent, his eyes narrowed.

"She's too dangerous, we can't risk letting her get away." When he spoke, his voice was cold.

Jarring.

Nikolai nodded in understanding.

It might have been a trick of the light from the moon, or the reflection off the blade he held between us, but I could have sworn his bottom lip quivered. Was he... scared? My gaze met his, but his eyes didn't betray him.

When Isaac spoke, it broke the unearthly silence that had fallen among us. Broke another piece of me, when I hadn't thought it was possible to break even more. His words set the Shades in motion, a flurry of flying blades, grunts, and blood.

"To the death, then. Kill them all."

25

Isaac moved first. He was faster than I had ever seen him before, his blade slicing out and barely missing my throat as I jumped back. I ducked, using the tree behind me to put space between us as I grasped my scabbard from my bedroll. I slid Stormslayer into its sheath at my thigh and grabbed the sword, sliding it free. I held it between us, my grip firm but apprehensive.

We were trying to *save* Isaac and Nikolai... we couldn't risk accidentally killing them. I moved back further, putting even more distance between us before stepping into the circle of another Nightshade, one I had no problem killing.

I turned towards her, a woman with hair the color of ink. I had never seen her before. A glance over my shoulder confirmed Isaac and Nik were lost in the melee. I needed to dispatch this Nightshade and grab the antidote.

Focus on Nikolai.

I ducked away from the blade that soared towards me, my leg sweeping out to kick the Noctani's legs out from under her. I needed to be careful not to let them get too close. If they stole my magic, it was all over. I was positive they had no qualms about stealing it now that Nikolai's protection had expired, orders or not.

The Noctani rushed me, sloppily trying to tackle me. I smashed my knee into her gut, slicing my sword down to cut across her chest. Her tunic opened, leaving a thin slice of blood to drip down her abdomen. She came up with her own sword quickly, parrying. Her blade met mine with a jarring impact, and I clenched my teeth together and groaned against the force.

I was no match for her strength, I needed to use my speed and smaller stature to overtake her. I pushed back hard, freeing my sword. I stabbed forward, but she hit my arm on an upswing, cutting the skin on my forearm. I let out a hiss, fresh blood dripping to the forest floor beneath me. The Noctani's gaze focused on the droplets of blood, as if she were locked in a trance.

I used her distraction as my opening and I cut forward, the sword in my grip burying itself in her neck. I hadn't used enough force to cut her head clean off, but her eyes rolled back before closing, her body slumping to her knees.

I used my foot to dislodge her body from my sword, her neck cut in half, her head rolling listlessly on her shoulders before her body crashed to the forest floor and didn't move again.

I turned quickly, sensing another Noctani at my back. I cursed, the Noctani smiling at me as it stood between me and my pack.

"Diana!" I could hear Zion calling out my name across the clearing, but he was too far away.

The antidote in my pack was the closest option.

I lunged, catching the Noctani off guard, their eyes widening as my sword came down across their shoulder. But they were faster. The Noctani had to be double my size, towering over me. He reached forward and grabbed my throat with his bare hand before I could dodge him, squeezing.

I sputtered—my air cut off. It felt as if he was crushing my windpipe.

I struggled and squirmed midair, trying to get out of his grip as he lifted me off the forest floor, my boots dangling in the air. I tried to swing my body, to gain purchase to kick at him, but to no avail. The sword in my grip was too long to use against him in this close of proximity. I let it drop from my grip, and its clang against the dirt resonated through me as if it were an earthquake. I quickly struggled to release Stormslayer from its sheath at my thigh and relaxed at the immense relief as my fingers closed around the hilt.

I pulled it free, stabbing upward.

Stormslayer pierced the flesh of his forearm straight through, protruding from the top. He released me and I fell to my knees as Stormslayer slid free, still in my grip. I was coughing, fresh blood spattering the ground before me. I couldn't catch my breath as he descended on me once more.

I clawed against the ground, dirt and blood embedding itself beneath my nails as I clawed at my own throat.

Had he seriously crushed my windpipe?

I could feel slow, labored inhales finally dragging into my lungs and relief flooded me once more.

No, he hadn't. *Thank the Mother.*

I rolled in the dirt, still out of air but needing to get away from him. He reached out faster than I could get away, grasping the back of my hair and pulling me to my feet as Stormslayer slid from my grip. I cried out as he wrenched my hair backward, exposing my throat to him.

A bloodcurdling scream tore from me as his lips lifted, his fangs only inches from my throat. As he bent his head towards me we both went stumbling to the side, his grip on my hair still tight.

Puck had found us.

The Noctani held me against him on the ground, one arm across my shoulders and the other buried in my hair.

"Another step and I kill her," he warned.

As his hand moved from my hair to my forehead, bracing. Panic leeched through me. He was going to snap my neck. Dread flooded me and I snapped my own head backwards, crashing into the Noctani with a force that made my vision go black. He let out a cry, releasing me. I rolled away, searching the forest floor for Stormslayer.

A glimmer of silver caught my eye, and I darted for it, grasping Stormslayer in my fist by the blade and cutting my hand open in the process as I turned towards the Nightshade once more. His eyes darted back and forth, unsure of whether to come after me or Puck. His moment of hesitation cost him, and Puck wasted no time burying his Katana deep in his gut. He pulled it free, and the Noctani fell to the earth.

Dead.

I braced my hand against my chest, my breathing labored.

"Are you alright?" Puck asked, wiping his Katana off on his jacket.

I nodded, taking in big, heaping gulps of air.

"Good. Get the antidote. Let's end this." He nodded at me once before turning and disappearing back into the melee. I could see him moving towards Tess to engage in the Noctani she currently battled with.

I turned back towards my pack, hoping I could quietly sneak inside it. I moved towards it quickly but silently, hoping not to draw attention to myself. My sword was long forgotten in the clamor of battle but Stormslayer was still tight in my grip, and Stormslayer was the blade I needed to administer the antidote.

My eyes never left the pack, my gaze focused on it as I moved towards it. As I neared closer, a pair of familiar boots entered the peripheral of my vision.

Nikolai stopped before me. He was equally as close to the pack as I was, and it lay mere feet away from me. I needed to dip this sword into the liquid. Coat the blade in magic.

I just needed to get my fucking bag.

"What's wrong, Firecracker?" he called over the mayhem, a sadistic smile across his lips. "Not going the way that you planned?"

My gaze darted towards the others. Kenna was on her knees, a dagger buried in her thigh as Saanvi rushed to her side. Puck and Tess fought a Nightshade that was faster than any I had ever seen before. Zion fought Isaac, and while I thought they would be equally matched, Isaac was easily overtaking him. Annelise and Amiyah fought, too. Three of the five resistance members who had joined us lay dead in the dirt beneath the glint of the moon. It appeared as if Kenna was going to join them soon if Saanvi couldn't get that blade out and heal her. And fast.

I didn't hesitate, I lunged for the pack.

I rolled in the dirt, my face and body coated in blood and dirt as I kicked up even more earth around me to distract him. Nik's eyes lit with surprise, as if he had half expected me to simply stand there and argue with him.

I grasped the pack and took off at a sprint. Nikolai was faster, he was always faster. He took off after me, close on my heels in an instant. I rushed through the trees, circling around them to put more space between us and buy me time as I pried the top of the pack open and slid my hand inside. When my hand grasped the bottle, I let the pack slip from my fingers, the antidote safely in my grip. I turned towards Nikolai, popping the top off and sliding Stormslayer inside.

He took a hesitant step back.

"What is that?"

"What's wrong, Nikolai? Are you afraid?" I asked, a teasing edge to my voice. Now that I had coated the blade in the antidote, I needed to bait him closer.

I could sense the spell down to my bones, a strong and heady pulse. It throbbed up the arm that gripped Stormslayer, syncing to the gallop of my beating heart.

Nikolai took another step back. My gaze traveled from the blade up to him.

This had to work.

It had to.

I sprinted forward headlong towards Nik, Stormslayer extended between us. I needed to bury it beneath his ribcage, lodge it in his chest. Then this would all be over. Nik deflected my first blow, smashing my arm with the blade off to the side. I held tight to Stormslayer as my arm smarted. I whirled, thrusting the blade upwards once more.

He blocked again, his mouth curving into a smile. "Having fun?"

I grunted as he kicked out hard, his boot connecting with my thigh. I buckled but managed to keep my stance, pain searing through my leg. Nik's eyes were eager as he moved forward, tackling me to the ground. The impact of his body crashing into mine was jarring, his leg wrapping around me to hold me down against the packed earth.

I tried to shrink away, but his grip on me was tight.

I was utterly exhausted. My hair was plastered to my neck with blood and sweat, my breaths coming in short, quick pants. But I raised my chin as I steeled myself, crashing my head back against his. Unlike the last Nightshade, he didn't release me, but I still saw stars behind my vision.

"Little devil—" But his words were cut off by a shriek that shook the very earth beneath us. It sent a tingle down my spine that chilled me to my core.

Nik had my forearms grasped in his hands as my gaze searched for the source as the scream continued, piercing the air with a shrill cry.

Annelise was on her knees, a Noctani holding a blade to her throat. Zion was shaking his head in disbelief, standing over a Noctani he had killed.

Puck was cradling Tess in his arms, rocking her back and forth.

Her eyes were closed, her body motionless.

No... she couldn't be. She wasn't. She had to only be injured.

And Isaac...

Isaac lay in the dirt beside them.

Puck's Katana buried deep in his chest.

26

In that moment the world as I knew it had shattered, my body going limp in Nik's grasp. I pressed my eyes shut tightly, praying that when I opened them, this would have simply been a terrible nightmare. That I would still be asleep in my bedroll beneath the night sky.

But I wasn't.

It was Annelise whose cry had broken us.

"I didn't have a choice," Puck kept saying, rocking Tess back and forth, his words on repeat. *"I didn't have a choice."*

Isaac was dead.

His heart had been run through with a blade not coated in the antidote.

I didn't have anything left within me to break. Not with Nik's life still hanging in the balance.

"There hadn't been time," Puck cried, his voice cracking as his body racked with sobs.

Even the few Noctani that remained alive were motionless. Still. As if they grieved him, too.

A flash of light blinded me and I lifted my hand to shield my eyes. It easily slid out of Nik's grip. When the blinding brightness finally dulled, my arm fell back to my side, the earth beneath Isaac glowing luminescent. The light dulled slowly until it was gone.

"What was that?" Puck asked in a cracked voice, his gaze snapping to Zion.

Zion didn't have time to respond, the Noctani had begun to move once more.

We needed to end this.

Now.

I wasn't about to lose Nikolai, too.

I drove Stormslayer up, jabbing Nikolai in the stomach. The wind left him and his grip loosened on my other arm as he fell to one knee. I crawled away, but only enough to turn around and face him.

I poised Stormslayer over his heart as the earth became still once more.

Isaac was dead.

Tess was gravely injured.

I couldn't stand one more loss.

One more disappointment.

If Alastir's spell didn't work... it would all be over. I wouldn't have the strength to go on. Whatever happened next, it would change us forever.

My gaze held Nikolai's as his mouth opened to speak.

But I didn't let him.

With tears streaming down my cheeks, I pushed forward. With one final thrust, I drove Stormslayer—coated in ancient magic—into his heart.

27

Nikolai's mouth was parted as blood poured forth, coating the corners of his chapped lips and his chin. His hand lifted, burying itself into my hair as I bent over him. I leaned closer, my ear at his mouth.

"Diana." My name was merely a whisper on his lips before he went utterly still.

His body fell fully to the forest floor. His inky black eyes were trained on the sky above him, unblinking. His arm fell from my hair to his side where it remained, unmoving.

His fingers didn't itch towards his weapon.

His chest didn't expand with troubled breaths.

Nikolai was dead.

I slid the dagger free, allowing the magic to mend what I had irreparably damaged. I dropped the blade in the dirt beside him, burying my fists in his tunic.

His skin had grown pale and chalky.

My gaze traced the lines of his face. His right brow that was slightly creased with a scar down the middle. His strong jaw, lined with stubble. The freckle on his left cheek. His parted lips, coated in blood.

A heavy moment passed, and nothing happened.

"Nikolai." My voice was a plea. A prayer.

My fisted hands shook him, his head rolling to the side.

"Nikolai, wake up."

I could sense the others at my back, watching over us. I pressed against him once more, shaking him roughly.

"I won't lose you. I won't let you die. Now wake up, you *stubborn bastard.*"

My gaze flickered momentarily to the scene behind me. Noctani and Shades alike were strewn about the forest floor.

Dead.

Tess was awake now, clutching her head in her hands. Zion stood over me with Annelise and Amiyah, their eyes expectant.

I tore the tunic at Nik's chest, the fabric easily parting beneath my dirt and blood caked fingers. I pushed it aside to see the wound over his chest, exactly as it had been mere moments ago, cut straight through one of his swirling tattoos.

It wasn't healing.

"No, no, no." I shook my head back and forth violently, a scream bubbling to my lips.

I couldn't lose them both.

I wouldn't.

"Alastir didn't make any promises." It was Zion's voice, soft in my ear as he placed a gentle hand on my shoulder.

I flinched, shrinking away from his touch. I pressed my ear to Nikolai's chest to listen for his pulse. For any sounds of breathing.

There was nothing.

"*God dammit!*" I roared, punching my closed fists against his chest. "No! I will not lose you!"

When he didn't wake, I placed my fingertips against his chest, my magic surging towards them as I let my eyes fall shut.

"Diana—" Annelise's voice held a warning note.

I shook my head back and forth, brushing them off. Blocking them out.

I almost lost Nik once before and had managed to save him. I would do it again, if need be. Even if he *did* come back as Noctani.

I didn't care.

My magic pulsed beneath my fingertips, thunder clapping loudly overhead as the sky darkened rapidly. I was pulling on too much magic, too quickly. But I didn't care.

Lightning lashed out so close the others jumped back, but I kept my focus on Nikolai. Concentrated on the sensation of my power burning beneath my fingertips where they were buried against his skin. Lightning struck again, and Zion jumped back as a bush next to him sparked with fire, cinders lodging themselves in his clothing. He patted the cinders against him until they doused, reaching his hand out to douse the brush fire with his own magic.

"Diana, rein your magic in." His voice was a command, but I barely heard him.

I lifted my gaze and his silhouette moved into my line of sight ahead of me.

"Diana—" His hand was held out towards me, as if he was going to physically stop me himself.

I bared my teeth at him, my eyes snapping to meet his wary gaze. He took a step back, his hand reaching for his chest as a soft gasp escaped his lips when he saw my eyes.

"How dare you command your queen."

The words didn't sound as if they were my own. They were glacial. Chilling.

"Your eyes—" He moved quickly, but to where I didn't see. All I knew was I couldn't see him anymore, thus I focused my magic back on Nikolai. A fresh surge of power jolted through him so sharply, his back arched off the forest floor to meet my fingers.

His eyes remained black. Open. Unmoving.

Swallowed in darkness.

"Diana, it's happening again... your eyes." It was Tess's voice in my ear now, a soft plea. "Please, Diana. If you don't stop, we will lose you, too. The magic has taken you. Your eyes... they swirl with amethyst and onyx. Please Diana, I beg of you."

I pressed my eyes closed firmly, squeezing them tight.

This had happened when my magic had taken over me, turning me into a bloodthirsty and unfeeling savage. The last time my eyes swirled with magic, I had killed my own people. The very people who had pledged their lives to me as their rightful queen.

The magic held me tightly and all consuming, it didn't want to let me go. I shoved hard against it with all my strength, but it reared against me. The only thing I could think to do was to sever myself from it temporarily. It wouldn't release me otherwise. I imagined a blade sliding between me and my power. When the power finally disconnected, I flew onto my back from the release of energy, my breaths coming in fast, labored pants.

My head sank into the forest floor as the dawn sky rose above me, Kenna circling with her raven wings overhead. A tear slipped free and trailed down the side of my face as I stared up, unblinking.

I sucked in a heavy inhale as Tess leaned over me, her face flooding my vision. Relief was plain on her face.

"Thank the Mother," she muttered, pulling me up and against her. "Diana, don't do that to me again."

She held me as tightly as the magic had only moments ago, and a sob escaped me as I buried my face in her shoulder.

He was gone.

Nikolai was truly gone.

Everything that had happened over the last few months tore out of me on a guttural scream. The last time my emotions had overtaken me, my magic had detonated. But I had severed that connection this time—there was no magic left in me.

All I felt now was a cavern where my heart should be.

I screamed until my throat was raw, my cries piercing the quiet forest air. I sobbed until there was nothing left, the tears dry and caked against my cheeks as I fell against Tess, utterly spent.

Tess held me as I cried for Nikolai. For my unbound magic. For my father Donika had murdered. For the innocents she had tortured and maimed. For the Stormshades who would never be free in Istmere because I had *failed*.

My auburn curls were stuck to my forehead, the back of my neck. I was covered in blood, dirt, and tears, limp in Tess's grasp.

I had lost *everything*.

When I had cried all that I could, when my emotional well was empty and had nothing left to give, I quieted. Tess gently stroked my hair as I fell silent. A morose stillness fell across the forest as Zion lifted me from the ground and out of Tess's arms.

He held me in his own, his apologies repeating into my ear as he stroked my back softly. I was limp in his hold, my body utterly and completely exhausted. He would need to carry me back to Prins. I wasn't sure if I could make it back on my own. Or if I would even live now that Nikolai was dead. Has his turning Noctani altered the bond somehow?

This was how it always was. First, I shattered. Then, I was numb.

"Diana... " It was Annelise's voice that broke the fragile silence, a note of hope in her tone. "Did he just... "

I peered over Zion's shoulder to see Annelise on her knees before Nik, his hand grasped firmly between hers.

His finger twitched.

"No... I had to have imagined... " my voice trailed off as I pushed away from Zion. He placed me gently down, and I joined Annelise on the forest floor. "Did you—"

She shook her head. "I did nothing. I did not heal him. I only came to say my goodbyes. His hand moved in mine."

My brow crinkled as I watched him, unblinking. I didn't want to risk missing a single movement. My eyes were open long enough that I wasn't sure if I had seen his eye twitch, or if it had been my own.

If I had simply imagined it.

"Did you see that?" It was Tess's voice behind me.

I nodded, afraid to move my gaze from his face. The forest was utterly still once more as we collectively held our breaths. The dead bodies were still strewn around us, the trees still devoid of all wildlife. There were no animals rustling in the brush. Everything became completely and utterly still.

All at once Nik's tattooed chest gulped in a breath, his chest rising off the dirt as his lungs filled with air, a gasp releasing from his blood caked mouth.

His eyes closed as his hand fisted in Annelise's.

His chest rose again with another tentative inhale.

Then another.

Great heaving breaths racked his body until he settled, his breathing evening out and becoming rhythmic once more. When he opened his eyes to gaze upon the morning sky of Akra they were impossibly, glacially, blue.

F or one impossibly long moment, I sensed the bond snapping back into place. A surge of magic sparked in my core, seeping through my veins, and my eyes pressed closed at the intensity of the power surging through me. I allowed myself one moment of shock before relief swarmed my body and I fell against him, wrapping his cold, blood caked body in my embrace. I didn't care.

Nikolai was *alive*.

And he *wasn't* Noctani.

He wrapped his arm around my waist, pulling me against him. His hand fisted in my hair as he held my face against his shoulder, soft sobs escaping me. I could sense the binding deep in my core, as if it had never left at all.

"Diana, Diana, Diana." My name was on his lips as if it were a chant. A prayer. Wonder laced his voice as if he couldn't believe it, and neither could I.

And then something in him shifted.

He pushed me away enough to gaze into my eyes—and in that moment—he finally broke.

Tear drops fell from his eyes, leaving dirt and blood stains across his cheeks. His hand held my cheek as he held my gaze with his own, the pain clear in his gaze.

"I'm sorry. I'm so sorry." His voice cracked.

"You have nothing to apologize for," I assured him, my hand clamping over his at my cheek.

"You're wrong." His eyes swam with tears, his face stricken. "You're wrong." His voice was a harsh whisper as his eyes fell to his lap, his hand falling with it.

I tried to hold his hand in mine, but he pulled away.

"Nik—" I wasn't sure what I was going to say.

That everything that had happened while he was Noctani was ok? That we could go back to the way things used to be? The binding constricted in my chest as he moved away, standing on shaky legs.

"Welcome back," Puck said, a smile lifting the corner of his mouth.

Nik's gaze met his and fresh tears sprang forth. He was likely thinking of how he had fought him. *Hurt* him. Knocked him out. He had done the same to me.

I could see the guilt swell behind his gaze as he stood and stepped backwards once. Twice. Putting distance between himself and the rest of us.

I stepped forward, wanting to close that distance, but Annelise grabbed my arm.

"Give him space. Give him time."

My gaze shot to hers, a witty quip on the tip of my tongue until her expression sank in.

She shook her head, her expression strained. "I know what it is to feel the sudden repercussions of your actions like this. How it is to betray the ones you love, even unwittingly."

I swallowed hard, my gaze flitting back to Nik.

He held his ripped tunic closed across his chest, gooseflesh breaking out across his skin. He gave me one last glance, his eyes filled with anguish, before turning away from me. As he walked away, his human footprints on the forest floor turned to those of a great wolf, and I could see his black, shaggy fur as his Nightshade form retreated into the forest.

I moved to protest, to go after him, but Annelise held me firm.

"He knows where we are. He will be back. He needs to process this on his own. We don't know what else happened while he was Noctani. We only know what he did to you. To Puck. To Tess. These wounds are likely deeper than we know."

My gaze fell to my boots as I gave a soft nod.

As much as I didn't want to let him go, despite how much it hurt to watch him walk away when I had just got him back, I understood. He was swelling with emotions, brimming with guilt, and he needed to grieve in his own way.

But I had already forgiven him. For everything.

It hadn't been *him*. Not truly.

I brushed my pants off, meeting Puck and Zion's gaze. Sympathy was clear in their eyes, and I almost couldn't take it. I wasn't the one they should be sorry for. It was Nik. I moved to my pack, stuffing the items that had spilled out of it across the forest floor during the mayhem of searching for the antidote bottle back into the rough canvas.

Isaac was still dead.

We hadn't been able to save him.

Zion held the second antidote out to me and I stuffed it inside the pack ruthlessly, an emptiness enveloping my chest. My gaze was drawn to Isaac's still form, motionless among the moss-covered forest. His eyes were closed, the reminder of his Noctani darkness hidden from my view.

"What was that?" I asked, turning to Zion at my side. "When the magic seemed to... swell around him. Into the earth. Was that his Stormshade magic?"

I had thought it was safely enclosed in Donika's serpentine staff, encapsulated for her to use at her every whim. We weren't sure what would happen to it if we had cured Isaac... or killed him.

Zion nodded, his gaze following mine. "When a Shade dies, their magic returns to the earth. To where it was first born. I wasn't sure if Isaac's would, with Donika having stolen it and him having turned into Noctani. But it appears that when a Noctani dies, so does their magic. It returns to them, then to the earth."

My gaze brightened a little. "That means Donika doesn't have storm magic anymore?"

"That's correct. At least one good thing came from this battle. We know now that killing the Noctani or curing them returns their magic to their bodies and the earth. Valuable knowledge for us to use in the fight against her."

I nodded. A small consolation.

Isaac was still gone, and we couldn't get him back, but at least Donika couldn't use his magic against me. Against us.

Isaac was as much of a father to me as he was a mentor. He was the first Stormshade I had ever met. The first Shade who had magic similar to my own and had taught me how to wield it.

I moved to his body, kneeling beside it. I reached for his hand—his skin cold within my grasp. I remembered how he had taught me more about my magic than I had ever thought possible. He had taught me how to shield, how to use my magic not only for offense but for defense. He had been by my side when my magic turned on me. He had helped me rein it in.

A single tear escaped my eye, and I wiped it away with the back of my hand.

"I will win this war for you, Isaac. I wish you could have known a realm where you didn't have to hide your storm magic." I bit back a cry as I gently placed his hand across his chest, fingers splayed out. "Thank you. For everything."

I stood, a sad smile across my lips as I gazed down at him.

"He needs a proper burial." I spoke to no one in particular, but it was Amiyah who answered.

"We will ensure it." She embraced me, her arm reaching around me to pull me against her side. When she pulled away, she held my gaze in hers. "You cannot save everyone. That is not your responsibility."

I hadn't been able to save Tyr either.

Despite her words, guilt settled forcefully in my gut.

Puck came up beside us, saying his own quiet goodbyes to Isaac. When he was finished, he stood, coming to my side and grasping my hand in his.

"I'm sorry, Diana. I didn't have a choice. He was killing Tess... strangling her. I could only save one of them. I didn't have the antidote."

I shook my head. "You don't need to explain—"

"But I do." He nodded, swallowing hard. His throat bobbed. "Isaac led the resistance in your stead. He was our best asset... and *I killed him.* Nothing I ever say or do can forgive it. I just need you to know that I'm sorry."

"Puck—" I wanted to console him. To assure him there was nothing else he could have done. But he left, joining the others to clean up.

Annelise took the longest to say goodbye. Her forehead pressed against his, her tears spilling against his cheeks. I had a hunch they were involved before, and it was clear now that there was more between them than friendship. Their relationship had been... complicated.

Amiyah, Zion, and Annelise used their magic to dig burial sites for the fallen Shades as Saanvi, Kenna, Puck and I gathered the bodies and prepared them for burial. It was the way of Shades for their bones and flesh to return to the earth where their magic was born. Not only their magic would return to the soil, but their very essence. We buried Isaac first, each of us saying a prayer to the Mother as we shoveled the dirt into the grave with our magic and our bare hands.

We buried the Noctani, too. Their magic returned to the earth when they died too, which meant they died as Shades.

They deserved properly burials, too. We were heaving the fifth body into the graves Zion, Amiyah, and Annelise had dug when Nik returned quietly, leaning against a tree in the distance and silently watching.

One of the Nightshades that had been killed in the battle was Antonia Finch. I hadn't even realized she had been here, hadn't recognized her when the Nightshades had come to reinforce Nik. We buried her last, her body returning to the earth beneath a tall evergreen tree, its long green branches reaching down towards her.

I wished I could have saved her.

I wish I could have saved them all.

When we had finished burying them and giving them their last rites, we adorned their graves with wildflowers we had found growing in the adjacent field. Isaac's final resting place was marked with a large granite boulder that we used magic to roll into place.

It was odd using my magic easily after so much time had passed. It was second nature, as if it had always been this way. This effortless. No thunder clapped overhead. No storm raged, threatening to steal my magic and turn me into a bloodthirsty monster. The magic sensation warmed in my core, filling me with a pleasant heat.

I had been able to sense the moment Nikolai had returned, and he bore his human form this time. His gaze focused on me as we worked, but he said nothing. He needed time... and I would give it to him. It had been weeks since he was turned—and Annelise was right—we had no idea what had transpired during that time.

What Donika might have made him do. Despite everything, even when he was Noctani, there was a piece of him that was *Nik*.

I gathered my pack, a silent question in my eyes as I turned towards Zion and Annelise.

"We should return to Amiyah's," Zion said as she joined us.

She nodded. "I think that's the best idea. We should return to the grimoire and regroup. Decide our next steps. We can return to Siraleth and reinforce the wards with their binding now intact. It should be safe there again."

Her head nodded towards Zion. "I guess you are the leader of the resistance now."

A sad smile lifted the corner of his mouth. "I guess I am. I never imagined leading a movement against my own daughter, but there's nothing else to be done about it. Istmere needs to be returned to its rightful queen, and the violence needs to end. It's time for a change."

I couldn't imagine how difficult this might be for him. How he had to put our family aside and work towards the greater good for the people of Istmere. It was as if he could read the thoughts on my face, his gaze burning into mine.

"It's what rulers do. Sacrifice. Make difficult decisions that benefit the greater good."

A humorless laugh escaped me. Donika had certainly not gotten that memo. She had let her thirst for revenge, her hatred for those stronger than her, to grow and fester. To destroy her... turning her into the worst thing for the realm.

As a group, we headed towards the Prins border and Nikolai moved into step beside us soundlessly.

"How long until we get there?" he asked, his voice strained.

I could see in his expression he was still being swallowed by his own thoughts. He was distracted, his shoulders as heavy as his conscience.

"Two days' time," I answered.

We said nothing more, traveling side by side in silence. This certainly hadn't gone to plan, and we could feel the loss with every step we took back towards the seaside cabin. We had saved Nik, but lost Isaac and many Shades of the resistance in the process.

Nik's steady presence was a balm at my side, but despite him being so close to me physically... he was distant.

I couldn't help but think that things had irrevocably changed between us.

And that thought terrified me to my core.

29

We were weary from the battle—our bodies tired and sore. It took us almost three days' time to make it back to the seaside cabin that was Amiyah's family home. It wasn't until the sound of crashing waves met my ears that I let my body relax once more. I hadn't realized how tense I had been on the journey back, as if my body were a taut bow string. I cracked my neck, stretching the tension out of my limbs.

I was happy to have the grimoire safely back in my possession, the cabin remaining unchanged since we left. It was handy to have a safe house this far from the cities of Istmere, in the far reaches of the mountains and shore.

Nobody would ever find us here.

We discussed how long to stay, but Zion and Annelise were anxious to get back to Siraleth and re-ward the cottage. To return to the library that held the most useful information for us. We would need to hone our battle strategies, call on the remainder of the resistance to join us, then march against Donika in the coming weeks.

The time for battle had come.

But as we made preparations, I needed to study the Kotova grimoire. To memorize as many spells as I could to use against Donika when I faced her. We knew more about the Noctani now, and we would know even more once Nikolai was ready to talk.

When we had returned to Amiyah's, Nikolai had retreated even more. He spent his days by the shore, his feet buried in the sand. He wasn't ready to talk yet, and I wasn't sure if he was going to be ready any time soon. He was more withdrawn and distant than I ever expected, but Zion and Annelise were firm with me that I needed to give him time. Instead, I should focus my energy on battle strategies. We would need to be sharp heading into the final battle, and should her army get the better of us... we needed to be ready.

I needed to train my magic now that it was bound once more, but I had no other Stormshade to train with other than my mother, now that Isaac was gone. Zion noted a few that he knew of in the resistance, but I didn't know them personally. They were perfect strangers.

I knew I could trust them, but training with them simply didn't feel right. Tess and Puck had offered to train with me, though their knowledge of my magic was limited. In the end, I knew I would have to rely on Annelise. She was a practiced Stormshade, her magic having been bound since long before I was even born. She and Zion had bound themselves to each other early on, Annelise never having to fear the repercussions of her unruly and unpredictable magic.

She was a formidable Stormshade in her own right, and I knew I could trust her to take over Isaac's training. Our relationship was still strained, but I hoped this would bring us closer together. Give us more time to bond.

When we decided to leave for the cottage underground the following morning, Annelise said there was one thing left to do before she joined us. When we set out towards Siraleth, she left us in Prins, on the north side of The Shadow. She promised she wouldn't be more than a half a day's time ahead of us, and that she would help us secure the wards when she returned if need be.

I was confident we could manage the spell without her. Amiyah had decided to join us, leaving behind her peaceful cabin for the first time in centuries and vowing not to return until we had put an end to this conflict.

By the time we had passed the two pillars reaching up into the sky signaling our entrance into Siraleth, the fact that Nikolai and I hadn't had a true conversation was threatening to drive me out of my mind. Tess could sense my frustration, and along with Saanvi and Kenna, they did their best to distract me on the journey back. The grimoire was safely tucked in my pack, and I could sense its gentle hum as we neared the cottage underground. Despite this being the site of our last battle against Donika and her men, this appeared to be where the grimoire was most at home.

Even if Donika knew we were here, we weren't fools enough to fall into another of her traps this time. When we finally made it to the cottage, we paused outside, leaving our packs by the door and standing in the center of the cobbled road. We joined hands, magic pulsing between the eight of us, easily reinforcing the wards so that neither Donika nor any of her men would be granted entrance. When we did march to battle, we would meet the resistance on the plains of Siraleth, not here at the cottage.

This safe house was only for us.

It had begun to feel as if a home before Donika had used Warrick to lure us out. I hoped it would feel that way once more when we were settled. I took the same bedroom I had last time, right across from Nik. We had taken to sharing a room before he had been turned, but when we had completed the ward spell and returned downstairs, he slipped behind the heavy wooden door of his own bedroom. Disappearing without a word.

My heart dropped, fear settling deep in my gut. I wasn't sure he was ready for what was going to come next. He was strong, but turning into Noctani had left him broken. He reminded me of how I had been when I had finally escaped the Stormvault, except the anger hadn't hit him yet. It was all despair... threatening to drown him.

I left him alone as the others had suggested and returned to the library, needing to brush up on the war council and Kotova spells. I was determined for the grimoire to become a part of me in these next few weeks leading up to our stand against The Stone City. I wanted its spells to live within me, always at the tips of my fingers. They were some of the most powerful spells in the realm, and it had been my family that had created them. Passed them down from generation to generation.

I wondered how many of them my mother had used before as I ran my hand across the tattered pages of the grimoire in the library, the afternoon sun peering in from the windows located high above. The shelves alongside me were brimming with brown, worn books. The heavy wooden door of the library opening startled me and I jumped, casting a gaze over my shoulder to determine it was only Tess.

I had been a little on edge since getting back.

She moved to the center table to join me, pushing the books out of the way so she could perch on the end of the table.

"Haven't seen you since we returned to Siraleth. I wanted to check in on how you're doing." Her smile flashed her pearly white teeth.

"It should be *me* checking in on *you*," I reminded her, closing the grimoire with a thud. "I wasn't the one that was almost strangled to death by a Noctani in battle."

Tess waved her hand in the air as if it were nothing.

I bit my lip, my gaze focused on the closed grimoire before meeting her gaze once more. "I don't know what I would have done if I lost you."

She took my hand from the table, clasping it in hers. "You didn't lose me."

I shook my head. "But I almost did. If it weren't for Puck... "

"Diana... " her tone was uncharacteristically stern. Tess was always light, even when the situation didn't call for it. "Please tell me you aren't blaming yourself for what happened in the clearing."

I wished I could tell her that. Everything falling apart... everything that had happened... I couldn't help but think things would have been different if it weren't for my actions. I was so hell bent on saving Nikolai that we lost Isaac and many other Shades from the resistance in the process. We almost lost Tess, too.

I opened my mouth to speak but Tess cut me off. "This isn't your fault, you can't think that for a single second. I can hold my own, you don't need to be watching my back all the time. You were focused on the mission, as you should be."

My gaze fell from hers. "But what if Annelise was right? What if I was willing to sacrifice too much to save Nikolai? What if it wasn't even what he wanted? Everything is all fucked up."

My breath blew out on a heavy sigh. I tilted my head back towards the library ceiling, my eyes tracing the architecture within the wood as I bit back tears that stung the back of my eyes.

"You can't think like that." Tess shook her head at me, but I could only see her out of my periphery. "None of this is your fault. Of course we were going to do whatever it takes to save Nikolai. Not just for you, but for all of us."

I pushed back in my chair, glancing at her once more. Her amber eyes held immense sympathy within their depths. So much compassion. I hit the lottery when I met Tess, and I couldn't help but think I didn't deserve her sometimes. She was the best friend anyone could ask for.

I stood, grasping her shoulder and embracing her. She let out a deep sigh against my shoulder. "I know it isn't my fault, but that irrational part of me simply won't be quiet."

She pushed me away, a twinkle of mischief in her eyes. "Sounds like you need something to get your mind off it. Sounds like you need an *adventure*."

I breathless laugh escaped me. "I'm not sure I could handle any more adventures at the moment. I've got my hands full... I think I've had enough excitement for this month. Or for a lifetime, really."

I collapsed back into the chair.

"Well once you're up to it, I say we explore Siraleth a little. There's so much here we haven't seen. This was the capitol city once, before the war. I'm sure there's lots to find. I'm dying to see the old ports."

A soft smile graced my lips. "I would like that very much. Once things are a little quieter."

"I'm not sure they will be until we kill this bitch," she replied, tossing her chocolaty straight hair over her shoulder.

Her deadpan delivery made me laugh. "When we do, I am going to sleep for three whole days, I can promise you that much," I replied, picking up the pencil and tapping it against the grimoire.

"Have you spoken to Nikolai?" she asked, her brow raised.

I inclined my head towards her as I laughed. "I knew you just couldn't wait to ask me that. Always wanting to talk boys."

"You know me." She smiled down at me, wiggling her eyebrows.

"How about we talk about *your* love life instead," I offered.

She shook her head. "Nothing to tell, everything is status quo."

I peered at her with a skeptical gaze, one eye squinting. "Tess Fowler, tied down. I never thought I'd see the day."

Tess laughed. "Me neither, to be honest. Puck isn't like other men. He's... kind. Strong. Gentle. Not to mention hilarious when he wants to be. But the dad jokes have *got* to stop."

Those same words could have been used to describe Nikolai, and a knot in my chest formed at the thought. He was so distant—I wasn't sure I even knew who he was at all anymore. Tess could sense the shift in my mood and she hooked her foot under my chair, dragging me back towards the table.

"Talk to me. What's going on?"

My jaw tightened as I thought about everything that had transpired since curing Nik in the Akra forest. It was like we were perfect strangers now. Tess could read the thoughts behind my troubled gaze.

"He will come back to you." She rested her hand on my shoulder, giving it a gentle squeeze.

"I'm not so sure," I told her, glancing up at her with a shake of my head. "He feels so far away. He wants space, time to deal with this on his own. But it feels as if he's already been gone for so long. I want to be able to fix things."

"But you can't," she reminded me. "You can't fix everything. You need to give him space to come to you, to take his time."

"And if he never does?" I asked, my brow raised. "All the others care about is that the binding is back in place. I can't even begin to tell you how immensely lonely it feels to be tied to someone—eternally bound—but they won't even speak to you. Won't even look at you."

"I'm so sorry, Diana." Her words were a caress across my skin, filled with the sorrow I felt. Tess was always good at comforting me. "He will come back to you. I promise you that."

I could almost hear the words she wasn't saying. "But not before we move against Donika?"

"I really don't know." She bit her lip, her gaze falling to her lap. "Zion and Annelise want to move in only one week's time. Take advantage of the element of surprise. Before she realizes her band of Noctani aren't coming back and the numbers of her soulless monsters have been cleaved in two."

"And it's a good plan." I nodded to myself. "But I fear that we aren't working as a team. That it will be our downfall if we can't work together when we wage war. I'm... scared."

"I am too." Her voice was soft now. "But we have your back. We have the numbers. We have your storm magic."

"So everyone keeps reminding me." I grumbled. "I sometimes feel as if I am a pawn, only needed for my magic and the prophecy that foretold it would be a new generation of Stormshade Kotova blood that would save the realm from darkness."

"That isn't true," Tess assured me. "We care about you. The council cares about you."

"I know," I replied, mouth thinning. "It's just complicated."

"What isn't?" Tess laughed.

I wasn't sure how long we had spent in the library but the sun in the arched windows had faded, night descending upon Siraleth and cloaking it in darkness. I grabbed the grimoire and held it against my chest.

"I'd better get some sleep. I have my first training session with Annelise tomorrow."

Tess raised her brow at me. "You'll have to tell me how that goes. I'd imagine you can't wait to go head-to-head with her."

"That's what I'm nervous about." My teeth worried my lower lip.

"But you won't lose control this time. You're bound," she reminded me.

"I'm not sure that's the problem when it comes to Annelise. I'm still angry with her for everything. I'm not sure anything but time will cure that." I stood, pushing my chair back into the table and heading for the library door, Tess following behind.

"Time heals all wounds."

"All?" I replied, skepticism in my tone.

Tess shook her head. "Yeah... maybe you're right." She laughed. "Time can't heal *all* wounds, but it *will* heal this one."

As we pushed out of the library and towards our bedrooms, I couldn't help but glare at Nikolai's door, hoping it would open. I said goodnight to Tess and turned my back on his door, everything within me urging me to walk across the hall and knock. He had asked for space, and I would give it to him, but that didn't mean it wasn't difficult to stay away.

I returned to my room, stowing the grimoire in the dresser and taking a long soak in the claw-foot bathtub among the lavender salts that were always stocked here. I had missed this place. I was happy to know it still felt like home to me, even after everything that had transpired over the last few weeks.

By the time I climbed into the satin sheets I was freshly scrubbed clean, my skin smelling of sage and lavender, my auburn curls wet against the pillow. I snuggled deeper under the covers and tried to sleep, but all I could think about was that the right side of the bed shouldn't be cold.

Shouldn't be empty.

That Nikolai should be here, with me.

When sleep finally took me, it wasn't to dreams of the future—dreams of a better Istmere.

It was to nightmares.

30

*T*he sensation of dream walking overtook me as I fell under, deeper and deeper. I hadn't felt this sucked into a dream in a long, long time. We weren't in the throne room, where my dream walking usually took me. We were in Donika's personal bedchamber. Donika stood at the vanity, a black sheer robe tied around her waist, her blue and white ombre hair falling in curated ringlets down her back.

She inspected herself in the mirror, pulling against the frown lines on her forehead, the textured skin at her cheek.

"I'll need more elixir soon," she said, casting her gaze to the wrought iron bed beneath the crescent window.

"Of course, My Queen," a voice purred.

I turned my gaze expecting Corian, but it was Zachariah Dragovya. Nik's father.

He lay across the sheets, shirtless, his skin spells on full display. He had other tattoos dancing across his chest, too. Just like his *son. He was barefoot, his arms folded behind his head, a deep grin playing on his lips.*

"I do believe the stress of losing my precious Noctani aged me ten years," she replied, leaving the vanity to join Zachariah on the bed.

She curled against him, her hand on his chest as she gazed up at him.

Oh... Mother above.

That was... that was twisted. I know Nik had said she was working with him, but I hadn't realized she was with him. After she had been with his son? She was much older than Nik, but I hadn't imagined anything going on between her and Nik's much older father when Zachariah had appeared at her side in Siraleth.

That answered the question of whether she knew of the fate of her Noctani, though. We had painstakingly taken the time to bury all the bodies—Noctani included—but somehow she knew.

"My Queen, you haven't aged a day."

Her dark gaze traveled down the muscles of his abdomen and I tried to push out of the dream, fearful that I might be forced to witness something I most certainly didn't want to.

"I wonder when Nikolai will be back," she mused, her voice taunting.

"You don't think he was killed with the others?" Zachariah asked, his brow raised as he gazed down at her.

Donika laughed, and the sound sent a shiver down to my toes. "You underestimate your son, Zachariah. Not only would they not have had the heart to kill him, but he would never let them. He is faster and stronger than even their best soldier."

"Then he will be back," Zachariah mused, nodding.

So... they didn't know Nikolai's location, and they didn't know about the antidote, either. That was good. Very good. We could use that to our advantage, especially with one antidote left to spare. It will come as a shock to Donika when we march against her, a perfectly mortal Nikolai at my side.

If he was up to it.

She couldn't know the damage turning him Noctani had caused him, not that she would care. They didn't call her the Black Heart for nothing.

"I must say, Isaac's passing threw a wrench into my plans," *Donika admitted, tracing her long, delicate finger against him.*

I wasn't fooled by her appearance, there was nothing delicate about her.

"You'll have the little Stormshade bitch's magic soon enough, you won't need his," he assured her.

"No... " her voice was cutting. "I won't need his, but I wanted it."

Zachariah laughed, his pearly teeth on full display. "My Queen, you will have so much magic you won't know what to do with it."

Her sinister lips lifted into a malicious smile. "I'll know exactly what to do with it."

Donika hadn't known we killed her contingent of Noctani until Isaac's magic had left her, another win for us. Another thing she hadn't planned. We might not have the upper hand in this, but she wasn't predicting our movements, and I was relieved at that.

"How many Noctani does that leave us with?" he asked, stroking his hand against her vibrant hair.

Donika thought for a moment, her gaze on the ceiling. "About forty, give or take." Her laugh made my stomach fall, a stone in my gut. "Luckily, the Araneoch are much easier to make."

No.

Oh no.

We had no idea how many of those she had created, and with their size and poisonous pincers they were equally dangerous. They couldn't steal our magic, but they could kill us all the same. I had never seen where she was creating the monsters, where she was keeping them. My dreams never showed them to me. How many were there, if they were so easy to make? Tens? Hundreds?

I needed to find out before we marched on The Stone City. I needed to figure out how to leave a token and dream walk wherever I wanted, as Corian had. I needed to find out what we were up against so that we weren't going in blind.

I tried to pull out of the dream once more, but it held me firmly. It was as if I were underwater, their voices becoming harder and harder to hear. I knew I was waking up, but it was taking longer than I would have liked.

"No one is as smart as you, my darling," Zachariah rumbled against her cheek, grasping her face in his palm and capturing her mouth with his.

It was time to go.

Wake up, wake up, wake up.

WAKE UP!

He pushed the sheer robe back from her shoulder, revealing a patch of bare, tanned skin. His mouth explored her decolletage, her neck, finding her mouth once more.

WAKE UP!

I shot up in bed with a start, sweat coating my back, my nightgown stuck to me in every place it touched my skin. I placed a hand over my chest, slowing my breathing.

The Araneoch.

They could turn the tides of the battle, and I needed to find out where they were. Needed to find out how many of them she had created. I needed to do more research on dream walking, and I needed to do it *now*.

I stood from the bed, wrapping a black robe around me. Despite the sweat coating my skin, a chill had settled in my bones. I slid a pair of slippers over my bare feet, treading out into the hallway. The torches were doused, the darkness clinging to the hallway in a menacing way.

It had to be the middle of the night.

I traced along the stone walls until I reached the library door, pulling it open and descending into the shadows. I found the table I had been working at yesterday by almost crashing into it, stubbing my toe in the process. I swore, rubbing at it until the sting dulled. I grabbed around blindly for the lantern on the tabletop and when I finally found it I struck the match, filling the space with warm light. I sat, wrapping the robe tighter around me as I pulled the dream walking books towards the front of the table.

I opened the first one, combing through the text to find anything I could about intentionally dream walking. If I could figure out how to leave a token behind, I could dream walk anywhere I wanted in The Stone Palace. I could find out where Donika was creating and hiding her Araneoch.

Annelise would be back to the cottage underground tomorrow and we were set to train. I knew I should head back to bed and get some rest, but my dream walking had unsettled me too much. We were running out of time, and we needed all the advantage we could leverage. We needed the upper hand. I was too anxious to sleep.

My eyes were bleary with exhaustion by the time I made it to the second book. The words were smudging together on the page as I peered down in the dim lamplight. The library door squeaked open, and I jumped, the book before me knocking the lantern over. I stood quickly, grabbing it and righting it before the light was doused.

I turned to see Nikolai standing in the doorway, his blond hair disheveled, his white T-shirt crinkled from sleep.

His gaze held mine for a long moment before he spoke. "I'm sorry, I didn't mean to startle you." He swallowed hard in the flickering lantern light, stuffing his hands into the pockets of his linen pants awkwardly. "It's just— I thought I heard something... then I saw the light on."

I nodded, falling back into the chair and sliding the lantern away from the edge of the table. "I couldn't sleep."

He moved forward, his gaze on my profile as I remained turned towards the table. We hadn't been alone together since I had administered the antidote, and I wasn't sure what to say. How to act. He had been pushing me away so thoroughly I was surprised he wouldn't have simply turned back around and gone back to bed when he saw it was me poring over the books in the library.

All the words I wanted to say to him were stuck in the back of my throat in a lump, allowing nothing to pass my lips.

"Bad dreams?" he asked as he squatted next to the table, his hands resting on its edge.

He was close enough to me that when I turned towards him, I could see the reflection of his glacial blue eyes in the warm light, flecks of gold spattered around the iris. His eyes were heavy with lack of sleep, his brow creased.

"Something like that." My eyes fell back to the table.

"You can tell me, Diana." His voice sounded fragile. Brittle.

"Can I?" My gaze swung to his once more, eyes narrowing. "You have been avoiding me like the plague, and for the life of me I can't figure out what I've done wrong."

He shook his head, one hand moving from the edge of the table to grasp mine from my lap. He squeezed, his palm warm against mine.

"You did nothing wrong." His voice was raw this time—strangled.

I shook my head. "Then why?"

"This has nothing to do with you and everything to do with me." His gaze fell to our combined hands in my lap. "You can't imagine the guilt I feel. Every moment of every day it threatens to swallow me whole."

He was punishing himself.

"Then tell me," I pleaded, inching towards him. "Tell me what happened. I can't help you if you don't let me. It eats me up inside to see you like this, Nikolai. So... fractured."

He let out a long exhale, biting his cracked lip between his teeth. "The things I did while I was Noctani... "

I scooted to the edge of the chair—my thighs spread so that he was squatting next to the table between them. His other hand moved from the table to rest on my thigh as he remained perched there. This was the first time he had touched me since we had been back, and the sensation of his skin against mine sent an electric shock running up my spine.

I had experienced that electric shock the first time we had ever touched back in the classroom in Silver Oaks. I had never had that happen while he was Noctani. Even after all this time, after everything, he still had butterflies swirling in my stomach.

I reached out with the hand not clasped in his, turning his chin up towards me. "There is nothing you can tell me that I would judge you for. *You were not yourself.*"

"But a part of me *was...* " His words trailed off. "There was a part of me that was still... me. I think it was because we were bound... before I was turned. It allowed me to have more autonomy than the other Noctani. If that weren't the case... I never would have let you go. Never would have let you keep your magic."

I shook my head. "You can't overanalyze your actions. You were *Noctani* for Mother's sake, bond or no bond. Dark magic was pumping through your veins, and there is nothing you could have done that would have changed that."

He tried to avert his gaze, but I held his chin firm.

"I still love you, Nikolai."

It was those words that broke him. He fell back, his legs giving way beneath him. A sob tore through him as he buried his face in his T-shirt, salty tears trickling down his cheeks as he tried to hide them from me. I crawled onto the floor with him, pulling him against me as the sobs racked through him, his body shuttering.

"I love you," I whispered, my hand rubbing circles across his muscular back.

He held my arm tightly against his chest as he pulled away enough for his gaze to meet mine.

"Diana—the things I did to you... I can never forgive myself." His breath caught in his throat as the words almost choked him. "Never—"

I pulled him against my chest once more. "You have nothing to forgive yourself for where I am concerned, Nikolai. I do not blame you for the things that happened in that house, or what came before."

His head still pressed against my chest, he shook it back and forth furiously.

"I hurt you. Suffocated you. Bit you. Drank from you. Took from you. *Diana, I touched you*—" His words cut off as his breath caught in his chest once more and he sputtered.

My voice was strangled as I spoke. "You didn't hurt me, Nikolai. Not truly. I am here, I am ok. You let me go." I squeezed him tightly against myself. "*You let me go.*"

"But the others... " His voice trailed off as he released a choked sob. "You don't even know the half of it. You only saw what I did while I had you in that house. Only saw me kill Giselle and Baker. There were so many others... so many lives I took and innocents I tortured. I'm a murderer, Diana. The fact that I still had a sliver of my humanity due to our bond only makes it worse. That there was a piece of me that might have been able to fight the compulsion, that I should have been stronger. That I was only able to fight against it when it came to you... "

His tears soaked through the robe I wore as I held him against me and let him cry. I had never seen him fracture. Never seen him shatter. It broke my heart to see the guilt eating him alive. A piece of me had known he would feel this way once he was cured. That he would have a hard time coming to terms with what he had done while he was Noctani. But I hadn't expected this.

When he pulled away and his eyes met mine once more, they gleamed with tears, bloodshot and exhausted. "Will you ever forgive me?"

My answer was immediate. "There is nothing to forgive. *Nothing.* Do you hear me? You only need to forgive yourself."

He scoffed at this, as if it weren't that simple. I clasped the back of his neck as I brought my lips to his cheek, placing a gentle kiss against his tear-soaked skin. It felt so good to have him back in my arms again, even if he was breaking apart as I tried to hold him together. Even if it would take more time to break down the walls that had been built up between us.

"We will not let Donika win. You are here, with me. You are safe. And I love you. She cannot take that from us. She *won't.*"

He buried his face in my neck as the tears subsided, his hand firm against my back, holding me against him. When his lips found my neck, the tears he had shed against my skin mixed with his kiss. He let out a shuddering exhale as he pulled away to meet my gaze.

A smile lifted the corner of his mouth despite the tears that had yet to dry tracking across his cheeks. "Leave it to you to pull me out of my own darkness. Always so strong. Always so brave. I wish I were even a fraction as courageous as you are."

He leaned towards me and I could taste his breath on my lips, cinnamon and coffee and spice. He was everywhere all at once, and I drank him in.

"I love you, Diana. You are strong when I can't be." His words were throaty, ragged.

"And you are my strength, too. When I left the Stormvault... " I shook my head. "I never could have healed without you. We are better together, Nikolai. Never forget that. Everything that happened before, it wasn't your fault. You can't blame yourself... not ever. Not for one second. You are the strongest man I know, and the only person to defeat black magic pumping through your veins. If that isn't strong... I don't know what is."

His gaze held mine, burning with reverence first... then hunger.

"I don't deserve you." His words were hoarse. Haunted.

It was my turn to scoff this time. "You do deserve me. You deserve *everything*."

Nik buried his hand in my hair as he pulled me against him, closing the distance between us. When his lips met mine, they tasted like redemption.

Salvation.

Deliverance.

I let him pull me against him, our chests pressed together hard enough that my breasts were trapped and aching between our chests with every heaving breath. We had kissed when he was Noctani, but it was nothing like this. *Nothing.*

My soul was on *fire.*

There was nothing I could compare to the sensation soaring through me as his lips devoured me. Worshipped me. I crawled into his lap, curling my legs around his back and hugging him close to me as he peeled the tear-stained robe from my body.

He held me against him forcefully. As if he thought I was going to disappear at any moment. As if this were only a dream.

And there—on the library floor in the middle of the night—he forgave himself for *everything* as he let me love him again. Let me kiss him until his lips were chapped and raw. Let me peel his shirt from his sun-tanned chest, exposing the tattoos I loved. Let me explore his skin with my fingers and my mouth as if it were the first time I had ever touched him like this.

And when I could feel him hard against me, he stood and took me into his arms once more, leading me towards his bedroom. I knew that when we came together, we would be whole once more. That whatever wall had been standing between us would be destroyed, and we could stand together as one.

And I needed that more than anything.

Needed *him* more than anything.

I couldn't go to war until I had him by my side. I needed him more than he could ever know. With him by my side, I knew we could achieve anything.

I wasn't whole without him, and as he touched me over and over again, I thanked the Mother for bringing him back to me. He didn't stop touching me that night until I vowed the only one I would ever pray to again was *him*.

31

When I woke, the sun was streaming through the open window, warming the skin of my face. I was naked—the sheets tangled around me—an arm stretched over my stomach. I turned to see Nikolai still fast asleep, his eyes closed, his face peaceful. The lines that had creased his forehead the night before were gone, as if last night had rejuvenated him.

Replenished him.

My hand found his golden hair, and I ran it through my fingers. The strands were the finest silk against my skin, and I thanked the Mother once more for letting me have this moment. I had thanked the Mother *a lot* last night, until I had begun thanking only Nikolai.

As if sensing my thoughts, Nik peeled his eyes open, a soft smile across his lips.

He made a humming sound, his head against my chest. "Good morning."

His voice was raspy from sleep, and the sound sent a shock of warmth pooling through me. My lips curved into a smile as I gazed down at him. "Good morning."

He propped himself up on his elbows, hovering over me, hunger igniting in his gaze once more. He brought his lips to mine, and I opened for him, allowing his tongue to caress me. He had been so, so broken last night, and there was still a glint in his eye that told me he hadn't forgiven himself fully, but that he was on his way towards it. I assured him over and over that I wasn't haunted by those memories, that whatever had transpired before this didn't matter because I was here, and I was safe. That whoever he had killed while he was Noctani had been under Donika's orders, and he couldn't blame himself.

"I have to train with Annelise today," I spoke, breaking the kiss with a heavy sigh.

We hadn't gotten much sleep last night, and it had left me ragged and exhausted. My body was sore in delicious places as I imagined his was, too. When he sat up, I could see the marks I had scratched down his back as I held him against me under the moonlight.

Last night had been nothing like the last time we had sex. It wasn't hard or rough, though I wouldn't mind that again in the future. He had worshipped me. Loved every inch of me. It had been slow and sensual. Passionate.

When he stood from the bed to move towards the washroom, the sight of his bare backside had me wanting *more*.

"Though I'm not sure when she's due back. Perhaps it can wait—" My words trailed off as he turned around, his hard length already at attention.

I raised an eyebrow at him as I sat up on the bed, the sheets pooling around my hips.

"Diana, I am always hard for you. *Always*."

"In that case..." my words trailed off as I crawled off the bed towards him, pulling his bare skin against me.

I captured his mouth with mine, kissing him slowly. I pressed myself against him, my peaked breasts against his chest, my wetness rubbing against his thigh. He let out a low groan as he buried his hand in my hair, holding me against him. I pulled back to gaze into his eyes, and when I saw the expression of adoration there, I fell to my knees before him.

Both of his eyebrows raised high as he gazed down at me.

It was my turn to worship him.

"Diana, you don't have to—" But his words were cut off when I grasped his length in my palm, the touch causing him to twitch.

His lips parted as he watched me. "The queen of Istmere, on her knees before me." There was a wicked note in his voice, one I had missed so, so much.

"Only for you," I whispered before taking him into my mouth.

My gaze held his as I tasted him, running my tongue over the wet bead already forming at the tip. His hand fisted in my hair as I stroked him with one hand, tasting him at the same time. He was so hard in my grasp, the sensation of him throbbing against me had wetness pooling between my thighs.

My other hand ran up my thigh towards that heat, and a moan escaped his lips as he watched me touch myself as I pleasured him. The thought sent a shock of desire through me, and his eyes fixed on me had me close to the edge in mere moments. I loved the way he watched me. I moaned, the sound vibrating through his length as I ran my mouth over him, my lips full as they held him.

"Diana—" my name was a prayer on his lips as his head fell back, his teeth capturing his lip as he bit down.

I ran my tongue up the underside of his cock, the thick vein that ran along him throbbing beneath my touch. I worked faster, sucking all the way down to the base of him and letting him fall out of my mouth, a bead of saliva trailing from my lips.

"Holy fuck—" He could barely speak, his words a gruff whisper.

"Praying to the Mother for release?" I asked, my brow raised as I pumped his length with my hand.

His voice was dangerous when he responded. "Diana, you're the only one I pray to now. The only one I worship. The only one I will call out to when *I* am on *my* knees."

His words made me cry out, my own fingers pumping in and out of me and the sound of his voice bringing me close. He tried to pull me up, to throw me down on the bed, but I shook my head, remaining on my knees. My fingers slipped out, wetness coating them as I used that hand to stroke him.

"I want to taste you."

A garbled sound left the back of his throat as my mouth found him once more, sucking him until his thighs were shaking. His grip in my hair was tight enough that I couldn't move my head even if I wanted to... but I didn't.

I wanted him. *All* of him.

When he fell over the edge, my mouth filled with the taste of him, swallowing each and every drop as I held his gaze with my own. When he was finished, I licked him clean, licking every ounce of wetness off my fingers with a wicked smile across my lips.

"My turn," he growled, grabbing me off the floor in one swift movement and throwing me down onto the bed.

He gripped my thighs and pulled me to the edge of the mattress before placing a hand on the inside of my thigh, spreading them before him. He fell to his knees before me as my own knees fell to the side of the bed, opening for him.

"My turn to taste you." His voice was raw with want.

It was my turn to fist his hair in my grip as his lips teased my inner thigh, leaving a trail of kisses along my hot, fevered skin.

I watched as his gaze met mine, a devilish smile across his lips, before he finally kissed where I wanted it most. His mouth met my wetness, slipping his tongue inside and sending a shock of pleasure through me. My head fell back against the bed as I cried out. I squirmed beneath him, but his hand found my stomach, pinning me down to the bed. He lapped against me. The sensation of his tongue against my flesh solidified that I would only worship *him* now, too. His name was a cry on my lips as his mouth found my most sensitive bundle of nerves, flicking it and then sucking, taking it into his mouth.

"Nik—" the feeling was almost too much, too sharp. I wasn't sure I could take it.

He laughed against me, his hot breath against my core as he continued, his fingers sliding into me.

"So wet. So perfect." His voice hummed against me as he worked, his gaze focused on me as he teased cry after cry out of me.

My back arched off the bed, but he held me firmly, his hand still splayed against my stomach.

"I can't—" I protested, biting my own lip.

"Oh, but you can, Diana." His gaze burned with want as he watched me writhe under his touch. His voice was wicked against my flesh. I had missed him so, so much.

I couldn't even count on one hand how many times I had thought of that voice. That mouth. My own hand slipping between my thighs at night while he had been gone.

I craved his touch. When he sucked my nub into his mouth once more, his fingers pumping in and out of me at a relentless pace, curling to hit that spot he knew I loved so much, it was his name on my lips as I came apart. I shattered into a million pieces beneath him.

I fell against the bed as he stood, licking the taste of me off his fingers as his gaze held mine.

I fucking loved him.

As he stood before me in all his glory, my legs still parted for him, all I could think about was how damn lucky I was. That he was *mine*, and nobody else would ever touch him. Ever love him. That every ridge of his abdomen belonged to me. I would be the only one to taste the muscles that led down to his beautiful, perfect cock. That his lips were *mine*, and I would be the only one he would ever taste on that wicked mouth ever again.

And when we came together again, we worshipped each other as if he had the same exact thought.

That I was his and his alone.

By the time we had made it out of bed, half of the day had already passed. I was sure Annelise was somewhere in the cottage waiting for me, despite not having set a time for our training session. Nik and I reluctantly dressed and made our way towards the library, where we found Tess and Puck.

"Any sign of Annelise yet?" I asked as I pushed the library door open, Nik following me inside.

Tess had all the lanterns lit already, one on each of the tables. The sun had begun to set, and I realized how much time we had wasted away between the sheets. I hoped for many, many more days spent like this. But for now... there was work to do.

Tess cast a glance over her shoulder. "No, not yet."

She did a double take when she saw that Nik and I were together, raising an eyebrow at me as I pulled the chair out across from her.

"I told you," she mouthed silently.

I kicked her under the table, a grin spreading across my lips.

The exchange gave me a sense of déjà vu from when she had first accused me of liking him. As always, Tess was right. Nik had simply needed time, and he had come to me when he was ready.

"I'm supposed to train with her today," I said as Nik settled into the chair beside me.

Puck exchanged an equally subtle grin with Nik and I pretended not to see.

"Seeing as the sun is almost setting, I would say that ship has sailed," Tess replied, her gaze returning to the book before her.

"Any luck?" I asked, eyeing the book upside down to see if I recognized it. If it was one I had already combed through.

"Not yet," she mused, running her finger along the tattered pages to keep her place in a large paragraph.

"I see you're helping." Nik laughed, gesturing to the empty table before Puck.

"If I read one more bloody book about dream walking, I swear I will pass out," he replied with a huff.

"Somehow, I doubt that," Tess replied, eyeing him with a narrowed gaze. "The least you could do is comb through the rest of this stack and determine which ones we should check out first." She gestured towards the stack of books I had left on the table the night before.

The cottage underground was a treasure trove of information, and we had found a number of books on the subject, but nothing mentioning a token yet. Corian would have made a good mentor if he weren't on Donika's side—he knew the most about dream walking. More than any of us. Tyr knew a good amount too, but we had never spoken about it before his death. Other than the time he had tried to pry the Kotova grimoire away from me...

I was anxious for Annelise to return so we could train. I had only worked with my bound Stormshade magic a handful of times before Nik had turned into Noctani, and I needed more practice. Bound magic was entirely different from unbound magic, but I believed the mechanics were largely the same. Annelise has been a bound Stormshade for two decades, and her knowledge on the subject was incomparable.

The library door opened again and Zion shuffled in, Saanvi and Kenna on his heels.

"I thought I'd find you lot in here," he said, joining us at the table and pulling up a chair.

"You found us," I sighed, pulling one of the books from the stack to begin reading.

"Annelise just got back." He leaned back in his chair so that only two feet were on the ground.

"Where is she?" I asked, pushing the book back and moving to stand.

Even if we didn't have much daylight left, we might be able to at least get a little bit done. And who said you needed daylight for magic anyway?

Right as I was about to leave in search of her, the library door squeaked open again. Annelise entered with her pack in her arms, a wide smile across her lips.

"Sorry it took me longer than planned. There was one thing I had to do first."

She stepped aside and behind her was an old, familiar face. One I hadn't ever expected to see in the cottage underground, let alone with the resistance.

His grey hair was combed back against his head, a pair of spectacles balancing on his wrinkled nose. He wore training gear, a black long-sleeved shirt, and a leather vest across his chest. A sword hung from his back, a dagger at his hip.

I leaned across the table, my brow raising.

The others turned, equally shocked.

"Alastir? What are you doing here, and why do you look ready for battle?"

32

Alastir had come back to the cottage underground with Annelise, and he was wearing training gear, no less.

"To what do we owe the pleasure?" I asked.

Alastir moved forward, and without answering my question, he came to Nik's side. He put a hand on his shoulder, squeezing tightly.

"I wasn't sure, I didn't—" but Nik cut off Alastir's words before he could finish.

"It worked, old man. It worked." Nik placed his own palm over Alastir's hand. "I owe you my life."

"It was only a spell that I conducted, boy. The blood, the blade, that was all Diana. It is her you owe your life to," Alastir replied, his mouth thin as he gazed down at Nik.

"I owe her much more than that." Nik's reply was gruff as he turned to meet my gaze.

I shared a soft smile with him in return.

"The Mother has worked her magic, once again," Alastir said, laughing to himself.

He turned towards me. He appeared younger than I had ever seen him before. The corners of his eyes were still creased with wrinkles, but there was something spritely about him.

"I heard there's a march to war in the coming weeks, one I would be sorry to miss."

"You're joining the resistance?" Puck asked, his arms crossed over his chest. "How many times have we tried to recruit you? Asked you to join? Your answer was always the same... 'I am too old for war.'" Puck's impression of Alastir had us all bent over with laugher.

"I am," Alastir replied, his lips curving into a smile. "But Annelise... her visit changed my mind. Osiris was my dearest friend, and I was his advisor for many, many years before his death. Annelise became like a daughter to me in her time in The Stone City. Diana is the true queen, and I would be honored to live long enough to see her take her place on the throne. To be a better ruler for Istmere than Donika or Osiris ever were."

"So... what you're telling me is that you like them better than us?" Puck jested, leaning back in his chair with a shake of his head.

"That's exactly right." Alastir laughed, and I had never seen him so joyful. "I'm not sure my skills will be with the blade, but I wish to help in... other ways."

"Thank the Mother." Tess pushed back in her chair, pushing the dream walking book away from her across the table.

"Because we desperately need your ancient knowledge to figure out this dream walking crap."

"Ancient?" Alastir asked, his brow raised in question.

"You've got to be what, one thousand years old by now?" Nik laughed, standing to allow Alastir to take his seat beside Tess.

Alastir narrowed his eyes at him. "You'd better watch yourself, boy. My magic can swallow yours whole. You know as well as I do that witches are *mortal.*"

"So just eighty-or-so then?" He laughed, backing away from Alastir with his palms raised in surrender.

"We've got no time to waste," Alastir said, ignoring Nik and pulling the chair he had offered up to the table.

Having Alastir as my council would be invaluable. He had known Donika wanted to recruit him and had been cloaking his location for years. She would be shocked to know we had him and his wide breadth of knowledge on our side.

"What is it we are researching?" he asked, pulling out one of the books from the stack.

"Dream walking," I replied with a sigh.

"When is the last time you walked in dreams?" he asked, his eyes glimmering as if he already knew the answer.

"A few nights ago," I replied, swallowing hard. I wanted to forget all about Donika and Nik's father in bed together. "Zachariah was... with Donika."

"What do you mean *with* her?" Saanvi asked.

"I mean... in bed."

"Ah yes, daddy dearest bedding the ex-girlfriend. That's not gross at all," Puck chimed in, his gaze on Nik.

We all shot him a glare.

"It isn't news to me... unfortunately. Donika didn't bother hiding her comings and goings with me while I was Noctani. She thought I was entirely devoted to her, and it had never even occurred to her that there might be a cure. She thought her secrets were safe with me for eternity."

"And did you find this... disturbing... as Noctani?" Puck asked.

Tess kicked him hard under the table.

"Let's spend a little less time psychoanalyzing the situation and a little more time focused on what we are trying to accomplish," Alastir offered.

"Agreed." I shot Puck a glare, and he raised his hand, miming that he was zipping his mouth shut. I doubted that would last long. "Her Noctani numbers have been greatly reduced since we saved Nik. Anyone in his band of allies was killed in the battle. Isaac included."

Alastir's expression was grim. "That I already knew, the Mother had shown me."

"The Mother is awfully discerning in her visions, isn't she?" Puck asked.

"What happened to zipping your mouth shut?" Tess asked, cocking her head to the side with a playful smile.

Puck gave her a grin that showed all of his perfectly white teeth. Alastir sighed, running a hand through his thinning hair. I could have sworn I heard him mutter *children* under his breath.

"What we don't know is how many Araneoch she has managed to create," I replied, bringing us back on topic. "Corian, her right hand, has managed to dream walk and pull me into a dream before because he had left a token in that location. We are trying to figure out how to do the same. How we can dream walk to wherever she is keeping her Araneoch to analyze her numbers. To leave a token behind to ensure that we can check back any time we need to."

Alastir sat back, stroking his long, grey beard. "That's quite simple," he replied.

"Simple?" I asked, my voice incredulous. "We have been poring over these books for days, and weeks before that the last time we were here in Siraleth. We haven't been able to find anything."

"Do you know much of the magic of dream walking?" he asked, his tone indicating that he already knew the answer... and that it was no.

"No," I confirmed sheepishly. "Only what we have been able to discern from these books."

"Well, dream walking in a certain place is quite simple—" Before he could finish speaking, I interrupted him.

"The problem is I don't know how to intentionally dream walk at all. Every time I have, it's been my subconscious pulling me into The Stone City."

Alastir shook his head, covering his eyes. "We will need to start at the beginning, then."

"I hate to cut this short, but my time is better spent elsewhere. Training and making battle preparations," Puck said, pushing back from the table. "Anyone care to join me?"

Saanvi and Kenna raised their hands, eager to get out of this history lesson.

"Nik?" Puck asked, his gaze turning towards him.

"I'd like to stay. I want to support Diana however I can."

Puck nodded, exiting the library with Saanvi and Kenna to make their battle preparations. I wouldn't be surprised if he was only going to clean and shine his Katana for the next hour to escape Alastir.

That left Zion, Annelise, Amiyah, Tess, Nik, Alastir and me to congregate around the library table. The sun had set, and I was thankful that Tess had already lit all the library lanterns to illuminate the space.

"Back to business. How do I dream walk intentionally?" I asked, leaning across the table towards Alastir.

"All you need is your magic, and an anchor. The anchor can be a person, or a place."

"I volunteer," Nik replied, pulling his chair to my side. "I can be her anchor."

I grasped his hand under the table and gave it a squeeze, my voice soft. "You already are my anchor."

His responding smile had a dimple popping on his right cheek, and I thought I might melt. I hadn't seen such a genuine smile from him in far too long.

Tess pretended to gag across the table, and I shot her a piercing glare.

"Ok, Nik is the anchor then. You will hold on to him and pull on your magic. Only enough to let it fill your core. Then... instead of letting it flow down your arms and reach your fingertips as you normally would, you want to hold it in your chest, here." Alastir brought his hand to his breast, hovering over his heart as he spoke.

"Got it, then what?"

"Then you want to let it fill you. Let it fill your thoughts. You want to *think* of where you want to dream walk, but unless you have left a token, it has to be someone you are familiar with. Donika should be easy enough, I presume, since you have dream walked with her many times before, and you have a blood connection. Corian likely uses Donika as his anchor, making it easy for him to connect with you through that same blood link. It has likely been your subconscious seeking out Donika during your sleep, though."

I nodded, closing my eyes to concentrate.

"Once you have thought of who you want to dream walk with, you will allow your magic to bring you there. Almost as if it were astral projection. Think about what they look like. The more specific details, the better. You don't have to be asleep to dream walk, but to dream walk *intentionally*, you *need* to stay with your anchor."

"This isn't the same as bringing Nik into the dream with me, is it? Because Corian did that once with Donika. He brought her with him and met me in Dragon's Hollow."

Alastir shook his head. "No, not the same. You just want to ensure your hand is connected to your anchor at all times. He will not enter the dream with you. That is a different technique entirely, which we can practice later."

I nodded my head, closing my eyes again to focus.

"Once the person begins to fill your mind, you will slowly see their surroundings. You want to grasp onto that image with your magic, and you will be thrust into their environment. To wake up, it is the same as when you have walked dreams when asleep. You simply tell yourself to wake."

Alastir explained it as if it were so easy, as if he was astonished we hadn't already figured it out.

"Waking up hasn't been the easiest part, either. The dreams seem to want to hold me there. Whether that is my own subconscious or not, I have no clue," I mused. "And to drop the token? We need to find where the Araneoch are and spy on them. If Donika isn't in the same location as them, that would prove impossible. We want to be able to walk dreams in a specific place."

Alastir nodded. He reached into his pocket and took out a tattered piece of paper with scribbled writing on it.

"You can use this." He offered me the paper, and I wrapped it in my grasp. "You will imbue this paper with your magic, and you will hide it in the location you want to visit again. Once you have found your desired subject, you can walk through the castle *with* them. It would be much easier to physically go there and leave the token yourself, as I assume Corian did. But in this instance, it is much too dangerous."

"Agreed," Nik replied, a muscle ticking in his jaw at the thought of it.

"So, I just have to spy on Donika enough until she visits the Araneoch... " There was a note of disappointment in my tone.

"Unfortunately, yes. You can't physically travel there to leave the token without her. You have to be lucky enough to be taken there. You can also dream walk with Corian if you are familiar enough with him, though that is a risk since he would know of your presence. Leaving a token right under his nose when he can see you would be tricky, indeed."

I shook my head. "He practically has eyes in the back of his head. I don't want to underestimate him. Better if I stay off his radar entirely."

"You'll have to practice, over and over again. Hopefully you get lucky." Alastir nodded to himself.

My gaze fell on Nik and he gave me a reassuring nod. We would need to check in on her frequently, and hope that Corian was busy elsewhere during this next week. Alastir had already given us more information than we had been able to glean after hours and hours of poring over these books.

"If there's nothing else, the travel has exhausted an *old man* such as myself. I'd like to retire for the night." The words 'old man' were emphasized as he narrowed his eyes at Nik.

We thanked Alastir for his help and Annelise, Amiyah, and Zion escorted him to his chambers for the night. An uneasy feeling settled in my gut as I realized I would need to try dream walking tonight. And tomorrow. And the next night. And any free moment I had, really.

As if reading my mind, Nik pushed back from the table, pulling me along by the hand.

"You'll let us know what you see?" Tess asked, grasping one of the lanterns in her long fingers and pushing back from the table to follow us out into the hallway.

"Of course."

I pulled her into a one-armed hug, careful not to burn myself on the lantern she held.

When I retired for the night to Nik's bedroom—diagonally across the hall from Tess—I turned to see her raising an eyebrow at me, making a crude gesture before I rolled my eyes and closed the door between us.

33

Nik led me towards the bed and we settled on top of the covers, my back against the headboard. He climbed onto the sheets with me, clasping my hand in his.

"I will be right here, your anchor. Always."

I gave him a soft smile as I squeezed his hand in mine. "Thank you."

I took a deep, steadying breath, pulling the piece of paper Alastir had given me out of my pocket. The first step was to imbue it with my magic, which was fairly simple. I clasped the paper between my fingers, letting my magic flow into it and back into me, as if it were an endless loop. Once I sensed the energy within the paper, recognized it as my own magic, I nodded.

"I'm ready."

Nik nodded, a reassuring smile across his lips. Intentional dream walking sounded fairly simple. I only prayed to the Mother that Donika was alone and not with Corian. Or Zachariah, for that matter. I had seen enough of that to last a lifetime.

I closed my eyes, focusing my energy in my core as Alastir had instructed. I didn't allow it to flow down my arms and towards my fingertips as I usually did. I let it simmer right beneath my breast. I sensed its warm presence against me as I pictured Donika.

Her black, endless eyes. Her flowing blue and white hair. Her chiseled cheekbones. Her perfectly painted red lips.

I could sense the intention swell within me and I pushed the magic outward. Behind my closed lids, I could faintly see Donika, the outline of her body, the silhouette of her hair against the night sky.

I pushed once more with my magic, harder this time, and as Alastir had said it would, the dream snapped into place.

Donika stood on a terrace, her perfectly manicured nails gripping the iron railing before her. Her hair was bound behind her in a braid down her back, but strands of it had come loose and were whipping across her face beneath the wind. Her eyes were narrowed on the scene before her. My gaze traveled with hers, dread filling my core when her view became mine.

She was gazing down on the field in front of the castle, and though it was the middle of the night, it was far from empty. Rows and rows of soldiers were lined up, their helmets secured, their breast plates donning the white wolf and her sigil. There were too many to count from this far up, a fine mist coating the sky and obscuring my line of sight towards the trees and the forest beyond.

I had seen this field once before. In a vision the grimoire had sent me.

When Annelise had been fleeing The Stone Palace—my body tightly wrapped against her as she ran.

Movement in my periphery caught my eye, and I realized it wasn't only her soldiers that were lined up before her. The Araneoch were pacing back and forth among the tall grass below, their black grotesque bodies visible even from up here.

I quickly counted them off.

From what I could see, there were about twenty or so. I had thought her numbers were greater than that of her Noctani since she had indicated that they were easier to make, but maybe that wasn't the case. Or was this not all of them? The monsters were huge, with poisonous stingers we would need to be wary of. One Araneoch brought the might of at least five trained Nightshade soldiers, if not more.

I didn't immediately see her Noctani on the field, though I was sure they were here somewhere, blending in among the soldiers.

Thankfully, Corian was nowhere to be seen.

Donika's lips curved into a smile as she glared down on them, assessing her own numbers. I wasn't sure if this is where she was keeping the Araneoch, but this was as good a place as any to leave the token. I could always create another token, imbue another item with more magic to leave in another location on another night. I would easily be able to come back here to spy, even if Donika wasn't present. I moved towards the stone wall, slipping the piece of imbued paper in between the stone and pushing it until it disappeared between the rocks.

I might not have gotten lucky enough to dream walk to the exact location she was keeping the Araneoch, but I was lucky enough that she was assembling her soldiers at this moment.

The sight of them lined up among the dark and mist had my heart beating rapidly in my chest, nausea rising up the back of my throat. Zion was confident in the numbers of the resistance… but seeing her army before me like this… I wasn't so sure.

"I've brought you here to prepare for the war ahead." Donika's voice rang out across the field as if it were amplified by a spell.

A resounding cheer emanated from the crowd below, soldiers raising their swords in the air.

"The battle is imminent. My spies among the resistance have seen what is to come, and the Stormshade bitch will march against us before the next full moon."

Fuck.

She still had a spy somewhere in the resistance, and they had told her what we planned to do. She didn't know exactly when—which was to our advantage—but to some degree, we had lost the element of surprise. I stepped up to the railing beside her, placing my hand on the iron mere inches from hers. I could see her clear as day. As if she were truly before me, and she had no idea that I was here. I wished we had consulted Alastir about this earlier… this ability to spy would have been incredibly useful.

I shook my head as if to clear the thought. There was no use ruminating on the past anymore. The only path left now was forward.

"I don't know about you," Donika mused, her voice laced with a hint of humor. "But I crave Stormshade blood!"

The soldiers roared once more, jeering and clashing their swords together. The raucous had me clasping my hands over my ears, squeezing my eyes shut. Were these soldiers truly hateful, or were they simply brainwashed by Donika? Did they not see that there was another way where Istmere could live in peace with all Shades?

Donika leaned over the railing, her braid swaying in the breeze behind her. Shadows snaked out from her, creeping down the stone walls of the castle and up towards the tall spires, until the entire castle was swathed in darkness.

"You will never find a queen as powerful as I am. The one to bring me the Stormshade bitch's head will be granted a seat on my council."

Another roar.

It seemed she wasn't keen on stealing my magic anymore. She wanted my head. Perhaps she was as anxious to end this war as I was... though I wouldn't go down without a fight.

"When she comes, we will be ready!"

Her voice was louder now, the soldiers below beating their closed fists against their breastplates, a chorus erupting among them.

"Nightshade Queen! Nightshade Queen! Long live Queen Donika!"

Did they know she had usurped the throne from Osiris? Pretended to be on his side, then slain him in cold blood, taking his throne? Osiris left an heir behind, and my blood was the rightful blood of the throne. I wanted a better future for Istmere, and all Donika wanted was more blood.

More destruction. More hate.

A flash of white caught my eye, and I turned to see a number of Noctani walking out onto the field, Corian among them. I quickly backed up, unsure if he had seen me standing beside Donika at the rail. I clasped my hand against my chest, taking a deep, stabilizing breath. His head turned towards the balcony, but I pressed myself against the stone wall where I had left the token, splaying my hands against it.

Trying my hardest to become invisible.

From this point of view, he shouldn't be able to see me. I was hidden by the wall and the alcove within.

I could no longer see how many Noctani were marching out onto the field from this point of view. Despite that fact I was confident the numbers were forty or less based on the information we had gleaned from my dream walking and those we killed in Akra. Nothing we couldn't handle with the right soldiers. Donika released her shadows, and they dispersed among the crowd. They dropped to their knees in awe before her.

I had seen what I had come to see, and I needed to wake up before I got caught here by Corian. To our knowledge, he was the only dream walker we had encountered in The Stone Palace, but he might not be the only one she kept close.

It was time to go.

Wake up. Wake up. Wake up.

I focused on the sensation of Nik's hand in mine, bringing myself back into the present.

"The Shade who brings me the head of my mother... now... that Shade will get a special reward, indeed."

Donika's words had bile rising up the back of my throat once more. How could she relish killing our own mother? She relished killing me because she was jealous. Jealous of my power. Jealous that Annelise left her and Zion to start a life and a family with Osiris.

She thought she had been slighted at every turn, when in reality her situation was one of her own making. She let her hate and dark magic consume her, taking her over and driving her to be devoured by it. I still found it difficult to believe she could feel nothing towards our mother. That she wanted her head as much as she wanted my own.

I shook my head, backing towards the French doors of the terrace.

Wake up.

Wake up.

I could sense my hand clasped firmly in someone's grip, and I focused on that. The sensation of skin on mine. A sweaty palm pressed against me.

The next time I blinked I was no longer in Akra, I was propped against Nik's shoulder in his bedroom in Siraleth. My eyes met his as relief washed over me. I leaned forward to capture his mouth with mine.

I had woken up much easier than I ever had in the past with Nik as my anchor. I imagined the bond pulling me back to him, and I could sense his presence on the other end of it.

"What did you see?" His voice held a note of desperation in it. "I hated seeing you like that. Unreachable. I pray you saw what you needed to and we don't need to do this again."

"I did, but that doesn't mean we don't need to do this again. I should try to spy as much as possible in the next week. Nik... she knows we are coming," I replied.

"How could she know?" His eyes narrowed in confusion. "We have been so careful about who we've told our plans to."

I nodded, biting my lip. "We have, but we must still have a spy in the resistance somewhere. Someone reporting back to her. But we can't worry about that now. She is assembling her army and her numbers are... vast."

"And the Araneoch?" he asked.

"Twenty," I answered. "Maybe more. It was dark, and her magic was swirling everywhere. It was hard to tell."

"And the Noctani?" He ran a hand through his mess of hair, his other still clasped in mine.

"Corian brought them out, but I couldn't let him see me." I shook my head. "I can't confirm. All I know is we took out a good number of them when we fought your contingent. The sooner we move against her, the less time she will have to create more."

Nik nodded in agreement. He rested his head back against the headboard, closing his eyes and releasing a pent-up sigh.

"I am bound, now. Her magic will be no match for mine," I told him.

He turned his head towards me. "You sound certain."

"I am certain," I said. Though I wasn't sure how much I believed in my own words or whether it was false bravado. "Alastir saw it. The last Stormshade of the Kotova bloodline would put an end to the violence in Istmere."

"Kind of a vague prophecy if you ask me." Nik let out a humorless laugh.

"You know that Alastir only sees what the Mother shows him. But this is what she showed him *decades* ago."

I snuggled closer to him, resting my head on his shoulder. He leaned his head against mine. Only days stood between us and the battle that could change everything, and seeing Donika's army only unsettled me further. We might not have dark magic or blood magic on our side, but we had a number of Stormshades whose magic was unrivaled, Annelise and myself included.

"I'm just so, so tired." Nik's voice was raw when he spoke.

I knew exactly what he meant. I felt, deep in my bones, that it was time for this war to end. No matter the outcome. I gave his arm a squeeze and slipped under the covers, leaning across the nightstand to turn the bedside lamp off.

He curled with me beneath the sheets, his legs intertwining with mine.

"Have you changed your mind about allowing me to follow you into the castle? To meet Donika head on?" he asked, his voice soft in the darkness.

"No." My own voice was stern. "You know why you can't be with me. She might not know it... but if she kills you... she kills me. We are bound, Nikolai. With the amount of spies and intel she has, I honestly wouldn't put it past her to already have that information. We can't risk it."

He let out a heavy sigh. "I know. I just hate the idea of you going in there without me. I know you don't need me—it isn't that. You are a force of nature. It's *me* who needs *you*."

I smiled at him in the darkness even though he couldn't see it. "You don't need me, Nikolai. You will lead our soldiers into battle fearlessly. You are one of the strongest people I know."

He scoffed. "I'm not sure about that."

I slapped his arm playfully. "Don't be self-deprecating. When I first met you, you told me you were an *incredibly* powerful Nightshade, do you remember that?"

He laughed, and this time there was genuine humor in it. "I was trying to impress you."

"Oh, please." I rolled my eyes as I curled my body against his, my arm across his chest. "There is no one else I would pick to lead the resistance against her army." I told him. "You know it has to be *me* who kills Donika. It can be no one else."

"I understand… but it doesn't mean I like it," he replied thinly.

"Get some sleep. You can come and train with us tomorrow if you want. I'm excited to put some of this bound magic to use," I said, wiggling my fingertips against his skin. I let a shadow snake out against his chest, caressing his collarbone before it disappeared into his hair.

He laughed, seeing his own magic seep through my fingertips. The corner of his mouth lifted into a smile as he pulled me closer against him.

I closed my eyes, memorizing the feel of him beneath me. The soft rise and fall of his chest as he took each deep breath. The sensation of his hot skin beneath my palm. My cheek. The soft sounds of his exhales as he fell into a deep sleep.

I had never felt safer than when I was wrapped in Nikolai's arms. Despite that feeling of security, it was thoughts of Donika's army that kept me from dozing off.

When sleep finally did find me, it wasn't the dreamless sleep I craved.

My thoughts were filled with nightmares. Araneoch and Noctani beating back our forces. Donika's sword slicing through my chest.

And me on that terrace... falling, falling, falling.

34

Annelise relentlessly pulled me from bed first thing in the morning, when the sun had barely kissed the Siraleth sky. I sleepily pulled on my training leathers, strapping Stormslayer to my thigh and leaving Nik twisted among the sheets.

I met her out where we had conducted the binding ceremony, a fine mist clinging to the air in a way that reminded me of when I had seen Donika last night. The morning air was cool, raising the hair on my forearms and sending a chill through me.

Annelise was also donning her training gear, a glistening broadsword strapped to her back as she waved me over. She unstrapped the sword, resting it against the rubble.

"I figured this was as good a place as any. Plenty of open space," she said, resting her hands on her hips. "You ready?"

I ran a hand through my mess of curls. "As ready as I'll ever be."

I stretched my arms upward, cracking my back and stretching from side to side. The last time I had trained with my storm magic had been with Isaac. Pain lanced through me at the thought. I still couldn't believe he was gone. That he had been the leader of the resistance and my number one cheerleader... and he wouldn't get to see this war come to an end.

As if Annelise could guess my thoughts she cleared her throat uncomfortably, casting her gaze away from me. "This won't be like training with Isaac," she said.

"No?" I raised my brow, expecting her to say something about how she wouldn't go as easy on me or something like that.

"No. Bound magic is different from unbound magic. Its control comes from a different place entirely. It will be... easier."

That was good news, at least. I could sense a pull on the other end of the bond and could tell that Nikolai had woken, the bedsheets empty but still warm beside him.

"We can start with some defensive magic," Annelise offered.

I nodded. "Isaac and I were working on that."

"This time you'll have another Stormshade to contend with." There was a ghost of a smile on Annelise's lips.

I narrowed my eyes at her.

"You'll need to truly fight me. I know Isaac didn't... but you need the practice." Her voice was cold as I met her gaze.

"I have no problem fighting with you."

She flinched ever so slightly. If I had blinked, I would have missed it.

"Good." Her mouth was tight as she turned her face towards the sky. "Bring up your shield, and I will try to penetrate it."

I nodded, focusing on the magic deep in my core and allowing it to flow easily through my hands, creating an invisible air shield around me. I had practiced this many times with Isaac, and this kind of magic now came easily to me. I could sense the bubble of protection around me as Annelise called on her own storm, the morning sky darkening rapidly with oncoming rain.

The storm formed quickly overhead, rain pelting against my shield and bouncing off. I remained dry beneath its protection.

"Good," Annelise called from across the clearing, her strawberry hair now plastered to her scalp beneath her own rainstorm.

She narrowed her eyes in concentration, her brow creasing as lightning streaked through the sky right outside my shield. I was startled, and my shield faltered for only a moment.

"Hold tight!" She called.

I nodded, focusing once more. When the lightning struck again it hit my shield, bouncing off. It was as if it were a bodily pressure. As if the shield were a blanket on top of me and I was physically repelling the electric strikes.

Annelise's lips curved into a smile. "Very good. I'm impressed."

"I had a good teacher," I called out over her storm. Both Isaac and Nik had taught me well.

"Can you go on the offensive?" she asked, taking a step back.

I didn't answer her, only let my magic reach out to the sky, sensing her own storm there. I funneled my energy into the forming clouds, creating one of my own. Two storms were warring in the sky, colliding together angrily against each other. Thunder shook the earth as the rain became a deluge. I held my shield in place, focusing my efforts on doing both things at the same time. The last time I had done this I had lost control... my storm had stolen my magic and lashed out at me, injuring me. I still had the scar on my shoulder to prove it.

Splitting my efforts as a bound Stormshade was much, much easier. Not only did the magic come easier to me, but concentration did as well. I found that I barely had to focus on the shield to keep it in place... as long as I didn't get distracted. I released the storm overhead as Isaac had taught me, stepping towards Annelise.

She inclined her head, watching me.

Once I had released the storm it was easier to coax the magic out of it, instead of using the power from my own core. *This* was the magic I had been yearning to practice. *This* was the magic that had the Nightshades turning against the Stormshades. I drew energy from the cloud overhead and lightning struck, Annelise barely avoiding it as she jumped back.

I was more confident than I had ever been before when it came to my magic. The storm I had created raged on overhead and I siphoned a little more power from it, a swirling tornado forming at the tips of my fingers. I released it as if it were a spinning top and it landed in the dirt before me, growing in intensity as I fed more magic from the sky into it.

I wasn't even the least bit tired.

Annelise reached out with her hand and redirected the tornado so it spun away from us.

A grin spread across my face as I held my hand out, fire reaching the tips of my fingers and crackling in the ball of my outstretched hand. I firmly held the shield in place but allowed the fireball to pass through, and Annelise raised her arms in a shield of her own before it made contact.

"Good. Again."

I pulled another fireball from the energy in the sky, throwing it once more. Annelise easily batted it away.

"Again."

When I went to pull the magic from the storm above this time it bucked against me, roaring in a thunderous clap overhead that had me wanting to cover my ears.

"You have to remember," Annelise called over the raging storm, pointing overhead. "It isn't *yours* anymore. It doesn't belong to you. You can siphon its magic, but it won't give it easily. You need to manage the power of the storm while taking its energy, little by little. You'll expend your own energy in the process, but it is a give and take."

I nodded in understanding. Using my Stormshade magic was all about balance. Multitasking. I couldn't lose control of the storm I had created and released, or I wouldn't be able to pull from its energy easily.

I pushed against the storm with my own magic once more—and though it pushed back—it relented after a few moments. When I was unbound, the magic of the storm had easily been able to overtake me. But now... *I was the storm.* I forced it into submission once more, siphoning more energy from it over and over again to create another fireball.

My eyes still on the sky I released the fireball, lowering my shields only momentarily to allow it to pass, and it hit Annelise with full force, throwing her back.

She fell against the rubble behind her, cutting her arms on the jagged rocks. I released my shield, rushing forward with my hands outstretched.

"I'm so sorry, I didn't mean—"

"Never apologize, Diana. That was quite impressive." Annelise pushed her wet hair back from her face and her hand came away covered in blood.

I extended my own hand out to her and helped her to her feet as both of our storms continued to rage around us. I had soaked through my leather training gear the moment I had let my shield down, my hair plastered to my face. My eyelashes were wet as I blinked away rain droplets.

"Are you ok?" It had been a hard hit, and her leather training vest had a fireball sized hole burned right through the center of it. "You need to see a healer."

"Diana... I am a healer," Annelise said with a laugh, her palm hovering over the wound.

She spoke a soft incantation under her breath and when she removed her hand, the wound was closing before my eyes. She did the same to the cut on her head. I had almost forgotten about her healing prowess from when I had known her as Liss.

"Perhaps that's enough for today?" I asked, pushing my wet hair back from my face.

Annelise nodded, placing a skin spell against her collarbone. She reached up to the sky with one arm and absorbed her own storm seamlessly.

I did the same, reaching out to the sky with my hand. I could see the storm as it absorbed back into me, a swirling haze at my fingertips. Pure energy. The magic was amethyst as it swirled back towards me. I knew the moment I had absorbed it all, the swell of energy in my core causing me to take a step back beneath the force of it.

Annelise was healed, the only remnants that I had hurt her at all the dried blood crusted on her forehead and across her abdomen. She smiled at me, the corners of her eyes crinkling. The morning mist had cleared, and the sun beat down on us now, warming me from the inside out. I dare say that was the best training session I had ever had.

"Thank you," I said, stepping towards her tentatively.

Her grin was encouragement enough, and I pulled her into a fierce hug. She was shorter than I was, the top of her head coming to my shoulder. I could feel her sigh against me as I held her, and for reasons I couldn't quite understand, tears stung the back of my eyes.

Was it... gratitude? Love? Relief?

I wasn't quite sure. But in this moment, I knew we were on our way to healing. That I was on my way to forgiving her. I might not understand why she did what she did, but that was in the past now. As I had told Nikolai, the only path now was the way forward. And I wanted to move forward with Annelise.

I wanted to forgive her.

I wanted a relationship with her.

I pulled away to meet her gaze, and a tear tracked its way through the dried blood and dirt across her cheek. We didn't say anything—we didn't need to. She could feel in that hug more than I could ever say aloud.

My hand on her shoulder, I gave her a gentle squeeze as she wiped away the tear.

"I knew I would find you two here." It was Zion's voice that rang out from behind us.

I turned, his body silhouetted with the rising sun behind him so that I had to cover my eyes in order to see him.

"How are you… dry?" I called out, assessing the state of him.

Mere moments ago there had been two raging storms here, and Annelise and I were completely soaked through. I was due for a long, hot shower.

Zion grinned down at us from the hill of rubble he stood on. "I stood out of striking distance of the storm until you two were finished."

He raised a brow at me as he assessed Annelise, the grime and blood caked on her.

"You got a hit in on her?" he asked, suspicion lacing his tone.

"I did," I said proudly.

Annelise appeared equally proud as she nodded. "She did. She is a natural with the magic. She did well choosing a strong binding partner."

"Does that factor into the equation? How strong the binding partner is?" I asked.

"Most certainly." She nodded. "If you bind to someone who can't share the magic, your ability to control will only weaken. Nikolai is a strong Shade in his own right. Though, with how much magic you have used today, you might find him a little tired."

"Zion doesn't look tired," I pointed out.

Annelise crossed her arms over her chest. "He has more practice with the give and take of storm magic. This was your first time truly using your power and pulling on that energy. Nikolai will never have sensed anything like that before. We should train daily, maybe even multiple times a day so that you both can become accustomed to the effects of the magic."

"I agree." I nodded. "I need Nik to be one hundred percent when we storm The Stone City."

Annelise placed her hand against my back reassuringly. "He will be."

"I didn't only come to check on your training," Zion said from atop the rubble. "Tess has found something that you both might find of interest."

We exchanged a glance that felt as if I was gazing in a mirror, and we both laughed as we trudged through the mud and followed Zion back to the cottage underground.

Before I joined Tess and Puck in the library, I desperately needed a hot shower. I was covered from head to toe in dirt and grime and I needed to scrub myself clean before I let anyone see me. I returned to my own room to shower, hoping Nik was still getting some rest. I drew myself a bath, scrubbed my skin raw, and washed all the grime from my tangled hair.

By the time I had emerged from the bathroom I was an entirely new person. Not only was I now squeaky clean, but I was a bound Stormshade with *control* of her magic. A renewed sense of hope simmered in my chest, despite what I had seen at The Stone Palace last night.

I slipped into the library, my hair still wet and braided down my back leaving a wet mark against my shirt. I found Tess and Puck standing, leaning over Annelise who sat at the table. She had the Kotova grimoire beside another book, her gaze traveling back and forth between the two texts. Nik stood across from them with Zion, his arms crossed over his chest.

I gave him a soft smile as I joined them, peering over Annelise's shoulder to see what it was they were gazing at.

"What is it?" I asked.

My gaze met Nik's across the table.

"Tess found the meaning of Donika's wolf sigil."

35

My head snapped towards Tess—eyes wide.

"You *what?*"

She held her hand out as if to stop me. "I didn't find the meaning itself, I only found the symbol in this book." She pointed to the one Annelise was referencing. "I don't read this language, so I needed someone to translate using the Kotova grimoire as a reference. Not to mention the Kotova grimoire won't as much as let me glance at it, let alone touch it."

I raised an eyebrow at the back of Annelise's head. "You can read this ancient language?"

She nodded, saying nothing.

She ran her finger along the page, reading the transcription from the grimoire and referencing the sigil drawn onto the page of the book Tess found.

"What book is that?" I asked.

Tess shook her head. "I have no idea. All I know is that it had a chapter on dream walking, so we had added it to the stacks to look at."

Annelise flipped it over, but the cover was bound leather, no inscription on it. The spine was the same. It was an unnamed book of some sort, and the pages were yellowed and worn. The writing and drawings were all done by hand, not printed.

"Is this someone's grimoire?" I asked, shock running through me as I registered the scribbles in the columns of the page.

Annelise nodded. "I believe so. But whose, I have no clue. It was here, in the library. Among the other texts. So very strange... "

Alastir burst through the doors, equally rejuvenated as he had been yesterday. He moved to Annelise's side silently, pushing us out of the way to take the seat beside her.

"Have you finished it yet?" he asked, sliding a piece of blank parchment in front of him and grabbing a quill from the ink pot at the center of the desk.

Annelise shook her head silently before sliding the book towards him so that it sat between them. Alastir worked quietly, writing down words that I didn't recognize and hastily sketching the sigil onto the piece of parchment.

I had done my best to draw it out of memory and had left the poorly done replication in the library for Tess and the others to reference. I had wanted to find out the meaning of the sigil since the moment I had first seen it, but it hadn't been our priority. I had forgotten all about it, to be honest. I was surprised Tess had recognized it.

Who could this new grimoire belong to, and why was it in this library? Had it belonged to someone who had passed, and there was no bloodline for it to be passed down to?

Alastir shook his head as he buried his nose into his work, translating the words that Annelise wasn't able to off the top of her head. We all watched in strained silence as they worked together. I wasn't sure if the translation would help us or hurt us, but I was anxious to know what it meant.

Donika was the only wolf I had seen with a sigil before, and a bloody one at that. When she had come to me in my dream, and when I had seen her wolf form in person in The Stone Palace, the sigil had been marked in blood. Trails of it dripped down its edges as if it were freshly applied and hadn't had time to dry, though it appeared that way every time I saw it.

Alastir and Annelise exchanged a silent glance that had Tess and I doing the same. I swallowed back my anxiety as Alastir returned the quill back to the pot at the center of the table and sat back.

"Well?" I asked, putting a voice to the tension all of us were surely experiencing. I glanced around the table and everyone was focused on the books before us.

Alastir turned to Annelise, allowing her to speak.

"Seven devils," she swore under her breath, pushing herself back from the table and running a hand through her strawberry blonde hair.

"What is it?" Tess asked, practically bursting from the seams.

Annelise hung her head, rubbing at her temples.

"It's... it's a dark spell in which she hoped to achieve immortality."

"Hoped?" I croaked. My hand flying to my chest as my heart threatened to beat out it. What did *that* mean?

"Hoped," Annelise repeated, "because I am not sure she succeeded."

"And why do you think that?" Tess asked, leaning over the chair Annelise sat in.

Annelise's voice was soft when she spoke.

"Because she tied the spell to *me*."

36

"What do you mean, she tied the spell to *you*?" I asked, taking a step back away from the table. "What does this all mean?"

Annelise turned towards me as she answered. "It's a way to keep her alive. She tied a piece of her soul to mine. If I were to die, she would simply take the piece of her soul back and place it in another. She is tying herself to someone living to ensure that if she is killed before that person is... she won't truly be dead."

"You can't be serious... " Puck shook his head back and forth, backing away from the table.

At first my heart had been beating out of my chest, but now it was a solid a rock, un-beating. This couldn't be right. It couldn't.

"The only way to truly kill her would be to—" Annelise began, but I interrupted her.

"Don't." My voice was hollow in my own ears as I backed away even more, hitting the table behind us. "Don't say it."

Annelise's gaze held mine as she finished her sentence. "Would be to kill me, too."

"And why do you doubt that she succeeded in achieving immortality?" Zion asked, his voice gruff as he ran a hand down his face.

Annelise paused before answering. "Because we already know where she left the piece of her soul. And there's an easy way to ensure it can't be passed on... "

My gaze cut towards her, but Zion spoke before I could.

"How do you know this? How do you know it was you that she left the piece of her soul with?"

Annelise swallowed hard. "A spell of this size wouldn't go undetected. It's similar to the binding spell. You wouldn't be able to ignore the feeling that you were connected to someone else. I have felt that way ever since that day in Siraleth, when Donika spared my life. She connected herself to me in some way, but I had no idea what it meant before now. That it was *this* spell. But now it all makes sense."

Annelise turned back towards the grimoires on the table.

"Whose grimoire *is* that?" Nik asked almost to himself, speaking for the first time and moving towards the table.

Annelise shook her head. "I have no idea. Your guess is as good as mine. It isn't spelled like the Kotova grimoire. But then again, most aren't... " she mused.

"Can you only link yourself to one person at a time? Leave one piece of your soul with another?" Tess asked, shaking her head.

"Yes," Alastir replied, "you cannot split the soul multiple times."

"Oh my God… it's a horcrux." Tess's hand flew to her throat as her eyes went wide.

"Kind of… " Annelise replied, her eyes still on the text before her.

"Mother above, she created a Goddamn horcrux… " Tess muttered, her gaze traveling to mine.

"And you think she chose you… why?" Nik asked, peering down at the grimoire.

As if the Kotova grimoire sensed his gaze, it snapped closed, almost catching Annelise's hand within its pages. She cast him a halfhearted glare as she closed the other book, stacking them atop one another.

"Some kind of sick punishment, I suppose. That to truly kill Donika, I would need to die, too. Donika has always been one for the dramatics, and it is quite poetic if you think about it. She never bore the sigil on her wolf form until after that battle. Until after she marked me."

"You saw her after that battle?" Tess asked.

Annelise cast her eyes down to her hands in her lap. "I did a lot of… spying in the years afterwards. I hid Diana in the human realm, but I… lingered in Istmere."

That was one way of putting it. She had kept a close eye on all of us, that was certain.

"Is there a way to be positive that it was Annelise who was marked? What if she marked another during that battle?" Nik asked.

Alastir nodded. "There is a way to confirm. A spell, written here in the grimoire. Without removing this piece of Donika from Annelise... we cannot kill her. Not completely, anyway."

"God dammit... " Tess muttered under her breath, flinging her arms up into the air in exasperation.

"And if it is Annelise that she marked?" I asked, crossing my arms over my chest. "I refuse to lose another person I care about. Another person I love."

Annelise's gaze flew to mine, surprise glistening in her eyes.

"We will cross that bridge when we come to it," Alastir said. "This... I'm afraid... the Mother did not show me. Now that it has been uncovered, perhaps there are other things she may deign to show me. A way out of this mess."

That was an understatement. This was a shit show.

It was less than one week until we marched against Donika and her forces, and she may have created a 'horcrux' as Tess had put it. This was the worst possible moment for us to figure something like this out. But at least we figured it out *before* we marched on Akra.

I prayed Alastir could find a way out of this. Zion was already deep in his war planning with his resistance committee and there was no turning back now. We needed to kill Donika, and we needed to save my mother. I wouldn't allow her to sacrifice herself so that we could break Donika's immortality.

I should have guessed Donika would try something like this. She was so hungry for power, so relentless. Of course, she would want to be immortal, too. No spell was too much when it came to Donika.

"What now?" Tess asked, letting Puck pull her against him. She nuzzled her head into the crook of his shoulder.

Alastir's voice was ragged when he spoke. "Now, we test her blood... and we wait."

I hadn't spent any time in the laboratory during my time in Siraleth, and my only memory of it was from when I had dream walked here. From when I had pulled the grimoire out of the dream with me and brought it back to the mortal realm.

I was biting my fingernail to the point where it had started to bleed by the time Alastir had rolled up Annelise's sleeve and taken her blood with a needle. It was exactly as one would in the mortal realm... no slice of the blade across a palm or anything like that. It all felt so... normal.

The next part... not so much. He had taken the syringe full of blood and emptied it into a beaker, setting it over a flame to the point of boiling. His hand poised over the glass—eyes closed as he spoke a murmured spell. He added ingredients for the spell to the beaker and mixed it. When he was fin- ished, a spark of light emanated from the beaker and the flame turned off, the blood inside sitting quietly for the first time.

He inserted his pinky finger into the mixture—then put that finger in his mouth—tasting it on the tip of his tongue. His gaze was downcast, a crease forming between his brows.

"Well?" I asked, anxious to know what the spell had told us, if anything.

Alastir shook his head so slightly I could have missed it. My gaze shot to Tess across the lab table, and she gave me a half smile that never reached her eyes. Nik placed a hand on my shoulder.

"It's as we feared. She has been marked."

"God dammit... "

I wanted to fling every single thing on the lab table to the floor, but I restrained myself. Barely. I leaned back against the work bench behind me, running a hand through my auburn curls and pushing it out of my face. I desperately wanted to hit something right now. My energy was swirling angrily inside of me when I felt a tug through the bond. My gaze flitted up to Nik's, and he wore an expression I couldn't quite read.

"Ok. We thought that might be the case. What do we do now?" Tess asked.

Always trying to be helpful. Not only was this one more thing that now stood between me and Donika, but it also made the fate of Annelise unknown.

Amiyah pushed into the room with a grim expression. She had obviously been listening at the door.

"We will do what we always do. We will find a spell to reverse it." She answered simply. As if it were that easy.

"And if we can't find a spell? If we run out of time? We only have a matter of *days* left." I pointed out.

Amiyah nodded, as if she understood the stakes.

It was always one step forward, two steps back, and I was brimming with frustration. We didn't have time for this.

"We have *two* grimoires at our disposal now. There has to be something in there to reverse the marking. We have Alastir, one of the most skilled Shades of our time. And we have *me*. Worst-case scenario, we figure out how to transfer the mark to me instead of Annelise."

"No." I shook my head, my hair falling in front of my face once more. "Not an option. That's out of the question."

"I am more disposable than your mother." Amiyah's voice was soft when she spoke. She was trying to be reasonable.

"No, you aren't. None of us are." My voice was ragged in return.

"Diana—"

I put my hand up to stop her. "I won't hear it. We won't sacrifice one person for another. We will find a spell to reverse the marking, or… "

"Or what?" Tess asked, her voice small.

I met her gaze once more from across the lab table and her eyes brimmed with fear.

"Or nothing. We will find the spell." I practically spit out the words. "Let's all get to work."

I could only pray that the Mother saw fit to save my own mother. That she would show Alastir a way out of this. Donika was dark and cruel, but she had found one more way to twist the blade. If she died, we would have to kill Annelise, too, in order for her soul to truly return to the earth from which it came.

This was so fucked up.

I stormed out of the laboratory and down the hallway, up the spiral staircase, and out of the cottage underground. I pulled my shirt away from my throat. It felt too tight. As if I was being strangled. I pushed my hair back again in aggravation, but all it did was fall forward once more, tickling my cheeks.

My head fell back, and I released a guttural, frustrated scream.

Lightning struck behind the cottage and I hadn't even realized I had released magic along with my frustration.

I screamed once more, and the rain began. In a matter of moments, I was soaked through, my vision blurry through the rain droplets clinging to my lashes.

I screamed in frustration again and fell to my knees, all the angst swallowing me. A hand on my back startled me. I flung my hand out without thinking clearly. Luckily, Nikolai was ready, and he deflected the fireball easily.

I startled, realizing what I had done. "I'm sorry, I wasn't thinking—"

He cut me off by grabbing me by the back of the head, pulling me against him. He kneeled in the mud with me, holding me as I cried. I had done the same for him when he had broken apart in the library, and now he did the same for me.

"I can feel it. Your anger. Your frustration." He pulled away only enough to capture my eyes with his. "Your eyes, Diana. They're swirling with your magic."

I pulled away slightly. "They haven't done that since I've been bound. I've been in control... I've—"

Nik shook his head. "Maybe it has nothing to do with control. Maybe it is the magic... taking a piece of you. Bound or not, that is the nature of Stormshade magic. It is always a balance."

I shook my head, tears dripping down my cheeks and mixing with the rain that pelted my skin. "I can never escape all this."

"You can." Nik pulled me against him once more. "This is almost over, Diana. We will finish this."

"And my mother?" I croaked against him, gripping his jacket in my fists. I held on so tightly my knuckles were white.

"I don't know. I wish I could tell you she would be fine, that we would figure it out and that everything was going to be ok, but I don't know if that is the truth."

I tilted my chin up to gaze at him. His eyes were the depths of the ocean, swirling full of emotion. "What will I do?"

"You will do nothing." His voice was raw when he spoke. "If it comes to it, I will wield the blade."

"But Donika is mine to kill," I protested.

"And she still will be," he said. "If a piece of her still lives in Annelise, that is not your burden."

"I can't ask you to do that, Nik."

A muscle feathered in his jaw. "You didn't ask."

I shook my head to protest, but his hand clasped my cheek, pulling my mouth to his. The kiss was salty and desperate, full of all the anger and frustration that drowned me. The guilt. I could taste the smoky rainwater and my own salty tears on his lips.

I pulled him against me, desperate to release every last kernel of anger that threatened to tear me under. He kissed me back just as fiercely, his rough lips claiming mine.

Marking me as his.

Whatever came next, he would be by my side. He would help me get through this. The only problem was… I didn't think I could tolerate losing one more person I cared about. I wouldn't survive it. Annelise and I had just started getting to know each other. I had just begun to forgive her.

When our lips parted, his were red and swollen, rainwater streaming down his cheeks. His blond hair was darkened and dripping. He looked as if he were plucked straight out of my wildest dreams. As if the Mother made him just for me. The corner of his mouth lifted into a smirk under the torrents of rain.

A warmth bloomed in my chest through the bond and I quirked my brow at him.

"Did you do that?"

He nodded—his lips parted ever so slightly. I ran my hand from his cheek, down his chiseled jaw, to a drop of rain at the edge of his lower lip. I captured it with my finger, dragging his lip down with it. I sent him a blast of warmth in return and his eyes heated, his jaw ticking as his smile turned wicked.

"Diana—" My name wasn't a prayer this time, more like a warning.

My smile turned sinful in return, thoughts of what we could be doing right now, beneath this rain running through my head.

But I knew he was right. We didn't have any time to spare. We needed to find a way to break the immortality spell and save Annelise… or come wartime, my heart would be broken once more.

And I wasn't sure how many pieces were left.

37

We had spent the last week combing through the Kotova grimoire and the one we had found in the library. We hadn't had any luck when it came to the immortality spell Donika had marked Annelise with.

I had continued to train with Annelise, my magic coming easily to me during our sessions together. There were times when my eyes swirled with my magic, and I could taste the bloodlust that had once consumed me at the battle in Prins. I wasn't sure what the repercussions of this magic were, but I didn't have time to over analyze it.

Annelise didn't know, either.

She wasn't as powerful as I was, but there were times when I could see cobalt swirling in her own gaze. She wasn't immune to the magic, either. Despite being bound, Stormshade magic was a balance of give and take. It was still unpredictable. We had done all we could to prepare. The rest was in the Mother's hands.

Tomorrow, we would begin our march against Akra.

It would take us two days' time to travel to The Stone Palace and breach its walls. The resistance would meet us on the plains of Siraleth and cross The Shadow with us in force.

We were in the library, moving the figurines across the map and finalizing our battle plans. My anxiety was at an all-time high, and I knew I wouldn't get any sleep tonight. I had already packed my bag, my outfit and Stormslayer all set out for tomorrow. I would also carry a sword on my back, and my throwing knives. I would be armed to the hilt.

I had my magic... but it was a blade that would take Donika's life.

Kenna and Saanvi had brought a large bottle of brown liquor into the library with us and we sipped on it. The tone in the room was both excited and bleak at the same time... if that was even possible. We were anxious to dethrone Donika and put an end to her reign of tyranny, but we hadn't found a way to save Annelise yet.

I tried not to think about it, but my thoughts kept drifting back to her over and over again. We had initially not wanted her to be a part of the contingent that would breach the castle, but with a piece of Donika's soul living inside her, her presence was needed there. Zion also wanted to go, but I insisted one parent was plenty. We couldn't afford to have any last-minute regrets and anyone changing their minds.

Donika might be a monster, but she was also their daughter. This would be difficult enough without both Annelise and Zion in the room with us.

We knew she would have Noctani protecting her, so we had selected fifteen of us to infiltrate the castle. Some of the passageways were narrow, only allowing for us to pass through single file. We also needed someone to lead us through them, and nobody knew them as thoroughly Annelise did. While Nik couldn't be with me, Puck would, and he had promised to lay down his life for me should the need arise—despite my stern objections.

Tess would be with me, too.

Zion, Nik, Saanvi, and Kenna would lead our forces on the battlefield, across the open plains before The Stone Palace. Annelise, Tess, Puck, Alastir, Amiyah and nine hand-picked soldiers from the resistance would join me in the hidden passageways, hoping to take out Donika before the battle became too bloody.

There was no way Donika would meet us out on the battlefield head on. She might think herself the most powerful Shade to ever exist, but she was also proud. She wouldn't risk being slain among her soldiers in the dirt. If she was going down... it would be on her throne she had fought so hard to keep.

The throne she sacrificed so much to obtain in the first place.

I kicked my feet up on the table, sufficiently exhausted from battle planning. I sipped the brown liquor Saanvi had handed me and it had a bite to it, but was smooth going down. Maybe it would help me sleep.

We had gone over the plan over and over again until it was seared into all of our brains. I couldn't help but think I should have been breaching the castle with Isaac by my side. I hoped he would approve of our plans, and come tomorrow, his death would not have been in vain.

Nik would also have to face his father.

He had seen him while he was Noctani, but there was only a sliver of his consciousness present at the time. If Zachariah didn't surrender, he would be killed among the other soldiers. Despite their turbulent relationship, it would be no easy feat. Just as I knew that when the time came, driving Stormslayer through Donika's heart would be difficult. Despite my hatred for her.

"I want to thank you all," Zion spoke, clearing his throat. He raised his glass in a toast. "Thank you for entrusting me with the position of leading the resistance. I know that nobody could ever fill Isaac's place, but I tried my hardest to make him proud. The day after tomorrow, we will see an end to the bloodshed and sacrifice that has plagued this realm for the last decade. We will see the rightful heir take her place on the throne of Istmere. I propose a toast to honor Isaac and the true queen, Diana."

He kneeled before me and I tried to pull him up, to no avail. I laughed, but my face sobered as the others kneeled as well. I wasn't sure how to feel, my friends and family on their knees before me. Their heads bowed—their glasses raised. I was only a normal girl. I wasn't anything special. My destiny had been seen and set in stone long before I had even been born.

"To Diana!" Their cheers rang out, and tears stung the back of my eyes.

Tears of gratitude.

Tears of loss.

Tears of happiness.

Tears of grief.

"And to Tyr!" I called, raising my glass.

The others whooped and hollered, and a smile was gracing Amiyah's lips when my gaze landed on hers.

"Cheers to the resistance!" Nik called, shooting back the brown liquor in one gulp and grabbing the bottle to refill everyone's glass.

"To the resistance!"

These eight people had become my family, and I was so, so lucky to have them. My gaze fell on each of them as we laughed, memorizing their smiles. Their eyes. The lines of their faces.

Tomorrow wasn't promised, and I prayed we would all make it out to see the other side. These people, this realm, had sacrificed enough. My gaze fell on Annelise last, a silent prayer running through my mind to the Mother. That she would show us a way to save her. That despite everything... I couldn't do this without her.

Nik kneeled beside my chair, leaning into me. His cheeks were flushed from the alcohol. I ran a hand through his hair and placed a soft kiss against his cheek. His was the face I wanted to memorize most of all. As if reading my thoughts, he stood, his glass in one hand, his other extended out towards me.

"I think it's time we get some rest, My Queen."

"I'm not your queen yet." I laughed, allowing him to pull me from the chair and against him, his arm sliding around my waist.

"You have always been my queen," he whispered in my ear.

I gave him a playful push before turning towards the group.

"I can't thank you all enough for joining me on this mission. For being by my side every step of the way. For putting the good of this realm before everything else. You are my family. The debt I owe you all can never be repaid." A tear slipped down my cheek, but I hastily brushed it away with the back of my hand. "What I'm trying to say is... thank you."

I almost burst into tears right then and there, my gaze falling on each of them as they smiled back at me.

"That's enough liquor for you," Nik said with a laugh, plucking the glass from my hand.

We all fell into a fit of laughter as he led me from the library, the door closing behind us and enveloping us in the quiet of the hallway. I could still hear the laughter and clinking of glasses through the door. I let Nik turn me from the library, leading me down to his bedroom, which he opened with his back, leading me inside.

My breath caught in my throat as I took in the room before me. A fire roared in the grate. Red rose petals were strewn from the doorway to the bed, where they were scattered among the black silk sheets. There was a bottle of champagne resting against the pillow.

"What is all this for?" I asked, quirking my brow at him.

"We never had a proper honeymoon," he answered, a smile curving across his lips.

I turned to him with an incredulous smile, eyes wide. "Maybe that's because we aren't married… "

"After our binding ceremony, I mean," he said, grabbing the champagne off the bed and popping the top off.

He didn't bother with glasses—he took a sip straight from the bottle and handed it to me. I did the same.

He smiled down at me and that dimple in his cheek popped, his throat bobbing. He grabbed the champagne bottle back from me, taking another sip before resting it on the nightstand behind me.

"Our last night together as fugitives," I said, placing my hands against his chest and peeling the jacket off his shoulders.

"Mmm," he hummed, "I quite like being a criminal."

"I'm sure you'll still find some laws to break," I said, running my hands underneath his T-shirt.

He shivered at the cold touch of my fingers, his gaze heating.

His hand captured the back of my neck and pulled me closer, his mouth close enough to mine that I could taste his breath on my lips. My eyes met his, and I could read so much emotion through them as he sent those feelings down the bond.

Warmth.

Love.

Want.

I could sense through the bond his growing need as his eyes narrowed, his lips parting. His gaze held mine for another moment, the tension so taut between us it was electric before he captured my mouth with his.

"You are so fucking perfect," he murmured against my lips, sliding his tongue into my mouth.

I groaned in response, warmth pooling in my core as one hand held the back of my neck, his other slowly moving down my back. When he reached the hem of my shirt, he slipped his hand underneath, splaying his warm palm against my back.

I leaned into him, tasting him back and nipping at his bottom lip. I pulled back, a slow bead of blood forming where I had bitten him.

"You know I love that," he said, his gaze filled with longing as his tongue shot out to lick the blood off. "So, so, wicked."

His hands gripped the hem of my T-shirt and pulled it up over my head, our bodies pressing together once more. My fingers found the hem of his and we pulled away from each other only long enough for me to slip it over his head.

My lips found his chest, and I tasted his skin there, kissing each tattoo across his neck, his collarbone, his chest, his arms. I wanted to taste all of him. He did the same to me. It was like we couldn't get enough of each other.

I wanted him to fill every void in me, every crack and every break filled with his love. Repaired by each kiss he placed against my skin. Donika hadn't broken me, not entirely, but there were fractures. Places where I had let her inside, fissures that were small but deadly.

Every time Nik's lips tasted my skin they closed, one by one, as if when he was finished, I would be whole once more. When he burned, I burned. When I hurt, he hurt. We were one and the same now, two pieces of the same whole.

We were bound.

I pushed him down against the silk sheets of the bed, and he smiled up at me. I leaned over him, unbuttoning his jeans and sliding them down his muscular legs, stopping to remove his shoes, too. I didn't want anything between us at all. I wanted to come together as one.

His length strained against his briefs as he propped his hand behind his head, the picture of relaxation. I moved to crawl on top of him, but he held out his other hand, gesturing for me to wait.

"I want to see you."

He wanted to devour me with his eyes. Every inch of me. When he looked at me like that, lust and love filling his gaze, who was I to deny him?

I slowly unbuttoned my pants, my gaze holding his. As I slid them down my legs, he never broke eye contact. When I pushed my panties down my legs and stepped out of them, his eyes were still on mine. His gaze finally broke as I reached behind me and unclasped my bra, my breasts popping free.

He watched me hungrily, his gaze studying every inch of me. He memorized the way my hair fell back behind my shoulders. My collarbone—my peaked, perfectly pink nipples. The freckles on my arms. The muscles on my abdomen. All the way down to my toes.

"Have you had your fill?" I asked, raising a brow at him.

When I had first been bare before him, I had been so nervous, so self-conscious. Now... I felt none of that. He gazed at me as if I were a goddess. The most beautiful thing he had ever seen.

"Never." His voice was raw, unbridled lust.

His gaze darkened as I climbed over him, straddling him. I could feel his cock straining beneath his briefs, pressing hard against my thigh. I was already so wet for him. I had never thought I could want someone this much in my life. I didn't just *want* him... I needed him.

He slipped a hand between my legs as I bent down to kiss him. I groaned against him as I rubbed against his hand, right where I wanted him. He slipped a finger inside of me and I threw my head back, a soft cry escaping my lips.

"So, so wet. That's my good girl." His voice was a whisper against my skin as I rode his fingers, the feeling of him inside of me so good, but not enough.

I wanted to feel all of him, all night long.

He flipped us over, his fingers never leaving me as he pressed down over me. He used his thumb to work my most sensitive place while he pumped his fingers in and out of me. When he removed his fingers, he licked them slowly, one by one, tasting me.

"Nikolai—" His name was a moan on my lips as I pushed at his briefs with my legs around his hips.

He laughed against me as I slipped my hand inside of them, grasping him. I would never get over the feel of him. The size of him. He was so hard against me and I pumped his length, his lips parting and his eyes closing. I pushed his briefs down his legs using my own and he kicked them off, leaving nothing between us now.

I placed him at my entrance and he needed no coaxing. He plunged into me and I arched my back off the bed, crying out at the sensation of him filling me so fully. He pulled back slowly, until only the tip was inside of me, then pushed back again all the way to the hilt. He filled me up so deliciously, as if I was made just for him.

He pumped in and out of me roughly and I held on, my legs clasped around his back, my hands on his shoulders. My head fell back with a cry when he hit that spot, the spot only he knew how to find. I hadn't even been able to on those nights when he was gone and I had found my hand between my own legs late at night, thinking of him.

"Fuck, Diana—" He watched me beneath him, writhing in pleasure.

"Harder," I whispered against his shoulder, my eyes falling closed.

My wish was his command.

He set a punishing pace, and I loved every second of it. His cock felt so, so good plunging in and out of me, and I was doing nothing to quiet my screams. We hadn't thought to spell the bedroom, but not even a trickle of embarrassment lanced through me at the thought of the entire cottage hearing the screams Nikolai was wringing out of me.

"I want to watch you ride me." His voice was against my ear as he grabbed my hips, turning us over once more.

I sat up, my hands on his chest, my legs straddling him. His hands fell to my thighs, his eyes on me, reverent.

"That's it, just like that," he said as I began to move.

I slid up and down, rocking my hips forward with each movement so that my own pleasure crested. My mouth fell open, eyes squeezing shut.

"Not yet baby, not yet." His voice was all breath now.

He watched me ride him, my breasts bouncing as he took them in his hand, squeezing. He leaned forward, capturing my nipple in his mouth. He swirled his tongue, biting at the sensitive tissue there. My head fell back in another cry of pleasure as he sucked.

I had half expected it to feel like a goodbye when we came together tonight, but this didn't feel anything like that.

It felt like a beginning.

He leaned back against the bed once more, his lust filled gaze watching me as I rocked my hips, back and forth. Up and down. Back and forth. I increased my speed and his breaths were coming more rapidly. I leaned back, reaching behind me to cup him and he pressed his eyes closed, almost falling over the edge.

"Not yet." I chuckled. Now it was my turn to tease him.

He laughed, his eyes still pressed together in concentration.

"You are so Goddamn sexy, do you know that?" he asked, sitting up once more and wrapping his arms around me.

My hands fell to his shoulders as I continued to ride him ruthlessly, the bed squeaking beneath us, my chest pressed up against his.

"I love you." I breathed the words into his mouth as his hand captured my cheek.

"I love you." He whispered back against my lips. "*You're mine.*"

Those words had me breaking apart.

He slid his hand between us and worked against me as I finished, falling over that edge of pleasure and crying out louder than I ever had before. My hair was a mess, tangled and coated in sweat behind me. He gathered it in his hand and pulled my head back, exposing my neck to him as I came down from the high. He kissed me gently at first, then he bit the skin across my neck and I let him know how much I loved it with my cries and soft whimpers. He held my head back as his mouth captured my breast again, his hips driving up into me as he chased his own pleasure.

Each thrust was heaven. When he drove up into me for the final time, filling me with himself, I came with him again, my mouth on his shoulder, biting down. My fingernails raking across his back. We would be bruised and bloody tomorrow and would certainly need to administer some skin spells if we didn't want anyone asking questions.

He had taken me rough before, but never like this. I *loved* it. *Craved* it. Every inch he would give me, I would take. I slid off his lap and went to the washroom, casting my gaze behind me as I went.

He was against the bed, spent, his hair pushed back from his face, and I had never seen anything I had loved more in my entire life. I made quick work of using the washroom, fixing my hair and splashing water on my face to rejoin him in bed.

I curled against him, sleep taking him quickly with the satin sheets pooled around his waist.

I had thought that sleep would evade me with the amount of anxiety I had been harboring all day, but when I closed my eyes against Nik's chest, his arm wrapped around me, all I felt was peace.

When sleep did finally take me, I didn't dream of the battle to come.

My only dreams were of his hair.

His eyes.

His mouth.

And that wicked, wicked tongue.

38

I woke fully rested for the first time in months. Nik was curled around my side, the dawn sky softly illuminating the bedroom as we lay tangled in the sheets. We woke and dressed wordlessly, stealing kisses and touches here and there.

There was nothing to be said.

Today we would march on Akra, and in two days' time Donika would be dead.

Or we would be.

I strapped Stormslayer to my thigh, stashing my throwing knives in my boots as well. I had always planned to take a sword too, but Nik wordlessly held his out to me.

"You want me to take yours?" I asked, my brow quirked at him.

He nodded, his gaze meeting mine. "So a piece of me will be with you when you face her."

I gripped the front of his jacket and pulled him towards me, capturing his mouth with mine. I would never get enough of the taste of his lips. The touch of his skin against mine.

He helped me secure it to my back, adjusting the strap to fit me. He disappeared to grab another blade from the weapons room down the hall to strap onto himself. We secured our packs and ascended the staircase towards the upper cottage for the last time, meeting the others out front.

Zion, Annelise, Alastir, and Amiyah were already out here waiting for us. Zion gazed at the cottage wistfully, as if it were the last time he would set eyes on the home. I knew how much it meant to him, and what it represented. It was his haven after the War of Siraleth. It was the home he raised Donika in. The home he fell in love with Annelise in. These walls had seen so many of the moments that had built his life.

It wouldn't be the last time he saw it if I had anything to do with it.

Saanvi and Kenna joined us and each pulled me into a hug, wishing me speed and luck in the battle to come. They hugged each other fiercely, and tears stung the back of my eyes. Kenna had almost lost Saanvi once already, and there was no guarantee we would all make it out of this battle alive.

I wanted my family to finally feel safe. I didn't want them to worry about whether they would come home again, whether they would ever see a loved one again. Whether they would be captured and tortured simply for the magic they were born with.

Tomorrow, I would fight for each one of them.

Tess and Puck joined us at last, Tess gripping me tightly. Puck gave me a gruff hug and mussed my hair with his gloved hand, laughing when it clung to me with static electricity. I gazed around at each of them, thanking the Mother for bringing them into my life. For allowing me to feel so supported and loved in these past months. That no matter what happened now, I would never be alone again.

The corner of my mouth turned up in a half smile at Zion who nodded, starting off towards the plains of Siraleth. We would meet the army of the resistance right before the two columns that reached up into the clouds—the entryway to Prins.

There was no haste to the pace which we set, as if we were walking towards something we didn't truly want to, but rather needed to. I was anxious to get this over with, but I wasn't anxious for what would come first.

Blood would be spilled on both sides tomorrow.

It was Puck who broke the silence as we walked. "It's too bad we can't march against Donika on horses, it would be so much more badass."

Nik laughed, shaking his head. His golden hair fell into his eyes. "Have you ever seen a horse in The Shadow?"

Tess tilted her head as if she were truly thinking about it.

Nik playfully punched Puck in the arm. "There are horses north of The Shadow and there are horses south of The Shadow. You try taking a horse down those steps."

"I never thought of it that way," Puck mused, his hand on his chin as he gazed off, deep in thought.

I couldn't help but laugh.

I was reminded of how things had been mere months ago, when winter had just begun and we had met Nik and Puck for the first time. The stakes were much less then, and everything was so... simple. Puck had always been the comedic relief of the group, and I hoped that never changed.

"I think if we really needed to, we could get a horse into The Shadow," he finally announced.

"But how many?" Nik countered. "If we were all to ride horses into battle... it just doesn't make sense, Puck. Think about it."

"Ok... then we get horses north of The Shadow. Simple."

"Sure... we will just buy a battalion of horses as if we come across that every day." Nik slung his arm around his shoulder. "I think you're going to need to let this one go."

"I'm only trying to see how we can make this more... epic," Puck replied.

"I think this will be epic enough without the horses, boys," Tess replied, rolling her eyes.

She was right about that. If the battle at Prins had shown us anything, this was going to be the fight of our lives.

Mist still clung heavily to the early morning air, and the scent of battle was tangible. It smelled of... hope. And fear. All mixed into one.

As we approached Prins, I could see the twin spires in the distance, and what lay beyond had me stopping dead in my tracks.

There were hundreds of Shades filling the planes of Sir-aleth.

No, not hundreds. *Thousands.*

I had never seen this many Shades in one place at the same time. My breath escaped me as if the air was physically pressed out of my lungs, my hand flying to my throat.

The resistance.

For all this talk of the resistance, we had scattered the numbers across the realm in hopes that we could keep pockets of us hidden. I had met many members of the resistance before, and fought alongside others, but I had never seen the force of them together before my eyes.

It was formidable.

Shades upon Shades filled the plains, leather gear adorning their bodies, blades strapped across their chests and at their waists. I recognized a few faces from the safe houses we had visited in Prins, and others from the battle. But the majority of the force I had never seen before, and I had no words for the amount of gratitude I felt seeing them in this moment.

Isaac and Zion at the head of the resistance had gathered a force that would rival Donika's. A force that would fight for the rights of every Shade in the realm. I bit my lip and tilted my head back, pushing back the tears that threatened to spill over.

Isaac should be here for this. He should have gotten to see this force with his own eyes. This was his work, after all.

Tess came up beside me, looping her arm through mine and grasping my hand in hers, giving it a reassuring squeeze.

Every Shade before us had been wronged by Donika, or knew someone who had. Had either been tortured by her or had hidden for over a decade in hopes of escaping her notice. Among these numbers were Stormshades who could never reveal their magic in their own home. There were Night-shades who had allied with the Stormshades in the War of Siraleth. There were Shades who were forced to pick sides or be murdered along with the others.

A sea of brown and black leather stood before me in the morning mist of Siraleth and I couldn't help but feel completely overwhelmed with emotion and gratitude.

Zion came up behind me, placing a hand on my other shoulder opposite Tess.

"You should say something." His voice was soft in my ear.

"Me?" My voice cracked as I turned towards him, eyes wide. "They don't—they don't even know me. I'm only a figurehead, something they could imagine when they thought of a better realm. A better life."

Zion shook his head. "You are much, much more than that. You are their leader. Their *queen*. They will look to you to rally them into battle."

"But they know you," I argued, "I've never even met most of them."

"That doesn't matter," Zion replied. "What matters is that you are here, and you have fought for their freedom as valiantly as they have. That you belong here, and that your blood is the rightful blood on the throne. Donika might be a Kotova, but she is not of the blood of Osiris. She is a usurper. You will usher in a new era in Istmere, one we have not seen in a long, long time."

My gaze flitted to Tess who gave me an encouraging smile, releasing my arm and giving it one last squeeze.

"How do I—" but my words were cut off as Nik snapped his fingers and a stone dais appeared before us in the grass.

"Is that… " I turned to him, brow raised.

"The dais from The Stone Palace?" he asked, shrugging his shoulders. "Shapeshifter magic. I had to take from somewhere, and it's the only platform I've ever seen with my own two eyes. I figured Donika wouldn't miss it."

I shook my head at him, a soft smile on my lips.

A hand grasped my shoulder and turned me. I was face-to-face with Annelise, her hand extended towards me.

"A skin spell, for amplification," she said, nodding at my forearm.

I nodded wordlessly.

She took my arm, rolling the sleeve up to my elbow before closing her hand around my wrist, a spell on her lips. When she opened her eyes and stepped away, a black rune marked my forearm. It quickly turned a charcoal color, then faded to grey. She nodded towards the dais and stepped back.

I steeled myself, inhaling deeply before slowly ascending the steps of the dais. I had never walked these steps before, but my blood had been spattered at their feet. Nik's hands raised and his shadows slithered out into the crowd.

A hushed silence fell among them, their attention turning towards me.

I was awkward and uncomfortable on the dais… who was I to claim the throne? To walk this dais and speak to these people? But my gaze fell on Zion, then Annelise. Alastir, Amiyah, Saanvi then Kenna. Puck, Tess, Nikolai. They all smiled at me from the grass below in reassurance.

I cleared my throat, and the sound echoed off the mountains in the distance. That was… quite the amplification spell Annelise had inked into my skin.

My eyes met the gazes of each of the Shades before me, and I searched what I could make out of their faces beneath the morning mist before I cleared my throat once more to speak.

"You might not know me—" my voice was tense as I cleared my throat once more. "You might now know me, but I know each of you, even if we have never met. I know that Donika has ruled this realm with an iron fist for too long. I know that she has tortured you, murdered your loved ones. Your family. Your friends. She murdered my father."

Whispers broke out in the crowd as I continued.

"My father Osiris wasn't a perfect man. He, too, fought to eliminate Stormshades from the realm. But I stand before you, blood of Osiris, blood of Kotova. *I am a Stormshade.*"

The whispers swelled as I confirmed what everyone had already suspected. That I was the last Stormshade of the Kotova bloodline, the one prophesized to lead them into battle. It appears Alastir wasn't the only one privy to the prophecy from the Mother.

"Donika may be my half sister, but there is no love lost. She has tortured me. Tried to kill me. Tried to steal my magic to use as her own. She has taken, and taken, and taken from me and I will not allow her to take any more!"

At this, claps rang out in the crowd as well as a few shouts.

"Istmere should be safe for *all* Shades. Nightshade, Stormshade, and Shade alike. We shouldn't need to hide who we are or choose sides simply to survive. Tomorrow... we will march The Stone Palace and take back what is *ours!*"

Swords clanged together and cheers rang out in the crowd. My face was flushed as I pulled my own blade free from the scabbard at my back and raised it in the air. I could sense my magic pumping through my veins as if it were my blood, my sustaining life force. Nik sent warmth down the bond and I glanced down at him, my eyes filled with amethyst magic.

I let thunder clap loudly overhead, joining the chorus of the resistance. Blue lightning struck the ground behind me, illuminating me in bright light. I released a little more magic, the clouds swirling overhead in a mixture of grey, white, and black.

"Tomorrow, we will bring an end to the tyranny that has *suffocated* this realm. Tomorrow, *we will take back the throne!*"

The crowd roared, raising their swords to match mine, silver blades cutting the air before me. My eyes brimmed with tears as I stared out at the crowd. The mist had risen, allowing me to see soldiers lined up as far as the eye could see.

There were Stormshades just like me in this crowd, and an open show of magic was something they had never had the chance to experience in their lifetime. Lightning struck again behind the dais before I reeled the magic in, the sun peering out behind the clouds.

"Tomorrow... we fight for every Shade who has been persecuted, tortured, or murdered. Tomorrow... we fight for a better future."

The cheers from the crowd were deafening, and the tears that brimmed in my eyes threatened to spill over. In this moment, I felt more hope than I ever had since arriving in Istmere. These people deserved a better future, and I would fight to give it to them.

"Tomorrow, we dethrone the malicious queen of Istmere once and for all! To Istmere!"

"To Istmere!" The crowd roared.

I thrust Nik's sword into the air and allowed a bolt of lightning to escape its blade, shooting across the sky. Nik rushed the dais and grabbed me, pulling me against him, his lips on mine.

"To the true queen!"

"To Diana!"

"To Istmere!"

The calls of the resistance filled my ears as Nik kissed me. When he released me, I steadied myself, trying to catch my breath. My hand rest against his chest as I gazed out at the resistance.

I wanted to memorize the feel of their power. The hope that was tangible among the crowd. The tears of happiness that fell from their faces and tracked down their cheeks. I would remember this moment until my end of days, and I did my best to sear it into my memory.

Tomorrow, we would fight for freedom.

And we would win.

39

When I stepped down from the dais it disappeared behind me, returning to the throne room in Akra. Magic pulsed through my veins, excitement pushing my heart to beat faster. The crowd parted as I walked among them, towards the front of the group.

Zion had done well when he had stepped into Isaac's shoes. He rallied a force I could never have imagined in my wildest dreams. As the crowd parted for me to pass, they dropped to their knees, bowing their heads before their true queen.

It was the first time I had felt like a queen in earnest. I was the daughter of Osiris, heir to the throne, and this army was *mine*. I led the troops through the docks of Prins, towards The Shadow.

The streets were empty.

The shops boarded up.

No laundry hung from the balconies of the town homes here—no taverns had patrons spilling out of them.

Prins was quiet.

We approached The Shadow as an army and descended the steps. I noticed more and more Shades leaving their homes to join our force. Shades were spilling out onto the streets to join us, to march against Donika.

With my magic bound and an army at my back, I had never felt so powerful. When we made our way out of The Shadow and the merchant district of Prins was behind us, we stopped to rest before the plains of Akra.

Donika wouldn't be able to see our force from here, but if she still had spies in the city—which I'm sure she did—she would know we were coming. We set up camp outside of the forest before the castle, pitching tents and starting fires to cook food and keep the troops warm under the frosty night air.

Summers in Istmere truly were unpredictable.

As I helped Nik set up our tent, I saw someone join Annelise and Amiyah out of the corner of my eye. It was Fleur, the woman from the tavern in Akra. The one who had given me a free meal when I had been battered and bruised, after I had escaped the house of Noctani I was being held captive in. The one who wore the glamour.

She shot me a wink before disappearing into the crowd.

Even the most unlikely of folks had joined our force in the end. I still couldn't believe we had managed to sway Alastir into battle after they had tried to get him to join the resistance for over a decade. Donika would surely be surprised when she saw him at my side when we stormed the castle. She likely hadn't seen him since the day she murdered my father.

We had each pitched our tents and retired for the night, excitement stirring the air and making sleep an intangible thing. I lay beside Nik on the bedroll he had laid out for me, surrounded by the resistance. I had never felt so safe, despite the construction of the tent being questionable at best. Nik had tried his best, but we all had our weaknesses.

As if reading my thoughts Nik threw his head back against his makeshift pillow and laughed. "What can I say, building tents isn't my strong suit."

I quirked a brow at him. "I thought you were good at everything?"

"We are safely out of the cold night air... are we not?" he asked, pulling me against him.

I buried my face in his neck, running my fingers through his hair.

"I wish you could be with me tomorrow."

He sighed heavily against me. "Me too. It isn't too late to change the plan—"

I cut him off with a deadpan glare. "You know why we have to be separate. It's the same reason Zion and Annelise have to be separate. The binding doesn't only bind our magic... it binds our *lives*."

Nik nodded. "I know, I know." He ran his hand along my shoulder blade, rubbing the muscles that had formed into a knot there. "I just wish I could be by your side, that's all. I hate to be apart from you."

I sent a wave of warmth down the bond and Nik tilted his head to gaze down at me. "You'll always be with me as long as we are connected," I told him. "It might not be words… but you'll know if I'm ok."

The corner of Nik's mouth raised in a half smile. "The moment it's over you'll come find me?"

I nodded against him. "Of course. Or you'll find me. The moment it's over."

We still had the obstacle of the immortality spell not being broken to contend with, but we had all decided that was a bridge we would cross when we came to it. Annelise had assured us she would figure out a way to transfer the spell, though she hadn't any luck with that yet. I didn't want Amiyah taking it on herself merely because she was blood. I didn't want anyone else to be linked to that sliver of Donika's soul. I didn't want her to take down anyone else in her desperate attempt at immortality. The only solution I could live with was capturing one of Donika's drones and allowing them to bear the burden.

I knew I needed rest, but sleep eluded me. Nik offered to add a sleep spell to my skin, but I refused. I didn't want to risk being groggy in the morning—I needed to be at my sharpest. It was the middle of the night before I finally fell into a fitful sleep, and only a matter of hours later woke to the clatter of the rising camp.

Nik and I assembled our packs and deconstructed his poor excuse for a tent. We stashed our packs in the forest, needing to travel lean from here on out. Once we made it onto the plains of Akra before the castle we would split off, Nik towards Donika's force on the open fields, me towards the mountain pass.

Zion had introduced me to the resistance members who would accompany me into the castle, and I was confident in his choices. A few of them I recognized from the battle at Prins, and I gave them my thanks for offering to travel with me into the secret passageways. Our task would be simpler in a way, but also more dangerous. We knew Donika would have a contingent of Noctani protecting her, and we needed to avoid them stealing our magic at all costs.

We still had one antidote we could use, but we had no plans of using it today. We didn't have the time, and we couldn't take the risk. We needed to bring down Donika and her army as quickly as possible—before the casualties stacked up.

The camp became eerily quiet as everyone packed their things, preparing for battle. The sun had barely risen and cast the camp in a pink glow. I wasn't sure if it was an ominous sign from the Mother or merely a coincidence.

"Red in the morning, sailors take warning," Tess breathed at my shoulder, her hand on the hilt of the sword at her waist.

I glared at her. "Thank you for that, Tess."

"I'm just saying," she replied with a shrug, backing up with hands raised.

I raised my own hand, flame swirling easily in my palm. "Have you so easily forgotten that *I* control the weather now?"

"That's right!" She patted me on the back hard enough that I took an involuntary step forward. "Powerful Stormshade and all that."

I rolled my eyes at her. Leave it to Tess to try to lighten the mood.

Though it was quiet, the atmosphere wasn't grim at camp. We were on the precipice of something, and the waiting was the worst part. This could go one of two ways, and the anxiety was palpable in the air. I had expected the quiet that had descended to bring with it a sense of calm, but it was the opposite. Electricity was a tangible thing, permeating everything and everyone.

As an army we bled into the forest under the cover of the rising sun. There was no way to hide our forces now. I gripped Stormslayer in my fist as the sun rose before us, reaching up into the sky to illuminate the marching resistance below.

Nik and Tess were at my side, the others fanning out behind me. An army of leather clad Shades in brown and black, willing and ready to take back what was rightfully theirs. As we approached the tree line, a feeling that we were being watched settled over me. I turned behind me to gaze at Kenna, and she wordlessly shifted into a crow and took to the sky.

She called out overhead as she swooped over the trees, towards the iron spires that rose in the distance. The Stone Palace appeared formidable from here, its black points reaching up into the morning sky. It was surrounded on the mountain by civilian homes, who would have the perfect view of the battle should they choose not to join in the melee.

Kenna came back in a whirlwind of feathers and claws, landing abruptly on my shoulder. She tilted her head to the side, one call escaping her narrow beak.

Donika was waiting for us.

I gave her a curt nod, and she pushed off my shoulder, taking flight once more.

I pulled on the magic in my core, allowing it to drift down my arms and out of my fingertips. The sky darkened with magic overhead, inky clouds swirling angrily against the pink dawn sky. It was only a matter of moments before the light was swallowed whole and we were plunged into the dark.

I moved forwards, casting the plains in darkness as I emerged from the trees, my gaze immediately latching onto Donika. She stood on the same balcony I had seen her on the last time I had been dream walking, where I had left the token as a magical tether should I ever need to come back.

Her army was fanned out beneath her, a sly smirk on her lips that I could see even from this distance. I couldn't wait to wipe it off her face with my blade.

Thunder cracked loudly overhead, the ground beneath us shaking. Some of her forces appeared rattled, glancing between one another as I funneled more magic into the storm than I ever dared before. They had never seen storm magic at work—they had never seen a Stormshade without iron shackles, cowering in the Stormvault.

But I wasn't *any* Stormshade.

I was a Stormshade of the Kotova bloodline in all her glory, bristling with power, and the storm that roared above us was *mine*.

I stepped across the threshold of trees and onto the open plains of Akra, the storm raging deafeningly overhead. Lightning coursed through the sky, sending torrents of dirt flying. Rain began to pour down overhead, and I turned my face towards the sky, a smile across my lips. I pushed the storm outward, expanding it. I could see Annelise out of the corner of my eye, her hand raised to the sky, her own magic intertwining with mine.

I narrowed my eyes at Donika from across the field, allowing lightning to streak through the sky dangerously close to her balcony. I tilted my head to the side, watching.

Waiting.

I knew Donika would make the first move, and she did. With a nod of her head dark figures shot out from the back of her army, gaining speed quickly from the left and right.

Araneoch.

She cast her gaze back down towards me for one more moment before spitting over the edge of the balcony. She turned, her black cloak wafting behind her, as she disappeared into the castle.

So predictable.

So cowardly.

I moved to follow but Nik grabbed my wrist, holding me back. Now was my time to move, and I didn't want to lose my window. My mind was only focused on one thing right now—vengeance thrumming powerfully through my blood.

That was, until Nik shot a sensation so hot down the bond it threatened to scorch the grass I stood on. He gripped the back of my neck and brought his mouth down to mine, tasting me one last time. My lips crushed against his, my fists gripping his leather jacket with my arm that held Stormslayer crushed between us. He kissed me so fiercely, sending that heat down the bond the entire time, claiming me in front of everyone.

When he finally broke apart from me I was panting, my lips swollen and red. My skin was flushed from the magic he had marked me with... as was his. I hadn't even realized I had been sending just as much magic back down the bond the other direction towards him.

The thunder exploded overhead, the storm descending into a deluge of rain. Raindrops fell from the angry black sky, kissing my cheeks as I held Nik's glacial blue eyes with mine for one long moment.

Finally, he dropped his hand from my neck, taking a step back.

"I love you." His voice was gruff. Raw. Unfiltered emotion pouring through the words.

"I love you, too." My own voice was ragged in return.

As much as this felt like a goodbye, I would make damned sure it wasn't one.

My only consolation was that if I went down during battle—or if he did—we would go down *together*. I shook my head to clear the thought. I wouldn't entertain that kind of negativity. We would come out of this victorious.

There was no other option.

I committed to memory the exact shade of blue that glimmered in his eyes. The texture of that golden hair I loved to run my fingers through so much. The freckles that bridged across his nose. The strong jaw that my fingers had already memorized the feel of.

He gave me one last reassuring smile, that dimple creasing his right cheek, before he shifted into his wolf form. He nodded his head once towards me, human blue eyes surrounded by a mountain of coarse black fur. My gaze lingered on him for one more moment before I turned away from him.

Away from the resistance.

Away from my friends and family.

Towards the very person that had threatened to take it all away from me.

40

The storm overhead roiled angrily—the sky streaked with dark, furious clouds. Lightning flashed through the sky with explosions of light as our group made our way through the forest, towards the mountain pass that would bring us to the back of the castle. I had let go of the storm raging above—it wasn't mine any longer. The Stormshades of the resistance could use it to pull energy from during the battle.

As we approached the edge of the thicket, the distant sounds of clashing blades and cries filled my ears. I pressed my eyes together, sending one last prayer to the Mother to keep my loved ones safe. Tess grasped my shoulder, and my gaze met hers with a question in my eyes. She didn't speak, only squeezed in reassurance. She had faith that I could do this. That I would get through what lay ahead. I knew in a matter of moments adrenaline would take over, pumping through my veins and driving me forward.

I relished my last moments of silence.

Despite every warning in my body telling me to turn back as the sounds of battle drifted towards my ears, I didn't. I pushed forward. Annelise led us towards the portcullis that led to the secret chambers beyond. It was open, the extinguished lantern resting at the entrance. Just as we had left it when we escaped the Stormvault.

I adjusted my grip on Stormslayer, wiping the sweat off my palms as we followed Annelise into the shadows. Alastir brought up the rear with Amiyah, Puck and Tess at my side. I had only a brief chance to meet the other resistance members that would follow us into the castle, but I thanked them for their bravery. While we weren't out on the battlefield facing Donika's forces, we were facing the villain head on.

This was arguably the more dangerous mission.

We ascended the first set of stairs and the sounds of battle trailed off in the distance until I could hear nothing at all except the soft breaths escaping me as my heart rate increased. We passed through the round room we had met Zion in that day we had escaped, passing through the passages single file until we reached the next antechamber. We had been lucky that we hadn't run into anyone thus far.

I found it hard to believe Donika still hadn't found the secret passages after we had escaped the castle. A suspicion settled in my gut that perhaps she *had*, and she was leading us directly into a trap. Letting us infiltrate the castle only to be slaughtered.

The hairs on the back of my arms rose as I watched the shadows of Annelise and the resistance members traverse the narrow passageways ahead of me by lantern light. Their silhouette's cast against the stone walls hauntingly.

I wasn't as familiar with the different parts of the castle having only been taken from the Stormvault to the throne room. Almost every time I was moved, I had been drugged and blindfolded.

Annelise knew the halls of this castle like the back of her hand—this had been her home once. She led us down the last stretch of hallway that would take us to the main part of the castle, but instead of passing through the secret doorway Puck had initially led us through, we took a sharp right.

The chamber narrowed here, and I cast my gaze backwards to ensure we were all safely filing into the passage. I was in the middle of the pack now, protected in case we were to be ambushed.

We had successfully breached the castle.

Step one in the plan was effectively in place.

I had no idea where we were headed now and had to trust that Annelise knew the way. We didn't know for certain where Donika would be hiding, but we had a hunch it would be the throne room. She would want to protect her throne at all costs, we suspected she was too proud to leave it unguarded.

We reached a hidden doorway and Annelise pressed her ear against it, listening. She brought a single finger to her lips, signaling for us to be as quiet as possible. I all but held my breath as she listened, her eyes narrowed.

I raised my brow at her in question.

She shook her head.

She couldn't hear anything in the chamber beyond. I tilted my head at her in question.

"The only way to find out, is to open the door," she whispered, despite the sound insulation the thick rock provided.

I adjusted my grip on Stormslayer. Setting my jaw, I nodded.

As soon as Annelise pressed against the door and the click of it opening could be heard echoing through the chamber, I rushed forward to slip through the narrow opening. Tess followed—Puck close on her heels as well as the rest of our group as we poured through the entryway.

I skidded to a stop on the familiar black-and-white marble checkered floor. That floor my blood had been spilled on *so many* times before.

The throne room was empty.

I turned back, my brow furrowed at Annelise as she surveyed the room, her sword held out before her. She approached the dais, searching for any marks that a spell had been cast, that maybe Donika was cloaking herself. Annelise turned back to me, her head moving back and forth in a finite shake.

Donika wasn't here.

Her throne sat atop the dais, unoccupied.

Unprotected.

The red velvet that adorned the seat was brighter than I had ever seen it. The marble sparkled as if it had been freshly scrubbed.

Confusion swarmed my thoughts as I turned. There was nowhere for her to hide. The room was long and narrow, windows with thin red drapes adorning them lining the walls. The throne and the dais were the only furniture in the room.

"Where is she?" I muttered.

Right as Annelise opened her mouth to reply to me, the throne room doors burst open. I was expecting Donika herself—a devilish grin across her lips—but the person who sauntered in was not the one that I expected.

He held his sword out before him, a breastplate signifying the queen's army strapped to his chest. A cloak was tied around his neck, billowing out behind him as he casually strolled in.

When my gaze traveled to his eyes, they were endless black.

He came to a stop halfway across the room from where I stood.

He set his jaw—feet apart—ready for battle.

I couldn't discern the amount of soldiers that filed in behind him, my only thought was that I was relieved he was the only Noctani among them. As they continued to fill the throne room a desperation settled deep in my core. I pulled on my magic, allowing it to travel to my fingertips, ready for when I called upon it.

Because I would need it.

It was no stranger who led Donika's forces towards us as we backed towards the dais... but one I was quite familiar with.

An expert swordsman.

One I had thought was dead.

Warrick didn't smile, he didn't even flinch as he set his shoulders, his expression determined.

Between one blink and the next, he moved.

41

Warrick's sword clashed with Puck's as he jumped in front of me, protecting me. I quickly slid Stormslayer back into the sheath at my thigh in favor of Nik's sword. I pulled it from the scabbard at my back just in time to clash with the blade of a Nightshade soldier from Donika's army. I grunted against the impact; the vibration traveling up my arms, my teeth clenching.

Donika had kept back more soldiers than we had projected, and as I had suspected… it was a trap. She wanted us to breach the castle walls. She *wanted* us to infiltrate the throne room. She had a force of Nightshade soldiers waiting for us.

There weren't so many that we couldn't defeat them, but there were certainly enough to keep us busy and to keep my fear singing in my blood. We needed to dispatch these soldiers and find Donika. Would she be in her personal chambers? Hiding like the coward she was?

I spun out of the way as the soldier brought his sword down towards me. It hit the marble floor with a spark; the soldier losing his balance and tipping forward. He hadn't expected me to be so fast. I took advantage of his slip and brought my sword up, swinging it towards the back of his head where the skin was exposed between his helmet and breastplate.

It lodged into his neck with a sickening thud and he fell to his knees. Blood spurted over me, coating my blade. I hadn't swung it with enough force to decapitate him entirely. Nik's sword was heavy, and I hadn't trained enough using it. I internally cursed myself as I pressed my foot against his shoulder, pulling the blade free. I swung once more, finishing the job. His head rolled to the marble floor, eyes fixed on the ceiling, unseeing.

"Diana!" It was Warrick's voice that roared from behind me.

I had no time to turn towards him. Another soldier was already upon me. This one was much smaller and faster than the first. He swung his blade, and it hit mine with a reverberating shock, but this time I had been expecting it. I pushed back with all my might, and he stepped back. I swung the blade down in the same moment, finding the sliver of skin exposed between his arm cuffs and hand. The hand holding his sword severed easily, falling to the throne room floor with a grotesque thump.

I had to stop myself from gagging as blood pooled around the stump, the soldier screaming out and grasping his now severed hand.

"Diana, I never meant for any of this to happen, but you brought this on yourself by coming here!" Warrick cried.

I turned to see him still locked in battle with Puck, and from the looks of it, they were evenly matched. Puck had never been able to defeat Warrick in our one-on-one training sessions, but Warrick was Noctani now. He was faster and stronger. He also had bruising across the back of his neck, the skin around his eye blackened. He had taken a beating—from who I wasn't sure—but if his fresh injuries were any indication, this wasn't his first battle of the day.

Another soldier stood between us, a smile on his lips. His lip was split open, blood coating his teeth as he peered down at me. He didn't swing first but rather came at me with his shoulder, trying to throw me off balance. I stepped back reluctantly, trying my best to keep my footing.

I swung my sword first, and he parried, holding off my blade. I hadn't had a chance to wipe it off, and it was still coated in the blood of the last two soldiers I had killed. The soldier let out a gruff moan as he pushed back, bringing his sword down again and again.

Each time I met his blows, surprise flitted over his expression. My fingers gripped Stormslayer, and I pulled the blade free from its sheath once more, gripping it tightly in my nondominant hand. When our blades clashed together once more, I used less power in my sword arm, allowing the soldier to fall towards me. Surprise flashed across his expression right before I plunged Stormslayer into his neck. Blood dripped from his mouth, coating his busted lip with fresh crimson.

He fell to his knees, gurgling.

I slid Stormslayer free and turned towards Warrick once more.

"He's mine," I ground out between my teeth.

Puck shot a glance at me over his shoulder as he watched me step up to them. He seamlessly backed away from Warrick, allowing me to step in.

"I didn't want it to come to this, Diana." Warrick's voice was strained.

"Too bad," I said, bringing my sword in an arc towards him. "I thought you were *dead.*"

He easily batted it away. Warrick was the one who had trained me, after all. After Nik. He knew my moves, and I knew his.

"I was," he ground out. "Diana, please. I need you to listen to me." His voice was pleading, and my brow creased in confusion.

"The time for talking has long past," I replied, my sword clashing powerfully with his.

His face was coated in blood and grime. Any light that had once been in his green eyes had been swallowed by darkness.

"How dare you wear her brand," I said, motioning towards the breastplate. "How dare you fight against us!"

I ducked low, swinging against the back of his knees. He quickly jumped out of the way before I could sever the back of his legs.

"I never wanted for any of this to happen," he cried, pushing towards me.

I shook my head as the level of emotion in his voice shocked me. I stepped back, mirroring his steps. "It doesn't matter what you *wanted*."

He stifled a sob as it tried to escape his throat. "I only wanted to save my family."

"*We* were your family. We could have helped them. There was never a chance in hell Donika would have given them back to you after you betrayed us. You are a *fool*. And now you are simply one of her monsters." My voice dripped venom as I let the sword fall to my side.

Warrick shook his head. "I didn't want any of you to risk yourselves to save them. Risk the resistance. I thought I was thinking about the bigger picture."

I narrowed my eyes at him. "Didn't want us to risk ourselves? But you were just as happy to turn us over to save them?"

He could see that I was backing him into a corner and his footsteps turned to the side, bringing us back towards the center of the throne room.

"That was never the plan. I wasn't going to turn you over to her. I wouldn't do that."

I raised a brow at him. "What do you think happened back there?" I asked. "You led her straight to us. And now? Now that you are *under her spell*?"

He laughed, but there was no humor in it. "I never wanted that. She *tortured* me!"

Spit flew from my mouth, my voice lethal as I cried back, "*I know all about Donika's torture, you fucking coward,* and not *once* did I give anyone up to save myself."

His black eyes dimmed, resigned. "Then you are stronger than I am," he replied.

I scoffed. "That's more than obvious. Torture is no excuse. *You betrayed us.* Turned your back on us. You'll meet your end at the tip of my blade."

Warrick swallowed hard as I brought my sword up again, moving towards him in earnest.

"What can I do to convince you?" he asked.

Pleaded. His voice was desperate.

"Nothing," I hissed, our blades clashing together again.

"She kept me here and tortured me, beat me. Turned me into this *monster*! Made me meet you here in the throne room. *I never wanted any of this.*"

"Made you? *No.* She didn't *make* you turn against us. Didn't *make* you battle us here, killing resistance members that you once called family. You *chose.* And you chose wrong. You are a coward and a liar."

When my blade met his again, he pressed me back, and I slipped against the blood-stained marble, scrambling to keep my footing. A sting pressed against my abdomen, right below my ribcage. My hand pressed against the flesh there, and when it came free, it was covered in fresh blood.

I narrowed my eyes in confusion.

Warrick's blade hadn't touched me.

I felt down the bond, but it was dull. As if I were wading through quicksand. A thick haze coated the emotions that were once so crystal clear.

Nik.

He was blocking me out.

He was injured.

I couldn't go to him. Couldn't run out onto the battlefield to protect him and make sure he was all right. I had to trust that the resistance would have his back, as they had mine.

If he died, I died.

We were wasting time. We needed to find Donika, and we needed to find her *now*.

Blood dripped from the wound to soak through my shirt, thickly coating my leather jacket.

Nik's wound was *my* wound.

Warrick stared at me—his mouth open. I used his distraction as my opening. I hit him across the shoulder with my sword and the blow took him by surprise. Before he could get his own sword up between us, I twisted to kick him, and he fell to his knees.

"I'll make it quick," I told him.

I raised Stormslayer between us.

His eyes fell on the blade, a soft smile crossing his lips.

He recognized it.

Recognized what it meant to me.

To Nik.

I glared down at him, my own emotions warring inside of me that Noctani could show such emotion. Such *humanity*. It went against everything we thought about them.

"Mother, forgive me," he whispered, right before I sliced Stormslayer across his throat.

42

Warrick fell to the marble tile before me, a pool of blood surrounding him as his black eyes turned green, right before they went still.

He was dead.

I had endured the same torture he had. I had experienced Donika's wrath first hand. Not once did I betray my loved ones to save myself. Not once did I give in to her. I had not let her break me. But she had broken Warrick.

I hoped wherever he was now, whether that was with the Mother or not, he was at peace. His magic would return to the earth all the same.

I wiped the blade across my jacket to clean it before securing it back to my thigh.

We had managed to kill the soldiers that had infiltrated the throne room, only losing one member of the resistance in the process. Annelise, Amiyah, Alastir, Puck, and Tess were all safe. I caught my breath, steadying myself as I glanced down at Warrick's lifeless body.

"You ok?" Annelise asked, sheathing her own sword in her scabbard.

I nodded, wiping my face. It came away bloody. At some point, I had split my lip, and it throbbed.

"What happened?" Tess asked, motioning to the wound at my abdomen that was no longer bleeding but had soaked through the fabric to leave behind a large wet mark.

"Nik," I explained. "He's injured."

"We better end this, then." Puck said, nodding towards Annelise. "Do you know where else she might be?"

Annelise thought for a moment before speaking, her eyes on the blood coated marble. "Her chambers? That's my next best guess."

"Do you know how to get there without taking the main hallways?" he asked.

I didn't relish the idea of traipsing around the castle hallways unprotected. Annelise nodded in response.

We followed her into the passage once more, closing the stone door between us and the carnage of the throne room.

Annelise led us forward through the corridor with the single lit lantern. Exhaustion wore deep in my bones, knowing we had another battle ahead of us. Donika was expecting us, but she had to have known that wasn't enough of a force to defeat us. She was likely hoping Warrick would tug on my heartstrings. But there was no love lost there. It was Warrick's fault that Nik was turned into Noctani. It was likely his fault that Isaac turned Noctani, too. Ultimately ending in his death.

His betrayal was no question in my mind.

We passed down the hallway towards a part of the castle I had never seen before, but I could sense the token I had left as if it were awakening. As if we were growing closer to it, and it sensed me and my magic.

It was a heartbeat, pulsing with growing intensity as we neared it. My magic recognized itself here. The balcony where I had left it must have been the balcony of Donika's personal chambers. She would have a firsthand view of the battlefield from there.

We ascended a set of steep stone stairs that were deteriorating to the point that I had to drag my hand along the wall to keep my footing. We weren't sure the stairs would hold all of us at once, so we went up them one at a time.

When we were all safely on the top landing, Annelise continued, only stopping when we reached an antechamber large enough for all of us to fit inside. She traced her hand along the wall until she met a stone that was loose. Her gaze met mine, and I gave her a nod before she pressed it.

The door swung inward—I raced forward into the room—sword at the ready.

The room beyond was familiar to me, having seen it in my dream walking. There was a vanity on the far wall, a four-poster bed with sheets draped across it in the center of the room beneath the crescent window. The balcony lay off to the right as well as the door to the washroom, which was closed.

The room was empty.

I approached the closed washroom door, my hand on the knob as I turned back. Annelise nodded at me, ready. I swung the door open and entered, but the bathroom was empty too.

My sword fell back to my side as I let out an exasperated groan. "Where is she!?"

Annelise's eyes roved over the room, taking in the delicate accents. I wasn't sure what I had expected the first time I had seen it... but this wasn't it. My gaze fell on the bed that Nik had once shared with her, and it felt as if a million little bugs were crawling all over my skin. I needed to get out of here.

Now.

"Where else would she be?" Puck asked, rejoining us at the center of the room after clearing the remainder of the space. "We need to move in case another force tries to ambush us like they did in the throne room. We already lost one soldier."

Annelise nodded, her gaze meeting mine. Her eyes were swimming with an emotion I couldn't quite name.

Was it regret?

"There's only one other place I can think of that might... mean something to her."

"And where's that?" I asked, sliding Nik's sword back into its scabbard.

"Osiris's old chambers."

I had been on my way back towards the hidden doorway, but her words halted me in my tracks. I turned back towards her, my arms limp at my sides. My chest was heavy.

"The room where you were born."

43

Tess let out a humorless laugh. "Of course... that makes the most sense. The room where you were prophesized to kill her. She wouldn't want it any other way. She would want that to be the room in which she killed you."

Annelise nodded, her lips pressed together in a thin line.

They were right.

It was almost... poetic. But I knew Donika hadn't chosen it for that reason. She wanted to take me out of this world in the exact place I was brought into it. Such an event would generate a *massive* amount of power. Power she could harness.

It was always about power with Donika.

No amount of power would *ever* be enough for her. She would first steal my magic, and then the magic my death generated.

Alastir raised a brow at Annelise. "The Mother prophesized *her* death, not Diana's."

Annelise nodded. "We have to trust that the Mother showed you the truth."

Alastir cleared his throat. "She has never shown me a falsehood, though she may not be the most forthcoming. She never shows me what I *want*, only what I *need*. In this, I am certain. The Mother has shown me that Diana will restore peace to Istmere."

"But at what cost?" Annelise asked.

Alastir swallowed hard. "The Mother did not show me the outcome. I do not know if Diana's life is the sacrifice that is required."

His words had me reeling back. "What do you mean?"

"My visions are not clear," he explained. "I do not know how the outcome will be reached, only that it *will be*. You will restore peace... but will it be because you kill Donika this day? I simply do not know."

Annelise opened her mouth to speak, but I moved back towards the opened stone chamber, interrupting her. "It's too late to go back now. Whatever happens, happens. We face Donika today and restore peace to Istmere one way or another. Whatever the outcome may be."

Puck and Tess joined me as we waited for the others.

Annelise's expression was sad as she joined us, sealing the door shut once more. We had no way of knowing what was about to happen, only what the Mother had shown Alastir. There was no point in dwelling on it now. Our forces were out on the battlefield *at this moment*, risking their lives fighting Donika's army and her demonic monsters to save this realm.

Today, we would end her rule of tyranny.

The mood was somber as we made our way to Osiris's old chambers, hoping we would strike luck at the third location. If Donika wasn't there... I wasn't sure where we would search for her next.

But there was a piece of me, deep down in my gut, that knew she would be there... waiting for us.

We descended the same set of stairs one at a time, rocks falling to the landing and disintegrating the structure even further. A few more passes and that particular passageway would be entirely unusable.

We passed through a long hallway and rounded a corner to the right before coming to a stop. There was no antechamber here, only a small piece of wood wedged into the stone. My hand found the wound on my stomach and I pressed against it, reaching down the bond to feel Nik.

I could feel him faintly, hear the distant sounds of metal clashing. Shades screaming.

There was a fire somewhere in his periphery, the rain that spit down around them was not enough to extinguish it.

He was *fighting*.

I swallowed hard, closing my eyes to steel myself.

Everything I had endured since finding out I was a Stormshade was about to culminate. Beyond this door... I would engage in the fight of my life. With my sister, no less. I would drive my blade through her flesh and end her reign. End the dark magic that trickled through her veins.

I took a deep breath, then another.

When I opened my eyes, Tess was before me, watching me. I gave her a reassuring smile, but it never reached my eyes. She nodded in understanding. Despite knowing what needed to be done, despite the anger and vengeance pumping through my own blood, I didn't relish it. Tess had been by my side through everything, and she would be by my side through this, too.

My gaze fell on Annelise and I could feel the love pouring out of her. I wasn't sure what was going to happen behind this door, because we still hadn't found a cure for Donika's immortality. A piece of Donika lived inside Annelise, and even if I killed her today, she wouldn't be *entirely* dead. Not while that piece of her still lived.

But it would buy us time.

All I needed was *more time.*

Time to figure out how to break the spell and release Annelise from the part of Donika's soul that clung to her. A tear slid down Annelise's cheek, and she moved her delicate hand to hastily wipe it away.

When she smiled at me, I could see her eyes burning with a memory from the last time she had been in this room.

I steeled myself one last time, swallowing back the fear that crawled up the back of my throat. When I opened my eyes once more, my gaze fell on Annelise with magic burning in my gaze.

I nodded.

Annelise moved forward, releasing the wooden wedge and swinging the door wide open.

44

As soon as the door opened, I rushed in, sword at the ready before me. I had been ready to leap into action... but the moment I scanned the room, I stopped. My feet frozen to the floor.

Donika lay across the wooden bed on the far wall, her legs crossed at the ankle, her back resting against the headboard. A wicked smile graced her lips. Her eyes narrowed at me. My attention had been drawn to her immediately, her position suggesting she wasn't even a little afraid of us.

And for good reason.

She was *surrounded.* I kept my gaze on her as I ticked off the Noctani out of the corner of my eye in my head.

One, two, three...

Four, five, six...

Seven, eight, nine...

We were evenly matched. Or... we would have been if we hadn't lost the resistance member among the bloodshed in the throne room. The remainder of her Noctani must be out on the battlefield with the Araneoch.

Donika moved slowly, her delicate legs flashing as she swung down from the bed, her blue chiffon skirt trailing behind her. She wasn't dressed for battle... no.

She was dressed like a queen.

I swallowed hard, my gaze focused on her as she crossed the room towards me.

"Ah, ah, ah... stay right there," Puck warned from behind me.

I didn't dare move my gaze from hers.

There were enough Noctani in this room to easily drain us all, stealing our magic and leaving us for dead. We needed to be careful. As we had expected... she hadn't surrounded herself with her normal Nightshade soldiers. She had saved only the best to serve as protectors for her. She never cared about the men who fought for her on the battlefield below... she only cared for herself and her own safety.

Donika quirked her brow at Puck. "I only need to give the word, and you'll be slaughtered where you stand. Don't think you can order me around in my own castle."

Her words were cold, voice cutting.

A prickling sensation settled over my skin as my magic surged forth of its own volition. I pressed it down carefully, letting it hum right beneath the surface of my skin. There was so much of it I practically expected my skin to be aglow when I glanced down.

The sun had made its ascent into the sky and it had to be midday, the rays of light peering in through the window and casting shadows across the floor. The storm still raged on outside, but the sun had managed to fight its way out despite it, peeking through the cloud covering. Donika stepped through those shadows, her heeled feet clicking against the worn wooden floorboards.

"So easy to predict you," Donika mused, her manicured fingers on her chin. "I knew you would check the throne room first, naturally. I would never be dumb enough to hide in my own chambers, either. But here?" She laughed, and the sound sent a cold shiver down my spine. I tightened my grip on Nik's sword.

She took another step closer, but I refused to step back. I would not cow before her.

She had imprisoned me in the Stormvault and tortured me, but she had not broken me then. She had turned Nik into a bloodthirsty, soulless monster... and that hadn't broken me, either. She had killed my father and countless resistance members, but still, she did not break me.

I was Diana Kotova... and I would *not* break today.

I was the most powerful Stormshade of the Kotova bloodline, and beneath a storm of my own creation, I would reclaim my throne.

My father's throne.

It had been stolen from us by someone only hungry for power, and today it would be returned. Istmere would be returned to peace once more.

Donika took another encroaching step.

"This room not only means something to you, Mother dearest, but it means something to me, too."

"And how is that?" Annelise asked, her voice strained.

I couldn't imagine how difficult it must be for Annelise to be here. This was the room in which Osiris cast her out of the castle. The room where I came into this world. So much pain had unraveled and endured inside these walls.

"Wouldn't you like to know?" Donika replied, a smirk lifting the corner of her mouth.

"Enough games, Donika. You know why we are here," I ground out.

Donika laughed once more, her head thrown back and her blue and white ombre hair shaking behind her.

"Little Stormshade, you are too funny. Of course I know why you're here. To defeat my army of trained Noctani and Nightshade soldiers and take your place as the rightful queen of Istmere. There is only one little problem... "

I knew she wanted me to ask what that problem might be... but I clamped my mouth shut, my teeth grinding together. I wouldn't give her the satisfaction.

She narrowed her eyes at me. "I have too many men for you to have any hope of defeating, of course."

She spread her arms wide, indicating the Noctani that lined the room around her. Thankfully, I didn't recognize any of them.

Zachariah and Corian were nowhere in sight.

"You think you have any hope of defeating them?"

She took another step.

"I have created the *perfect* Shade. Both more powerful *and* stronger. And the best part? They only take orders from *me*."

This had my mouth twitching into a smile of my own despite my best efforts to keep my face a mask. "Is that so?"

Donika's expression turned sour. She had to be thinking of Nik.

"Ah, my one failed experiment, yes." She shook her head. "Perhaps he would have been better off dead."

"Don't speak about him that way," I replied through my teeth. My jaw was aching from the tension.

"Or *what*?" She threw her head back and laughed once more. It was always a performance with Donika. She always put on a show.

My left hand twitched towards Stormslayer—Nik's blade still held firmly before me.

"He warmed my bed once, but I tired of him. Though I must say... playing with him while he was here in the castle really was a *treat*."

Anger simmered in my blood, my palms sweating. She was trying to get a rise out of me, and I couldn't let her. I needed to remain calm.

"I see another warms your bed, now. And what about poor Corian? I thought he was your second hand," I taunted.

The mention of what I had seen in my dream had her bristling. Her eyes, despite being endlessly inky black, were alight with a fire I had never seen before.

"Zachariah and Corian both have their uses," she mused.

I scoffed at this. Leave it to Donika to not only use her soldiers to fight for her, but for her own pleasure. Everyone was disposable to her, including her own family. People were merely pawns for her to move around the board as she saw fit.

"Enough of this," I spat, taking my own step towards her.

She raised her brow at me in surprise.

"Little Stormshade, none of it will matter in the end. Your forces are being slaughtered on the battlefield below. You will join those numbers soon enough." She shrugged, feigning nonchalance.

If I wasn't paying close enough attention, I would have missed the slight shake in her hand as she raised her fingers to inspect her manicure, shadows swirling around her blackened fingertips.

"You're right, Donika. None of it will matter... when you are *dead*."

She giggled, and for one mere moment, she sounded very, very young. "You think you can kill me?"

I inclined my head as I watched her with narrowed eyes. "I know I can."

I allowed my magic to spark through my fingers and the blade in my grasp illuminated with amethyst magic. Thunder cracked overhead so loudly the floorboards beneath us shook.

It was my turn to smile.

Donika's gaze flitted away for a mere moment, but not before I could read the confusion in her expression. She had to know of the binding ceremony, with our own mother being bound. Hadn't she ever wondered how Annelise had been able to use *and* control her own magic all these years without it swallowing her or betraying her?

Realization dawned in her gaze as her eyes darted towards the window.

She mustn't have known I had found myself a binding partner in Nikolai. She had underestimated our connection to one another. Did she also know the stipulation of the binding, that if I died, Nikolai would too? And that the same was true in reverse? If she could only kill Nikolai—which might be easier for her—that would solve her 'little Stormshade' problem.

I stepped into her field of vision, blocking her view of the window beyond.

"It's too late now." As soon as the words were out of my mouth, she gave a soft nod, and one of the Noctani moved to leave the room.

Alastir raised his hand, an incantation spilling forth from his lips before anyone else could so much as blink. In a matter of seconds, a glimmering ocher barricade encapsulated the doorway, pulsing.

"No one leaves." His voice was gruff when he spoke. "It ends here."

Donika's eyes sparked with recognition as she took him in for the first time.

"Alastir?" Her voice sounded... small.

Alastir set his jaw. He might be older, but he was one of the most powerful Shades in the realm. He was blessed by the Mother herself. Donika would have known him from when she was a soldier in Osiris's army, training at the academy with Alastir daily.

His expression was sad as he took her in. There was so much history there, passing between them. Donika had killed Osiris, his oldest friend. And now Alastir would help to avenge his murder by killing his protégé.

The Noctani who had tried to leave the room banged uselessly against the magical barrier before turning towards us, letting a hiss escape her fanged mouth.

Donika raised her hand, signaling for her to quiet. To wait.

Just as a trained dog might, the Noctani settled into submission, quietly taking her place back by the wall.

The tension in the room was palpable. The hairs on my arms were raised as Donika smiled to herself. Whispered words escaped her lips. I wasn't sure if they were a spell or a prayer. I wasn't sure she even prayed to the Mother at all anymore.

With no other warning she raised her hand, and the Noctani surged forth.

45

I slipped Stormslayer free of its sheath on my thigh and wielded it with my non-dominant hand, Nik's sword tightly gripped in the other. The first Noctani moved forward so quickly I could barely track her. The space in the room didn't allow much room for us to outpace one another. That could be used to my advantage. Level the playing field. She snarled as she came at me, her fangs showing, dripping with saliva as she went straight for my neck.

I easily pushed her back, burying Stormslayer deep in her chest. She hadn't even tried to protect herself—she was only focused on one thing: *my blood.*

The Noctani might be faster and more dangerous, but they weren't necessarily smarter.

Another Noctani was on me in a mere moment and I did my best to keep him back, crouching down as he wielded his sword, swiping over my head in a smooth arc. He was fast, but so was I. He had to be at least twice my size if not bigger, and there was no escaping this room. Alastir had ensured that.

We were all trapped here.

I called on my magic to propel me faster, lightning streaking through the sky right outside the window. The bright flash drew my attention, and out of the corner of my eye a deluge of rain poured down from the sky right outside the window.

The sun was no longer in sight.

I allowed more magic to simmer to the surface, my amethyst coated blade clashing with the Noctani's. His own sizzled and disintegrated, as if my magic were the antidote to whatever dark magic had created it.

The Noctani stared at me in shock. I took his split second of distraction to my advantage. I sliced Nik's sword forward and the Noctani's head fell clean from his body, thumping to the wooden floorboards beneath us.

Two down.

The small space was working to our benefit. The Noctani weren't able to move as quickly to evade us, which was one of their only strengths. As I turned to see where Donika was, I felt the wound on my abdomen re-open—as if it had been freshly stabbed again.

The pain of it caused me to press my eyes closed, falling to one knee. I gripped the blades tightly in both of my hands, trying to push myself back up to my feet and off the floor. I ground my teeth, a cry escaping me as I forced myself up.

My eyes found Donika, alone in the corner of the room. A wicked smile creased her lips as she watched the melee unfold.

She might not have been able to send the Noctani onto the battlefield to kill Nik, but she had somehow gotten a message to them, regardless. Had it been Zachariah? Corian? Was she connected to them in a way I didn't know about?

I stormed towards her, my footing slick against the blood spilled across the wooden floor. Before I could make it to her, a third Noctani intercepted me, this one with an axe in one fist and a sword in the other. She had her hair tied back, bite marks decorating the column of her neck. Her eyes were as black as Donika's as she stepped into my path and advanced towards me.

I surged towards her first, allowing my magic to propel me forward faster than her eyes could follow. She crossed her arms, throwing me back at the last moment. But not before I broke the skin against her forearm with Stormslayer.

She recoiled with a hiss, spittle flying from her fangs. She ducked low and before I could push more magic out, she swiped the axe across my leg as I backed away. A hiss escaped my own lips as she tore through my skin.

Blood trickled down my leg as I circled her, both of our hands filled with weapons. She tracked my every movement with her black eyes, not underestimating me as the others had. She surged forward and our blades clashed. As she snarled—pushing back—I allowed magic to sear through my blade and into hers. She dropped it with a clatter, craning her head back only to bring it back down with force, smashing into my own temple.

I staggered back, my vision spotting black for a moment. In that singular instant where my vision had gone dark, she had composed herself, regaining her blade. I blinked away the spots, focusing my gaze back on her.

Blood trickled into my eye, a wide gash must have opened on my forehead where she had bashed her head into mine. I bit my lip as I surged forward again, sliding across the floor and swiping the sword against her outer thigh. She caught me as I slid by, wrenching me back by my hair.

A cry left my mouth as she grabbed a fistful of it, tilting my head back to expose my neck.

No, no, no. I couldn't let her bite me. *Anything* but let her bite me.

If my magic was stolen, it was all over.

I steeled myself, and as she brought her head down towards mine—my hair still fisted in her grip—I brought Nik's sword up. It sliced straight through her open mouth, protruding out the back of her throat.

She fell to her knees beside me, her eyes opened in shock. Her grip released on my hair and I stumbled to my feet, sliding the sword free from her. Somehow she wasn't dead yet. As she gargled on the ichor that poured forth I buried the sword in her chest. Her body fell to the bedroom floor beneath me, motionless.

I turned to see Puck approaching Donika, the remaining Noctani occupied with fighting the other resistance members.

"Puck, no!" I cried over the melee.

She would kill him without a second thought. He couldn't stand against her.

She was *mine* to kill.

Puck met my gaze and stepped back, arms raised. He moved to help Tess with the Noctani she currently battled with across the room.

I approached Donika slowly, her back pressed against the wall, her hands hidden behind her. She watched me advance—her expression unreadable. The battle parted as I made my way towards her, whether by choice or by spell, I wasn't sure.

"It ends here," I called over the sounds of clashing metal.

"I agree," she said, pushing back away from the wall and coming towards me.

My feet were shoulder width apart, Stormslayer in my left hand, Nik's sword in my right. The wound on my stomach was throbbing, but I sent a pulse of magic down the bond and received one back.

Nik was ok. For now.

The battle was wearing on me, my muscles becoming sore, my energy depleting. I pushed more magic into the storm in the sky and released it, thunder rattling the windowsills as it snapped free.

The storm was its own, and I allowed that magic to siphon back into me, energizing me once more.

I could tell that Annelise was fading and would need energy soon. Luckily, she could pull from my storms, too.

A sense of calm settled over me as Donika approached, her steps slow and careful across the floorboards. She didn't make a single noise as she approached me, her eyes on the darkened sky through the windowsill at my back.

I reached out to one of the storms and pulled more energy, the storm bucking against me at first but quickly relenting. I allowed the energy to fill me until I thought I could burst from it, as if it were filling every inch of me with raw, unfiltered power.

Right as I was ready to detonate, to end this once and for all, Donika brought her hand forth from behind her back. In her palm was a spinning ball of raw, dark energy.

It was black magic streaked with grey, a hurricane of power within the palm of her hand.

Her eyes tracked my body from my feet, across the weeping wounds on my legs, the stab wounds on my abdomen from Nikolai, across my chest where my tunic was torn. Over my forehead where the gash still bled into my eye.

Before I could register what was happening, before I had a chance to release the energy I had collected from the storm above, she hurled the black magic at me.

I felt Alastir's border spell snap as my body went sailing across the room, falling through the glass window.

46

When the black magic touched my skin, I thought a million needles had pierced me. As I fell from the window, my only thought was that my skin was *burning off*. That by the time I landed, I wouldn't have any skin left at all.

The landing came much quicker than I had anticipated, and I fell against a balcony and not the battlefield that warred beneath. The wind entirely left my lungs and I gasped, struggling to capture any amount of breath I could. No matter how hard I tried, I couldn't fill my lungs with air. My hand clutched against my jacket, peeling it away from me.

I was choking.

The rain came down in sheets around me, the biting wind whipping my already sopping hair across my face. The storms above were furious, raining their anger down. Out here on the balcony, I could hear the sounds of battle clearly.

My eyes were on the sky as I saw Donika appear in the frame of the shattered window above, her skirt whipping around her beneath the whipping winds. She smiled down at me for only a moment before she jumped into the spitting rain.

She landed in a crouch on the balcony beside me. I had fallen with both Nik's sword and Stormslayer in my grip, but at some point they had clattered away from me on the stone terrace.

I swallowed, pressing my eyes closed as I tried to capture any breath I could manage to fill my lungs with. I gasped, clawing once more at my chest as I allowed the energy I had pulled from the sky to fill my lungs instead.

My magic breathed for me.

My lungs filled once.

Twice.

My breaths were coming in stuttering gulps now, but I could breathe. I turned away from Donika to locate my blades, but her foot across my back stopped me. She pressed down, but not enough to crush me or cause any injury. The sound of her laugh filled my ears as the rain cascaded down my face, filling my mouth with rainwater and blood.

"Tsk, tsk. Not so fast."

She allowed me to turn over, her heel now pressed flush against my chest. If she truly wanted to, she could likely drive that heel right into my heart from this vantage point. Another ball of dark magic swirled within her palm. It appeared as a fire of darkness, licking against her skin as if it were made of flame.

How much of her soul had she had to sacrifice for that power?

As if reading the thoughts on my face, she pressed her heel down harder into my chest, causing me to wince. I tried to recoil, but with my back to the terrace stones, there was nowhere for me to go. As I watched her above me, I pulled more energy from the sky. Lightning struck out and hit the iron railing next to us.

It sparked, causing Donika to take a step back.

This time I didn't hesitate—I extended my palm towards her and released the energy I had siphoned from the storm overhead. My magic shot out of my palm as a steady, pulsing flame. Amethyst energy colliding with hers.

She took another step back beneath the force of my power.

Then another.

I pulled more magic from the sky when I felt myself tire, the continuous stream of energy pushing Donika farther and farther back. I spotted Stormslayer beneath the railing and bent to pick it up, comforted by the blade safely back in my grip.

Donika's own palm was extended towards me, her energy met mine. Black fire mixing with violet. They pressed against each other mercilessly, the terrace groaning beneath us from the weight of all the energy we were wielding. We appeared evenly matched, her dark energy holding back mine for the time being.

Unless she cut herself and performed a new blood spell, she would eventually run out of energy. My energy was already in the sky, and the only way I would run out is if I sucked all the energy dry without allowing time to create a new storm.

The storms above us were furious, spitting and crackling with energy I had never seen before. It was truly a sight to behold.

I pulled more.

And more.

Until I was so full of energy, I thought I could fly. My skin was glistening violet as I pushed against her. I was certain my amethyst magic swirled furiously in my eyes. The light of our battle illuminated the surrounding sky, sending a beacon of light directly upwards where our magic clashed.

Donika was straining to hold me off, both hands extended towards me, her teeth ground together from pain.

I bet she wished she wore more practical shoes.

I took a step forward. Then another.

Donika stepped back away from me, conceding. Another few steps back and she would be pressed against the iron railing of the balcony. The slash of a blade across my side almost dropped me to my knees, my focus broken for a single moment.

Nik had been hurt again.

Donika used the momentary lapse in my concentration to press forward, but I was ready. I pulled even more energy from above to fill the void of what I had already expended, and she was forced backwards once more.

Her back was pressed against the iron railing now, my magic threatening to push her over. We were a few stories up, but a fall like this wouldn't kill her. It would take more than a little height to kill the queen of blood magic.

Was that... *fear* I saw in her black eyes?

I shook my head, banishing the thought from my mind.

Donika would never be afraid. That was a human emotion, none of which belonged to her anymore. She was growing weaker, my magic funneling straight from the sky and into my core. I would need to push more magic back up into the sky soon, and I prayed that Donika would break before then.

Right as the thought crossed my mind, Donika buckled, falling to her knees, her chiffon skirt so wet around her that it clung to her legs as she fell. Her black energy blinked out, but my magic continued to surge forth.

It exploded into her with such force that I was propelled backwards myself. I twisted my body to land as gracefully as I possibly could, pushing myself back up onto my hands and knees. My breathing was labored, my wet clothes plastered to my skin. I was utterly drained, but vengeance pushed me to continue once more.

Donika lay in a heap across the terrace from me, her white blue hair streaming around her head against the terrace stone. I pushed myself to standing, slowly approaching her with Stormslayer held tightly in my grip.

She hadn't regained herself, her head limp against the terrace. I used the edge of the blade to turn her face towards me, as she had done in the throne room to me so many times before. When her gaze met mine, her black eyes were filled with sorrow. I wasn't sure what I had expected... but it wasn't this. I pressed the tip of my blade to her chest, pressing down only enough to pierce the skin.

When her blood poured forth across the bodice of her bejeweled dress, it was as dark as midnight. The same ichor that pumped through the veins of her monsters. It pooled at her collarbone, a laugh escaping her lips and causing it to spill over her shoulders and onto the stone below with the vibration.

"Why are you laughing?" I asked, pressing the blade harder against her, my brows drawn together.

The ichor mixed with the torrents of rain that still fell from the sky above, causing it to turn a milky charcoal color. The storms overhead had weakened due to the amount of energy I had pulled from them, but the rain continued to fall.

"Because in the end, I always knew it would be you, little Stormshade."

I glared down at her in confusion. "What are you talking about?"

Her hand fell from her stomach to lie against the stone terrace, straight into a pool of her own blood. It instantly soaked through the delicate lace of the sleeve, but she didn't have the strength to move it. She had exhausted all of her energy. All of her power.

"I always knew you would win."

"And how did you know that?" I asked.

It had to be a trick. There was no other way Donika would concede defeat, even if my blade was poised over her heart.

"The Mother told me," she replied, coughing up a mouthful of rain and ichor. My magic had hurt something deep inside of her when it had blasted through her. Something irreparable.

"The Mother?"

She nodded. "She visits me often. She has tried to… tried to save me. Tried to convince me to join the light once more. There was never any hope of that… but it didn't stop her from trying."

The Mother had visited Donika? Alastir was the only one I had known to communicate with the Mother. She had chosen those that she sent visions to with great care.

To think that she would speak with Donika… and often…

I shook my head, blinking away the rain that coated my lashes.

"She told me what would happen… but I didn't believe her," Donika said, her head inclining towards me. "But it doesn't matter. I am ready to join her."

"I'm not sure that's where you are going," I spit out, pressing the blade deeper.

She wouldn't save herself with pretty words about being saved or the Mother trying to convince her to leave the darkness behind. She was a monster… and there was only one way for this to end.

Donika reached up to grasp the back of my head and I reared back, careful to ensure the blade was still pressed into her flesh right above her heart. As she moved closer, she pulled herself further onto my blade and the ichor poured forth in earnest now, coating the both of us in the slick, black liquid. She gripped my head with her hands, bringing her mouth to my ear.

The words that she whispered were words I *never* thought I would hear in this lifetime, or the next. When she released me and fell back against the wet stones, I could see through the terrace doors that the others had joined us. They were watching from the open doorway.

They had successfully defeated her Noctani in Osiris's old bedroom above.

The battle still raged below us, but it would come to an end in only a matter of moments.

The shock of her words still reeled within me as I kneeled, gathering the leverage to press the blade home.

Annelise must have stood right over my shoulder, because Donika's dark eyes were filled with wonder as she met her gaze. I had never thought such an emotion could be possible with that depthless black. Annelise kneeled beside us, gripping Donika's hand tightly in her own.

Donika was still weak from the blast of storm magic, her nose trickling the black ichor that was still pooling on her chest. That same ichor dripped to crease the corners of her mouth. My magic was killing her, eating her from the inside out.

She was dark where I was light. The energy I had filled her with was too much for her constitution... they weren't compatible. Even without the help of my blade, she wouldn't make it.

A humorless laugh escaped her as she tilted her head, glancing over my other shoulder.

I inclined my own head to see out of the corner of my eye that Zion had joined us on the balcony. He kneeled too, his hands capturing Annelise's and Donika's. I met Annelise's and Zion's gaze with a question in my eyes.

I know I had been the one to say we couldn't afford any last-minute changes of heart—that Annelise and Zion would be a liability when it came down to it. But it was *me* who somehow hesitated now... confusion swirling in my chest. We had never been whole as a family until now. Zion, Annelise, Donika, me... the only one missing was Osiris.

Annelise answered my unspoken question with a soft, sad nod.

Despite everything, I would put her out of her misery. Even if she didn't deserve such a kindness.

My gaze fell on Donika one last time, and she tightened her grip on Annelise's and Zion's hands as I plunged Stormslayer into her heart.

47

Donika paled, her lungs filling with one last gasp before her head fell against the stone terrace. For one brief moment, right as Donika took her last breath, her eyes had turned as blue as the sky.

It was as if the dark magic had bled out of her, leaving nothing but the innocent girl she had once been behind.

She was still.

I slid Stormslayer free, and the ichor continued to pour forth as the life force left her. I stood, letting the rain cascade over me and cleanse the ichor from my skin. It stung where it flowed over my open wounds before it fell to the ground.

I could hear the roars of the battle below us.

"Donika is dead!"

"Long live the queen!"

"Queen Diana!"

"Long live the queen!"

I had thought I would feel victorious when this was all over. What I felt was nothing. I was hollow. I didn't have the heart to turn from the terrace to glance at the battle below. I was sure it was coming to an end now that the Black Heart was dead.

But not *all* of her.

My gaze met Annelise's, and a tear slipped down her cheek, mingling with the rain that still fell from the sky, cleansing us all. Zion stood first, gripping Annelise and tugging her with him. He held her for a long moment, and I glanced away.

I couldn't imagine what it felt like to watch your own daughter die… and by your other daughter's hand, no less. There was no helping Donika if even the Mother couldn't save her, but that didn't make it any easier. It didn't erase the memories of her when she was young, her hair flowing out behind her as she swung from the old oak tree outside of the Siraleth cottage. Her death didn't erase the feelings of failure they must be drowning in.

I turned towards the doors and Tess rushed forwards, enveloping me in her arms before I could fall. I sent a beat of energy through the bond and felt Nik respond in kind. He was still down below, but he was coming. I didn't have the energy to go down to the battlefield to find him.

Tess held me up, her arms gripping me tightly as she ran her hand across my wet scalp, soothing me. She hushed into my ear, telling me it was alright, when it most certainly didn't *feel* alright.

I turned to Annelise, a question in my eyes.

What do we do now?

Donika was dead, but a piece of her still lived in Annelise because of the spell she had performed. She could find a way to resurrect herself if we didn't manage to kill that piece, too.

"I'm sorry, Diana." The words that left Annelise's mouth were barely above a whisper.

My brow creased in confusion.

Sorry for what? We had all known what a burden it would be to wield the blade against Donika. I had been prepared. Or I had thought I was...

Zion pulled away from her, a hand on her shoulder. He pressed his mouth to hers, capturing her in a passionate kiss. When he pulled away, Annelise met his gaze with a fierce nod.

Before I could even register what was happening, before I could free myself of Tess's arms and stop them, Zion had grasped both sides of Annelise's head with his large hands, placing one last kiss against her forehead.

In a movement so fast I almost missed it with my tear-stained eyes, he snapped her neck.

48

"NO!" The hoarse cry that left my lips roared out of me, piercing the air. I fell to the stone terrace, crawling away from Tess towards my mother's body.

"Did you know? Did you know that they planned this?" I cried, my accusatory glare landing on Tess.

She shook her head, her gaze filled with sadness. "I didn't know, Diana. You have to believe me... I had no idea."

I crawled among the ichor, blood, and rain that covered the balcony to Annelise, pulling her body into my lap. I raised my face to Zion, angry tears slipping down my cheeks.

"How could you?" My voice cracked as I glanced up at him.

"It was her choice." His voice was quiet among the racket of the soldiers down below, so quiet I could barely hear it.

Right as my gaze dropped to Annelise, my hand stroking the dying rain away from her cheek, Zion fell in a heap beside us. My mouth opened in shock, a fresh sob tearing free from my chest.

They were bound.

By killing Annelise, he had effectively killed himself.

"NO! No! *Fuck!*" I cried over and over, cursing the Mother. Cursing Donika. Cursing Annelise and Zion. Cursing this fucking realm. That we had finally killed Donika, but I had lost my parents in the process. All because of that God-forsaken immortality spell. The moment she had marked Annelise in Siraleth, she had cursed her to die with her.

This couldn't be happening.

Screams of agony poured forth out of my mouth as I rocked Annelise back and forth, my tears falling into her strawberry blonde hair. The rain had begun to dissipate, but as my anger escaped me… so did my magic. The sky darkened once more.

I'm coming.

It was Nikolai, sending me a message down the bond. He was coming as fast as he could, but it wouldn't matter. There was nothing he could do that would bring them back.

Alastir crouched next to me, and despite the glare of warning I shot him, he did not glance away. "I knew of their plan, and for this, I am sorry. But do not let their sacrifice be in vain."

"Why didn't you tell me?" I gasped, gripping Annelise so tightly it would have left bruises behind.

If she had still been alive.

"This was *her* choice. Her sacrifice for you. For Istmere. One life for the lives of *so many*." His voice was soft as he spoke, as if he were speaking to a frightened child. I didn't want to hear it.

"But it wasn't just one life," I cried, motioning towards Zion's motionless body that Amiyah now kneeled beside.

Puck moved forwards, gently pressing Zion's eyes closed and flipping him onto his back.

"No, no, no. This isn't real. *Isn't real.* We are a *family.* We were finally together." I shook my head back and forth furiously, denial settling deep in my bones.

"I can save her," I sputtered out.

I lay her gently against the stone, kneeling beside her body, my hands poised over her chest. "Yes… I can save her."

"Diana, no," Tess shook her head, all-encompassing sadness filling her expression. Tears brimmed in her eyes and when she blinked, they spilled over, streaking down her cheeks.

Donika was finally dead… but so were Annelise and Zion. Alastir had said there was a price to the cure, but he couldn't tell what that price might be. Was *this* the price I would have to pay for the dark magic spell that saved Nikolai?

I wasn't ready to pay it. Couldn't stomach it.

I had just started getting to know Annelise. We had just begun mending our broken relationship. I wasn't ready to let her go yet. Not ever.

She was my *mother.*

I let my magic spill through my fingertips towards her, and her chest rose towards the energy, lifting her off the ground.

"Diana, NO!" Tess darted forward, grasping me tightly around the shoulders. Puck joined her, pulling me away from Annelise's limp form.

"Let go of me! Let me go!" My cries were swallowed by the storm raging overhead, lightning streaking the sky and hitting the terrace, sending stones flying into the air.

Right as I was about to combust, about to let the magic inside of me detonate, a tug from the bond caught my attention. Not warmth or even words like he had sent before, but a pull that was undeniable. Nik was *taking* my grief. My anguish.

Sharing the burden of this turmoil with me.

Another choked sob escaped me as he appeared in the doorway of the terrace, cheeks red, his chest rising and falling as he panted for breath. He ran all the way here.

I ran to him, falling into his arms as he lifted me against him. I pressed myself against him so forcefully the air left my lungs, our bodies flush against one another. I cried into him, gripping him so tightly against me I thought my fingers would have to be pried apart. I could feel the hot blood of his wound between us, knowing we needed to get him to a healer. But the bond between us told me he was ok… for now. I tore against his jacket, wanting to erase any molecule of distance between us.

I had never felt so broken.

The others stood quietly as the anger and sadness escaped me. I couldn't be here anymore, couldn't see her limp body next to Zion's. I had lost so many people in the fight for this realm… and it was a hefty price to pay.

I released Nik, my gaze capturing his for only a moment before I scooped my blades off the stones. I secured Storm-slayer to my thigh and carried Nik's sword behind me.

I needed to be alone.

They let me walk off, staying behind to take care of the bodies. A pulse of understanding shot through the bond. That Nikolai recognized I needed to grieve and he would be waiting for me on the other side of this. I wandered through the castle, the sword dragging and sparking against the stone as I let it trail behind me. I didn't have the energy to lift it up.

I wasn't sure where I was going... only that I needed to get as far away from that balcony as possible.

A laugh escaped me as I found myself before the double doors that would lead to the throne room. I pushed the doors open, unsurprised to find the battle scene from earlier still remained.

I stepped over the bodies and narrowly avoided the pools of blood on my way to the dais.

I ascended the steps, the sword clanking against the marble in a way that set my teeth on edge. I threw the sword down and it clattered against the blackened legs of the throne. I stood before it, hatred and anguish bubbling up within me. I pulled against my own hair as another scream of frustration and anguish tore through me. I was bent in half, all the rage and sorrow tearing out of me.

I screamed until my throat was sore.

Until my voice couldn't possibly withstand another sound.

Until my legs were tired, my back aching.

It wasn't until I was utterly and completely spent that I turned, sitting on the throne, gently placing Nik's blade across my lap.

In the end... Donika *had* broken me, after all.

49

Deep in the halls of The Stone Palace, Annelise and Zion lay in white, narrow beds in the infirmary. The castle had fallen silent, the soft sounds of celebrations lingering outside and bleeding through the stone walls.

Their limbs rest at their sides, their eyes gently closed.

Their bodies were cleansed of blood and ichor.

But slowly... softly... the sound of a beating heart filled the castle.

Then two.

If one were to listen closely, the sound of a spine mending could be heard, snapping softly back into place. As if a collective breath were being held, the castle fell impossibly silent for one long moment.

Somewhere deep in The Stone Palace of Akra, ancient magic was at work.

Annelise's blue eyes flashed open, a gasp escaping her pale pink lips.

50

The moment Tess had come to fetch me, to tell me Annelise and Zion were alive, I raced through the hallways of The Stone Palace. I wasn't exactly sure where I was going, only that I needed to go to her. Needed to see her. I didn't know if it was instinct alone that drew me to the castle infirmary or something deeper, but I burst through the doors to find Annelise sitting up in bed, Zion at her side.

They were *laughing*.

I thought I had left every tear I had back on that throne, but they spilled forward once more as I rushed towards them.

But these tears were different—they were happy.

They captured me in a hug so tight it felt as if they were piecing me back together.

I pulled back only enough to search their faces. "How?!"

Another set of footsteps entered the room, and I should have known it would be the smug seer behind all of this.

"You?" I asked, confusion clear in my voice.

Alastir nodded, coming forward to rest a hand against my shoulder. "I didn't tell you, because I wasn't sure it would work. In the chance that it didn't... I didn't want to be the one to break your heart should I have failed."

"If *what* failed?" I asked, searching their expressions.

"The antidote." Zion's voice was resonant when he answered.

I shook my head back and forth, confusion creasing my brow as my mouth fell open.

"The antidote we created in The Shadow with your blood wasn't only a cure for siphoning, but a cure for *dark magic*. I thought it might work, but I couldn't be sure. When the antidote was administered to Nik and the Noctani parts of him died but left the rest of him whole, I thought perhaps the same could be true for Annelise. It would kill the piece of her that was dark, the piece of her that was *Donika*, but she would live. The spell that I used to save Annelise was a sister spell to the one that saved Nikolai. All Annelise had to do was drink it before the battle... no coating of the blade necessary since it wasn't Annelise herself whose heart had been changed by the darkness."

"And Zion?" I asked, glancing back and forth between them.

"If Annelise wasn't dead, Zion wouldn't be either. The same magic that saved her, saved him too. It took a little longer for it to work than we initially thought... but that's not what matters. What matters is that it *worked*," Alastir explained.

A tear slipped down my cheek, and I hastily swiped it away with the back of my hand. For the first time in a long, long time, the tears I shed were those of joy. I took a deep breath, allowing my body and taut muscles to finally relax and unknit themselves.

Annelise and Zion were *alive*.

Nik, Tess, Puck, Alastir, Amiyah, Saanvi, Kenna, they were all safe.

My family was safe.

And Donika was dead.

I buried my face in Annelise's shoulder and she brought her arms around me, holding me tightly. From the moment I met her, I had wondered what it would feel like to find comfort in her arms.

It felt *right*.

With my mother embracing me, I felt whole.

Tess joined our little reunion, laughing as she threw her arms around our trio. Then Puck appeared at the doorway, no hesitation in joining us.

"I'm not one for a group hug, but I won't be left out... " Nik muttered as he entered the room and threw his arms around us.

"Come on, old man." Nik nodded towards Alastir. "Join us."

Alastir lifted his lip as if he was repulsed by the idea, but after a long moment passed, he reluctantly joined us. We drew him into the middle, a fit of laughter shaking us as he appeared as uncomfortable as humanly possible.

The sounds of true, genuine laughter filled my ears and I was already lighter. There were tough decisions and hard times to come in the days ahead, but I would savor this moment.

I glanced around and seared their faces into my memory.

The way Nik's dimple stuck out on his right cheek when he smiled widely. The way Puck's mess of curls covered his forehead like a used mop. The way Tess's pearly white teeth were displayed as she threw her head back with genuine laugher. How Annelise stared at me as if I were a miracle. *Her* miracle. The way Zion looked at Annelise as if *she* was *his*. How Alastir begrudgingly joined our hectic little group, a smile across his lips despite his grumpy nature.

These were the moments I *never* wanted to forget.

51

None of us wanted to spend any more time in The Stone Palace than we needed to. I wanted to return to Siraleth. To the grimoire safely tucked away in the cottage underground.

I knew I had responsibilities... but I wanted to return *home*.

I could rule the realm as queen easily enough from Siraleth. There was no reason for me to remain in Akra after we buried the dead and had a ceremony to honor their memories.

There weren't many soldiers who did not sway to our side, many of them having been forced into service by Donika. They had been threatened and tortured, the same as every other Shade in Istmere. For those that were loyal to Donika and couldn't be swayed, they found a home in the prison cells of the Stormvault.

Donika's death and the return of my crown was a weight that had been lifted off my shoulders, and I imagined much of the realm felt the same. But before we could move on officially and begin anew, I knew we needed to honor those that had fallen in battle.

Peace had been restored to Istmere, and Stormshades, Nightshades, and Shades alike would be welcome and could call this realm home. No one would be persecuted for the type of magic they were born with.

No one needed to hide any longer.

But make no mistake, the happy ending we all deeply craved came at a steep cost. I had sacrificed so much to see an end to Donika's reign. I knew that there was no other ending than Donika dying at the end of my blade, but it still left behind a heavy weight that I couldn't shake. I couldn't stop thinking about the what-ifs and could-have-beens if things had been different in Istmere during our childhood. If Annelise was never called to be the royal healer and had stayed to raise Donika herself. Donika might have been evil, but she was still my sister.

My blood.

I was mourning the relationship we never got to have, and I'm sure Annelise felt the same way. If Alastir hadn't been able to craft a spell to save Annelise and Zion, they would have been lost to this war, too.

Alastir had said there would be a cost to the spell that cured Nikolai and returned his humanity. I would never know if that cost was almost losing Annelise and Zion, or if the consequences of that magic were yet to come.

Isaac never got to see the end of this war, and the thought was a lead weight in my gut. Tyr, too. So many had died and sacrificed their own lives for a better realm, for a better future.

The mood was solemn as I led the resistance through the plains before the castle in Akra, my friends and family following closely on my heels. I wore a white sundress that fell to right above my ankles, the customary color for Shade burials. Today, all the Shades lost in this battle would return to the earth from which they came, their magic returning to the source and the Mother.

I wasn't sure what came after this, but I prayed they found peace. We had chosen a spot between the castle and the forest to bury them, and it was quite the undertaking. We used our magic to dig the graves, but it still took the better part of the day to complete. By the time we had buried every single fallen Shade, we were utterly exhausted, our faces dripping with sweat and covered in dirt.

I gazed across the burial ground before approaching the hill to our right, the vast expanse of dug up earth unsettling me.

There had been so many casualties in this battle.

So many dead.

The sheer amount of graves we had dug today had gooseflesh breaking out across my skin, my tongue thick in my throat.

I stood atop the hill and clasped my hands together behind my back, clearing my throat before speaking. I knew my voice would be thick with emotion, but this would be my first time addressing the residents of Istmere as their queen, and I wanted to appear strong.

The Shades before me turned towards me, murmuring among themselves, their brows drawn. They carried the same heaviness in their chests, the gravity of the situation weighing on them. While Istmere would see a new dawn, there were far too many that died here and would never get to see it for themselves.

"I wanted to thank you all for coming here today, to honor those that have fallen during the battle here in Akra. While we may be victorious, it did not come without cost. The Shades we have returned to the earth have made the ultimate sacrifice for the future of this realm."

My gaze met each of theirs as I searched the crowd. When my gaze finally fell on Nikolai, my shoulders relaxed, my brows softened.

"We have buried not only the Shades of the resistance here today, but the Nightshades who stood against us. They may have been loyal to Donika, they may have been manipulated and abused into following her. We will never know. They deserve the same respect and honor of returning to the Mother that all Shades do."

A murmur swept through the crowd and I could see some nodding their heads, some scowling in disapproval. I would never know the motivations of those that had fallen. The thought of treating them all as traitors when some of them had only been trying to save their families—when they had endured the same torture I had—didn't sit right with me.

"Whether you agree with this decision or not, I know in my heart that this is the right thing to do, the right way to begin my reign as queen of Istmere. I do not want to continue the plague of discrimination that has tormented this realm for far too long. I do not want to further the hate that has permeated for decades."

I could see pride twinkling in Nik's gaze as he sent a wave of warmth down the bond that I could sense beneath my skin.

"While there are brighter days ahead, I want to take this time to reflect on those that sacrificed for our cause. Those that will never get to see what this realm should have been all along. Those that may have been misguided or forced into servitude. Those that lost their way and paid the ultimate price. To honor those friends and family members that have fallen, I want to speak their names. Please call out their names to remember them. To honor them. I will start." I cleared my throat as tears stung the back of my eyes. "Isaac Chamberlain. Tyr Kotova. Antonia Finch."

The other Shades began to say the names of those they wanted to remember among the crowd, a moment of silence for each name that fell from their lips.

"Fletcher Price. Kane Price."

"Ivory Percival."

"Destria Godwin."

"Christopher Hawthorne."

"Warrick Dragovya."

"Theo Aldrige."

"Giselle Norwood."

The names went on and on.

By the time we were finished honoring those that we had lost, the sun had set beyond the stone castle and cast the burial field in a dark, purple glow. The only light we could see by was the blush of the moon and the magic grasped within our palms.

As the final names were spoken and we prepared to return to the castle, Nikolai found me, wrapping me in his arms. I pressed my face against his shoulder, his white tunic capturing the tears that trailed down my cheeks.

"Sometimes I wish I didn't feel everything so deeply," I whispered into him.

"But that's what makes you so special," he replied, his arms tight around me, pressing me against him. His words were muffled by my hair.

A humorless laugh escaped me as I clung to him. I wished I could remember each and every name spoken here today. Each and every life lost to this war. I knew that there would be a price for Istmere to free itself from tyranny, but it was a heavy price indeed. I would never allow myself to forget about the sacrifices those around me had made. About the sacrifices I had made.

We had made it to the other side—and I was grateful—but with victory came the bitter tinge of sadness. Without sacrifice, it wouldn't have been possible to defeat Donika.

Nik grasped my hand and led me back towards The Stone Palace. The other Shades returned to their homes or returned to the castle with us, where we would hold a memorial banquet that would last well into the night.

As we passed the stone archway into the castle foyer, I could sense the energy of the Shades simmering under my skin as if it were a tangible thing. There was sadness, but beneath that, there was also hope.

My last thought as I grabbed a goblet of wine from Tess was that I prayed Tyr and Isaac were with the Mother—wherever that was—and that one day I would see them again.

52

The banquet had, in fact, lasted well into the night. Nik and I had called it quits by midnight and returned to our quarters to curl up together. We stayed in The Stone Palace for another few nights while we got things in order before traveling back to Siraleth. I was anxious to leave Akra and return home to start anew, but each night, right as I was about to fall asleep, a flash of memory crossed my vision.

Donika, with piercing blue eyes.

In her last moment, I had seen a glimpse of the humanity that still remained, buried so deep there was no hope in pulling it back out. She had shown a moment of humanity during the War of Siraleth when she had spared our mother, but that had been fleeting. Who knew how many dark spells she had performed over the last decade, letting her soul darken little by little until it could no longer be saved.

Each night, I wondered if I had done the right thing. If there truly was no way to peel back the layers of darkness that encased her in order to set free the lonely girl that lay beneath. In the end... I knew it had been the only choice for Istmere.

But that didn't make it easy.

A seed of regret was growing deep within me that I hadn't honored her during the burial ceremony. She might have been the reason for all of this, but beneath the layers of dark magic and cruelty there was merely a girl who had never stood a chance. Not once she had slipped into the shadows that would claim her. I snuck out to the burial ground, and though her magic had returned to the earth once more, I could still sense the energy emanating from where she had been buried.

I rubbed my arms against the chill in the night air, the only thing covering me was the nightgown I had been wearing when I went to bed. Beneath the stars, alone on the burial ground, I whispered her name into the darkness.

She would be remembered by everyone in Istmere as the cruel and malicious queen, but she would be remembered by her family as something far more complex. It only felt right to whisper her name, if nothing else, to release me from the nightmares that plagued me and the guilt that had settled in my core. There was no doubt in my mind that whether I had snuck out here tonight or not, for better or for worse, Donika would be remembered. When I returned to bed Nik was awake, but he said nothing. He had likely felt my stirring emotions through the bond. I think he knew where I had gone, and what I knew I had to do.

He wrapped his arms around me, caressing my neck with his lips until I fell back into a fitful sleep. I hated staying in The Stone Palace, but now that I was queen, it was one of the many sacrifices I needed to make to ensure a smooth succession. I kept having to remind myself that it would only be a few more nights.

That was the first night I didn't dream of Donika.

The following morning, we prepared to leave for Siraleth. The army of the resistance was now the queen's army, and some of them were staying behind in The Stone Palace to clear it of any trace that Donika may have left behind. They would also care for the prisoners who refused to submit to my rule.

Siraleth had fallen in the war where Donika had initially gained her power, and it only felt right that we planned to restore the capital city. Siraleth would be restored to its former glory, and I was anxious to return there and begin building a new castle.

A fresh start.

We had planned an ordinary, yet comfortable stone castle where I would rule. Atop the hill where Nik and I had shared our first kiss.

Annelise and Zion would be returning to the cottage where they had raised us when we were young. Tess and Puck would be joining us in the castle, as would Kenna and Saanvi.

Amiyah was set on returning to the far shores of Prins, her seaside cabin calling her home. She promised to visit often, and I did too. There was a peace I couldn't explain about her home that faced the Myrene Sea in all its solitude, waves softly crashing against the shore.

Alastir was insistent on returning to his shop in Dragon's Hollow and his family home in The Shadow, despite our protests. He wanted to keep a close eye on Phineas, and I couldn't fault him for that. His whereabouts remained to be seen, and we all thought it awfully suspicious that he had conveniently not chosen sides and stayed out of the battle. I could understand Alastir's unwillingness to leave him behind just yet. He had raised one of the realm's most dangerous thieves, after all.

By the time we left The Stone Palace, I had regained most of my strength, and the passage to Siraleth was a breeze as we made our way on foot. I was filled with a sort of optimism I wasn't sure I had ever experienced before. Things were already looking brighter for the realm, despite things still needing to settle down. It was all so fresh and so new.

I was thankful that the building site of the castle in Siraleth was also close to the portal to the mortal realm. I could go back to the other realm to visit Mom and Jake whenever I wanted.

To think I had almost lost Annelise right when we had begun repairing our relationship...

I shook my head, approaching the ruins atop the hill where Nik and I had first kissed. First danced in the rain. The first storm I had created with my own magic. I could sense the swell of my bound powers deep within my core as I stepped forward, towards the stone table that lay in fragments beneath the cracked ceiling of the old building. I pulled the grimoire out of my satchel, placing it atop the stone and stepping back.

The grimoire was home, too.

It felt odd, in a way, to simply leave it here. There was no longer the fear that it would be stolen and used for evil. It was quite the discerning book—and had only just begun to allow Annelise to use it once again. Sparingly.

It favored its queen.

I stepped back, the sun glinting off the gem in the center of the leather binding. I exhaled deeply through my nose as Nik approached me from behind. He didn't turn me, instead placing his hands against my shoulder blade, massaging the taut muscles there.

"You've got another thing coming if you think this is the end of our training." I could hear the smile in his voice, and imagined he had the left corner of his mouth lifted up in a smirk.

I shook my head, a piece of auburn hair falling in front of my shoulder. "Never."

"Good," he murmured into the skin at my neck, placing a chaste kiss at the junction where my shoulder met the column of my throat.

"I've got big plans for us, and none of those involve becoming so out of shape I can't make it from Siraleth to Akra in at least two days' time." I told him, my eyes still on the grimoire.

He made a humming noise against my skin that sent a shiver down my spine. My magic swelled in my core to meet him, reaching towards my fingertips. Before I could stop it, my magic sent a spark against his skin.

His laugh warmed something deep within me, and it felt like healing. Like happiness.

Like *home*.

He wrapped his arms around me, pulling me flush against him. I could feel him pressing against me in an entirely inappropriate way, and I let out a laugh of my own.

"Tsk, tsk. Always so ready for me," I said, leaning back into him.

His responding laugh shook my shoulders as he tucked his head against me.

"Always, My Queen."

"That will have to wait until later. We have lots of work to do." I motioned to the surrounding rubble that covered the hilltop.

"Whatever you say, Diana."

Annelise and Zion were only a few hours' journey behind us with Kenna and Saanvi. Tess and Puck had already gotten to work clearing the rubble at the port down the hill. Siraleth would be a bustling trade city again in no time.

Nik had promised me that we would visit the islands, too. Myrene and Drakellia were said to be beautiful, and I was anxious to see every inch of this realm now that I was its caretaker. No one had stepped foot on Dragon's Way in decades, apparently, and I was anxious to visit that island, too. It came with its own lore and stories I couldn't wait to hear.

I sighed into Nik, enjoying the touch of his warm skin against mine. Savoring this moment of peace that I wasn't sure I would ever be granted with him at my side. The bond was stronger than it had ever been before. I had never thought it possible to send more than emotions down the bridge between us, but I was beginning to hear murmurings and thoughts as clear as if they were spoken that zapped their way down the bond. He was hearing the same from me.

If we continued to grow closer each day, I wondered if we would soon be able to hear each other's thoughts. It was simple to block off the bond, but there was nothing that I wanted to hide from Nikolai.

He had all of me. Forever. Nothing would ever come between us again.

I had asked Annelise if that was the case for her and Zion, but she had simply replied that every bond was different, a knowing smile on her face. She wanted us to discover the ins and outs of the bond ourselves.

That was half the fun, she had told us.

I was enjoying seeing this side of Nikolai. I had never seen him so carefree and lighthearted. We hadn't yet spoken about Zachariah, but he had told me he was slain in the battle. He had refused to surrender.

I wasn't the only one that had spilled from my own bloodline that day, and I could see in the quiet moments, the way his eyes would darken, that it haunted him still. I was here for him when he was ready to talk about it, if that time ever came. His relationship with his father had always been strained, and it was entirely possible that it might be something he simply wanted to leave in the past.

The only thing that could heal those wounds was time. And love.

I was happy that the Araneoch and Noctani had fallen on the battlefield when Donika had, their life forces tied to hers through dark magic. I had wished we had the opportunity to cure some of the Noctani, but in the end, there were too many of them. The only way to truly stop them was for them to die with Donika.

We had burned every molecule of paper we found that spoke of siphoning and the making of monsters that we had found in The Stone Palace, hoping that we had purged everything to do with that dark magic.

There was one person we had never seen during or after the battle, and that was Corian. I had expected him to be at Donika's side in her final stand, and when he wasn't, I could only assume he had joined the battle down on the plains of Akra. Fighting among his Araneoch and Noctani. Nikolai had confirmed that he hadn't been there, either. We had tried a locator spell though we didn't have anything physical of his in nature to use, and had sent scouts out into the realm, but to no avail.

It was as if he simply... disappeared.

"Are you two going to help us or not?" Tess called out.

I turned and spotted her, standing in a ray of sunlight that poked between the cloud cover overhead. Her hand was over her brow, blocking the sun from her eyes as she peered at us atop the hill.

"You look like you have it well in hand," Nik called, turning towards her.

He unwrapped his arms from me, but kept his hand at the small of my back.

Even from this distance, I could see Tess narrow her eyes at him, and a giggle bubbled to my lips. I was glad to see their bickering was back in place now that we had saved the realm.

"I'm not getting any younger down here," she called up the hill, her gaze drifting towards me with a pointed glare.

"We're coming," I called back in reassurance.

I turned to Nik, my hands around his waist, pulling him against me.

His breath fanned across my face and I closed my eyes, wanting to taste him. As if reading my thoughts, he leaned down, capturing my mouth with his. My lips responded without thought, devouring him. His tongue pressed against me and a low groan escaped my lips.

He laughed against my mouth, and it was easily the best thing I had ever heard. I wanted to bottle that sound so that I could listen to it—over and over again.

"Soon we will be standing here, but not among these ruins. But in a castle of our own making. I cannot wait to make love to you in our own bed beneath the moon of Siraleth. To claim you over and over again until there is no doubt in this entire realm that you belong to me."

"Always," I sighed against him, pulling his mouth back down to mine. "You're mine."

"I'm yours," he whispered against my lips, breaking the kiss for only a moment to utter the words.

Beneath the Siraleth sun, we began building our future. Began repairing a broken realm.

I was anxious to get out and see the people, to stay in every part of the realm and learn its deepest secrets. But first, I needed to rest. To build our new home. To worship every inch of Nikolai's body with my own. To cherish the moments I thought I would never be lucky enough to experience.

To grow closer with Annelise and build our relationship from scratch.

To appoint Zion the commander of the queen's newly established army.

To properly grieve Tyr and Isaac.

But most importantly... to treasure the friendships I was lucky enough to make along the way. I wasn't sure I would see the other side of this war, and I needed to take a moment to process it all.

I was the queen of Istmere. The rightful heir to the throne.

Daughter of Osiris and Annelise.

Sister to the late Queen Donika.

Best friend to Tess Fowler.

Lover to Nikolai Dragovya, and hopefully more one day.

I'd be lying if I didn't say I thought he would make an amazing king.

His eyes narrowed at me as if he was reading my thoughts through the bond. I moved a hand to brush back the lock of golden hair that had fallen across his brow. It was growing too long, and I certainly needed to make time to cut it at some point in the coming days.

Tess cleared her throat loudly from the bottom of the hill, and I laughed when the realization hit me that she hadn't left. She stood there, hands on her hips, tapping her foot impatiently.

I captured Nikolai's mouth with my own one last time before turning to join Tess. Puck was behind her, a wide grin spread across his face.

I might not be Diana Barnes anymore... but I was Diana Kotova.

The last Stormshade of the Kotova bloodline.

The war was over.

And I was home.

EPILOGUE

When Zion had shown up in Siraleth with an enormous contingent of soldiers from the newly established queen's army, I was not surprised when the time it took to build the new castle was chopped in half.

Scratch that, we built it in a quarter of the time.

Nik had made good on his promise to make love to me beneath the Siraleth moon in our own bed. Many times.

Months had passed and The Stone City and its deteriorating castle were a thing of the past, but that didn't mean it hadn't crossed my mind from time to time. I hated to have the castle sitting empty atop the hill in Akra except for its prisoners. We needed to repurpose it in some way.

The new castle in Siraleth was called Stormspire, for obvious reasons.

I was incredibly lucky to call Stormspire my home. It was built of stone similar to The Stone Palace in Akra, but it had a tower that reached up into the sky with an iron crescent at the top. That's where Nik and my room was.

Siraleth was coming back to life before my eyes, and I relished the growth I had seen in the realm in these last few months. Homes were being rebuilt, merchants re-established their trade, the port city open once again. The portal on this side of the realm was seeing more use than it ever had before.

"What are you thinking about?" Tess asked, breaking through my thoughts.

My gaze flitted to hers as I zoned back in. We were setting up the new throne room, and I wanted to make sure it was *nothing* like the throne room Donika had. I still had nightmares of that marbled, checkered tile. Visions of the blood that had stained the dais that day we had stormed the palace to kill her.

The memories of that day might haunt me forever.

I shrugged, throwing a pillow at her. She caught it with one hand, placing it atop the cushion on the throne.

It wasn't dark as Donika's had been, but golden. Streaks of lightning were gilded down the arms, the cushions a royal purple. It still sat atop a dais, but this time there were *two* thrones. I had opted for a natural stone floor that resonated with the Siraleth countryside. There were no windows lining a long walkway, only windows behind the throne that cast rays of sunshine down onto the stone inlaid floor.

In merely a week's time I would be having my coronation here, and I would be kneeling among these steps as I was crowned the queen of Istmere. It was only a formality, of course, seeing as I had been ruling since the day Donika perished. But the realm wanted to see me crowned properly, and a celebration of grand proportions would follow suit. I was equal parts excited and nervous—it would be the first celebration at Stormspire and the thought sent a spark of excitement down to my toes.

"I know that look," Tess mused, fluffing the pillow on the seat and chopping it in half.

I shook my head. "It's nothing."

Tess turned toward me, an eyebrow raised. She held my gaze as she plopped herself down on the throne. I burst into a laugh so deep I doubled over, holding my stomach and trying not to wheeze.

"Oh, it's funny, is it?" she asked, propping her leg up over the armrest and making a show of relaxing.

She didn't look very comfortable. As if reading my thoughts, she flounced out of the chair with a huff.

"I don't plan on spending that much time there," I told her, indicating the throne before us. "I don't think it needs to be terribly comfortable."

"It wouldn't hurt anyone to make it a touch more... plush. That's all I'm saying," she offered, eyeing it, hands on her hips. "It needs to match your crown and be equally decadent."

I laughed, tossing her the other pillow, which hit her square in the chest, causing her to let out a grunt. She tossed it against the second throne, not bothering to fluff it.

"Nik doesn't get the royal treatment?" I asked, my brow raised at her.

She shrugged noncommittally. "It's not his... yet."

I smirked at that.

It was true that it wasn't his yet... but we all knew it would be. Soon.

Tess moved to Nik's chair and sat in it, patting the throne beside her. "Sit."

I did as she commanded, throwing myself down into the chair beside her. Much to my dismay, she was right. This was terribly uncomfortable.

She read my expression with a soft laugh. We sat in relaxing silence for a long moment before she spoke.

"You never did tell me."

I turned my head towards her, hands gripping the arm-rests. "Tell you what?"

She gave me a knowing look and my gaze moved back towards the open doorway beyond the dais. Another moment of silence passed.

"What did she say?" Tess asked, her voice gentle.

"Hmm?"

"Diana. What did Donika say? She whispered something to you. The moment before she passed. What was it?"

I hadn't told anyone.

Not Nik. Not my mother. Not Tess.

Nobody.

I wasn't sure what to do with it. What it meant. Why she told me at all. What was the point? In that moment, she knew that she was on the precipice of death, but she had chosen to spill her darkest secret, anyway.

Why did she tell me?

My gaze fell to my lap before once again landing on Tess.

"I haven't told Nik yet," I admitted.

Tess had always been my best friend. My go-to. She always knew everything first. But the bond between Nik and I had strengthened increasingly over the last few months, and we were able to send words down the tether that held us together now. He could likely sense in this moment how uneasy I was, despite me trying to shield it from him. Despite him being in Prins on an excursion with Puck to see Alastir.

Tess smiled conspiratorially. "I get to know first?!"

"I didn't say I was going to tell you," I replied, mouth scrunching. But she could gauge in the tone of my voice that I had, indeed, decided to.

She scooted closer to me, grasping my hand off the armrest and capturing it in hers.

"Whatever it is, you can tell me. You know the anticipation has been *killing* me. I'm not a patient person... "

I cut her off by raising the hand not currently pressed between hers. "Fine, I'll tell you."

She made a noise halfway between a squeal and a screech, and I had to stop myself from covering my ears.

"So... what did she say?" she asked once more, practically spilling out of her chair.

I took a deep breath, letting the air fill my lungs, then slowly releasing it. "She told me... she told me that she... " As the words left my mouth Tess was visibly on edge, though I wasn't sure if this would be received as good news or bad.

"She has a son."

Tess cocked her head to the side, clearly not the answer that she had been expecting.

"A what now?" she finally replied, her eyes cast towards the throne room floor, brows knit together.

"A son. Donika has a son. And she asked me to find him."

"Find him? What do you mean, *find him*? She didn't know where he was?" she asked.

I shrugged. "I've got no clue. That's all she said. 'I have a son, Diana. Find him.'" My impersonation of her voice was a terrible rendition.

"And then what?" Tess asked.

"Your guess is as good as mine," I told her with a shrug.

"Sweet Mother... why do you do this to us?" Tess asked the empty room as she tilted her head back, falling against the chair and releasing my hand.

I stifled a laugh at her expression.

"What does this mean?" Tess asked.

I shrugged again. "I've got no clue. I can't imagine when she would have had a child. How old he might be. Who the father is," I said.

Tess shot me a glance with a brow raised.

"*Don't*," I told her, hand raised. "Nik confirmed they never got... that far. He is not the father of her illegitimate love child."

"Well, thank the Mother for that. I thought we were about to be on a seriously messed up episode of Jerry Springer, the hidden realm edition. I mean... we still could be if the father was Zachariah, and Nikolai has a brother out there... "

I fell back against the throne, letting out an exasperated sigh. I shook my head at her before meeting her gaze once more. "I'm not sure how I am supposed to find him when I know nothing about him... including his age."

Tess let out a laugh, but there was only a little humor in it. "It never ends, does it?"

A smiled at that. "What, the responsibility of being a queen?"

"No," she huffed, "the *drama*."

That had us both reeling with laughter.

I stood from the throne, giving Tess a playful slap as she slumped into the chair. After a moment, she followed me down the steps of the dais and out of the throne room, into the foyer.

I wasn't sure about any of the details pertaining to Donika's child, but I knew that I did need to find him, one way or another. I didn't think I owed it to her. That wasn't quite the right way to put it. But something in me stirred at the thought of a nephew of mine out there in Istmere right now.

Did he even know who he was?

I was scared of the repercussions of her blood magic and dark spells. How might that have affected a child? Was there another dark Shade out there that we had no idea about?

Donika Kotova had a son.

I had a nephew.

And I wasn't sure how that was going to affect the realm, for better or for worse. There was only one thing I *was* certain of.

I was going to find him.

Acknowledgements

Where writing When Storms Ruin felt like a fever dream, writing When Storms Collide felt like wading through quicksand. I knew where the story was going since before writing book one, but that didn't make it any easier to write the conclusion of this story. This was by far the hardest book of the trilogy to get down on paper. I knew that at the end of this book I would be saying goodbye to Diana and Nikolai, and a part of me didn't feel ready. I cried tears of joy and sadness after writing the last words of the epilogue, but as you now know, this isn't our last visit to Istmere.

Thank you to my Mom and Dad who helped me complete a garage addition smack dab in the middle of writing and editing this book. A special thank you to Grammy Frohman who is always my #1 cheerleader, always looking over my shoulder and encouraging me.

A thank you to my sister Jennifer and my brother Eric. I know you don't understand why I prefer to be buried in a book vs doing literally anything else, but your support means the world. To my nieces Layla and Lexi, I can't wait for you to be old enough to read these books. For now...you flip through the pages and get excited seeing my name on the cover and you'll never know the happiness that brings me.

A special thanks to my friends, without whom I would be eternally lost. Jenn, Lisa, Laura, Brian—I hope you enjoy this book as much as you did the first two.

I also need to thank my incredible book team, without whom this wouldn't have been possible. Emma Jane at EJL

Editing for her amazing editing skills (I'm sorry about all the improper dialogue tags...again. I promise I will get them right some day!), Fran at MerryBookRound for this incredible cover that is quite possibly the most gorgeous thing I have ever seen (aside from the first two books, of course). To Rachael at Cartography Bird Maps, and Marialuna Grassi for bringing my characters and the realm of Istmere to life in their amazing artwork.

And lastly to you, the readers.

Thank you for taking a chance on this series. None of this would be possible without you, and I am forever thankful for your support. This might be the final chapter in Diana and Nikolai's story, but it is not the final chapter in Donika's or the last time we will visit Istmere.

I know I said I was finally going to write a book that didn't end in a whopping cliffhanger... and *technically* I did. The epilogue doesn't count, right?

ABOUT THE AUTHOR

Michelle Frohman is a writer, avid reader, and devoted animal lover with a passion for crafting captivating fantasy and paranormal romance tales. She resides in New England with her three beloved cats—Kasha, the spicy one; Kiwi, the sensitive one; and Peach, the fluffy one—who provide endless inspiration (and occasional keyboard interference). When she's not lost in a book or writing her next novel, she can be found indulging in her love for interior design, riding horses, or drinking an arguably excessive amount of peach tea.

instagram.com/michellefrohmanauthor

tiktok.com/michellefrohmanauthor

facebook.com/profile.php?id=100094541655815